Praise for John Dickson Carr:

"One portentious day in 1930 saw the publication of a first novel by an American-born Englishman and the detective story has never since, to its eternal benefit, been quite the same. How many reviewers in that year foresaw even a measure of the heights John Dickson Carr would climb in succeeding decades?"

—*New York Times Book Review*

**Other John Dickson Carr titles
available from Carroll & Graf:**

The Bride of Newgate
The Curse of the Bronze Lamp
Dark of the Moon
The Devil in Velvet
The Emperor's Snuff-Box
Fire, Burn!
The Ghosts' High Noon
Nine Wrong Answers

PAPA LÀ-BAS

JOHN DICKSON CARR

CARROLL & GRAF PUBLISHERS, INC.
NEW YORK

First Carroll & Graf edition 1989
Second edition 1997

Carroll & Graf Publishers, Inc.
19 West 21st Street
New York, NY 10010

ISBN 0-7867-0502-7

Manufactured in the United States of America

To Miss Margaret Ruckert, of the New
Orleans Public Library; to Dr. John H. Gribbin,
of the Howard-Tilton Memorial Library at Tulane
University; to Mr. J. E. Litchfield, the present
British Consul, and to others *sur le terrain* who
so patiently answered my often idiotic questions,
this book is gratefully dedicated.

CONTENTS

PART I:

Dusk

I

He had been conscious of disquiet for many days
before anything actually happened. Then, at dusk on the evening
of Wednesday, April fourteenth, as New Orleans drowsed in
mud-flats beside the Father of Waters . . .

Immensely broad Canal Street, stretching north from the levee
like a busier *Champs Elysées*, separated the Creole districts of the
city towards the east from the Anglo-Saxon or 'American' districts
towards the west. Number 33 Carondelet Street—though on the
American side of the dividing line, elbowed by offices, shops,
banks, and counting-houses in that prosperous business area—had
been built like one of the French or Spanish houses from the Old
Square east of Canal Street.

It was of brick and black cypress timbers, plastered over
against subtropical damp. Through the grey wall fronting the
street its *porte cochère* and covered way opened into a courtyard
or patio fragrant in shrubs and flowers, with a circular fountain in
the middle and an iron-railed gallery round two sides of the floor
above.

At number 33 Carondelet Street lived and worked Mr. Richard
Macrae, Her Britannic Majesty's Consul in New Orleans. Tonight
at dusk Mr. Macrae himself sat by the fountain in the patio,
smoking a postprandial cigar and feeling worried.

Easter Sunday, in this year 1858, had fallen on April eleventh,
three days earlier. Carnival-time was over; the great heat had not
yet come, with yellow fever or cholera or whatever else it might

3

bring. The social season was ended too. Wealthy families, Creoles from Esplanade Avenue and Anglo-Saxons from the Garden District alike, now talked of leaving town for White Sulphur Springs or even Newport and Saratoga in the far north. But it would be weeks before their departure; hardly a mosquito yet foraged.

The fountain in the patio had been turned off. From the direction of St. Charles Avenue, parallel with this street and only what Americans called a block away, Macrae could hear a low growl of wheels and voices past the St. Charles Hotel, past the St. Charles Theatre, past bars, restaurants, night-houses under the flaring gaslight. New Orleans, city of revelry and of ghosts, seemed as quiet as it could ever be at any hour.

Dick Macrae tapped ash from his cigar and sat up straight in the iron-ribbed garden chair.

"There's nothing wrong!" he said aloud. "There can't be anything wrong!"

Talking to yourself, they claimed, indicated a slate loose upstairs. Which was nonsense: it indicated merely a touch of loneliness. If Dick Macrae sometimes felt lonely, he had always told himself that he preferred it so. For he never need have been lonely at all.

A studious bachelor of thirty-seven, conscientious but easygoing, he fitted well into the life of the city. Some of its leading citizens, men of culture and wide interests—Judge Rutherford, Mr. Slidell, Jules de Sancerre, Senator Benjamin—were good friends. Tom Clayton, son of a former American Minister to Great Britain, was his close friend.

And now?

Though his duties here could never have been called exacting or onerous, the new Foreign Secretary was sending him a consular assistant. Lord Derby's Tory government had taken office in England. The appointment of young Harry Ludlow as consular assistant at New Orleans, Macrae knew, had been no more than a political gesture to please that influential West Country family.

Harry Ludlow was in America; letters from him had been arriving with fair regularity for almost a month. After landing at New York in mid-March, Harry had visited Boston, Philadelphia, and

Washington before taking the B. & O. Railroad west to St. Louis. A message by electric telegraph, handed in at Baton Rouge that afternoon, informed Macrae that his new assistant was now well down river aboard the great steamboat *Governor Roman*.

SLOW PROGRESS [the telegram concluded], THIS TEA-KETTLE HAS BEEN STOPPING WHEREVER IT CAN. PILOT PREDICTS ARRIVE NEW ORLEANS ABOUT NINE A.M. TOMORROW THURSDAY. REGARDS.

Dick Macrae seldom dined at home. But he had dined at home tonight. He was well looked after by a youngish middle-aged mulatto couple, Sam and Tibby Glapion, free man and woman of colour, whose twelve year-old son Rob ran errands and carried such letters as must be delivered by hand. With creature comforts once established, the consul had few wants beyond books, writing materials, an occasional day's riding or shooting in the bayou country round Lake Pontchartrain.

Well, with so much to make life pleasant, what *did* trouble him?

Nothing that he cared to mention publicly; nothing, in fact, that he could analyze or even define. But there it was. Confound this sensation of being so constantly followed and spied on, in particular at night, by some alien or malignant watcher: almost always present, lurking just beyond eyeshot, yet never there when you wheeled round in challenge!

The sense of being followed was no new thing; it had begun during a sober Lenten season after Ash Wednesday ended the frolic of this year's carnival. Usually felt outdoors, though once or twice even at home, this presence seemed to skulk at his heels or peer from doorways, close enough to reach out and touch. Sometimes the feeling would disappear for twenty-four hours altogether, only to return more oppressively than before.

Could it be more than imagination or some buried fear from his own brain? Could the whole business be as real as the *banquette* he walked on, perhaps the work of an enemy? Hang it, what enemy? He had no enemies here; or none, at least, of whom he had ever been aware.

But it seldom left him, a spider-twitch at the nerves. It had become almost an obsession. It blotted out even the memory of one brief, joyous, unfulfilled encounter, which did belong to carnival-time, with a girl he was never likely to meet again. The unseen watcher, forever following . . .

What was that noise just now?

A yellow glow spilled into the patio from two windows and a glass-panelled door giving on the upstairs gallery along the east side. The noise he heard had been made by no alien presence; it was only Sam, his servant, moving through the drawing-room to light the gas-jets. Sam did not close the curtains. Craning round and up, Macrae saw him silhouetted against glass panels as Sam emerged on the gallery near the head of the outside stairs.

At the same moment hoof-beats clopped along quiet Carondelet Street. The iron-grilled gates of the *porte cochère* at number 33 were never closed. Under the covered way into the courtyard, wheels rattling and harness a-jingle, rolled a small closed carriage, black with red wheel-spokes, drawn by one skittish black mare. On the box, in high beaver hat and brass-buttoned livery, sat Uncle Cicero, Jules de Sancerre's stately coachman.

With something of a flourish Uncle Cicero descended to open the carriage door. The woman who emerged, its sole passenger, stepped down gracefully to the flagstones. Faint light from above shone on glossy black hair and the short vertical side-curls that framed her cheeks. She wore a lilac-coloured gown with bell sleeves and monstrous crinoline, and had an Empress Eugénie shawl round her shoulders.

Some men wondered audibly, even profanely, how such immense skirts could be manoeuvred through narrow quarters. Dick Macrae, a bachelor neither prudish nor uninitiated, did not wonder. It was several years since the hoopskirted crinoline must be ballooned out by half a dozen horsehair-padded petticoats to give it shape. Crinolines now swelled on a watchspring framework so pliable that they could be compressed into spaces far smaller than that of the diminutive carriage.

Macrae dropped his cigar, trod on it, and stood up. Lean, wiry, not ill-looking in dark-blue frock coat and grey trousers, his silk hat on the rim of the fountain beside him, he bowed over the newcomer's extended hand.

"Your servant, Madame de Sancerre!" he said.

Isabelle de Sancerre, though past forty and the mother of a famous beauty, had herself been a beauty; she remained one. The light touched flawless complexion and vivid amber-coloured eyes set off by dark lashes. Unlike some Creole ladies, she did not affect ignorance of English or mangle the language when she spoke it. The soft voice, the demure manner, were more typical of her kind. But she was half breathless from strong emotion; the amber eyes held almost a look of anguish.

"Will you forgive this intrusion, Mr. Macrae?"

"You could never intrude, Madame de Sancerre."

"La, sir, I believe you mean that!"

"Indubitably I mean it, as I think you know."

Isabelle de Sancerre peered up at him.

"In one sense," she continued, "I felt no hesitation in paying an unexpected call at such an hour. As an old married woman of fairly good repute, I risk little from the breath of scandal. In another sense, alas, I have been hesitating for some time. After all . . ."

"Yes, madam?"

"Oh, you British!" She was very near to pouting. "So cold! So formal! So reserved!"

"Have you yourself, Madame de Sancerre, found me unduly formal or reserved?"

"Well—no. And my errand is so good, so immediate, so urgent! And you're such a good friend of Tom Clayton's! But this is not a social call, Mr. Macrae. One might even say I am here on business."

"I should be very sorry, believe me, to have a matter of business intrude on any meeting of ours. However!" Macrae raised his voice. "Sam!"

"Yassuh, Mist' Richard?"

"For the moment, at least, you may forget upstairs rooms. Be good enough to light the gas in my office."

"Yas, suh!"

His office, a good-sized if rather damp place on the ground floor below the drawing-room, had the severity of consular premises anywhere. Over the mantelpiece hung a steel engraving of Queen Victoria. Two sash windows faced the patio. Against the wall under the right-hand window was a kneehole desk, with a straight chair behind it, an upholstered armchair beside it, and (for visitors less favoured) another straight chair on the far side.

After Sam had kindled the green-shaded gas-lamp on the desk, Macrae ushered in his guest and rolled the armchair closer to the lamp. But Isabelle de Sancerre would not sit down. The crinoline swayed as she paced back and forth, nervously opening and shutting the clasp of a beaded reticule. He remained standing behind the desk.

"Something worries you badly," he said. "Can I persuade you to tell me what it is? And then may I invite you to more comfortable quarters for a glass of wine? I should be very sorry, let me repeat, to have a matter of business . . ."

" 'Business' is a mean, hard-hearted way of putting it. And yet (let's not be hypocritical) we can't avoid that aspect, now can we?"

"Will you favour me with your confidence, Madame de Sancerre?"

"Mercy on us, that's why I'm here! It's my daughter; it's Margot! And you know Margot. But then you don't really know her, do you?"

"No, I fear not. I have been in New Orleans for just over a year. During that time I have been honoured with invitations to so many dinners, balls, concerts, and theatre parties that it seemed inevitable I must meet one who is the belle of every ball. Yet by some fatality of accident I have always missed her. She has been away, or ill, or with a great friend of hers called . . . is it Ursula?"

"Ursula Ede, General Ede's daughter and a sweet girl. You've not met her either, I think."

"Your daughter, madam, is very much a topic of polite conversation. From every side I hear her praises sung with full-throated fervour. I hear of her beauty, her charm, her accomplishments . . ."

Isabelle de Sancerre spoke sharply.

"Is that all you hear, Mr. Macrae? There is something else, is there not?"

"What else should there be?"

"Do you remember what Byron wrote of Lady Caroline Lamb and her 'damned crinkum-crankum,' meaning her moods? You've heard of *Margot's* crinkum-crankum, surely?"

"To no great extent, since most opinions have come from men."

Here he spoke less than strict truth. Somebody had dwelt on the matter not long ago.

"Margot de Sancerre?" had said an informant whose name or face he could not remember. "Real smasher for looks, and no fool either. She's her mother's daughter: same eyes, same hair, same colouring. Prettier than her mother, of course. But look sharp when you meet her, I'm warning you; she's got a touch of the devil her mother never had or wanted to have."

That seemed to be the general opinion. Here in the office Margot's mother shut up her reticule, dropped it on the desk, and faced him over the lamp.

"High spirits," she cried, "are all very well in their way. *I* was high-spirited as a girl. This goes too far! You call me worried; in sober truth I'm half out of my mind. But what would you know of feeling worried, phlegmatic one? Nothing on earth could ever trouble you!"

(Nothing could, eh? Well, never mind.)

"May I point out, Madame de Sancerre, that you have not yet told me what the trouble is?"

His guest struck a pose.

"Marriage!" she burst out. "Margot's marriage! It's high time she *was* married, and to Tom Clayton too. Don't you agree?"

"Tom Clayton agrees, I know."

"Of course he does. Tom's in love with her and she with him, only the girl's too wilful and perverse to admit it. Now hear me, sir! Leonidas Clayton is one of my husband's oldest friends. Uniting the families has been the dream of us all since Margot was seven years old and Tom was a boy of fourteen or fifteen. It would be *entirely* suitable; there is not even a religious problem. The Claytons are Episcopalians, as you may know."

"Yes?"

"Because we're a Creole family, many people think of us as Roman Catholics. The de Sancerres, it's true, *were* Catholics up to about sixty years ago. Then Jules's father had a most awful fight with Luis de Penalver y Cardenas, the first Bishop of Louisiana; he wanted to marry a Protestant, and threatened to turn Protestant himself. The bishop was furious. 'Would you forsake the true Church?' 'Your true Church,' yelled old Raoul de Sancerre, 'may go and . . .' It was very vulgar; I won't repeat it. So *he* joined the Episcopalians, which is how it has been ever since. If nowadays we're seldom seen in any church at all, that's laziness and not irreverence or disbelief."

"But I still don't understand—" Macrae began.

Isabelle de Sancerre would not listen.

"Really!" she said. "Any objections to Tom Clayton as a husband are only seeming objections. He drinks too much, as some men do. He's wild and he's got a temper, more like the popular notion of a Creole blade than the descendant of Virginia forebears he actually is. But underneath everything he's as sound as George Stoneman's bank. And Margot loves him, and yet the idiot won't—!" Here she broke off. "Speaking of marriage, dear sir, can't we find some eminently suitable girl for *you?*"

"Many thanks, but I beg you won't try. I will not be conspired against, dear lady, even for what friends conceive to be my own good. Surely that is no part of the business you spoke of?"

"No, of course not! Still! You have been with us for a year; you are most eligible. Don't you like us at all, Mr. Macrae? Isn't there *someone, somewhere,* who has caught your fancy?"

Macrae cleared his throat.

Just as he could never have told her about the unseen, omnipresent shadow which haunted him and shook his nerves, so for different reasons he could not even mention a certain episode of carnival-time, or the girl in the mask with lace edges. He must shut away even the thought of that tawny-haired charmer, who belonged only to dreams; he must . . .

"I have been trying to say, dear lady, that I still don't understand your problem."

Isabelle de Sancerre shut up her reticule, dropped it on the desk, and retreated with fingers at her lips.

"The problem is Margot! She's a girl of good heart: *de bon coeur*, they would put it in French. But she's been spoiled, Mr. Macrae. Though I mislike saying so of my own daughter, she's rotten-spoiled! Since she could walk and talk she's been spoiled by her father, by her uncles, by every servant from Mammy and Cicero down! Margot has come to believe she may do anything she likes at any time she likes. That's where I so desperately need your advice. Considering the mood she's been in for days and days . . ."

"Forgive me; one moment!"

"Yes, Mr. Macrae?"

"When you arrived here tonight, you said that your errand was both immediate and urgent. The essence of the question, I take it, is that Miss de Sancerre must be persuaded to marry Tom Clayton. It's a desirable end, no doubt. However, since I am not even acquainted with the young lady, how can I advise you? And why is the matter so immediate or urgent?"

"It's the mood Margot's in: what caused it, and how to cure it. Didn't I explain that?"

"No."

"Then I will do so. If we could find some reason for the change that's come over her, I shouldn't have to bother you with all this. Mooning and brooding at the same time! Asking me questions about . . . well, you'll see. I think you're familiar with our home, at the corner of St. Charles Avenue and Holywell Street?"

"It's always a pleasure to be entertained there."

In his mind, as his guest spoke, rose an image of that great white house in the Garden District, set back on its deep lawn beyond a fence of iron fretwork, amid live-oaks and multicoloured flowers. Isabelle de Sancerre gripped her hands together.

"You may not at once see how the house comes into this. But you will. One popular belief about New Orleans is that the Garden District, uptown and up-river, is sacred to the homes of Anglo-

Saxon Americans, whereas Creole families hold stubbornly to the Old Square and Esplanade Avenue downtown.

"That's not entirely so; it has not been so for some time. There is no longer any friction between Creole and American. The oldest house in the Garden District—built in 1830, before the Garden District had been named or laid out—was designed and occupied by Thomas Toby, a Philadelphia architect who married into a Creole family and raised eleven children there.

"Then there's our home, *one* of the oldest. Jules and I were married in May of 1834; remember that. The house had been finished by that time; towards the end of March we inspected it with—never mind! We moved in before autumn of '34; we're always in residence except when we're at the plantation down-river. Margot was born there in April of '35. She's twenty-three now. If she's not married by St. Catherine's Day two years from now, she'll be an old maid.

"Oh, Margot!" breathed Margot's mother. "Up to this spring always so gay, so laughing, so talkative! Sometimes with her own little moods, of course, and vexing enough when she had 'em; but nothing in the least like *this*."

"Like what?"

"Haven't I told you? Mooning and brooding over something she won't explain. Getting precious little sleep either. Looking, in the morning, as though she'd been away dancing all night like one of the six dancing princesses in the fairy tale. But she hasn't been away all night or any part of the night. She's never left the house. We've made certain of that, because . . . well, we've made certain.

"You see, Mr. Macrae, that's a part of the awful trouble. It used to be beaux and parties, beaux and parties, whenever there was anything to do or assist at. Now she seldom *will* leave the house, daytime or night either. Mooning and brooding, mooning and brooding!"

Here Isabelle de Sancerre swept forward and grasped the back of the armchair.

"It's not a love-affair; I could understand that. But it's not a love-affair, so what in God's name *is* it? And the questions she asks me, when she can bring herself to speak at all! She's like a girl under a spell. And don't you tell me it's a Voodoo spell or I'll scream!"

Macrae held hard to common sense.

"I had no intention of talking about Voodoo," he said. "You have every reason to be worried; it's a puzzling situation. And yet there may be some clue in the questions she asks. Questions about what?"

"About a horror that took place here, if it really did take place, fully twenty-four years ago."

"Yes?"

"You, sir, are a man of the world. Even so humdrum a woman as your obedient servant may fairly claim to be *femme du monde*. Knowing our world, we're aware that certain persons—fortunately not too many—take a perverse and dreadful pleasure in performing or watching acts of sheer cruelty. We may not understand such people. But we know they exist, don't we?"

"Yes, of course. There was Mrs. Brownrigg in England during the last century; they hanged her. Did something of the same kind occur in New Orleans?"

"So it's alleged, which really frightens me when it seems to concern Margot. Now Margot at her best is far from perfect. She loves to tease; certain beaux have been driven half mad. But actual physical cruelty she abhors as I abhor it. Why, then, does she exhibit passionate interest in one who by repute committed the most bestial cruelties years ago? And why, when she asks no questions concerning that, does she go on about Marie Laveau, the Voodoo Queen?"

2

" 'BESTIAL CRUELTIES . . . VOODOO QUEEN'?"

"The two have no connection with each other. And this must stop." Isabelle de Sancerre drew herself up. "Come! A fit of hysterics will achieve nothing. I must be steady; I must be sensible; I must see all things as they are. Will you listen to me?"

"Willingly."

Madame de Sancerre seemed to have come to a decision. She sat down in the armchair, smoothed out her crinoline, and spoke with what coolness she could assume.

"In New Orleans, Mr. Macrae, legends pleasant or unpleasant grow and flourish like tropical flowers. The most persistent legend stems from the War of 1812; it deals with Andrew Jackson and with Jean Laffite, the buccaneer. By one account General Jackson met Jean Laffite at the Laffite brothers' blacksmith shop, where together they planned the Battle of New Orleans. Or they planned it over drinks at the Absinthe House. Both stories are absurd. According to Barnaby Jeffers, our best-known local historian after Mr. Gayarré, there is no evidence that the 'blacksmith' premises ever sheltered a blacksmith. And the Absinthe House had not even become a tavern at that time. Are you acquainted with Barnaby Jeffers, by the way?"

"Yes, though only slightly. I had called on him the night I met . . ."

"The night you met whom?"

"It's of no consequence. You were saying?"

14

"Well," and Isabelle de Sancerre lifted one shoulder, "let's return to our sheep. The next most persistent legend, which may have far more truth, is a grisly one. Have you heard of Delphine Lalaurie, the notorious Madame Lalaurie, and the so-called haunted house at the corner of Royal Street and Hospital Street in the French quarter?"

Macrae stared at her.

"Yes, I do seem to have heard *something*. Is that the affair which so fascinates your daughter?"

"It is, worse luck! The whole truth of it remains untold to this day; it may never be known. Madame Lalaurie has been dead for sixteen years. She may have been entirely innocent, as most Creoles still maintain. She may have been all her enemies said she was. Or the truth may lie somewhere between those two estimates. I shall have to quote dates offhand, but I think I have everything straight. You see, before she left New Orleans I knew her."

Isabelle de Sancerre paused for a moment.

"Delphine Lalaurie, born Delphine Macarty, was very wellborn despite that unromantic name. She came of ennobled French-Irish stock. And she had three husbands.

"In 1800, when she was eighteen or nineteen, she married Don Ramón de Lopez, a distinguished young Spanish diplomat. Four years later her husband was recalled to Spain by royal command, to 'take his place at court.' In Havana, while the young couple were *en route* to Madrid, Don Ramón died suddenly. Only a few days afterwards the widow gave birth to a daughter, and returned with the child to New Orleans.

"Her second husband, whom she married in 1808, was a very wealthy merchant and banker named Jean Blanque. She began to glitter as a society hostess of the most endearing sort. By Jean Blanque she had four children, three girls and a boy; he remained her husband for just over eight years. But in 1816 *he* died suddenly, and . . ."

Strange, explosive forces seemed to be gathering in that room round the green-shaded lamp. Macrae bent forward.

"Forgive the interruption," he said, "but are you suggesting . . . ?"

"Please! I am no scandal-monger; I suggest nothing; these things are matters of record. If in a moment I must indulge rumour or speculation, it's because there is no way of avoiding it.

"Well! This time Delphine remained a widow until June (all her marriages took place in June) of 1825. Her third husband, Dr. Louis Lalaurie, was a colourless, rather ineffectual soul who had left France to set up in medical practice here. But he never mattered. It was Delphine who held the purse-strings, having inherited Jean Blanque's fortune. It was Delphine who drew every eye. No misfortune befell *this* marriage except the disaster that overtook Delphine herself.

"She commissioned the building of an ornate house at the corner of Royal Street and Hospital Street, which was finished and occupied in 1832. How it shone with lights for her famous dinners! What joy to be welcomed under that roof! Her children had grown up and married; she held the stage on her own. And she was the darling of Creole Society.

"I met Delphine Lalaurie in that same year, '32, when I was eighteen years old. How kind she was to an inexperienced girl of not very good sense! Though she must have been at least fifty, no friend has ever exaggerated her magnetism; she would have charmed birds off a bough. God knows she charmed *me!*

"Jules and I were married two years later, as I have told you. At the end of March in '34, as I also said, we went out to inspect what was to be our own new home in the Garden District, then nearing completion. Delphine Lalaurie accompanied us. With her was somebody else about whom an odd story is told, but it needn't be repeated because it has no bearing on the scandal of Madame Lalaurie.

"Did I say scandal?

"There had been ugly whispers for some time. Many house-slaves served her in Royal Street; how kind she seemed to *them!* And yet—though sometimes at dinner she would hand the lees of her wine-glass to the slave behind her chair, saying, 'Take this, my friend; it will do you good,'—some people insisted that all her slaves looked haggard and woebegone except one who appeared to be her favourite: the sleek black coachman, Bastien.

"I heard no such whispers, and would not have believed them if I had. She was at her best that day she accompanied us to the Garden District; I can still see her face when she smiled. Who could have foretold what happened less than a fortnight later?

"On April tenth, when madame was away from home, an aged cook set fire to the house. Neighbours, hurrying in to fight the flames and remove furniture or valuables to safety, stumbled on a scene out of hell. Before the fire could be put out, they found six or seven emaciated wretches chained in the slave-quarters. Eye-witnesses or alleged eyewitnesses, quoted by the French newspaper *L'Abbeil*, testified that these victims bore marks of repeated bloody floggings with a cowhide whip. *Et madame s'amuse comme ça?*

"Word-of-mouth rumours added to confusion and wrath: that she was accustomed to whip her slaves as a daily stimulant, or that Bastien did the whipping while she looked on in ecstasy: finally, that other slaves had been murdered at this pastime and buried in the courtyard. Five days later, on April fifteenth, popular fury boiled over.

"Death to the Jezebel! Down with her!

"Inspired by their fiery young ringleader, a mob that had been gathering outside burst into the mansion and began to wreck it. The Lalauries fled. Even as invaders stormed through the house, smashing mirrors and hurling clocks from mantelpieces, madame and her husband were bundled into a carriage by Bastien, who whipped up the horses and made off along Hospital Street. The rioters had to be dispersed by a company of regular troops called in at the appeal of the sheriff.

"The Lalauries escaped. Reaching a friend's home in Mandeville, across Lake Pontchartrain, they crossed to Mobile, Alabama, where they took ship for France. Delphine died abroad in 1842, though her body was secretly returned to New Orleans and buried here.

"At so late a date it's ironic to remember (this is truth, not rumour) that the ringleader of those rioters on April fifteenth was a twenty-three-year-old law-student named Horace Rutherford; he has since become eminent as Judge Rutherford of the Louisiana Bench. Poor Judge Rutherford!"

Macrae, who had been sitting in the straight chair opposite his guest, sprang up and strode across the room before turning back.

"Why do you say 'poor' Judge Rutherford?" Macrae asked. "His lameness, which he says was caused by a fall from a horse long ago, never impedes him much. He may walk with a cane, but he's spry enough; he will run upstairs and strike a dramatic attitude at the top. In fact, he seems to strike a dramatic attitude whenever he can."

"And that's just what he mustn't do, don't you see? Horace has developed a bad heart, Amelia Rutherford tells me; undue exertion could kill him. But he won't listen to anybody, Amelia says. Also, incredible as it may seem today, other rioters on that tumultuous April fifteenth were young George Stoneman, now president of the Planters' & Southern Bank, and (though I'm sure he would deny it) a scholarly historian called Barnaby Jeffers.

"To all New Orleans, as you're aware, Delphine Lalaurie's house has become the 'haunted house.' Nobody will live there, though various families have tried since it was renovated after the Lalauries fled. Cries, shrieks, the agony of tortured slaves! Sensible people deny the existence of ghosts. But we can't deny the existence of superstition."

Isabelle de Sancerre looked up in desperate appeal.

"Now that whole story, Mr. Macrae! How much was truth, how much falsehood? Delphine Lalaurie has never lacked defenders or apologists. A very few slaves, it's conceded, *may* have been chained to keep them in order. Everything else, say the defenders, was only journalistic exaggeration or the malice of jealous enemies. There were no floggings. And there were no buried bodies, which seems to have been true. The worst tale of all—about a small slave-girl who jumped from the roof to her death rather than endure more of Delphine's whip—is almost certainly false. And yet . . . and yet . . . what do *you* think?"

"May I ask a very important question?"

"Of course."

"What happened to such slaves as actually *were* chained?"

"I don't think I follow you. Not one of the rioters was arrested, in spite of the sheriff and the troops being there."

"*Imprimis*, madam, let's not begin with the riot of April fifteenth. Let's begin with events attending the fire five days earlier. Neighbours, entering to put out the fire, found certain slaves chained in their quarters and, we'll assume for the moment, badly beaten as well. Were the chained ones released from their shackles?"

"I don't know."

"But the inference, at least, is that these good neighbours were struck with horror?"

"It's more than an inference. They *were* struck with horror!"

"Then what did they do to show it? The sheriff was there on April fifteenth. Did anybody call him five days earlier? Surely there was some kind of investigation?"

"I don't know. I don't think so. Is that important?"

"*Now, damn it all, woman . . . !* I do beg your pardon, dear lady!"

"Mr. Macrae, pray don't apologize for saying damn. I say it myself, not infrequently, and you should hear my husband when he's in a temper. But will you please explain?"

"With pleasure. The crux of it, the cause of the whole explosion, is the question of whether slaves were flogged or otherwise tortured. Did one responsible eyewitness say they were? It's testimony we don't seem to have. When the Lalauries fled, I gather, they took no servants except Bastien. Certain slaves, tortured or not, were still there at the time of the riot. Who observed them then? What happened to those slaves eventually? Therefore, in determining whether the hospitable lady of Royal Street was guilty or innocent . . ."

"Please, Mr. Macrae! I'm only a woman; you must allow me to think like one. In my heart of hearts I don't really *care* whether she was guilty or innocent. All that concerns me, as I've tried to tell you, is the effect of all this on *Margot*. My Margot! A sheltered creature, *jeune fille bien élevée*, yet brooding and questioning about things that happened before she was born. It's so vexing

I could weep. As I remarked to Mr. Benjamin only this morning . . ."

"Mr. Benjamin? You mean Senator Benjamin?"

Isabelle de Sancerre extended her hand as though for a mesmeric pass.

"Judah P. Benjamin!" she said. "He *is* a United States senator, of course; and I'm sure he's needed there, with all these dreadful abolitionists and the threats they make. But *I* think of him as the finest lawyer in the South, perhaps in the country; as a wise man who can give good advice—at solving any kind of problem by logical analysis, Jules says, he has no equal—and, best of all, as an old family friend.

"Just think of his career, sir! He was a poor boy, born in your British West Indies. His family moved to Charleston when he was still a boy, still poor; his father had no head for business in spite of being Jewish. Three years at Yale; left without taking a degree because his father couldn't afford to keep him there.

"Then New Orleans, with only five dollars in his pocket; studied law, supporting himself by working in a notary's office and giving English lessons to Creoles. Met Natalie St. Martin, daughter of Auguste St. Martin de la Caze, when he was teaching *her* English; married her the year before I married Jules. Mrs. Benjamin and their daughter live in Paris now, though I know he wishes Natalie had stayed at home. How his star has risen since the days of poverty!"

"Madame de Sancerre . . ."

"Mostly he's in Washington, you see; his main practice is before the Supreme Court. But he still keeps bachelor rooms here, and the law-firm of Benjamin, Bradford & Finney has never closed its doors in Canal Street. In addition to which . . ."

"I am acquainted with Mr. Benjamin, you know."

"I do know, and he thinks highly of you. A moment ago you mentioned the Senate; so did he, when he dropped in to see us this morning. The Senate's in session, he says; he ought to be there, because he rarely misses a roll-call. But there's some legal matter to handle for Benjamin, Bradford & Finney, so he risked taking a few days off duty. I told him I hoped to see you here tonight; I told him why. You must both forgive me: I was so *horribly* burdened and oppressed that I poured out the whole story, just as I've poured it out to you."

"And what did he say?"

"He said he himself might like to call this evening. That is, if you have no objection?"

"Objection? Anything but an objection; quite the contrary!"

"We must not expect him, Mr. Macrae; I must warn you not to expect him. Business apart, he says, he has little to occupy his mind beyond reading history or translating Horace, and he welcomes something to puzzle at. But that's just the trouble. There's such an appalling *lot* of work he must get through, dozens and dozens of things to unsnarl, though you'd never guess it to hear him talk. He won't be here because he can't get here. If I were in the habit of betting, as all the men do, I would offer odds of a thousand to one. There is not the least, the most remote possibility that . . ."

Outside the door of this room, in the wall towards the south, a passage ran west to the side door giving on the patio. Along this passage lumbered the heavy footsteps of Sam, Macrae's majordomo. Sam threw open the office door. Broad, light-brown, nearly bald, he was very conscious of his own importance at a time like this. Moving to one side, he drew himself up and inflated his chest.

"Senatuh Judah P. Benjamin!" he boomed.

"Something of a fanfare, I'm afraid," said a well-modulated voice from the doorway, "for rather an unimpressive guest."

The man who entered, unimpressive or not, would have been noticed anywhere. His smile was compelling: the ease, the good humour of his manner put everyone about him at ease too. Short and stout, though with strong shoulders—his favourite sport, Macrae knew, was the dangerous one of devil-fishing—Senator Benjamin had twinkling dark eyes in a fleshy face completely encircled by sidewhisker-cum beard trimmed so short it resembled a strip of dark fur above collar-points and the broad dark-blue bow of the tie.

Despite his age, the late forties, little grey tinged his hair. But frock coat, waistcoat, trousers were all the same shade of grey, and he had handed his pearl-grey top hat to Sam.

"Madame de Sancerre, your most obedient!" he went on. "My dear Macrae, how are you? Though far from being unannounced, it would seem I am unexpected. If I am also unwelcome . . . ?"

Macrae returned his bow.

"You are never unwelcome, Senator Benjamin. —Sam, that will be all for tonight; you may go to bed."

Sam departed, leaving the newcomer's hat on a table beside the door. Macrae made a hospitable gesture.

"Madame de Sancerre and I, sir, were about to adjourn upstairs for a glass of wine. Will you join us?"

"Right willingly. But not, with your permission, just yet. This meeting has the air of a conference I should be reluctant to interrupt. May I suspect that the lady has just finished giving you the same account she gave me this morning?"

"Often and often," said Isabelle de Sancerre, who had craned round towards him, "I can't make you out! You hide behind that smile as though you wore a mask. I asked for your opinion, and you wouldn't tell me!"

"I begged time for reflection, no more than that. There is a single remaining chair, I see: another straight one. Again by your leave, I will occupy it and lower this gross flesh. So.

"Now why is it," pursued Senator Benjamin, lifting his forefinger impressively, "that no client ever brings me a criminal case? They never have; they never will. For that they brief John Grymes or Christian Roselius. To me come long, tedious litigations in which clients of doubtful honesty try hard to split estates and succeed only in splitting hairs. Sometimes I yearn for a good criminal case like this one."

"Now really!" cried Isabelle de Sancerre. "Do you call my daughter's problem a criminal case?"

"Gently, old friend! Go gently here. Whatever may possess the fair Margot, it must be traced back to the business of Delphine Lalaurie in '34. And what a business! Reflect on it yourselves. Villainy or mere slander, it has every artistic element Mr. De Quincey calls indispensable to the best work in crime. 'Design, grouping, light and shade, poetry, sentiment!' They are all there."

"Well," interposed Macrae, "have *you* reflected? May we hear counsel's opinion now?"

Up went Senator Benjamin's forefinger.

"The issue before this c—the issue before us, good friends, is at least clear-cut. Were the slaves of Delphine Lalaurie thrashed or otherwise ill-used by an inhuman mistress? If they were, the case against her becomes a strong one. If they were not, the case falls to the ground. What happened to those slaves, then and afterwards?"

Isabelle de Sancerre flinched as though stung. She looked at Macrae, then at the lawyer and back to Macrae.

"Dear Lord!" she breathed. "Almost exactly the same words *you* spoke!"

"Did he so? Then I congratulate him," Senator Benjamin said with a touch of vanity. "I myself," he continued, "lived here at the time. But I was only a fledgling advocate: newly married, and with perplexities of my own. I paid scant heed to the case then. However, if only as a favour to an old friend, heed must be paid to it now by doing what is always necessary. We must examine evidence; we must look to the record."

"What record?" Macrae demanded. "Madame de Sancerre seems to think there was no record, and no investigation either."

"My dear fellow, of course there was a record! There had to be!"

"How so?"

"The law of Louisiana rules that, if any slave or slaves be cruelly used by the owner, such slave or slaves shall be sold at public auction and the proceeds go to the state. At least one municipal officer, the sheriff, surveyed that scene on April fifteenth. In any case at all, let alone so sensational a *cause célèbre*, he would have been obliged to make a report. Nor could the matter have ended there. Though our authorities may overlook many things, they seldom overlook a source of revenue."

"Then there's some chance of discovering . . . ?"

"I trust so. In '34, as for some years afterwards, the seat of local government was at the Cabildo in Jackson Square. When the increasing weight of the American vote shifted it to our present City Hall, Lafayette Square, all public records were transferred as well.

"Now more than one person at City Hall owes me a favour. This afternoon I called there and had a word with Mayor Waterman. As I was leaving I encountered Tom Clayton, who figures so prominently in Madame de Sancerre's speculations about little Margot."

"Yes?"

"He told me, did young Clayton, that he had just seen you here at the consulate, and that undoubtedly you would spend the evening at home. You expect a consular assistant, do you not?"

"Harry Ludlow, the son of an old friend. When Harry wrote from St. Louis, I wrote back with some instructions. I promised to meet his boat at the levee if he let me know its name by electric telegraph."

"Which telegram, Tom said, arrived this afternoon. The *Governor Roman* tomorrow morning? But that," and Senator Benjamin dismissed it, "is hardly to our purpose now."

The lawyer stood up. Instantly soothing, paternal, all concentrated persuasion, he bustled round to stand in front of Madame de Sancerre and hold her with his eye.

"Come, Isabelle: be of good heart and good cheer! If pertinent records exist, Mayor Waterman's staff will find them. There should be news in a day or so at most. Meanwhile, I charge you, let there be caution and reflection!"

"Really, Benjie, where's the need for so much caution or reflection? Horace Rutherford always says—"

"May I quote you another Horace, Quintus Horatius Flaccus of the Sabine farm? Moderation, the golden mean in all things, with feelings at never too high a pitch! If these documents exist, I say, if they have not been lost or suppressed, we must hope with some fervour that Delphine Lalaurie was as innocent as Little Red Ridinghood or the Mary who owned the lamb."

"Is that so important?"

"It's of the greatest importance, believe me. Suppose her to have been guilty of every cruelty, and suppose such facts became public knowledge? Though this may have happened long ago, it presents a picture of life in the South more grotesque than any dreamed by Mrs. Beecher Stowe herself. What our enemies could do with it may readily be imagined."

"Yes, but—!"

"Nor is that all. Two of Madame Lalaurie's daughters, I remember, took husbands from families of great prominence here. We must not expose ourselves to a suit for slander; we must not unduly rattle old bones."

"Benjie, don't lawyers ever do anything except try to put people in the wrong? *I'm* not anxious for trouble; I'm not trying to defame anybody. As I told Mr. Macrae here, it's a matter of indifference to me *what* the wretched woman did or didn't do. Even if we discovered everything about her, how on earth could it help us learn what ails Margot?"

"Giving advice in family matters, Isabelle, is something we should all try to avoid. I have known Margot since she was a child. And yet for the most part I feel I don't know her; I can't fathom her."

"What I feel," retorted the other, "is that *I* can't fathom *you*. Can anybody fathom you, or see behind your Oriental ways? I told you the whole story; I asked you to be frank with me. And so I have a question for one who usually does the questioning. Were you frank with me, Fra Torquemada? Are you being frank even now?"

"And I," Senator Benjamin said gently, "have the same question in return. You have told me a certain story, yes. Were *you* being frank with *me*?" Then his voice rang out. "In short, have you been telling me the whole truth?"

3

"Now if I am to be called a liar . . . !"

Senator Benjamin shook his head.

"No, Isabelle. Your worst enemy, if you had one, could not call you that. But your emotions lead you into a certain confusion, as emotions do with us all."

"Mercy on us, in what way am I confused?"

"You have stated that Margot, 'mooning and brooding,' seldom speaks except to ask you questions, in the main about Delphine Lalaurie. What kind of questions?"

"*All* kinds. Never one about whipping slaves, though!"

"Then what questions? Try to be specific."

"How well did I know Delphine? Was Delphine really beautiful, or only charming? Did all the men truly run after her, even as a woman past her prime? Did I think that *she*, Margot, would have so many beaux or be so sought after if she were not Jules's daughter and endowed with almost a surfeit of worldly goods?"

"H'm. Other questions, you have stated, show strong interest in Marie Laveau, our famous, mysterious Voodoo Queen, whose reign has lasted for well over twenty years. What is the connection between your daughter and Marie Laveau?"

"What is the connection between my daughter and Delphine Lalaurie, who left New Orleans before Margot was born? Really!"

"Is Margot acquainted with Marie Laveau?"

"Good heavens, no!"

Taking up her reticule from the desk, Isabelle de Sancerre

opened it to produce a small green bottle of smelling-salts, which she unstoppered and touched to her nose. Her gaze travelled past the lawyer's shoulder.

"As a newcomer if not a stranger, Mr. Macrae," she asked, "what have *you* heard about Marie Laveau?"

"Only that she is a mulatto, a free woman of colour. Of the Voodoo cult itself I have heard little beyond hints and oblique references."

"Few people learn more than that," observed Senator Benjamin, turning towards him, "though I have my own sources of information. Voodoo, imported by slaves from Haiti during the eighteenth century, is a form of devil-worship. Satan (in local patois called *Papa Là-bas*) has as his symbol a great serpent which the Voodoo Queen wears wrapped round her body. To such crude ceremonies Marie Laveau, who would call herself a good Catholic, has added touches of Christian ritual for wider appeal.

"The stories about her are endless. You will hear of a yearly orgy beside Lake Pontchartrain, with a scattering of white women among the Negroes, on St. John's Eve at midsummer. You will hear of more frequent orgies in the back yard of her cottage on St. Ann Street. And with Marie herself, a clever woman, as the moving spirit for every occasion."

"If she ever did anything like that," exclaimed Isabelle de Sancerre, replacing smelling-salts in reticule, "she's stopped doing it now. Why, the woman must be into her sixties!"

"She is."

"Then what are we talking about?"

"That is what I wonder. A question or two more, if you will permit them. Was *Delphine Lalaurie* acquainted with our Voodoo Queen?"

"I'm almost certain she wasn't. Stay, though! Your devil-worshipping paragon may have done Delphine's hair at one time."

"Done Delphine's hair?" Macrae repeated.

"Yes! Before she launched into Voodoo—ages and ages gone, when she was still young—she used to go into the better homes as a ladies' hairdresser."

"Thereby," Senator Benjamin made an arresting gesture, "learning the secrets all women tell their hairdressers, as useful information to be stored up. Among slaves she still has adherents, perhaps spies as well, in half the households of our city."

"*I* thought you were going to say 'our fair city.' You're a famous orator, Demosthenes, but don't try it on *us*. And this isn't helping at all! When do we get back to Margot?"

"We are about to do so. Margot, then, has been preoccupied with the late Delphine Lalaurie; and, to a lesser extent, with the still-living Marie Laveau. How long has this hypnosis been going on?"

"I . . . no, wait; I can tell you almost exactly! It began a day or two after *Mardi Gras*, which this year was the twenty-third of February. That, at least, was when I first noticed. The point is, when will it *end?*"

A day or two after *Mardi Gras* . . .

Macrae sat up straight.

Of the two windows facing the courtyard, his desk with the lamp stood under the right-hand one as you looked out. It should have been placed under the left-hand window, of course; with his own chair on the far side; a man sitting there to write would then have daylight over his left shoulder. Or he could have swung the whole desk round in its present position. Still! This had been the arrangement when he took over from the preceding consul in 1857; Macrae, a conservative soul who hated change, had never altered the furniture. Besides, with the light over your left shoulder you would have your back to the door.

But he was not now concerned with desks, or with lights, or with doors either. For a moment the mature beauty of Isabelle de Sancerre, the concentrated eyes and forehead of Judah Philip Benjamin, the office itself seemed to fade from his mind.

It was a day or two after *Mardi Gras* that he had first become conscious of somebody watching, somebody following, the malignant presence just beyond eyeshot. Could his own obsession, or perhaps hallucination, bear any relation to the obsession of Margot de Sancerre? Could the two have a common origin? It seemed impossible, nonsensical, any strong word you cared to use!

And yet . . .

Rising to his feet, skirting past Madame de Sancerre in the armchair with Mr. Benjamin standing before her, he went to the left-hand window and stared out.

Under clear starlight there was nobody in the courtyard except Uncle Cicero, sitting with majestic patience on the box of Isabelle de Sancerre's carriage. No alien presence, no sense of pressure, no spider-twitch at his nerves.

But it wasn't all on one side, he found himself thinking; it wasn't all nightmare. If it had been a day or two after *Mardi Gras* that he became conscious of surveillance, it was just a week before the same date when he met the girl with the tawny hair and the speaking eyes, whose face he had seen so briefly before she put on the mask: the girl who had walked through his dreams ever since, and whom he would never be able to forget.

'Got to forget her!' he said to himself. 'This is all foolishness!' The dream washed over him and rolled away; he returned to his chair.

Senator Benjamin was speaking.

"When will it end, you ask? That will be easier to predict when we have determined its cause. In the meantime . . ."

The stout little lawyer had been thinking hard, a vertical furrow between his brows. Reaching into his inside pocket, he took out a leather cigar-case; realizing the impropriety, he put it back again. Then he stood teetering, forefinger impressively raised.

"One last question, dear lady, after which we can ponder the information we already have. Are you sure there has been no contact between your daughter and Marie Laveau?"

"*Contact?*"

"Come!" The senator was indulgent. "In the past, it is well known, many fashionable young ladies have visited that little St. Ann Street house; no doubt they still do. They go to buy *gris-gris*, the Voodoo charm that will bring them their heart's desire. They go secretly and by night, leaving the carriage waiting. If the first *gris-gris* fails, they go again. Are you sure that Margot herself . . . ?"

"Oh, fiddledeedee!" cried Margot's mother. "Yes, of course I'm sure! What could the poor girl want that she hasn't got already? Anyway . . . !"

Here Isabelle de Sancerre rose up, with the effect of a flounce, and swept her great skirts over to the left-hand window, where she stood looking out as Macrae had done, with her face turned away.

"When I came here tonight, Benjie, I was worried about two or three things. Ever since you started these ridiculous questions, you've had me worried about at least a dozen.

"Really," she went on, "how inconsiderate I am! Servants *are* human beings, though the abolitionists say we don't treat them as such. There's poor Uncle Cicero like a black statue. Margot keeps him waiting for hours, which is what made me think of it. That doesn't matter, because he adores her. But *I* should set a better example, surely? Perhaps I ought to have sent him home; I'd have done it, so help me, if I had any way of getting home myself. And yet it doesn't seem *right* to dismiss one's coachman before *I'm* ready to go."

Senator Benjamin twirled the gold watch-chain across his waistcoat.

"If that is the pressing problem, Isabelle, I can solve it at once. My own hackney cab, with one of those Irish jarveys who affect so unintelligible a mixture of English and French, attends me in the street outside. And the tedium of the longest wait may be assuaged by a sizable tip. My rooms are in Polymnia Street, at no great distance beyond your house. Should you care to accept my hospitality, I shall be honoured to see you home."

"Oh, thank you! Will you excuse me for just one moment?"

"If it's to dismiss Cicero, dear lady, *I* can . . ."

"Am I so inept or so smothered in cotton-wool that I can't give a command to my own servant? Pray excuse me."

Out she went, compressing her crinoline through the doorway. Light footsteps rapped towards the side door. Very faintly they heard her voice from outside. Cicero rumbled something in reply;

there was a snap of reins, a clop of hoofs and jolt of wheels as the carriage backed and turned. When it had rattled off under the covered way, Isabelle de Sancerre returned in something of a hurry. If her manner had seemed strained when she left the office, it was still more strained now.

"Mr. Macrae!"

"Yes?"

"Did *you* see it?"

"See what?"

"At the far side of the courtyard, the garden part of it. Isn't somebody skulking there, watching us through these windows?"

Again evil forces seemed to gather and press close. But Macrae would not acknowledge it.

"You are mistaken, Madame de Sancerre. There's nobody there; nobody at all!"

"Oh, very well. You ought to know, I suppose. Now, Mr. Judah Benjamin, what's all this about Margot slipping out at night to visit Marie Laveau?"

Senator Benjamin made a deprecating gesture.

"I don't say she did that, old friend. It suggested itself as a possibility, no more. When you described the girl as so often looking wan and haggard, as though she had got little sleep the night before . . ."

"I also told you, I think, that up to this morning the poor child has seldom stirred out even in the daytime? And never once has she left home at night; I *know* that!"

"How can you be sure of it?"

"Because we've had the house watched from sunset till dawn."

" 'We'? You mean you and Jules?"

"Oh, very well; I have had the house watched. Do you think I'd let Jules learn anything of this unless it couldn't be avoided? Anyway! As though Margot would consult a dirty, dingy old witch-woman with a pet snake! For one thing, she would be too fastidious."

"I am more than inclined to agree. But you have not considered every possible explanation."

"If you're saying my Margot is a wicked girl, and that some

young man comes to visit *her* . . . ?"

"No, I don't say that either. God forbid! The answer, I am sure, is quite an innocent one."

"Is there any *other* answer?"

"Well, yes. There is the answer that—" He stopped.

"That what? Are you being mysterious again, Benjie?"

"Not mysterious, Isabelle; merely cautious. Tomorrow, for instance," Senator Benjamin drew a deep breath and expelled it, "I must glance at certain records much easier of access than those appertaining to Delphine Lalaurie. We must have evidence; we must nail it down. Also, though I seem unduly to be playing Grand Inquisitor, a moment ago you used words that intrigued me. You said that 'up to this morning' Margot had seldom left home even in the daytime. Did she go on any kind of outing today?"

"Yes, she did. She's back safe and sound now, with no harm done; but a rare old fright she gave me while it lasted!

"Do you remember, Benjie? Neither Margot nor Jules was at home this morning. When you asked how they were and where they were, to begin with, I just mumbled something vague. I don't think I could have borne it if either had been within listening-distance as I got down to telling the story."

"Well?"

"At eight this morning Margot came downstairs; she seemed less broody and more like herself. Jules has been at the plantation for a day or two, making sure the overseer has things in order. Margot said *she* was going to the plantation; she said there was something she wanted to fetch. She took the little carriage, the same one I used tonight.

"And I made no objection; I thought it would do her good. It was barely nine when she left.

"You know, sometimes Margot looks so much as they say *I* looked twenty years and a bit ago that . . . well, it scares me. But I wasn't properly scared until at past one in the afternoon Jules himself turned up from the plantation, riding Crusader, and said she hadn't arrived there.

"It shouldn't have taken her much more than an hour to get to

Bellegarde. Jules didn't panic; I almost did.

"Jules said she had probably just changed her mind and gone on to see her friend Ursula Ede, at General Ede's plantation a mile or two beyond ours. We put Hezekiah on a fast horse; we told him to ride to General Ede's and make sure Miss Margot was there.

"And that's what *had* happened, as we learned when Hezekiah reported back. Margot didn't seem to have been enjoying herself, though. She was sitting on the lawn with Ursula, Hezekiah said, but 'seem lak missy been in a tantrum,' or something of the sort. Margot promised to return before nightfall.

"It wasn't much past five before Cicero drove her back: beginning to be odd and moody again, hardly answering when you spoke. 'I've been neglecting poor Ursula,' she said, 'and I mustn't neglect Ursula!' When I asked her what she had wanted to fetch from Bellegarde, she said she hadn't wanted anything, because she was all prepared. Those were her exact words, 'all prepared.'

"And she hadn't cheered up much when I left home this evening," cried Isabelle de Sancerre, her voice rising high. "And what does it all mean? And why, when Margot once went out on her own a month ago, did she cash a cheque for five hundred dollars at the Planters' & Southern Bank? And there *is* something out there," a finger stabbed towards the windows, "and it's getting closer now!"

"If there is anyone in the courtyard, Madame de Sancerre, it's only Sam."

"I beg your pardon, Mr. Macrae; it is *not* Sam. Or Tibby or the boy either. You told Sam to go to bed. And your slaves obey you implicitly, which is more than can be said for ours."

"Sam and Tibby aren't slaves, you know. They are both free: as their son is also, of course. Her Majesty's government would never allow—"

Tactfully he paused. The lady had not even heard him.

"Dear God, aren't you going to go and *see*?"

"Yes, of course."

Macrae crossed to the door and opened it. Madame de Sancerre's voice went shrilling up.

"If it *is* Voodoo after all . . . !"

"Control yourself, Isabelle!" said Senator Benjamin.

Macrae squared his shoulders. Despite all common sense, dread touched his heart as he strode out into the passage. Was he to meet the enemy at last?

The passage, carpeted with dingy straw matting, stretched away to a glass-panelled patio door that stood wide open. One bluish yellow gas-flame made a fluttering noise in its wall-bracket beside the door. And just outside hovered a shape Macrae could not make out; the light was in his eyes.

"Who's there?" he called. "Stand forth and speak! *Who's there?*"

Relief flooded through him, with a shock of anticlimax too, as the Cockney voice sang back.

"Only me, that's all! Beggin' your pardon, sir, but are you the consul 'isself?"

"I am. Who are you? What do you want?"

Crossing the threshold, the shape from outside became a stocky, square-jawed young man in pea-jacket and flat-crowned hat. Respectful but insistent, uncertain yet determined, the newcomer touched his forelock.

"Name o' Jack Dowser, sir. Able seaman, brig *Bombay Girl,* out o' Liverpool for Havana."

"If you're in trouble of some kind, Dowser . . ."

"Not wot yer might call *trouble*, sir. Not this time, anyroad! No fight over a bit o' skirt. No layin' aboard so much drink yer gets knocked on the 'ead and robbed. Wot I 'as need of now, sir, is advice on a kind o' delircate matter."

"If you're in trouble of some kind, I was about to say, my duty is to help you all I can. And my advice is at your service for what it's worth."

"Thank'ee kindly, sir. You *are* a gentleman!"

"But, unless there's some very great emergency, it must be done during the proper hours. Those hours, as you may have seen on the plaque outside . . ."

"Couldn't see a ruddy thing, sir; black as yer 'at. Still! I did

see yer through the winder: you and the lady and the other gentleman too."

"Those are personal friends here on private business of the
most confidential nature. It's only by accident we are in the office
at all. Now be a good fellow, Dowser! Go home; return to your
ship. Come back tomorrow, and I shall be most happy to . . ."

"*Sir!*"

The young man spoke with such agony that Macrae hesitated.

"Yes, Dowser?"

"I 'ope I knows me place, sir, and I knows good will too. If you
says that, then I says fair enough and no buttin' in. I'll cast off; I'll
sling me 'ook and shut me potato-trap till I gets leave ter open it.
No word o' me own woes, though they may be closer to yours
than yer knows of. I'm not a chap as interferes, usually. *But—!*"

"But what?"

"Voodoo!" the other blurted. "When yer 'ad the door open
back there, just fer a second, the lady up and skreeked out about
Voodoo in a voice fit to raise me 'air. Avast, sir! If yer don't think
much o' me—as why should anybody?—at least take warnin'
from a lubber 'oo knows wot 'e's a-torkin' abaht!"

"You want to warn me of something: is that it?"

"I wants ter warn *all* of yer! If I promises to be'ave meself,
couldn't I come in fer just two shakes of a bo'sun's whip?"

"Now look here, young man—!"

"Oh, let him come in!"

Isabelle de Sancerre, her lilac-coloured gown somewhat rumpled, had emerged from the office and stood with one hand on the
knob of the door.

"Do let him come in, Mr. Macrae!" she pleaded. "I *was*
screaming, I confess it; I seem to have no pride or dignity left. But
it's more than a question of pride or dignity, isn't it? He seems a
well-meaning young man, at any rate. Possibly he can help us;
possibly not; it's worth listening, I suggest. Do please let him come
in!"

Jack Dowser had snatched off his hat. Determined but powerfully embarrassed, shifting his weight from one foot to the other, he followed the other two into an office which seemed suddenly to have grown darker and gloomier.

"The gas-pressure," remarked Senator Benjamin, indicating the lamp, "quite often grows low of an evening. Have no fear: the light won't go out. But it flutters and struggles, as we observe; it can be something of a strain on the eyes and the temper. Our seafaring visitor, now . . ."

"Our seafaring visitor," Macrae said, "has been the innocent cause of uproar. You see, Madame de Sancerre? You were alarming yourself unnecessarily. *He* was the only one out there."

"*Was* he the only one, Mr. Macrae? I don't think so; I still think . . . And I wish it weren't so *dark!* But—"

"Permission ter speak, sir?" begged Jack Dowser, who was waving his hat at Macrae. "Permission ter speak, f' Gaw's sake?"

"Granted; you have it. Well?"

"Don't matter 'bout me. I'm a rough sort o' cove, always 'ave been, so it don't matter. I'll 'andle me own business; I'll face it; I'll go up through the futtock-shrouds like a man. But you and you and you: you're gentlefolk if I ever see 'em; you oughter *know!*

"Steer wide o' Voodoo, I'm a-beggin' yer! Clap on sail and be 'ull-down 'fore they gives yer a 'ail. Mind! There's a lot less danger 'ere, I reckon, than in Port-au-Prince or Port Royal either. This Voodoo Queen o' the town: never met 'er, no more me mates 'ave neither. All the tork is, anyroad, she's more fer the show o' the thing, like a penny gaff with *everybody* drunk, than fer strikin' a cove down or choppin' 'is 'ead off with the big sharp blade they calls a masheety. All the same! Play no tricks with *Papa Là-bas*, and 'ands off 'is women too! Permission to tell yer why?"

"Yes, of course. Well?"

"*I'd* rather he said no more!" cried Isabelle de Sancerre. "This has gone too far already! Besides—"

"It was you, dear lady, who called spirits from the vasty deep," said Senator Benjamin. "Let's see if they attend us, shall we? Go on, young man."

"It wos me first berth, so please you, and me not fourteen year old. They'd signed me as cabin-boy aboard the *Nabob*, a square-rigged Indiaman with a rough skipper and an even worse chief mate. The marster was Cap'n Darcy; the mate's name was Sullivan. I mind 'em both yet.

"We wos anchored at Port Royal in Jamaica, with drums a-going in the 'ills. The mate goes ashore for a look-see and never come back. I dunno wot 'e done; no woman in it, far as we 'eard. Maybe 'e was just too curious, and they didn't like it. They found 'im; they cort 'im; they cut 'is 'ead clean off.

"*That* worn't so bad, yer see; there's 'ands killed every run. It was *returnin'* the 'ead as done it: the means they took to return it, chucking it like they done.

"Late at night, see, I'd just served the skipper a last grog in 'is cabin under the quarter-deck, with all the big winders aft, when we 'eard oars in rowlocks, and a little boat coming under our counter. We couldn't see nothing then; we didn't see much when they got away. But one of 'em must 'a' stood up in the boat, holding Sullivan's noggin by the 'air. All of a sudden, afore we knowed wot was wot . . ."

"Stop!" cried Isabelle de Sancerre. "There's a man out there now! He's going to throw something at us, and *it* looks like . . ."

Then she screamed and dodged.

There was a bursting crash of glass. An object heavy and roundish, flung with some force from the middle of the courtyard, shattered the left-hand window in a near-dark room. It struck the carpet, bounced, and rolled into the corner beyond the door.

4

"HELL OF A BUSINESS, EH?" DEMANDED TOM CLAYTON.

"It wasn't, you know," Macrae told him.

"Wasn't what?"

"Wasn't a hell of a business. And it wasn't a human head, though for a second or two we thought so. The power of suggestion; we saw what we expected to see."

"What *was* the thing, Dick?"

"One of those biggish earthenware jars, heavily glazed and painted brown or green, they sometimes hang in patios to catch rain-water. Roughly the shape of a head, rather larger, with the top of the skull gone. If you look through the window of my office, the window that isn't broken, you'll see it on my desk; it doesn't belong here. Why the thing didn't smash I can't tell you. Who threw it, or why, is equally a mystery."

"Somebody's having a game with you, old son. What happened after it hit the floor?"

There was a grey, uneasy sky that Thursday morning. In the courtyard at number 33 stood a handsome open carriage, of the sort locally called *calèche découverte*, with a pair of matched greys between the shafts. On the box was Walter, Leonidas Clayton's coachman.

Dick Macrae, walking-stick in his right hand and a copy of yesterday's *Picayune* in his left, paced back and forth beside the carriage. Tom Clayton paced beside him. Tom—loose-limbed, craggily handsome in a dark-complexioned way, something of a dandy with fawn-coloured frock coat, embroidered waistcoat, bottle-green trousers, and fawn-coloured hat—had been here for almost an hour.

"What happened after it hit the floor?" Tom repeated.

"Senator Benjamin and I raced out here. We found nobody; there was nobody to find. Jack Dowser left in a hurry, saying no more except to repeat over and over that he was a strong, silent man who knew the world. Then, after the rest of us had a drink, Senator Benjamin escorted Madame de Sancerre home. The senator—"

"Quite a lad, old Benjie; you'd never take him for the man of action he is. Has he got any idea what's been bothering Margot for nearly two months?"

"I'm sure he knows. The trouble is that he won't tell."

"Well, I wish I knew. I'm in love with the cursed jade, hoity-toity ways and all. But see here, Dick! What's this yarn you were spinning at breakfast: being followed and watched at night, as though by the old evil eye itself, for as long as something's been at Margot too?"

"Improbable as it may sound, it happens to be true."

"Fine kind of friend *you* are! Why didn't you tell me this before?"

"What could we have done if I had told you?"

"What's going to be done now, God willing! We'll set a trap for this joker and wring his damn neck."

"It may not be so easy, Tom. There's one incident I still haven't related, but that can wait. Meanwhile . . . !"

Leaving his tall companion muttering to himself, Macrae strolled under the covered way towards the street. The house's main staircase ascended from beneath that covered way; he could hear Sam and Tibby, somewhat impeded by their small son Rob, preparing the guest-room upstairs. Reaching the entrance, he glanced out along Carondelet Street. On the other side of the road, past Hookson's Bank, past Danforth the Wine-Importer's, past a sign reading *Sturdevant & Sons, Coach-Builders*, he could see the livery-stable where he hired his saddle-horses.

Macrae returned to the courtyard.

"You know, Tom," he continued, "this is life made easy. You arrive here with the family carriage while I'm having breakfast. The carriage, you announce, is at my disposal. We will *both* meet Harry Ludlow when the boat comes in, and give him a welcome New Orleans style. What gave you that idea?"

"Least I can do, seems to me!"

"On the contrary: it was a generous thought, and is much appreciated. I had meant to get a carriage from Will Likins at the livery-stable. That won't be necessary now. But you heard young Rob when he dashed back from the levee and yelled at us. The *Governor Roman* was coming in a quarter of an hour ago; they'll be discharging passengers now. Unless we make haste . . ."

"Don't look at *me*, old son; I've been ready all along. Jump in; that's it; plenty of room in this thing. Walter, forward! You know where to go!"

Out they rattled under the overcast sky. A right-hand turn into Common Street, another right-hand turn past the towering bulk of the St. Charles Hotel, then to the left down Julia Street towards their destination. They were nearly there when Tom, who had been sitting back with his hat over his eyes, adjusted the hat and straightened up.

"This Harry Ludlow—his father's something of a bigwig, *my* old man says—sounds like a pretty good fellow. How well do you know him?"

"I haven't seen him since he was a boy of ten. But I'm not likely to miss him. Harry can't be more than twenty-four now, still wrapped up in sport. At Lord's two years ago he played for Oxford against Cambridge, and by all report he's a very decent sort."

"Are you sure he'll know *you*?"

"That's been arranged. I'm to have a walking-stick in my right hand," Macrae held it up, "and a newspaper in my left." He thrust yesterday's *Picayune* into his pocket. "There's quite a mob ahead, Tom. These boats . . ."

The huge steamboats plying between St. Louis and New Orleans, called floating palaces by some or sinks of iniquity by others, had their berth at the levee between the foot of Canal Street and the foot of Julia Street. Several famous names were in: the *Grand Republic*, the *Princess*, and, last to arrive, the newest and most gaudy on the Mississippi.

Rearing three decks to a lofty height—boiler deck for roustabouts and less privileged passengers, upper deck for ladies and and gentlemen, texas deck for officers' quarters, pilot-house atop all—the *Governor Roman* loomed white and shiny against the yellow-brown river. A gilt emblem swung on its chain between two tall chimneys; the stage or gangplank had been run out over the port bow.

On the levee, amid cotton-bales piled high in both directions, the crowd seethed and struggled. Tom Clayton called a halt when their carriage was still some distance back.

"I'll stay here," he said. "You go ahead and find our man. I hope he hasn't been cleaned out in a poker game, or got left behind between here and Baton Rouge."

"And *I* hope . . ."

Macrae jumped down, shouldering through the throng. There seemed to be very few passengers left aboard; they were preparing to unload cargo. *He* hoped the young idiot had had sense enough to wait, according to instructions. If Harry Ludlow hadn't waited . . .

But Harry had.

Almost alone against the rail of the upper deck leaned a fair-haired, strongly built youth in one of the new-style short-coated lounge suits and new-style bowler hats with the curly brim, scanning all faces below. He caught Macrae's eye, raised his hand, and received a signal in reply. Picking up the carpet-bag at his feet, the new assistant retreated into the main salon, to appear twenty seconds later on the deck below, striding down the stage and tossing a coin to somebody as he passed.

"Sir!" he called.

Seen close at hand, Harry Ludlow had one of those boyish, fresh-coloured faces which can remain boyish when its owner is of mature age. He gave every sign of being what Her Majesty's consular representative had heard he was: not over-intelligent, perhaps, but willing, hearty, good-natured, guileless without too much gullibility. He greeted Macrae as he might have greeted an uncle or even a grandfather.

"Awfully good of you to meet me, sir! It's a great pleasure to be here."

"It's a pleasure to welcome you, Harry. How's your father?"

"Just as grumpy as ever, when I saw him last. Sent you his regards, though."

"Did you have a good journey down?"

"Not bad at all, and the food was first-rate. Only . . . Steve White . . . oh, confound the fellow!"

"Who is Steve White?"

"Chap I met in St. Louis, and shared a cabin with (they call it stateroom) on the way down. Lives in New Orleans, or used to. Behaved rather oddly, in a way, but I hardly thought about it until this morning. Then, without warning, he absquatulated."

"He—*what*?"

"Absquatulated! Hooked it! Cleared out in a hurry! He wasn't there when I woke up. One of the waiters said he'd nipped ashore in the first rush, without even staying for breakfast."

"Well . . . if you missed no money, and I gather you didn't? . . . never mind. Is that carpet-bag all your luggage?"

"My trunk will be coming by rail. Take some time, they said, but I didn't want to be burdened with it. And I couldn't even tell 'em where to send the thing! That's the point, sir: where *am* I going? Aren't there two famous hotels here?"

"There are, and you must have a drink at both. I have a better suggestion, however, than putting up at either the St. Charles or the St. Louis. Until you can find a place of your own, why not move into my guest-room?"

Harry's face glowed.

"*May* I do that, sir? I say, this is better and better! It's Carondelet Street, isn't it? The address I've been sending all the letters to?"

"It is, but you had better be warned about something. You speak French, don't you?"

"I'm supposed to speak pretty fair French; that's one of the reasons they chose me for this assignment. Why?"

"Unless you're talking to a Creole, never give street names the French pronunciation you used just now. Anglicize 'Carondelet' and sound the t. Chartres Street they call Charters, Bourbon Street is pronounced like the name of the whiskey . . ."

"What whiskey?"

"Corn whiskey, Harry: discovered and first distilled by (of all people) a Baptist preacher, the Rev. Elijah Craig. Speaking of Creoles, though . . ."

"Whatever you say, sir, but who *are* they? Before I left home, one of the nobs at the F.O. called me in and went on for an hour about Louisiana and its people. Most of it I couldn't make head or tail of. Who *are* these Creoles, anyway?"

"They are descendants or alleged descendants of French and Spanish families, mainly French, who settled here before the Louisiana Purchase of 1803."

"Creoles aren't coloured people, then?"

"Lord, no! Never ask that question, never so much as suggest it, unless you want to find yourself under the Duelling Oaks one morning at dawn. Now come this way; you must meet a friend of mine."

"I'm no hero," Harry confessed. "And I can be discreet; you trust me. But—oh, deuce take it! This whole American situation, North versus South, has got yours sincerely as confused as a cross-eyed batsman facing a fast bowler. It's all they go on about wherever I visit. Are things as bad as everybody says, sir? Is there really going to be trouble, even war?"

"That's a question nobody can answer. It's also a question in which you and I must conceal whatever opinions we may hold. And no more politics now, please! Here we are."

The carriage waited just ahead. Walter scrambled down to take the newcomer's carpet-bag. Tom Clayton descended with more dignity, beaming craggily on Harry. When Macrae introduced them, they shook hands with obviously mutual liking.

"Get in, both of you," Tom said. "Walter, drive back by way of Canal Street if you can avoid all these drays and cabs.

"Now then, young fellow," he continued, as they bumped along a course parallel to the river, "what seems to be on your mind?"

"Clayton," muttered Harry, who had been pondering. "Clayton . . . Look here, Mr. Clayton—!"

"Just 'Tom' will do. Any friend of Dick Macrae is a friend of mine."

"Thanks, Tom. Wasn't your governor the American Minister to Great Britain some years back?"

"My—oh, my old man? Yes; the *paterfamilias* did have a fling at diplomacy when James K. Polk was President. How's London these days?"

"Pretty dull, as it mostly is."

"Dull, eh? I can't accept that, young fellow. What do *you* say, Dick?"

"Let Dr. Johnson reply. 'The man who is tired of London is tired of life.' "

"And that's a fact!" Tom almost whooped. "I spent my impressionable twenty-first year there in '47. I heard Jenny Lind sing; I saw Macready play *Macbeth*. But we're not knocked endways by Macready, or by Jenny Lind either. Here's to more dubious amusements: to the night-houses off the Haymarket, and the women you could pick up there! The nymphs of the Haymarket, gentlemen, were something to remember in those days!"

"They still are," muttered Harry, his colour rising a little. "Got to be discreet about it, of course."

"Yes, of course!" Tom said lyrically. "Tell me, Harry: how did you fare aboard our best-thought-of steamboat? Did you admire the mirrors, the gilding, the red plush? Or did you find such *décor* 'vulgar and ostentatious,' according to the view of my esteemed mother?"

"Some of it was jolly fine, *I* thought!"

"He seems to have been most impressed," Macrae put in, "by rather a mysterious and peculiar character, one Steve White, who made off without a word of leave-taking as soon as the boat came in. However, since no sharper's tricks were attempted and no cash is missing . . ."

"Excuse me, sir," protested Harry, "but Steve wasn't exactly mysterious. And I didn't say he was peculiar."

"You said he behaved oddly."

"Dash it all, sir! It's only that he wasn't as free-and-easy as most people I've met. He seemed to be avoiding the others aboard, and kept *me* away from everybody as much as he could."

"Kept you away from everybody, did he?" Tom demanded. "Including women as well?"

"Yes; how did you know? There were two girls, dashed pretty girls at that, in a cabin (stateroom) near ours. I could have sworn one of 'em smiled over her shoulder, and I thought they mightn't be too offended if we spoke. Steve wouldn't hear of it."

"Whereas *you* wanted to meet 'em, eh? You'd have given a lot to meet 'em?"

"I wouldn't have minded. The brunette in green . . ."

"Well, well!" mused Tom, with a gleam coming into his eye. "Well, well, well!"

"And Steve did me one great favour, at least. He warned me about a notorious river gambler, flashily dressed chap known as Square Nat Rumbold, who had started some kind of game in the bar. Since I'm not too fond of cards or dice anyway . . ."

"I'm acquainted with Nat Rumbold, Harry; your mysterious friend did you a favour after all. No losses at poker or twenty-one? No regrets except for the brunette you didn't meet? What did you find to occupy you?"

"I ate too much and drank too much. There was nothing else to do."

"If you stay with us long, and accept much hospitality at the plantations, they'll have you drinking juleps before breakfast. Never mind. You're all right, young fellow!

"Now this is Canal Street," Tom pursued, as they turned into that broad thoroughfare, "and what can we do to entertain you on your first night? If you had a taste for games of chance, it would be easy. The finest gambling-house in town, where all croupiers and dealers must wear evening clothes, is at number 4 on the same street as your own consulate. Still . . ."

"This Carondelay Street, which I'm to call Carondelette, must be all things to all men! Isn't there a British bank, Hookson's? My governor's opened an account for me there."

"That's close by also. Like to be introduced to the manager?"

"Yes, thanks, but not just yet. I cashed a big draft on New York; I'm still laden with the ready."

"Well! If you don't fancy games of chance, I was saying, it's easy to see what you do fancy. And I've got it, young fellow! As the clerks say in the shops, I've got just the thing! Dick, may I have that newspaper?"

Macrae handed over yesterday's *Picayune*. Tom opened it to an inside page and folded the paper flat.

"Here we are, among the advertisements. Now be respectfully silent; hearken and attend.

" '*The Washington and American Ballroom, formerly Globe, corner of St. Claude and St. Peter Streets, abreast of the Old Basin. Thursday evening, April 15, and every Thursday until further notice, a society ball will be given . . .* ' "

"A society ball?" gasped Harry. "Do they advertise 'em in the newspaper?"

"It's not a society ball, as you'll see very shortly, but it's not an experience to be missed either. Shut up while I read the conditions.

" '*No ladies admitted without masks . . . Gentlemen, fifty cents—ladies, gratis . . . Doors open at 9½ o'clock. Ball to commence at 10 o'clock . . . No person admitted with weapons, by order of the council . . . A superior orchestra has been engaged for the season . . . The public may be assured of the most strict order, as there will be at all times an efficient police in attendance.*

" '*Attached to the establishment is a superior bar, well stocked with wines and liquors; also a restaurant, where may be had all such delicacies as the market affords. Ladies are requested to procure free tickets in the mask room, as no lady will be admitted to the ballroom without one.*'

"Then there's the manager's signature, and that's all."

Again Harry Ludlow found his voice.

"It's quite enough, thanks very much! No weapons? Strict order? Efficient police? Oh, crikey, what *is* all that?"

"It's a quadroon ball."

"What's a quadroon ball?"

"An institution peculiar to this city," Tom informed him, "which might well be copied elsewhere. Dick, will you do the explaining?"

Macrae, riding backwards and facing the other two, shifted in his seat.

"I'm far from being an authority, remember. I've never attended one of these functions, even to look on, and I'm not sure I understand it all myself. Will you keep your ears open, Tom, and correct me if I go wrong?"

"I'll correct you *instanter*, old son. Fire away."

Macrae contemplated his new assistant, who had regained composure and looked eager.

"In New Orleans, Harry, there are many mulatto or quadroon girls: half white or three-quarters white, sired by white fathers who may not acknowledge them publicly. They form a special class of their own, superior to black but still below the level of white. Most of them are pretty; they have good figures and wear clothes with *chic*. Some are well-educated and accomplished, the unavowed father having paid for it. Not a few are beauties, in appearance as white as any of us; they may even have fair hair and blue eyes.

"Now what may such a girl expect in life? To become a maid or a hairdresser? Sometimes, yes. As a rule, however, she is carefully brought up by her mulatto or quadroon mother for one particular purpose: that she may be chosen as paramour, less mistress than a kind of unofficial wife, by some well-to-do young man of the ruling caste, Creole or American."

"Sir, are you saying . . . ?"

"The situation exists, and must be faced; let's have no moralizing or cant!"

"I wasn't going to do that, though at home they'd say . . ."

"The young man will approach her mother, a hard-headed woman of business who arranges terms. The girl, potentially a home-maker, is rewarded with a trim little house in Rampart Street or thereabouts, and such luxuries as her protector can afford. If she won't always rest content at home, where may she appear in public with a male escort? Only at a quadroon ball among others of her kind, where everybody is masked and the girl *must* be masked."

"And that's not all!" Tom interposed. "It's the place where still-unattached charmers go on display. If the masked beauty is accompanied by a man, just look the other way; she's somebody's property or about to be. If she's accompanied only by a masked duenna, probably her mother, then don't hesitate to say hello; that's what she's there for. It needn't go further than a dance and a *tête-à-tête*; you're under no obligation at all. Anyway, there they are: a whole roomful of dazzlers to suit every taste. Gentle and affectionate too, or so I'm told. Would you like that, young fellow? Do you think you'd like it?"

"Would I like it, by Jove? Oh, crikey-lordy, would I *like it*? It's just what I've dreamed of! But—!"

"But what?"

"A fight with fists is one thing; I'm your man for that any time. Aiming a pistol at somebody's guts is something else altogether. If I'm ever challenged to a duel, I hope I can be steady and do myself credit. But I don't claim I'd enjoy it, or that my knees wouldn't knock together. If I get called out on the very first night I'm here . . ."

"Called out, my foot!" roared Tom. "Nonsense and humbug and balderdash! Keep your hands off a woman who's spoken for, and those affairs are as decorous as any ball at the *Salle d'Orléans*. They've got to be! If that's your only reason for hanging back . . .?"

"It's not my only reason. What would Mr. Macrae say?"

Macrae looked at him.

"Well, provided you behave yourself, what *would* I say?"

"You've never attended it yourself, sir! At your age, and remembering dignity . . ."

"Damnation, Harry! I'm not stricken in years or ready for a wheel-chair just yet. If you and Tom decide to do this, I've more than half a mind to go with you and look on."

"Shall we call it settled, then?" asked Tom.

And yet a shadow had crossed Tom's face.

They were bowling at a good clip along Canal Street, and had almost reached the point at which Walter must make a left-hand turn against oncoming vehicles along the far side of the road. Tom Clayton folded up the newspaper and returned it to Macrae. He did not seem happy.

"We will attend the ball, gentlemen," he declared. "There will be no duel-challenges, Harry, or I'll take 'em on myself and save you trouble. You may go unhesitatingly; your boss will be there to back you up. We will attend the ball, I say, with high hearts and expectant senses. And yet I'm not sure we ought to attend after all."

"Deuce take it," cried Harry, "you're the one who's been so strong for this! What's the matter?"

Tom rose to his feet in the carriage. Balancing as well as he could, hooking his left thumb in the armhole of his waistcoat, he took a reflective survey of the street.

"I'm a gloomy sort of cuss, young fellow, when I'm not excited about something. The Clayton ideas are excellent, granted. But the Clayton premonitions have been highly esteemed since their origin with my forbears in old Virginny. And I have one now.

"You don't know the pressure of oddity that accumulated last night, and may be accumulating still. Some joker on the prowl with his unfunny ways! The jar thrown through the window instead of a human head!

"Duels or rowdyism? I'm not disturbed by those. I *am* disturbed by the joker. He's too persistent; he won't let go. I can't help a presentiment that some damn thing or other will explode in our faces before the night's over. I can't help feeling . . ."

Tom did not continue. But he was right.

5

ALONG BOURBON STREET IN THE OLD SQUARE, AT A QUARTER
to ten that night, the same open carriage behind the same horses,
with Walter again on the box, jolted east towards the Washington
and American Ballroom.

A gleam of carriage-lamps touched pastel-coloured house-
fronts with iron balconies and shop-signs in French. Despite one
or two rain-squalls that day, the night had turned fine; a clear,
luminous sky showed the edge of a moon.

The same three passengers now wore evening clothes: heavy
black broadcloth, starched shirts with very broad white tie, and
gossamer silk hats. Harry Ludlow, his own 'goss' having not yet
arrived, had bought another hat in Canal Street.

Accepting thirty-two-year-old Tom Clayton as a contemporary,
Harry still behaved towards thirty-seven-year-old Macrae as he
might have behaved towards a well-meaning but formidable uncle.
Tom, irrepressible, had given Harry some account of last night's
events. But he had touched only lightly on Macrae's sense of being
watched, for which that harassed gentleman felt grateful.

There was one incident Tom had not mentioned, and would
have had the tact not to mention in any case. However, since he
knew nothing of a certain lithe girl with tawny hair and grey-blue
eyes, he could not have referred to her if he had wanted to.

Harry, in an excited state all day, was now preoccupied with his
new life.

"I say, Tom! That restaurant where we had dinner this evening, with the *bouillabaisse* and all. What's the place called?"

"McDonald's, Gravier Street."

"Some rather rum customs you've got here, if you don't mind my saying so. That earlier meal, the one I never expected! In the big underground bar at the St. Charles Hotel."

"Well, what about it?"

"You walk up to the bar-counter and name your poison. The barman spreads a strip of cloth on your side of the counter, and puts down your glass on his side. On the strip of cloth, before you've said a word, he sets out an elegant little repast from cold prawns to salad. When you ask what there is to pay, he says it's included in the price of the drink."

"That's a St. Charles invention called the free lunch; it'll spread elsewhere some day. Anything else on your mind, young fellow?"

"Yes, rather a lot! Is it much farther to where we're going?"

"Not unduly far, no. We bear left at St. Peter Street, and your destiny will soon be upon you. Feeling nervous already?"

"Already, you say? I've been on wires the whole evening! I *want* to be there, understand? It's only that . . . that . . . Suppose one of these girls does take my eye: what's the manner of approach? How do I *treat* her?"

"Treat her exactly as you'd treat any young lady at a ball in England. Don't expect her to be brash or coarse; you'll find her anything but that. At first she may be coy about lifting up her mask so that you can get a good look; insist firmly but gently, on your best behaviour."

"Yes; only . . ."

"Perhaps I should explain," Tom made a boxed motion with his hands, "that the Washington and American Ballroom, formerly Globe, is in fact several rooms of a building set in its own grounds with a wall around. In the grounds, at either side of the building, there's a paved yard where carriages wait. Behind it is a garden.

"We go into the place; we buy tickets in the lobby, and pick up masks in the room adjoining. Men aren't obliged to wear masks, but it's advisable. You can never tell what friend you may meet there, and you want to embarrass him no more than he wants to embarrass you. That's all there is to it until the orchestra strikes up. Just trust your natural address, Harry, and don't worry your head about a thing."

"Tom, you yourself . . ."

"Will you be *quiet*, for God's sake?"

Few vehicles seemed to be abroad, and few wayfarers either. They had travelled for some distance along St. Peter Street when Harry craned sideways and peered ahead. Macrae, once more sitting with his back to the horses, twisted round for a glance in the same direction.

Just ahead, at the junction of St. Peter Street with St. Claude, a torch blazed in its link-bracket at either side of the arch in the wall, beyond which lamps were twinkling from a pillared building in a paved courtyard. Macrae turned back.

Then it happened.

Walter, juggling his reins, was about to negotiate the arch when another two-horse open carriage, with top-hatted driver and one passenger, came rattling up out of St. Peter Street close behind them. The flames of two torches shone on the face of the solitary passenger, a girl in a low-cut blue gown frilled at the bosom.

Hair light-brown and yellow for the effect of tawniness, done into fashionable short curls framing her cheeks. Complexion a soft golden white crossed by the red of the lips, which were half parted. Eyes long and heavy-lidded, grey-blue against strongly luminous whites.

For one instant, with a sense of shock like a physical stopping of the heart, Macrae looked her straight in the eyes.

The fair unknown gasped and turned her head away. Her right hand whipped up a spread fan to hide the face completely. And Tom Clayton glanced back over his shoulder.

"Walter," he called, "be good enough to let the lady's carriage precede us. Pull up, can't you?"

Walter pulled up. The other equipage swept past through the arch, and swung left over muddy stones.

"Was that one of 'em, Tom?" exclaimed Harry Ludlow. "Damme, Tom, was that one of 'em?"

"How should I know? Yes, probably it was. But keep your voice down and don't yell. Walter, they turned to the left; you turn to the right; why embarrass *anybody?*"

To the right of the low-roofed building with the pillars, over whose portico a medallion-head of George Washington had been superimposed on a shield of the national colours, perhaps two or three dozen vehicles awaited the end of the evening. There were carriages open and closed; there was even a hackney cab. Most drivers had gone to refresh themselves in one way or another. Walter chose a spot near the east wall, and his passengers alighted.

"Well, here we are," began Harry, who was shifting from one foot to the other. "I'll go ahead and get the tickets, shall I?"

Tom seized his arm.

"Oh, no, you don't! You're not paying for *everything*, Young Innocence, as you paid for those drinks at the St. Charles and tried to pay for the dinner too. I'll get the tickets; the price is modest enough; in the great days of these affairs it would have been two dollars a head. Dick, what's the matter with *you?*"

"There's nothing the matter. Nothing at all! You two cut along in; I will stay here and smoke a cigar before I join you. Keep an eye on Harry, Tom; restrain and hobble him, if need be."

"Are you sure nobody needs to hobble *you?* I have a distinct feeling . . .".

To avoid argument by ignoring it, Macrae said no more. Leaving the others to their own devices, he strode back past the front of the building and round to the other side.

Fully as great a clutter of vehicles had been left here. Near the arch into St. Peter Street, its single horse facing outwards as though ready for departure, waited an equipage which seemed vaguely familiar; so did its coachman, very much in attendance.

But he could not now concern himself with this. He was looking for a *calèche découverte* with upholstery of oystershell grey, against which a blue gown and white shoulders had stood out so vividly by torchlight.

He found the carriage, also facing outward, well back in the courtyard near the luxuriant garden at the rear; he found the fair unknown. She sat motionless behind a motionless coachman, a gauze scarf round her shoulders, her hands clasped on the fan. He saw her by the gleam of carriage-lanterns roundabout.

But she saw him too. And she did not hesitate. Supple of body, lithe of movement, managing the great crinoline with a kind of fluency, she descended from the carriage and ran off into the garden, where shadows swallowed her up.

'If there's another way out of here,' he was thinking in some desperation, 'I've lost her again!'

The luminous sky, draining flowers of their colour, gave just light enough for pursuit. Gravel paths wound maze-like through a head-high wilderness heavy with tropical fragrance. One single broad path, straight through the centre of the garden, *might* lead to an exit. He heard light footfalls hastening along it, and increased his own pace to a run.

There was no way out. The path ended in a cul-de-sac, a semicircle of tall hedge in which a marble statue of Diana, rather less than life size, stood on its pedestal as though in a niche.

The girl stopped and turned below the statue of Diana. Though the fan was again spread in her hand, she did not lift it. He could hear her quickened breathing and feel her agitation, but there was some other emotion besides agitation or alarm.

"Will you forgive this unmannerly performance, madam?" he said. "I had no choice. At our last meeting . . ."

Her voice, low and sweet, held not a trace of French accent.

"Are you under the impression, sir, that we have met before?"

"It's more than an impression, believe me. At that meeting, our only meeting, your dress was the russet colour of leaves in autumn; and in your hand, as you are now holding that fan, you had a black domino mask edged with lace. The occasion, may I remind you . . . ?"

"I have no choice. If you insist on addressing me, it must be endured."

"I will take that for permission. The occasion, then, was the night of Tuesday, February sixteenth, exactly one week before *Mardi Gras*.

"At the invitation of Mr. Barnaby Jeffers, the local historian, I had called on Mr. Jeffers at his house in Second Street, off St. Charles Avenue of the Garden District. I went there in a hackney cab, bribing its driver to wait. When I left the house at a little past eleven o'clock, the street was empty. Someone had given the driver a larger bribe and made off with the cab.

"There was nothing for it but to walk home to Carondelet Street. I set off along St. Charles Avenue, and had gone two or three hundred yards when I passed one of those big houses in its own grounds behind an iron-railed fence.

"For some entertainment of a sort common during carnival season, the whole house (whose I can't say) was a blaze of light. I had come abreast of this house when *another* hackney cab loomed up from the west, also proceeding towards town. It was moving so slowly that I assumed it to be empty. I raised my hand; the driver slowed still more . . .

"I was too precipitate; very well, let that be admitted. But it was only relief at finding a cab that made me precipitate; I had no other motive. I ran into the road, I pulled open the door of the cab, tumbled inside, and slammed the door. Then I discovered that it was not unoccupied. *You* sat in the far corner, muffled in a cloak over your evening gown, with the mask in your hand. Do you doubt my veracity now?"

"Not only your veracity; I begin to doubt your sanity too. Really, sir . . . !"

"I tried to explain the mistake; I tried to tell you my name. You asked what my name mattered, and I was obliged to confess that it mattered little. You thought, or appeared to think, that I had done this deliberately in order to molest you. You put on the mask in haste; you begged me, if I had anything at all of gentlemanly instinct, to get out of the cab and leave you in peace.

"Again there was no choice. I jumped down, slamming the door. As for my next action: call it undignified or ungentlemanly or even ludicrous, but . . ."

"Well?"

"I ran along beside the cab and called to the driver. I said I did not suppose he knew your identity; he replied that I supposed correctly. In my watch pocket I had a five-dollar goldpiece. I offered him this goldpiece if he would tell me where he was taking you."

"Now why should you have done *that*? If in fact you did anything of the kind?"

"Why should I wish to trace you, learn your name, see you again? For the answer, madam, consult any mirror. You have more than mere good looks, *belle inconnue*. You have the quality which some call magnetism and others call by a grosser name. But my own thoughts or intentions, pray credit me, were and are the reverse of gross. May I conclude the story of that night?"

"There's no stopping you by main force, is there?"

"Much as he would like my money, the driver said, he didn't know where he was taking you. He said you had hailed him from the pavement a quarter mile back, seeming much upset; that you had told him to drive anywhere, anywhere at all. A few moments later, as I ran beside that infernal cab, you put your head out of the far window and told him to whip up his horse, which he did. But not before he had added something which makes me wonder why you are play-acting at this minute."

"*Play-acting?*"

"Doubtless you have good reasons; permit me to explain. He had slowed down when I hailed him, the cabby said, because he could have sworn you yourself called out and asked him to slow down.

"Nor is that all. When I first tumbled into the cab, landing with great clumsiness on the edge of your crinoline, there was enough light from the house opposite to show your face distinctly. Just before you began your accusation of dishonourable intentions, you looked at me from close at hand, closer than we are now. I could have sworn there was a kind of intimacy about that look, as though in spirit we were very close, and as though your eyes—what eyes they are!—would convey some message I ought to understand."

She had backed towards the statue of Diana; the eyes in question seemed very near tears.

"If I am to be called the worst of liars and hypocrites," she said, "what are *you*?"

That was when the music began.

From the back of the low-roofed building which housed the Washington and American Ballroom, its windows muffled in thick curtains, the unseen orchestra struck up a quadrille. You could imagine the dancers pairing off in an ornate room, four couples to a set. But Macrae, on whom the solution of certain puzzles was beginning to dawn at last, could think only of his fair unknown.

Her face had grown as white as that of the statue above her; she moved her shoulders as though in pain, and seemed to be nerving herself for a last effort.

"You had no hesitation in accosting me that night, when I was alone and unprotected. But aren't you *just a little* afraid now?"

"Afraid?"

"You find me at a quadroon ball; you must know what I am."

"Must I, madam?"

"A woman of my sort comes here only accompanied by a duenna, or to meet the gentleman who is her current protector. You see no duenna, do you? What if my protector should resent your attentions tonight, and were minded to issue a challenge?"

"I must risk that."

"Are you immune or immortal, then? Even a crack shot like yourself, Mr. Macrae—!"

She stopped dead, though her expression did not change.

Macrae sketched out a mimicry of applause.

"We are getting on, I see. You know my name; you are good enough to call me a crack shot . . ."

"Even a quadroon hussy," she flashed at him, "may learn the names of her betters. Why shouldn't my protector avenge me?"

"Because you are not a quadroon hussy, and you have no protector either. You did not come to attend the ball, or even to' venture indoors. If we may drop this pretence of being total strangers, if you will honour me by taking my arm and walking back in the direction of the carriages, I will hazard a guess or two concerning who you really are, and why you did come."

"I—I must do that too, I daresay?"

She was trying to preserve an icy dignity, but icy dignity did not suit her. Her relief was as evident as the willingness with which she took his arm; even that slight contact gave him a thrill of pleasure.

"They are only guesses, remember," he continued, guiding her along the path. "They lack the logical analysis that could be supplied by Senator Benjamin, and parts may be mistaken. But to their general rightness I will swear. In any matter which concerns *you*, my masquerade lady of carnival-time, I have eyes to see through a brick wall. May I believe that?"

"I *want* you to believe it!"

"Out of the garden, now . . . past your own carriage . . . along a murky lane with the firefly gleams of the lanterns . . ."

"Where are you taking me?"

"Not much farther. Towards the front gate, as you see; towards . . ."

"Oh, good heavens! If you really *have* guessed everything, though on my soul's life I don't see how you could, please tell me! Who am I, then? Why *did* I come to the wretched affair?"

"I think your name is Ursula Ede, and that you are here as an act of friendship in support of someone else. You observe the small closed carriage, black with red wheels, its horse aimed at the gate as though for instant flight?"

"Well?"

"One such carriage looks very like another. But it seemed familiar when I passed a while ago, and I am now certain. It was used last night by Madame de Sancerre when she visited me at the consulate. It is used much more often, however, by Madame de Sancerre's daughter, your great friend. Margot is here tonight, is she not? And in disguise?"

The girl dropped his arm and recoiled as though from a blow in the face, but her eyes had already told him he was right on all counts.

"Really," gasped Ursula Ede, "this is almost past belief. I had heard you were reliable, Mr. Macrae; I had not heard you were a magician."

"Nor am I. There is a question Margot de Sancerre has been hammering at her mother for almost two months. Would she,

Margot, have so many beaux or be so sought after if she were merely herself and not the well-dowered, socially prominent daughter of Jules de Sancerre?"

"How do you know Margot asked her mother that?"

"Information received, as they say among the detective police in London. And so Margot, already a law unto herself, must prove herself too? She would go masked to a quadroon ball, and in that guise or disguise bring all the men to her feet as she usually does?

"The plan, I think, came to maturity yesterday; she told her mother she was prepared. She visited you at your father's plantation, probably begging you to put on a mask and go with her. You refused to play the quadroon beauty in the ballroom, which put her into the tantrum a servant described. But you promised to be on hand and lend moral support. Is that a fair guess too?"

Ursula Ede gestured helplessly.

"I told Margot it was too risky and not worth all the trouble. She called me dishonest and a prude: which I'm not, truly I'm not! I was dishonest with *you*, I know. But that was only my awful, accursed training; it wasn't me at all!

"The truth is," she hurried on, avoiding his eye, "I've wanted so much to meet you since that day last fall when I was out with my father, and I saw you shooting near the lake. But they told me it would be wrong and unladylike to make any kind of approach . . .

"Do you think *I* don't remember the Tuesday night before *Mardi Gras*? I had been to a masquerade at the Hendersons'; the boy who took me got so drunk he fell downstairs and knocked himself out. I didn't wait for someone else to drive me home at the end of the evening. I snatched up my cloak, ran out of there, and hailed a passing cab."

"You told the cabby to drive you anywhere? But eventually, no doubt, to take you home?"

"Yes."

"All the way to the plantation?"

"We don't live at the plantation all the time, any more than Margot's family lives at theirs. We're in town too, mostly, at a house not very far from them.

"Well! Of course you thought the cab was empty, as I knew at the time. And I did tell the cabby to slow down. Then, when you jumped in as I hoped you would, the awful, wretched training of years wouldn't let me be natural or behave as I wanted to behave. My father, my aunts all seemed to be there and talking. I lost my nerve; I carried on as though I really thought you meant what I intimated you meant. Please! Am I forgiven?"

"There's nothing to forgive, you know. Any real problem, perhaps an immediate one, concerns your friend Margot. Anyway, how can she manage the business alone? In this refined sort of slave-market, isn't every unattached girl supposed to have her duenna?"

"Margot's got one."

"Oh?"

"You see, there's nobody at the de Sancerres' who could possibly have played the part. But we've got a mulatto house-slave named Samantha who's perfect for it."

"And Margot borrowed her?"

"Yes, of course; that's one of the reasons she wanted to see me. I gave my permission; I wrote a note Margot could read to Samantha. And we arranged it.

"Samantha is permanently attached to the house in town. Margot was to give her money for cab fare, and any clothes Samantha needed in dressing up for the part. They were to meet here between half-past nine and a quarter to ten. Margot would bring her own mask, an elaborate domino, and Samantha would get one of the kind they provide. There's the carriage as proof of everything: Margot is dancing in all her glory, just as you explained. Is there anything we *haven't* explained?"

"Yes, and it's important. Did she think of this scheme on her own, or did somebody put her up to it? In short, who's been whispering to her and hypnotizing her for the past seven weeks?"

"I don't know! That's another of the things she won't tell me! There *is* someone, I'm sure from hints she's let fall: someone who suggested a trick she mightn't have thought of for herself."

Perplexed, distressed, Ursula stretched out a hand towards him and then withdrew it.

"Margot has a great deal on her mind, I'm afraid. Part of it concerns Voodoo, of all things; part of it concerns a woman dead long ago, a woman named Delphine Lalaurie. But what relation there can be between Voodoo and Madame Lalaurie, or whether either has affected this ridiculous game tonight, is all a part of the same mystery! Do you think there's going to be trouble here?"

"That's impossible to say. Much may depend on how far the girl goes in her acting. Did she tell you what her tactics would be?"

"No!"

"She may carry it off, of course. On the other hand, since Tom Clayton is here in his most swashbuckling mood . . ."

"*Tom Clayton's here?*"

"He was in the carriage with my new assistant and myself. Didn't you see him?"

"I *saw* two others; I didn't *observe* them; I was thinking only of hiding my face from you!"

"The others didn't see your face; you were too quick with that fan. We thought . . ."

"I know what you thought. And Margot . . . oh, this is ghastly! Will you excuse me for just one moment, Mr. Macrae?"

"You won't run away again, will you?"

"I won't run away again; I promise. And I'm only going as far as my own carriage, in case it matters. If *you* don't desert *me* . . ."

Adjusting the gauze scarf round her shoulders, giving him a look from under lowered eyelids, she slipped away into obscurity

The music from the ballroom, which had ceased a few moments ago, now swelled up again in muffled volume. Macrae glanced towards the portico with the pillars.

Three broad, shallow stone steps led up to that portico. Double doors, emitting a glow of shaded lamps, stood wide open to the lobby. Of the lobby, from this position, he could see little more than a side wall with a gilded cornice, the edge of a desk, and one or two shadows, presumably those of attendants, passing and re-passing against the light.

From the yard itself came a clop of hoofs and jolt of wheels. The *calèche découverte* with the oystershell-grey upholstery, ex-

pertly guided by Ursula's coachman, skirted the press of other
vehicles and took up a position only a short distance behind the
little closed carriage on whose box sat burly old Uncle Cicero. In
the *calèche*, on the left-hand side facing forward, sat Ursula herself.

"Mr. Macrae," she began, "you have been so kind to me that
. . . may I take up a little more of your time this evening?"

"All the time you want, and whenever you want it. I am entirely
at your disposal."

"Will you get into the carriage, please? And sit over at the right-
hand side?"

"There!" he said a moment later. "Is this far enough away?"

"It's not a question of being far away! It's not that at all! But
from where you're sitting you can see . . . Will you go on helping
me in something that may seem rather silly?"

"You know I will, Miss Ede."

"My name is Ursula. It's a horrible name, of course; it suggests
a saint or an old maid or something dreadful like that. Still! If you
can bring yourself to use it . . . !"

"It will be a pleasure to use it. What do we do now?"

"We wait. You see, you were right about another thing. Margot
did think she *might* have to leave in a hurry, and jump in that
carriage and go like blazes. I can make guesses too, and inspired
ones. My guess is that it's going to happen, and very soon. Of
course, there may be a long wait for nothing."

"In your company, Ursula, I have no objection to waiting."

"But I'm taking you away from your friends!"

"They will excuse me, I know. What happens if she does beat a
hasty retreat?"

"We follow." Ursula indicated the coachman. "Jared has his
instructions. Wherever she goes, and at whatever pace, he's to
keep behind that carriage and never lose sight of it."

"Here's what I want you to do, if you will. From that position
you can watch the right-hand door of Margot's carriage, while I
do the same with the left. Please, please never lose sight of it! We
must make sure of two things: first, that Margot herself doesn't
open the door to leave of her own free will; second, that nothing

else opens the door to catch her and pull her out."

"Did you say 'nothing' else?"

"Yes! I'm afraid of the first possibility: that she may suddenly have decided to desert family and friends, and hide herself away somewhere. Margot's afraid of the second. She thinks something, meaning something not human at all, is on her trail and after her."

" 'Ghoulies and ghosties and long-leggity beasties'? You don't expect to find 'em in the streets of New Orleans?"

"I don't expect anything," Ursula cried, "because there's no way of telling what may happen. I do know I must keep an eye on her as far as anyone can. And my own guess wasn't such a bad guess after all. Here she comes now!"

6

At the double doors to the lobby of the Washington and American Ballroom, in the direction Ursula indicated, there had been a kind of minor explosion.

Out under the portico, now enraged and wearing no mask, stalked a dark-haired, imperious-looking girl in yellow brocade gown and overjacket of green-and-gold velvet. If you had not known her for a reigning beauty, you might have taken her for a professional actress. She turned round to glare briefly at the hovering shadows just inside; Macrae had a distant glimpse of her face in profile.

Margot de Sancerre was much taller than Ursula Ede, who measured little more than five feet one. Margot's resemblance to her mother could not have been mistaken, though she had youth's freshness, youth's self-assurance, and (clearly) youth's bad temper.

Whipping up her mask, a black one with rhinestones round the eyepieces, Margot put it on and adjusted it. She turned her back to the doors. She ran down the three shallow steps, and, without so much as glancing at Ursula and Macrae in the *calèche*, hastened across the yard towards the waiting black carriage, at which Uncle Cicero had descended to open the door.

And then, at the entrance to the lobby, there was a major explosion.

Tom Clayton, himself without mask, his hat on the back of his head, stalked out under the portico. Two others followed him.

One of these, fat and with the air of manager or proprietor, seemed to be expostulating. The second, a lean figure with a flowing moustache and evening clothes of exaggerated cut, was in a state of grievance. He overtook Tom and tapped him on the shoulder.

"I spoke to you, sir!" he said.

"Did you, now?" Tom exploded. "Did you, by God!"

Their voices rang in the quiet night.

"Gentlemen, gentlemen!" yelped the fat man. "None o' that, now! None o' that *here!* 'Tain't as if—"

"You shall answer me, sir," said the aggrieved one, "and you shall answer *to* me. Do you hear what I say?"

Tom's exact move was a little difficult to follow. His left hand seemed to go behind the aggrieved one's back. His powerful right hand fastened round the aggrieved one's chin, and he uncoiled all his weight in a mighty shove.

The man in the exaggerated evening clothes flew backward through the open doors as though shot from a catapult. There was a crash as he landed somewhere inside. At the same moment Harry Ludlow ran out under the portico.

"Do you know who that was, Tom? Do you know who it was you shoved?"

"I don't give a whistling damn who it was. Look there, will you?"

And Tom stabbed his finger in the direction of Margot, who had compressed her great skirts into the little black vehicle with the red wheels.

"There she goes, curse the conceit of all women. She needs a lesson, that young lady does, and this time she's going to get one!"

"I say, though! What can you *do?*"

"I'll tan her behind, that's what I'll do! I'll put her across my knee and . . . Call Walter and the carriage! Bring 'em around here quick! Wherever she goes, home or any place else, she won't get away from me again!"

Cicero's whip had cracked like a pistol-shot. Jared's whip cracked a scant three or four seconds later.

The black carriage, plunging for the arch, might have made a right or left turn into St. Claude Street. Instead it darted straight ahead, gathering speed due south along St. Peter Street, with Ursula and Macrae in pursuit at no great distance back.

Once or twice, especially during Tom's outburst, Macrae had feared his companion might faint; Ursula's eyes seemed glazed. But his fingertips at her elbow reassured him of her steadiness.

"Don't touch me!" she said. "I mean: don't touch me *now!* Stay on your own side and watch that door; lean out if you must, but don't ever lose sight of it! Margot . . ."

"She'll have quite a lot of company, it seems. Tom and Harry will be along in a moment. Tom's suggestion of tanning her . . . Tom's suggestion, though it lacks subtlety and might have been expressed in choicer words, is not without a good deal of merit. It may be the best way of meeting the situation after all."

"But that mustn't happen either, don't you see?"

"Not altogether, no."

"I've wanted to smack Margot myself. Many's the time *I've* wanted to smack her, or at least give her a good shaking. But she's bigger and stronger than I am; I couldn't have done that even if it weren't conduct unbecoming a lady. And Tom mustn't either! He mustn't tan her— That is, I mean, if Tom and that fair-haired boy really do follow?"

"Dey comin', Miss Ursie!" Jared said from the box. "Dey comin' sure nuff!"

"Mr. Macrae and I mustn't look back, Jared; we must look straight ahead. But . . ."

"Dey comin', Miss Ursie! Don' you *hear* 'em?"

The clatter of another open carriage had become distinctly audible.

"Jared," Ursula called, "under no circumstances must Mr. Clayton overtake and pass us! We've got better horses, anyway; he can't pass us! Nobody must pass us! And really, Mr. Macrae," she added with sudden severity, "you find nothing *comical* in all this, I hope?"

"Well . . ."

"Do you?"

"There's a certain piquancy about the chase, at any rate. It's not a midnight chase, though it ought to be. The ball explodes with a lovers' quarrel. Away dashes Margot, fearing bogles in the dark. Away *we* dash, fearing we don't know what. And after us all roars Tom Clayton, intent only on . . . what he *is* intent on."

"It's not funny; it's horrible! Do you think Margot knows she's being followed?"

"She knows, right enough," returned Macrae, who had seen the glass in the right-hand door of the black equipage briefly lowered, and had seen the face of Margot de Sancerre peering at them before the glass was raised again. "She's just looked out and dodged back in. We've become quite a flying procession, which should interest Mayor Waterman and the council. Let's hope it won't interest the police too. I could be more alert for malignant ghosts if I had some notion of where we were going."

He was answered as to direction, at least. Damp night or no, horseshoe-iron struck fire from the road as the carriage ahead made a sudden right-hand swerve into Royal Street, and pelted west with its two tiny lanterns agleam.

"Headin' lickety-split fo' Canal Street, we are," Jared volunteered. "Miss Margot goin' home, you ask me!"

It looked like that. Down the rest of Royal Street nothing stirred except a drunken man who reeled out of the Gem Saloon just before they crossed the dividing line into the American sector.

The St. Charles stretch, for the first three or four hundred yards, showed more life. Gaslight flared on faces and on advertising posters. A troupe of minstrels was appearing at the St. Charles Theatre. Then saloons, oyster-bars fell behind as the three carriages swept on into darkness. Whips cracked; once or twice Macrae could hear Tom Clayton swear.

"Nobody's gaining ground," he said, "but nobody's losing it either. And Margot does seem to be going home. From where we are now, how far do you estimate it is to St. Charles Avenue and

Holywell Street? A mile and a half or so?"

"Something like that, perhaps a bit less. Are you still keeping watch?"

He was, being conscientious. But concentration had grown increasingly difficult. Ursula's nearness, within touching distance, her intense femininity, disturbed him and induced thoughts he shouldn't have had. Ursula herself may or may not have been conscious of this. Though her own eyes never wavered from the left-hand door ahead, she had dropped the gauze scarf from her shoulders. She was still trying to be severe, with no success at all.

"I ought to scold you, Mr. . . . what's *your* Christian name, by the way?"

"Richard. Hadn't you better . . . ?"

"That's a good name, that's an awfully good name! But I'd much rather call you Quentin. Do you mind if I call you Quentin?"

"Not at all, but why Quentin? Is it the name of somebody you know?"

"I've never known *anyone* called that! It's just a silly fancy, which I'll explain sometime. I ought to scold you, I say. As an Englishman . . ."

"I am a Scot."

"Oh, then I *must* call you Quentin! Being British at all events, Q-quentin," and Ursula went rather pink, "you ought to preserve a seemly dignity and not treat my worries with any ill-timed sense of humour. I don't know, though; maybe it's better to give way to a sense of humour; I wish I could!"

"Well, why don't you?"

For some reason she was so upset by this 'Quentin' business that minutes passed before he spoke again.

On they flew along broad St. Charles Avenue. The uneven paving jolted them and more than once almost jolted them together, at which both scrambled back to the point of duty.

And then stately houses bowered in trees began to loom up right and left. Macrae suddenly drew her attention to the left-hand side of the road.

"Over there, I think, is the place where we first met. Holywell Street, if memory serves, is four or five turnings further on, also at the left. But *there*, outside that house . . ."

"The old Cavendish house. You jumped into the cab, and I behaved so badly!"

"On the contrary, Ursula, you behaved with extreme correctness."

"Yes, that's what I mean! And we're almost at Margot's house, as you say," she added a few moments later. "Jared, Cicero's making a wide turn to cross. You make a wide turn too, please, and we can keep both sides of the carriage in sight!"

Jared followed instructions. The big white house with white pillars, lifting three tiers of windows in spacious grounds, had its main entrance in St. Charles Avenue at the corner of Holywell Street. Both lower floors were illuminated.

Ursula pointed at the scrolled-iron gates in the tall iron-railed fence fronting the road.

"Those gates are wide open," she said. "Usually they're shut; a visitor pulls the bell at the side, and somebody comes out to answer it. But they're open now, and . . . what are you muttering about?"

"I asked you a while ago, Ursula, why you didn't exercise the sense of humour you so obviously have?"

"Oh, is there anything *f-funny* about this?"

"It's not farce, let's admit. But it's not Voodoo magic either. Where's the spell that should paralyze our wits and limbs? Has any dark force swooped down to pluck her out by the hair? She's safely home now, or will be in a few seconds more. Cicero's slowing down, Jared's slowing down; even the redoubtable Walter is slowing down behind us, or we'd all pile up together. Ursula, that place is almost as brightly lighted as the other house was, the one outside which you and I met. Are the de Sancerres entertaining tonight?"

"They're not entertaining formally, so far as I know. They do tend to keep open house, and people drop in."

A broad gravel drive stretched forty feet to the house's portico, where it divided left and right. Jared, at Ursula's signal, followed the little carriage so closely that, when Cicero swung it broadside with its left-hand door towards the steps up to the portico, its immediate pursuers had swung into the same position close behind.

There was a silence in dew-damp air heavy with the fragrance of magnolia blossom. Marcus Brutus, major-domo of Jules de Sancerre's household, opened the front door. And the third carriage, with Tom Clayton leaning out at one side while Harry Ludlow leaned out at the other, came clopping up the drive and stopped head on.

Ursula lifted her hand as though about to cry a warning, but it was not necessary. Tom, shoulders back in a kind of magisterial stateliness, descended slowly and drew himself up.

"I'm not mad any longer," he proclaimed to the world at large. "At least, I'm not as *damn* mad as I was thirty minutes ago. There will be no physical chastisement, much as the spoiled brat deserves it."

"That's better, Tom," said Harry, jumping down beside him. "That's much better! During the wild ride out here, you know, you were so *deuced* explicit about what you'd do to her that you had me thoroughly alarmed. Can't talk like that, old chap; it's not done."

Tom flicked his fingers at his hat-brim.

"Hello, Ursula!" he called. "When and where did you take up with my friend Dick? Never mind. You're supposed to be a good influence on Margot, being three or four years older. But I wonder. To judge by your conduct and Dick's conduct this evening . . ."

"Our conduct?" cried Ursula. "What do you think we've been doing?"

"What does it look as though you've been doing? Never mind; we're all human." Tom turned to Harry. "But, if I won't demean myself or Margot by applying the good right hand where it ought to be applied, if I've got too much dignity and self-control for that, it doesn't mean the damn woman's to escape. A few well-chosen words, spoken as only T. Clayton can speak 'em, ought to bring her at least partly to her senses. Stand aside!"

He stalked to the black carriage and threw open its right-hand door. He glanced inside, then put his head in for a closer look, and finally whirled round towards Ursula and Macrae.

"Look here, you two! How did you come to let her do that?"

"Tom, what are you talking about? Let her do what?"

"Let her slip away," Tom said, "while you two were carrying on. She's not here; she's gone!"

At the back of Macrae's brain stirred a vision of nightmare. But there was no time to contemplate this.

Ursula's rich pink colour had become a deathly pallor. Picking up scarf and fan, she alighted from the carriage with the blue crinoline billowing. Macrae followed, his left hand under her elbow, and she did not draw away her arm.

"Tom," Ursula began, "this is ridiculous. It's utterly r-ridiculous! We've watched both those doors every second of the time until this minute, and we can both swear she didn't leave!"

"Well, she did leave, because she's not here. Come and look for yourselves!"

They both went to look. Harry Ludlow hastened forward to do the same.

Both windows of the carriage were now lowered. On the dull-red upholstery of the seat lay Margot's black domino mask, its eyeholes outlined in rhinestones. Of Margot herself there was no other trace except a faint perfume.

"It's absolutely impossible!" said Ursula. "I didn't see her lower the left-hand window . . ."

"And I didn't see her touch the right-hand window," Macrae agreed, "except once when she very quickly opened and shut it again to look back during the journey."

"But that means nothing at all," Ursula insisted, and again Macrae agreed, "because the doors didn't move. If either door had opened as much as a couple of inches, we couldn't have missed seeing it. At the pace we were going, as you know very well, she could never have jumped out without hurting herself. But the doors didn't move, and that proves it. I tell you, she can't have gone or been taken!"

"Been taken, eh?" repeated Tom. "Been taken? Oh, I see. It's the logical result of last night's prelude, is it? It's old Marie Laveau, and some *gris-gris* to make Margot vanish like a soap-bubble. You're on about Voodoo doings too?"

Marcus Brutus, the major-domo, who had been standing at the open door like an ebony statue in evening clothes, suddenly turned and belted back into the house.

"Just a moment, Tom!" Macrae interposed with some sharpness, though he felt his own sanity dissolving. "We mustn't allow imagination to run away with us. This thing happened; let's face it."

"I know it happened, old son. What I want to know is: how the hell *did* it happen?"

"We're all interested to learn. There's some explanation, probably a very simple explanation when we find it. Meanwhile, try to understand that Ursula and I have been telling you the sober truth. Our attention was fixed on that carriage . . ."

"Your attention was fixed on each other, you mean. Both you and Ursula are slow starters, old son, but you're like to bust the boiler when you get steam up. Even now there's an air about you that a blind man couldn't mistake."

"Just don't tell us *we* were blind, that's all!"

"I'm not saying you're blind, Dick. I'm merely saying the idea in both your heads (and who's blaming you?) so shut out other considerations that you let Margot slip away when you weren't looking. What do *you* say, Harry?"

"If you don't mind," and Harry shifted uncomfortably, "I'll make no comment in the presence of my esteemed superior. Besides, aren't there worse troubles? What are Miss de Sancerre's parents going to say when you tell 'em what you're bound to tell 'em? That you found her playing quadroon at a quadroon ball?"

"You must let *me* explain that, please!" Ursula begged. "The truth has to be told, whether we like it or not, and I'm as much to blame as Margot is. You must let *me* tell Aunt Isabelle!"

"This young lady . . . er . . . I don't think I . . . ?"

Macrae presented Harry to Ursula. Harry made polite noises with his hat over his heart, and then addressed Tom.

"Miss de Sancerre, now!" he continued. "Just as she was being asked to dance by that gambler fellow, Square Nat Rumbold, you walked up to her in the ballroom and took off her mask in public. You didn't make it very easy for her, did you?"

"She didn't make it very easy for me, did she?"

"No, maybe not. She pulled off *your* mask and then slapped your face. But we've got to allow a lady some privileges, haven't we? Don't you ever do that in the South?"

"We *always* do that in the South, and it's caused half our troubles."

"Then the rest of it!" Harry was rapt. "She marched out of there, looking like fire. You marched after her, and the gambler followed you, trying to attract your attention. I thought you said you were acquainted with Square Nat Rumbold?"

"I'm acquainted with him in the sense that I've seen him here and there. Couldn't notice the fellow tonight; couldn't be bothered. I didn't use him with much ceremony, did I?"

"Ceremony? You grabbed his chin and chucked him a good fifteen feet. They say he always goes armed, Tom. If he carries this further . . ."

"Let him try any games with me and I'll blow his God-damn ears off. But see here, Dick!" Tom turned to Macrae and resumed his main theme. "Fair's fair, now. You can't seriously believe Margot was shut up in a kind of box?"

"It's better than believing I ought to be shut up in a padded cell. Kindly accept the fact that Miss Ede and I were not behaving as you seem to think, and that . . ."

"So it's 'Miss Ede' now, is it? Well, well, well! You didn't even *want* to behave that way, I suppose? Stick to your story, old son; claim what you like. But if Margot ever looks at me as I've seen Ursula look at you . . ."

Ursula had turned away. Isabelle de Sancerre, as *soignée* as ever in a gown of green silk trimmed with lace, swept out of the front door and stood at the top of the portico steps with light from the hall behind her.

"Who mentioned Margot, pray?" asked Madame de Sancerre. "And what has Marcus Brutus been babbling about? He even went upstairs to babble it at my husband. Good evening, Ursula;

it's something of a relief to see *you*."

"Good evening, Aunt Isabelle. Aunt Isabelle, this is Mr. Macrae, the British Consul."

"I'm already acquainted with Mr. Macrae, dear. I wasn't aware you knew him."

"We met some time ago," Macrae said, "under rather unusual circumstances. This evening . . ."

"This evening," proclaimed Tom Clayton, groping in the air, "as Dick was smoking a cigar outside some place on St. Claude Street, and Ursula drove past in her carriage . . ."

"Please!" Ursula cut in. "No gentlemanly lies, either of you! The truth must be told, as I've already said, whether we like it or not. Aunt Isabelle, may I have a word with you in private?"

"Yes, dear, of course. But it's so *provoking!* Judge Rutherford is upstairs with Jules in Jules's study. They won't come downstairs to hear Miss Partridge sing, and it's most discourteous of them; but what can one do with men like that?

"You see, Judah Benjamin arrived with some news to tell me. He's had no chance to tell it; who should turn up but Miss Partridge? She discovered, as usual, that quite by accident she happened to bring her music. So of course we must ask her to sing, and she's going to do some of Tom Moore's Irish melodies. It's not that she's a bad singer; she's got a really fine soprano voice; it's just that she makes so much *noise*."

"Aunt Isabelle . . ."

"What *was* Marcus Brutus gabbling about? I don't know where Margot's been tonight, and I'm half afraid to ask. But if she's been with you, Ursula, I'm sure everything must be all right."

"Aunt Isabelle, *could* we go into the house?"

"This way, dear. I do wish Horace Rutherford, with his lame leg and his bad heart-condition, wouldn't prance around and strike poses everywhere. If he had a fall it would kill him, and what would Amelia Rutherford say then? And it was just this day twenty-four years ago, come to think of it, that Delphine Lalaurie fled the country with her house in ruins and the mob howling after her. But it's barely half-past ten in the evening, you know; the day's not over yet, is it?"

7

Ursula had ascended the four steps to the portico. Isabelle de Sancerre, with the air of a woman who expects bad news but is prepared for it, took her hand and led her into the house.

Moving close to the portico steps, between the back of the closed carriage and the heads of the two horses behind it, Macrae could look into the familiar hall he had seen so often before.

The light of half a dozen gas-globes emphasized its height and depth. Walls panelled in glossy white wood rose from a darkly polished floor. At the rear of it the broad black-and-white staircase mounted to a carpeted landing with the door of Jules de Sancerre's study opposite the head of the stairs.

To the left, down here, would be the front drawing-room, with the dining-room immediately behind it. To the right would be the library and the back drawing-room. It was to the back drawing-room, inside which somebody could be heard plunking experimentally at the keys of a piano, that Isabelle de Sancerre ushered Ursula.

They were just carrying their crinolines through the doorway when the door of Jules de Sancerre's study opened. De Sancerre himself burst out of it like a cuckoo out of a clock. He stumped down the stairs, crossed the hall, and emerged under the portico to greet the newcomers.

A smallish, brisk, no-nonsense man in his early fifties, he had an amiable eye and dark hair shot with grey. His moustache and

fox-brush of imperial beard, after a style made famous in pictures
of Emperor Napoleon III, were completely grey. Cigar-ash spat-
tered his shirt-front. His voice, like his wife's, had no French
inflection at all.

"Ah, Tom!" he said. "Your servant, Mr. Macrae! And our
young friend here . . . ?"

Harry Ludlow was duly and formally introduced. Jules de
Sancerre mused.

"If I don't invite you in, gentlemen, at least until that woman
has finished her customary two or three selections, it's from consideration of your feelings rather than any lack of hospitality.
There's no nook or cranny here in which you can't hear Flossie
Partridge when she really opens her lungs. She's the terror of the
district. So unless Isabelle insists, as is sometimes the case, I won't
subject my guests to cruel or unusual punishment. Well, what's
been happening?"

Tom Clayton braced himself.

"Tonight, sir," he began respectfully, "all of us here (as well as
Margot and Ursula too) were at a certain place in town. At the
moment, with your permission, I won't say what the place was.

"Ursula is now telling Mama de Sancerre about it. Or, at least,
she *will* tell it if she can nerve herself to the sticking-point. It's not
easy to get at this, sir; we're all more embarrassed than we care to
admit.

"Let me say simply that Margot and I quarreled. Margot left
hastily, alone and in a huff; Ursula and Dick followed in General
Ede's carriage; Harry and I followed *them*. I will now tell you
what happened next, concluding with what we discovered when
we got here. You can then compare my version with Dick's, and
decide for yourself which of the two is the more sane and reasonable."

In his account of the chase and its ending, Tom made no
reference whatever to any suggested impropriety on the part of
Ursula or her companion. He told the story without trimming or
innuendo, while Harry merely nodded.

"They ought to have known Margot would try some trick or
other," Tom concluded. "They ought to have been on the alert. It

was sheer carelessness, that's all!"

"Any carelessness," Macrae said, "I categorically deny. The fact is, Tom . . ."

Both of them had powerful voices, which were beginning to clash in the night. Jules de Sancerre raised a hand for silence. Though he had listened with attention and concern, he did not seem in the least upset.

"I see," he remarked. "Or, if I don't altogether see, it's of no consequence at the moment. Marcus Brutus has been pouring out much the same sort of tale; Judge Rutherford is still questioning him."

"About Mama de Sancerre, sir: I don't think your good lady can have understood what Marcus Brutus was saying!"

"Well, I understood. Margot has been playing tricks, has she, and made herself vanish like a soap-bubble?

"The girl is full of tricks, I allow; she has been playing them since she was in the nursery. The meaning of this one, or how she managed it, I confess myself at a loss to understand. But we must not 'take on,' as they say, at the *fait accompli*. Margot's mother may have hysterics, and probably will; her father begs leave to preserve a more detached attitude."

Jules de Sancerre seemed to be looking into the distance.

"I have always thought, gentlemen, that we keep our women too swathed in cotton-wool: that they are better able to take care of themselves than we prefer to think. Let Margot absent herself for an hour, two hours, even a night! Shall I tear my hair, beat my breast, stamp the house down?

"But it is a problem, assuredly it's a problem. —*Cicero!*"

"Yassuh?"

"That will be all for tonight. You may put the carriage away and," he glanced at the horse, "have Zeke see to Bessie."

"You see, gentlemen," their host went on, as Cicero swung round the right-hand curve of the drive and disappeared, "not even in a moment of madness could I believe . . ."

"Believe what, sir?" asked Tom.

"That a carriage we have owned for several years contains some sort of secret panel, as in *The Mysteries of Udolpho*, by which a passenger could drop through the floor unseen by her pursuers. A passenger in a crinoline? And travelling at the pace you have described?

"I can't believe that," said Jules de Sancerre, "and I won't believe it. But I will examine that *voiture* with great care. In the face of Mr. Macrae's extraordinary positiveness (and, I presume, Ursula's too) about the doors remaining closed, it is most of all mysterious that—"

He broke off abruptly as the noise began.

Macrae had heard aforetime of Miss Florence Partridge, that chesty and tireless soprano who accompanied herself at the piano. They now heard Miss Partridge in the flesh.

If the few notes of the introduction were smitten with assurance, it was as nothing to the assurance with which Miss Partridge's voice smote her rendition of The Harp That Once Through Tara's Halls.

It soared up in a kind of aesthetic agony; its volume shook the gas-globes and would have made picture-frames rattle had there been any in the hall. But the song contains only two verses, and was soon over. From the back drawing-room, where Miss Partridge's captive listeners were presumably Isabelle de Sancerre, Ursula, and Senator Benjamin, came a spatter of polite applause.

The group outside the house made no comment. But Jules de Sancerre, evidently so steeled by long experience that he had not even winced, pointed at Tom Clayton, who was brooding and muttering to himself.

"Before she begins again, my boy, have you anything to add to the testimony? What is it *now*?"

"I'm a fool, maybe," said Tom. "But I'm not a stubborn fool or a damn fool."

"Well?"

"I was thinking of a very remote contingency. It's just barely possible—not at all likely, but just possible—that Margot may have been kidnapped and may be in serious danger. If you don't mind, sir, I want to ask one last question. What's your stand on the Voodoo aspect of this business?"

"The *what* aspect? Who said anything about Voodoo?"

"Didn't Marcus Brutus?"

"Great Scott, no!"

"Well, he should have; that's what scared him away. And it seems to have been common talk for some time. Hasn't Mama de Sancerre mentioned it?"

"There is much," and Jules de Sancerre sighed gently, "they don't tell me or any other husband. You will learn that yourself some day. Meanwhile! If it's suggested that my daughter's disappearance may have been the result of dabbling with Voodoo practice . . ."

"I don't suggest that, exactly!"

". . . in such an event, frankly, I must own to feeling a trifle disturbed. The devil has some faithful retainers too. But I am a practical man; let's be practical. If you don't suggest that 'exactly,' then what exactly do you suggest?"

"I wish I knew!" Tom glowered. "At first I thought Ursula and Dick must have been dreaming. Now I'm not so sure. Behind everything that's been happening, I seem to see a joker with unfunny ways and a lot of persistence. He's there like a spider; he may be working up to some climax, with this as a part of it. It seems to me . . ."

Jules de Sancerre had stiffened.

"Whatever you were about to tell us, Tom, be quiet and don't tell us just yet. We have another visitor, I think. There is someone walking up the drive now."

It would be impossible to say that a chill of dread touched them all. For one thing, Miss Partridge had begun again. Refreshed by that brief pause, she was walloping *Oh, Believe Me, If All Those Endearing Young Charms* with virtually every quality of a steam calliope aboard a river-boat. Doubt or fear would have been blown wide before such sound and fury.

Also, as the newcomer approached, his face picked out by one lantern of Leonidas Clayton's carriage, it proved to be nobody more alarming than Mr. Barnaby Jeffers, the historian, who lived not far away in Second Street.

Mr. Jeffers alone was not in evening clothes. Lean, stoop-shouldered, his oblong spectacles down on his nose and his beaver hat hiding a bald head, he wore the frock-coat and trousers of everyday wear. He himself should have seemed the essence of the everyday.

And yet . . .

The man looked ill, or at least oppressed and hagridden. His pale-blue eyes seemed to have turned inward. There were many lines in the thin face. He had been moving at a very slow pace. And now, as Miss Partridge finished her tribute to the endearing young charms, he stopped.

"Rosette Leblanc!" he said suddenly. "That was her name, of course! Rosette Leblanc!"

"That was whose name?" asked Jules de Sancerre. "And what do you happen to be talking about?"

"Forgive me!" said the historian. "Sleep seemed impossible. A brief stroll before bedtime, I thought, might be conducive to slumber. Seeing your lights, and knowing your collective reputation as night-owls . . . Forgive me."

"Not at all!" crowed their host, fingering his imperial beard. "You are acquainted with everyone here, I believe, except the latest addition to the staff of the British Consulate. Harry Ludlow, Mr. Barnaby Jeffers. Delighted to see you at any time, Barnaby! What seems to be the trouble?"

"If you don't mind, Jules, I prefer not to discuss it in public. I have been turning over old diaries; I have been remembering a certain anniversary. 'A thousand ghosts and forms of fright have started from their graves tonight, to drive sleep from mine eyes away.'"

"Tut, man! As bad as that?"

"No, of course not! Consider it merely the hyperbole of my advancing years." Barnaby Jeffers wiped his mouth. "We grow old, my friend: our hair falls out, and most of our teeth too. But do we ever really learn? I am that figure of fun, an old bachelor. For the past twenty years my life has been exemplary. Before then . . ."

"My own life, I very nearly regret to say, has always been exemplary. For I might have enjoyed myself more, confound it! I seldom gambled recklessly, my worst excess being an all-night poker game. I pursued no women except the lady who became my wife. I never even went to a quadroon ball, in the days before those functions had become stale by repetition. Speaking of quadroon balls, by the way . . ."

Had there been a gleam in Jules de Sancerre's eye?

"Yes, sir?" interjected Tom Clayton, watching him. "Speaking of quadroon balls?"

"I recall one devil of a scandal in my youth, a few years before Isabelle and I were married."

"Well, sir?"

"A famous Creole beauty of the time was Cécile de la Plage, Henri de la Plage's daughter. Some of her friends dared her to attend a quadroon ball disguised *as* a quadroon, and see what scalps she might collect without going too far. She ran smack into the young man whose engagement to her had been bruited for months, and the roof all but blew off. Her father did not disown her or turn her out of the house; we don't do such things here, though old Henri had an apoplectic stroke. *Au fond*, did the uproar matter? It did not. She married a distinguished lawyer from Alabama, and is now a grandmother."

"I may remark tritely," cried Barnaby Jeffers, "that there are scandals *and* scandals. There are lawyers *and* lawyers. Have you seen Horace Rutherford recently?"

"As a matter of fact, he is upstairs in my study at this minute. And *I* will remark on a coincidence. 'A *thousand ghosts and forms of fright have started from their graves tonight.*' That's Longfellow, isn't it?"

"Mr. Longfellow," returned the other, "is not Shakespeare or Milton. But he is one of our few authentic voices, and need not altogether be consigned to limbo as some critics have done. Must a man stand rebuked for quoting him?"

"I mentioned a coincidence, no more. As these young people here raced up with a rather peculiar story, Judge Rutherford and I were examining a parcel of books just arrived from Boston. One of the books contained Mr. Longfellow's latest, a blank-verse effort called *The Courtship of Miles Standish*."

"I have seen the work. It bids fair to become popular, and to perpetuate another Puritan legend as untrustworthy as the title itself. Or am I carping and tedious to remind you that Captain Standish wrote his first name as M-*y*-l-e-s?"

Barnaby Jeffers's voice had begun to tremble.

"Jules," he burst out, "you must pardon my conduct tonight. I am not myself; I have lost my poise and seem to be losing my head too. But the nightmare that haunts me may be more desperate than anyone has guessed. Do you think I might see Horace Rutherford alone for five or ten minutes?"

"Yes, of course, and very soon. At the moment, gentlemen, you had all better grit your teeth. There goes the piano again!"

Miss Partridge's third selection, her gustiest yet, was *Come, Rest in This Bosom, My Own Stricken Deer*. Though of the wrong sex to be so concerned about an erring fair one, she gave it her whole heart and lungs. Marcus Brutus, on his way down the staircase at the back of the hall, stopped short and stood motionless before completing the descent. The last notes died away. From the back drawing-room issued another spatter of applause. Jules de Sancerre retreated into the hall, beckoning the others.

"Now that, with any luck, should be the end of it. Come in, all of you! Come in, be comfortable, and we'll find you a bottle of something good."

Macrae followed Tom Clayton and Mr. Jeffers into the hall, blinking for a moment against the light. Then their host remembered.

"Marcus Brutus, are you listening? You might go up and ask Judge Rutherford . . ."

It was unnecessary to summon Judge Rutherford. The study door opposite the head of the staircase, already ajar, was thrown open and left open. Judge Rutherford himself, cane in his left hand, lumbered out at the gait which gave his shoulders a misshapen look, though it came only from lameness.

He was a giant of a man, silver-haired and ruddy of face, but with a bluish tinge to his lips. He shouldered to the top of the stairs, drew himself up, and spoke in his booming voice.

"Can't get a word of sense out of that one," he called, pointing in some disgust at Marcus Brutus below. "Bad tactics, damn bad tactics! Don't ask *him*; ask those who were there and know. Stay where you are, all of you; I'm on my way."

Barnaby Jeffers found his voice.

"No, stay where *you* are," the historian called back. "I'm coming up. Jules's study will do for us."

"Jules's study will do for what? The rumpus *down* there," and Judge Rutherford indicated the back drawing-room, "I understand only too well. The rumpus *out* there, with you yelling like an auctioneer or a court crier, was a little beyond me. Will somebody kindly explain . . ."

"Horace," shouted Mr. Jeffers, "are you ever afraid of retribution?"

"In the religious sense, you mean? Well . . ."

"No; in the practical worldly sense!"

"Barnaby, are you crazy? Retribution for what?"

"For *her*," said Mr. Jeffers. "The son was born in '19 or '20. If he's still alive, he'll be a man of nearly forty. And he *is* alive. That note I got— He never knew his mother, of course; he never knew Rosette Leblanc. It wasn't his mother he loved and idolized; it was Delphine. Are you too insensitive to see it even yet?"

"Barnaby, for the love of . . . !"

"We thought we acted for the best; we thought we were justified. That's not the point. Never mind what judgment you'll face in the after life. Isn't there any *living* enemy you're afraid of? Now stay where you are; I'm coming upstairs!"

Barnaby Jeffers started to cross the hall, but stopped short. Jules de Sancerre made a mouth of despair. Once more the unwearying piano keys had riffled from the back drawing-room; once more a powerful soprano gathered and smote.

> Oft in the stilly night,
> Ere slumber's chain has bound me,
> Fond memory will bring the light
> Of other days around me:
> The smiles, the tears,
> Of boyhood's years,
> The words of love then spoken:
> The eyes that shone,

Now dimmed and gone,
  The cheerful hearts now broken.
Thus in the stilly night,
  Ere slumber's chain has bound me . . .

Miss Partridge never finished the verse.

Judge Rutherford, poised and teetering on the topmost step, had just snorted a contemptuous, "Enemies, for God's sake!" when the change occurred.

His big shoulders gave a sudden outwards lurch. The cane slipped through the fingers of his left hand and went clattering downstairs. His upraised right hand clawed at the air. His eyes rolled up, his mouth fell grotesquely open. He pitched head foremost, straight down, his great weight striking the treads as with a shock of doom. He rolled over, thudding on each step, and came to rest at the foot of the staircase, face up, in an inert mass of black broadcloth and white linen. The eyes were still open, but they did not respond to light.

There was a jangle of piano keys from the back drawing-room, and then silence.

Macrae glanced quickly at the faces about him: at Barnaby Jeffers, like a man paralyzed; at Jules de Sancerre, shocked but still alert; at Tom Clayton, thunderstruck and yet as though half expecting something like this.

For perhaps ten seconds nobody moved. Then Jules de Sancerre went over to that motionless figure and knelt beside it. He tried first for a pulse at the wrist, then for a heart-beat by running his hand inside the shirt. Finally, opening his gold watch, he manoeuvered its crystal close to lips still bluish in a face no longer ruddy.

"He's gone, poor devil," their host reported, putting away the watch and standing up. "We'll send for Dr. Andrews, but there's no doubt he's gone. The doctor told him this might happen, and it has. He struck a heroic attitude just once too often, and he slipped. We all saw it: he slipped!"

"Well, sir," Tom roused himself from dreaming, "it depends on what you mean by 'slipped.' "

"I mean what I say. We saw it happen, didn't we?"

"Yes, sir. We also saw that jerk of his shoulders as he fell. To me this looks more like dirty work of a pattern that's been observed before, and it looks like murder too. The shock to his heart killed him, yes. But he's dead because somebody gave him a shove that sent him toppling!"

"*Murder? Gave him a shove?*"

"It certainly looked—" began Barnaby Jeffers.

"There was nobody up there with him, was there? Did you see anybody near him, Tom?"

"There was nobody, I admit!"

"Well, then! If your view were the correct one," declared Jules de Sancerre, "then *I* could believe in goblins and werewolves and Voodoo magic too. For, unless some invisible murderer slipped out of nowhere to hurl him down, what explanation besides accident can there possibly be?"

PART II:

Darkness

8

"IT'S PAST MIDNIGHT," SAID SENATOR BENJAMIN, "AND THIS is sheer lunacy. We have gone over the facts too often. Let us see where we stand."

He himself stood with his back to the empty fireplace, pudgy features intent. As though to point his words, a little gilt pendulum-clock on the mantelpiece rapped out the quarter hour after twelve.

The big library at the de Sancerres', with oak mausoleums of bookcases and marble busts on top of them, stretched away into shadow. It might have been the library at a club, since at this moment the company was entirely male.

At one side of the fireplace Jules de Sancerre, a dead cigar in his fingers, occupied a padded chair draped with an antimacassar. At the other side sat Barnaby Jeffers, nervously fiddling at a gaudily painted music-box which he had found on a shelf, but which he could not persuade to work.

On the large mahogany table in the middle of the room, a paraffin lamp shaped like a pagoda shed its light on boxes of notepaper and envelopes, a tray of pens, a silver inkstand, and a sand-caster for drying the ink. An abashed Harry Ludlow sat fidgeting by the table, while Macrae paced beyond it. At one bookshelf along the east wall stood Tom Clayton, his back turned.

Senator Benjamin, eyeing them all, raised an admonitory forefinger.

"You have asked me to take charge," he continued, "and there

89

is much that you lay to my care. Margot de Sancerre has mysteriously vanished. An old and valued friend has died under circumstances as mysterious as they are tragic. His body now lies in that back drawing-room there, once a place of song and what for want of a better word may be called entertainment. Mrs. Rutherford will be informed in the morning, when she will be better able to bear such news.

"You have heard Dr. Andrews's verdict. Judge Rutherford died of heart-failure. Dr. Andrews conjectures that the shock of knowing himself to be falling—with such a look on his face as several of you describe—may itself have caused the stopping of the heart, and that he may have been dead before he struck the stairs. Or the bruise in the middle of his back was perhaps caused by the fall; it is all conjecture; we have no means of knowing with positiveness.

"Judge Rutherford's death *may* have been an accident, as some of you think. Taken in conjunction with other circumstances, however, it at least deserves the closest scrutiny.

"I have been permitted a private interview, separately and individually, with each person present tonight, excepting just one. I now have such information as you can give me, together with certain information of my own. But that is only a beginning."

"A beginning of what?" demanded Tom Clayton, whirling round. "Where do we go from here?"

"Gently, young man! *Suaviter in modo*, if you don't mind. There are two things we must do, and do at once; both should have been done ere this. We must . . . Stop! Where are the ladies?"

"Yes, yes! I am aware," and the senator made harassed gestures, "I am aware that our excellent Miss Partridge, in tears and a fit of megrims, was conveyed home more than an hour ago. But there are other ladies more immediately concerned. Where are Madame de Sancerre and Miss Ede?"

"In the front drawing-room across the hall," answered Macrae, who had stopped pacing. "I was a little disturbed when Ursula disappeared . . ."

Senator Benjamin stared at him.

"*Miss Ede* has disappeared too?"

"She has returned now, wherever she went. It's no part of these upsets tonight."

"Then it must be a unique event. In the front drawing-room, are they? Will you favour me, my friend, by stepping across there and asking the ladies if they will be good enough to join us?"

Macrae nodded and left the library.

Every gas-globe still burned in the hall, though the jets had been lowered to bluish flame-points that threw wavering shadows. But the front drawing-room, after the white-and-black simplicity of that hall, looked as cluttered and confused as an immense jewel-box.

Rosewood furniture, its edges carved and scrolled to tortuousness after the prevailing fashion, seemed to take up every inch of space round the walls and a good deal of floor-space too. Brocaded upholstery of peacock's feather colours stood out against pink walls crowded with pictures in gilt or ebony frames.

In the midst of this confusion, under gas-globes a little brighter than those of the hall, Ursula Ede sat back alone on a brocaded sofa with her hands folded over the short silvery cape across her lap. But she did not seem at ease; she was trembling a little. The moment he met her eyes, the long, grey-blue eyes with heavy lids and strongly luminous whites, he realized how alarmed he had been for some time.

"Hello, Ursula."

"Hello, Qu—hello, Mr. Macrae! You weren't looking for *me*. were you?"

"Yes, of course. Madame de Sancerre, now . . ."

"Aunt Isabelle's gone to bed. She swore she wouldn't sleep, but she also said she'd take a few drops of laudanum. She's behaved much better over all this than anybody could have expected, hasn't she? It's not as though she were deliberately absenting herself."

"Speaking of somebody absenting herself, where have *you* been for the past hour and a half?"

"Did you notice I was gone?"

"*Notice?* It seems generally agreed that Judge Rutherford tumbled˙ down these stairs at not much later than a quarter to eleven . . ."

"It was ghastly, wasn't it? Poor Judge Rutherford! I've always thought of him as something of a latter-day buccaneer, like Jean Laffite. But I *liked* him! Everybody liked him!"

"Yes, agreed. As soon as we determined he was dead, there was a good deal of shouting and rushing about: general confusion. At the direction of Papa de Sancerre, Tom and I picked up the judge and carried him to the sofa in the back drawing-room. You weren't there; nobody seemed to know where you were. I looked all over the place. Finally I looked outside, and your carriage was gone.

"You must have slipped away in the uproar. At first I supposed you had simply gone home. Then I started to imagine all sorts of things, including abduction and God knows what. Even now . . . forgive me, but is it possible you know more about Margot's disappearance than you've acknowledged so far?"

"I don't know *anything* about Margot's disappearance, I swear!"

He could not doubt Ursula's sincerity. She rose to her feet and approached him, looking up steadily.

"There was nothing mysterious about it. I—I can tell you what I did do, if that's of the least interest to anyone?"

"It's of interest to me."

"Well! When Aunt Isabelle first took me back to that room, with Mr. Benjamin sitting there, and Miss Partridge all ready at the piano, Miss Partridge didn't begin her little concert at once, as she usually does. She waited a bit before she opened with *The Harp That Once Through Tara's Halls*. Do you remember?"

"Yes."

"That was because of me, I'm afraid. I had to tell Aunt Isabelle at once, while I still had the courage. So I drew her over behind the big folding screen in the corner, and whispered to her. When I said Margot and I had both been at the quadroon ball, I thought Aunt Isabelle would have a fit. But she didn't. She quieted down, muttering something about a girl named Cécile de la Plage, whom I've never even heard of. Then she whispered that it was very dreadful, but that whatever happened a good hostess must remember her guests, and we were being very rude to poor Miss Partridge. Out we went from behind the screen, and . . ."

"The noise began?"

"Yes. That was when *I* remembered something and somebody I'd clean forgotten. Samantha!"

"Who?"

"Samantha! Our Samantha. The mulatto woman who played the part of Margot's duenna at the ball. Or didn't I tell you?"

"You told me."

"Both Margot and I had run away and left Samantha stranded at that place. Margot was supposed to have given her money for cab-fare both ways. But what if Margot had forgotten, or Samantha couldn't find a cabby who was willing to drive a coloured woman? So I had to go back for her, don't you see?"

"You went back to the Washington and American Ballroom?" Ursula, though upset, faced this too.

"Really and truly, what else could I have done? I slipped away from here, as you say, and nobody noticed me. (*You* didn't notice me, did you?)

"But I had to have a mask, and I just couldn't bring myself to use one they give you at that place. So, before I told Jared to return, I went round to the carriage-house at the back here. Cicero had put away the little carriage Margot used and disappeared from, but her mask with the rhinestones was still on the seat where we saw it last. I took that mask, and away I went.

"The ball was still in full swing; it'll go on until all hours. There was Samantha in *her* mask, sitting against the wall and looking as proper as any duenna at the *Salle d'Orléans*. And that gambler, the one Tom Clayton grabbed and threw like a discus . . ."

"Square Nat Rumbold? Let's hope we're not being haunted by Square Nat Rumbold too."

"*He* was there, and without a mask. He accosted me—quite politely, I must say—but I'm afraid I wasn't very nice to him. That's all there is. I took Samantha home as an end to the adventure. Was it so very awful of me, really? Do you think I did wrong?"

"Wrong?" He nearly took her in his arms at that moment. "You're a brick, Ursula! You're more than a brick; you're a whole beautiful house, a dream-palace where any man might . . . Stop! I mustn't carry that metaphor too far."

"Oh, don't be afraid of carrying *anything* too far! Still! If you're not going to berate or even frown at me . . ."

"The treatment I had in mind was rather different. But *was* it an end to the adventure?"

"How do you mean?"

"Tonight, Ursula, you've several times referred to your father. Though you haven't mentioned a mother, aren't there several real aunts as opposed to a courtesy aunt like Madame de Sancerre?"

"Indeed there are. Aunts Susan, Becky, Emmeline, and Kate!"

"What happened when you went home? Didn't you have any music to face?"

"They were all asleep, every last one of them! Not a sound in the house. I hid the mask in my bureau. It had turned rather chilly, so I put this on," Ursula held up the short silvery cape, "and I . . ."

"You came back here. Forgive this over-inquisitiveness, but why did you come back here?"

"You have every *right* to be inquisitive if you *want* to be! I had my reasons; let's just say I had my reasons."

With a toss of her head she swept away from him and then swept back again, her eyes searching his face.

"You know, Q-quentin, I'm getting awfully tired of having to be so very prim and proper, though who am I to talk of being proper after tonight? If there's any music to face, I'll face it later. Anyway, unless someone actually catches me when I go home for the second time, I can always get Mammy to swear I never left the house.

"But I'm doing all the talking; you haven't said a word. I gathered from Aunt Isabelle, before she went up to bed a few minutes ago, they're not much closer to discovering how Margot vanished or what happened to poor Judge Rutherford?"

"No, unless Senator Benjamin has some ideas. He's in charge. There was a good deal of argument, which took some time. Just as the argument waxed hottest, Senator Benjamin took each one of us into the dining-room, separately and individually, for a private interview. I know I for one told him something I hadn't intended to mention to anybody except Tom Clayton."

"Could you bear to tell *me?*"

"Readily. The sense of being followed and watched and spied on, especially at night and even at home, by someone I can never catch or drive into a corner. It may only be fancy, but it's gone on as long as Margot's own obsession, whatever that is.

"Well, the private interviews also took considerable time. Finally, Senator Benjamin suggested it might be more comfortable if we all adjourned to the library. The rest of them trooped into the library: except Madame de Sancerre, who drifted out of the front door under the portico."

"That was when *I* came back?"

"Yes. I was the last one into the library, and I was just closing the door when to my unspeakable relief I heard your voice. You came into the hall with Madame de Sancerre; you both made straight for this room. Now I've been sent to ask whether you'll join Senator Benjamin in the library."

"Good heavens, what can *I* tell him?"

"He didn't actually say you could tell him anything, though no doubt there are questions. He wants to see Madame de Sancerre too, but she can be excused if she's retired. He just said there are two things that must be done at once. Do you mind going, Ursula?"

"No, not really. It's horribly vexing and upsetting, not knowing where we are or what's happened. But I don't mind so much if you're there, and I like Mr. Benjamin a lot.

"There's a question I might ask you too," she continued as they moved towards the door, "about why you felt so relieved when you knew I'd returned. But I won't be coy; I won't; I've been quite coy enough already! Just let me take your arm, as I did when we were in that garden with the statue, and *be there.*"

In the library across the hall there was an atmosphere of strain. There was also an atmosphere of tobacco-smoke.

Senator Benjamin, not unimpressive in black and white, with

the dark hair fluffed out over his ears and the brush of dark whisker encircling a round face, still stood with his back to the fireplace. He had a guarded look in his eye and a lighted cigar in his hand.

The others were in their previous positions: Jules de Sancerre in a chair to the left of the fireplace, Barnaby Jeffers to the right of it, Harry Ludlow beside the table, Tom Clayton standing at a wall of bookshelves. The three seated ones stood up as Macrae rolled forward an upholstered chair for Ursula. When she had settled her skirts into it, they sat down again.

"Ah, Miss Ede!" Senator Benjamin greeted her. "Our hostess," he added, exhibiting the cigar, "permits smoking in the library and in her husband's study. Do *you* object to it?"

"Me? No, not a bit! I like it. Aunt Isabelle couldn't object even if she wanted to. She's gone to bed, I'm afraid, and won't be able to answer your questions. What did you want to ask *me*?"

"At the moment, nothing at all."

Jules de Sancerre, who was also smoking, looked up with less than his customary good humour.

"Then what are we doing here?" he asked. "*Enfin*, man, stop being so mysterious and get to the point!"

"Am I being mysterious?"

"At least you're not making much progress. What are these two things we must do?"

"The first and more obvious," Senator Benjamin replied, "should have been done long ago. We must send for the police."

"Now if you imagine," snapped Jules de Sancerre, "that I will expound the circumstances of my daughter's disappearance to some greasy illiterate from a precinct station . . . !"

"As regards the young lady's disappearance, use your own discretion. The death of Judge Rutherford is another matter. We *must* report it; we have no choice."

"But . . . !"

"Nor need you fear ham-handed interference; this is no water-front beating or stabbing. The death of a man so distinguished as Judge Rutherford will be investigated only by someone from the small group of plain-clothes officers attached to the district attorney's office at City Hall. If I may make a suggestion . . . ?"

"Anything, anything!"

"The man we want is a certain Sergeant O'Shea, who has been on all-night duty for the past week. Though hardly an ornament to the most polished society, he is no greasy illiterate either. Whether a summons from me would bring him I have no means of knowing. But there is one among us from whom a word to the same effect would get immediate results."

"Oh? And who is that?"

"Our friend Macrae," answered Senator Benjamin, turning his eyes on the gentleman in question. "Sergeant O'Shea, unlike so many Irishmen, has no hatred of English overlords. On the contrary. Before he came to New Orleans he belonged to the detective branch of the London Metropolitan Police under Commissioner Mayne, another Irishman. He knows Macrae, and likes him very much. Will you lend us *your* help in the business, my dear fellow?"

"It's certainly an idea," declared Barnaby Jeffers, and fiddled at the gaudy music-box he still held. "Police protection, after all . . ."

Macrae looked at his new assistant. "Harry!"

"Sir?"

"Pen, ink, and paper are before you. Write a brief line or two addressed to Sergeant Timothy O'Shea: room 46, City Hall, Lafayette Square. My compliments to Sergeant O'Shea; can he manage to attend us here on a matter of the greatest and gravest importance? Then I can sign it. Will you do that, please?"

Harry, who had been trying to make himself look as inconspicuous as possible, made wig-wagging gestures.

"Of course, sir, if you tell me to. But may I say something?"

"What do you want to say?"

"Dash it all, sir! *I'm* supposed to have been on duty since this morning. And you haven't given me one single assignment or instruction. All I've done is eat a couple of good meals, drink rather a lot, attend a—" He stopped short.

"Attend a quadroon ball," supplied Jules de Sancerre. "Say it, young man! Say it and shame the devil! After all the talk tonight, including our interviews with the good senator, my daughter's whereabouts before she disappeared are now no secret to anyone, including her mother and father. She went to the quadroon ball. And our well-behaved Ursula . . ."

"Yes, I was there!" Ursula confessed. "I was there more than once, in a kind of way. And I'm sorry I wasn't here to be interviewed, but I had an errand that wouldn't wait. What's the matter with poor Mr. Ludlow?"

Harry addressed Macrae.

"Sir," he said, "hadn't *you* better write the note to this Irishman, so he'll know it's authentic? Then I can take it as my authority, and go and fetch him here myself."

"Go and fetch a police-officer," echoed the amazed Jules de Sancerre, "when any one of a dozen servants can take the message?"

"Before I left home, Mr. de Sancerre," said Harry, "the people at the F.O. went on at me like a whole pack of Dutch uncles. How seriously I must take my duties! Whenever possible, make personal contact and do it yourself! I know people think, even at the F.O., it was a political appointment to please my governor. But this is my first chance to justify myself, even in a small way; the F.O. would agree. If Mr. Macrae allows it, and Tom will lend me his carriage . . . ?"

"You bet I'll lend you the carriage, young-fellow-me-lad!" Tom said heartily. "Just tell Walter to go to City Hall, find room 46, and Bob's your uncle. Always do it yourself, see people personally: that's the ticket, that's what we believe in this country, and what the hell's the F.O.?"

"Foreign Office. Part of the Circumlocution Office, if you know your Dickens. Well, Mr. Macrae, sir? May I?"

So it was arranged. Harry departed on his errand, carrying a note from Macrae.

"And now," said Jules de Sancerre, "may we proceed to the second consideration which our master of legal hocus-pocus believes to be so important. In short, Benjie, what's the word? What do we do next?"

"We pool our information; we determine our problem; we make

sure we know just what the problem is."

For some moments Senator Benjamin seemed to have been lost in a dream. The cigar was held motionless before him; he kept two fingers at his left side-whisker; only by the far-away glitter in his eye could they tell he was paying any attention at all.

Then he put down his cigar in a little dish on the mantelpiece, and turned back to them with his chin in his hand.

"As I consider the evidence so far," he went on, his orator's voice rounding the syllables, "I have the feeling that sometimes comes to me when I hunt the devil-fish in Port Royal Sound, South Carolina.

"Has any of you ever hunted the devil-fish? You should try it. I began many years ago, in the company of a young Negro named Hannibal who is now an old Negro with grandchildren, but still hale and willing. You hunt the devil-fish from a small boat, with stout lines attached to a couple of harpoons, and you will find him quite a quarry. He is wily, vicious, and a fighter; he can move like lightning in the water."

"Really?" Ursula cried in patent disbelief. "I shouldn't have thought one of those big squishy things with the eight arms could make any speed at all."

"Oh, you're talking about an octopus, aren't you?"

"Yes! I thought . . ."

"Some people do. The devil-fish, believe me, is a different species altogether.

"He is fifteen to twenty feet long, with powerful feelers projecting several feet beyond his mouth; he might even be called a monster. You will find him plentiful in Port Royal Sound, where he comes to feed on shrimp and other crustacea of the Carolina coast.

"Run as close to him as good judgment suggests; drive in your first harpoon. Off he darts at express speed, unreeling forty fathoms of rope in a few seconds, and dragging your boat after him. Play him until he exhausts himself, no matter how rough a time he gives you; then throw your second harpoon for the kill. Even then he may not be finished. He will fight every second until his death, and he has been known to charge the boat."

"Now I must confess," Jules de Sancerre remarked, "that I should like to try that game for myself."

"Not for me, I thank you," observed Barnaby Jeffers. "The contemplative life . . ."

"Not for me either!" cried Ursula. "It's *horrible!*"

There was a twinkle in Senator Benjamin's eye.

"But you take the analogy, ladies and gentlemen? We hunt a devil-fish of human intelligence: wily, vicious, apt to turn on us before we have thrown the first harpoon. You take the analogy?"

"I take the analogy," roared Tom Clayton, "and I score another for intuition. You feel it too, do you? The same joker behind all this, moving and planning?"

"Well, let us see. Our problem, as already indicated, divides itself into two parts: the disappearance of Margot de Sancerre and the death of Judge Rutherford. These two events may have no connection with each other. The first may be a mere prank, disconcerting but essentially harmless, like the young lady's attendance at the quadroon ball. Judge Rutherford's demise may be one of those disconcerting accidents which make all life so uncertain. But if my views have any value, which they may not, I will tell you what I believe."

The master of ceremonies picked up his cigar, and sighted at them along it as though along a rifle-barrel.

"I believe the two events are connected: that they depend on each other and interlock. They may well have had their origin at the same source."

"Good for you, Senator!" blurted Tom Clayton. "The same slippery joker managed both, eh?"

"I did not say the same hand managed both. I said they may well have had their origin at the same source."

"Isn't that a distinction without a difference?"

"Not at all. More immediately confronting us," and Senator Benjamin sighted at their host, "is the fall of our old friend down the stairs. You have asked what the word is, Jules, and you deserve a reply. The word, I greatly fear, *is* murder."

9

Jules de Sancerre threw his own cigar into the fireplace and sat up straight.

"You yourself keep insisting," he said, "that we have been over the facts too often. Very well! I will mention certain circumstances just once more, and then consider the subject closed. Come with me."

"Where?"

"Only out into the hall. You too, Mr. Macrae, by your leave."

Ursula, Tom, and Barnaby Jeffers did not stir as the other three trooped out into the hall. Jules de Sancerre left the library door open.

"The gas has been lowered since that unfortunate event," he commented, "but it is still possible to see clearly. Mr. Macrae, stand where you were standing when Horace fell. I will do the same.

"From this position (observe, Benjie!) we can see virtually the whole south side of that upstairs hall. There is the door of the study, opposite the head of the stairs and some ten feet back from it. To the right of the study door, perhaps a dozen feet away, another door leads to a spare bedroom now unoccupied. To the left of the study door, the same distance away, a third door leads to a second spare bedroom also unoccupied.

"Complete the stretch of hall at the back. On the extreme right, the west end of the house, is a room used by my wife's dressmaker for sewing and fitting and the like. On the extreme left, the east end of the house, is my daughter's room, now as unoccupied as any guest room. You note all that, Benjie?"

"It is duly noted."

"Need I flog the self-evident or hammer at the obvious? Though a balustrade stretches on either side of the staircase up there," and their host pointed, "its white-painted spokes do not in any way impede our eyesight. Under bright gaslight, in full sight of five witnesses—Mr. Macrae, Barnaby, Tom Clayton, young Ludlow, myself—Horace pitched to his death. There was not another living soul on that floor, let alone anyone near him. Before we are so casual with words like 'murder' or 'pushed,' hadn't we better determine how it was done?"

"You tell me only," groaned Senator Benjamin, "that I don't yet *see* how it was done. This is a very high hall; the floor up there is carpeted; and from this position we can't . . . oh, never mind! Back to the library!"

His cigar had gone out, becoming an embarrassment. He looked round for an ashtray, saw none, and thrust the cigar-stump into his pocket. Then he strode into the library, with the others following, and again assumed his master of ceremonies position at the mantelpiece, a man half out of his wits.

"If it were possible to determine the exact moment when Judge Rutherford died, we might know the how of it too. That bruise in the middle of his back, for instance . . ."

Barnaby Jeffers, so cadaverous with worry as to seem almost corpselike, had stood up with the music-box in his hands.

"Mr. Benjamin," he said, "I lay no claim to being a man of practical affairs, as Jules does. But I fail to see the relevance of your point. It's a wonder, I should say, he was not more bruised than seems actually to have been the case. Still, why are we discussing bruises? Why should a bruise or two be important?"

"Because dead men don't bruise. If shock killed him before his body struck the stairs, it means one thing. If he died during the fall or at the end of it, it means something else altogether. We don't know; we can't tell. And therefore . . ."

"To me," cried Mr. Jeffers, "only one matter of the most desperate urgency has emerged tonight. That matter has not been discussed or even so much as mentioned in conclave. If you don't understand what I mean . . ."

"I understand what you mean, and we are coming to it. It brings us back full circle to Margot de Sancerre."

Margot's father looked at him, but said nothing.

"For some time, then, the young lady has been preoccupied (over-preoccupied, it might be said) with thoughts of two persons who themselves are almost legendary: the late Delphine Lalaurie and the still-living Marie Laveau. So much is common knowledge. Even her father must have remarked it."

"How gratifying," murmured Jules de Sancerre, "that you should say 'even' her father! To speak the truth, everybody, I am a more perceptive fellow than the ladies of my household think. When I suspect or learn something, however, I have found it more conducive to domestic peace if I keep the discovery to myself. What are we getting at *now?*"

"We are wondering, for one thing, in what way these legendary women could have influenced Margot's own conduct. Has her closest friend no suggestion? Can't you help us, Miss Ede?"

Ursula had been leaning forward intently.

"I'm sorry!" she breathed. "Margot *has* been preoccupied about both of them. And somebody's been seeing her secretly and influencing her in some way. That's what I—I told Mr. Macrae when he asked much the same sort of question. I can't tell you any more, because Margot wouldn't tell me. I wish I could help you, but I can't!"

"Then we must see if we can't help ourselves." Senator Benjamin grew confidential. "Last night, Jules, I assured Isabelle that we could let public records confirm or demolish the alleged infamies of Delphine Lalaurie. I also promised to investigate other public records, much easier of access, about a certain other person. The other person, of course, was Marie Laveau, the Voodoo Queen. Hear what I have learned; you should find it suggestive."

From his inside breast pocket he drew out a sheaf of notes closely written. He sat down at the big table, bent over the notes, and then straightened up.

"Marie Laveau, free mulatto, was born here at New Orleans in

1794. There seems no doubt about her beauty in youth, though not much beauty can remain at sixty-three or sixty-four.

"Tales of an illustrious if left-handed ancestry can be dismissed as fables self-created for glamour; her father may have been anybody. In August of 1819 she married Jacques Paris, also a free mulatto. He died in May, 1822, less than three years later. There were no children of the marriage.

"About 1826—the exact date is uncertain, since she never went through a wedding ceremony again—Marie Laveau formed an alliance *derrière l'église* with one Christophe Glapion, still another free man of colour, who is said to have been only one-quarter Negro. This irregular union produced no less than fifteen children, the eldest being a daughter born in 1827. And the as-good-as husband survived until three years ago.

"That is all we know with certainty about the Voodoo Queen, who can scarcely have indulged in many public orgies during the years when she was bearing fifteen children. Informants tell me that today she almost never leaves her St. Ann Street cottage, the gift years ago of a man who believed Voodoo magic had saved his son from the gallows. But the facts shed a good deal of light on our present problem, don't you agree?"

"If you're looking at me," said Jules de Sancerre, "no! I don't agree, damme, because I don't understand at all."

"I don't understand either," proclaimed Tom Clayton, "though the old intuition is working full blast and I'm beginning to think I could see through a millstone. Look here, Senator—!"

"If you had asked *me*," Barnaby Jeffers said querulously, holding the music-box in one hand and adjusting his oblong spectacles with the other, "I could have told you any and all of those things with no necessity to consult birth-certificates or parish registers. And we're straying from the point again, aren't we? Since you mentioned Delphine Lalaurie . . ."

The door of the library was thrown open.

"Yes," said Isabelle de Sancerre's voice, "you mentioned Delphine Lalaurie. That is why I intrude now."

Handsome but pale, her eyelids pink and swollen, she closed the door and stood with her back to it, the green crinoline billowing out.

"Mr. Macrae," she added, "you must pardon me if I was distraught when I first greeted you tonight, and talked rather wildly. I am not at all the foolish rattle I must have seemed, though there is much to make me more distraught now. Judge Rutherford dead in our house! Margot still missing!

"It was useless, gentlemen, to make a pretence of retiring. Even with the aid of laudanum, I knew I could never sleep. So I crept downstairs again. I have been shamelessly listening outside the door."

"My dear Isabelle . . ." began her husband.

"Last night, Jules, the most eminent of lawyers assured me that Mayor Waterman's staff would determine the guilt or innocence of Delphine Lalaurie in the charge of torturing her slaves, and that he would have news for me soon. Well, sir, what did they find?"

"They found nothing," replied Senator Benjamin, and seemed to brace himself.

"You mean they didn't look?"

"Oh, they looked; they are still looking. I mean there was nothing to find. Following the flight of Madame Lalaurie and her husband in April, 1834, no slaves were sold at public auction, as the slaves must have been sold had they been cruelly used. Either the lady was entirely innocent, and has been much maligned, or . . ."

"Or what?"

"Or the record has been destroyed. I think that unlikely, though I state the fact. The investigation of her affairs, however, was not entirely fruitless."

"But you said—!"

"I said only that the lady's guilt or innocence could not be determined by existing records. Are you interested in such records as *do* exist?"

"For heaven's sake, Benjie, don't put on your mask! What is it?"

Senator Benjamin, now standing beside the table, shuffled through his notes.

"Before she left this country forever," he said, "Madame Lalaurie signed a power of attorney putting her American business affairs—she had enormous interests abroad too—in the hands of her elder son-in-law. Her husband, Dr. Lalaurie, signed a power of attorney for the other son-in-law. Finally, provision was made for the future of a fourteen-year-old boy whom she had informally adopted as her ward. This boy, one Stéphan Leblanc, was the illegitimate son of a French girl named . . ."

"Rosette Leblanc!" said Barnaby Jeffers. "Have you come to the point at last, sir, without being driven there? Rosette Leblanc!"

"May I explain, Benjie?" asked Isabelle de Sancerre.

"By all means."

"I tried to tell you in the dining-room, sir!" Barnaby Jeffers insisted. "I tried to tell you when we were decently private. But I was not myself; I could not frame the words. Now the whole wretched tale can be told; it *must* be told, else which of two more guilty men is safe?"

Madame de Sancerre fluttered back and forth.

"Really!" she said. "I won't sit down, thanks; pray don't keep pushing chairs at me, any of you! I must speak the truth as I know it, but I seem to know either too little or too much.

"That boy, Rosette Leblanc's son. Last night, when I was telling Mr. Macrae about Delphine Lalaurie, I referred to him without actually naming him because, as I said at the time, he seemed to have no real concern with Delphine's story. Now, considering certain things Mr. Jeffers has blurted out at odd times tonight, I'm afraid the boy grown older may be all too horribly concerned.

"Let me see what I remember, now.

"We women of favoured lives are so accustomed to having a personal maid in *some* shade of colour that an ordinary Caucasian maid comes as a positive shock. Delphine had one. During her second widowhood, after the death of her banker husband, she engaged Rosette Leblanc on a visit to Paris about 1818. Rosette came of bad stock, her parents being known criminals. But she was pretty and had fetching ways, though she had a savage temper too. Delphine took pity on her, brought her to New Orleans, and was always unfailingly kind.

"She had need of kind feelings for the girl. Much as I dislike mentioning such matters in mixed company . . . sorry, Ursula . . ."

"It's all right, Aunt Isabelle!"

". . . the sordid fact is that somebody in our own circle—it's never been known who the man was—took advantage of Rosette and seduced her. Rosette's child was born early in 1820, long before I, a mere child myself then, had made Delphine Lalaurie's acquaintance at all. Rosette herself died of yellow fever that same summer.

"The average employer would have packed the child off to an orphanage or got rid of it somehow. Delphine did nothing of the kind. The boy was brought up as a member of her own family. Delphine indulged him, even petted him, as she had scarcely done with her own.

" 'I feel guilty about him, for some reason,' she once said to me. 'I'll see he has a chance!'

"In another woman this cherishing of so dubious a brat might have excited comment, even scandal. With Delphine it didn't. Later they accused her of a taste for the most bestial cruelties. She was never accused of being immoral.

"Then came the explosion; then came the day of disaster. In that beautiful spring of 1834 . . . Do you remember, Jules?"

"Do I remember what?"

It was hard to tell whether Isabelle de Sancerre had become lyrical or cynical.

"You and I," she said, "were to be married in May. On a day at the end of March we came out here to look at this house, then a new house not quite finished. Delphine Lalaurie accompanied us. And in worshipful attendance on *her* was the boy, fourteen years old. Do you remember that, Jules?"

"Not with any degree of clearness, I'm afraid."

"Nor do I, except for a memory of Delphine's face. And of the boy's devotion, amazingly unembarrassed for fourteen. How he ran up and down the stairs, inside and out! How he hung about Delphine like a true knight errant, drinking in every word!

"Well, you know what happened. On April fifteenth, twenty-four years ago, Delphine fled. But she had provided for the boy. (It's said that his father secretly provided for him too, whoever the father may have been.) Later in the same year Delphine summoned him to Paris, where he was dispatched in the care of one of those slaves who *weren't* sold. They sent him to school in

England, then fetched him back to Paris to work for a bank in which Delphine was interested.

"What's become of him since then? After Delphine's death in '42, Harriet Cavendish—dead these eight years, poor woman!—met him once at the bank in Paris. He said, Harriet told me, that one day he would return to New Orleans and put right the wrong that had been done Mama Delphine. Harriet swore he looked horribly grim when he said that, as though he meant every word.

"And maybe he did mean it. He had seen his beloved Delphine hounded out of the country. He had seen her house wrecked at the hands of a mob led by a law-student named Horace Rutherford . . ."

"Well supported," cried Barnaby Jeffers, "by two other young intemperates. One of them is now himself the president of a bank. The other . . . !"

"Just a moment, all of you!" snapped Jules de Sancerre. "Isabelle, sit down in that chair and control yourself. Is it being seriously suggested that Rosette Leblanc's son *has* returned?"

"Why not?" Barnaby Jeffers asked. "I myself have received a note in French, a distinct threat, signed *Papa Là-bas*. The boy came of tainted stock to begin with. His mother's parents were known criminals, however pretty she may have been when she—when she—!"

A convulsion went through him. The music-box, of wood painted with a pastoral scene impossibly Arcadian, slipped through his fingers and crashed on the floor. That jar to its mechanism did what all his tinkering had been unable to accomplish. There was a metallic click; the box, twitching as though with life inside, whirred and began tinklingly to play.

> Oh, believe me, if all those endearing young charms,
>   Which I gaze on so fondly today,
> Were to change by tomorrow and fleet in my arms . . .

Mr. Jeffers pounced on it; the tune stopped. Lifting the box in hands that shook uncontrollably, he set it on the ledge of the mantelpiece.

"That girl's son, let me repeat, came of tainted stock. He left here a boy of fourteen; he would return a man in his late thirties. After nearly a quarter of a century, who could possibly recognize him? If he changed his name . . ."

"By all the thunders of Jupiter," shouted Tom Clayton, "he wouldn't even need to change his name!"

"Tom," said Ursula, and twitched her head round, "what on earth are you talking about?"

"It's my intuition, angel-face; ten to one I've come up with the answer. He hasn't changed his name; he's just anglicized it. Stéphan Leblanc! Steve White!"

"I have a feeling," cried Isabelle de Sancerre, "there's something else about him I ought to have told you. But I can't remember what it is!"

Senator Benjamin made a face of despair.

"Will someone tell *me* the meaning of all this?" he begged, turning towards Tom and spreading out his hands. "Why should Stéphan Leblanc be Steve White? And, in any case, who is Steve White?"

"You'll hear about him soon enough, Senator. The only one of us who's actually talked to him didn't think he was important and hasn't mentioned him to you. But he slipped ashore as soon as the *Governor Roman* docked this morning, and the police had better find him before . . .

"No, that won't do!" argued Tom, interrupting himself. "The pranks of our merry joker began long before 'Steve White' could have been anywhere near here. I was wrong and I apologize. He can't be the joker, but who is? Any ideas, Senator?"

"Before every one of you started explaining," replied that harassed gentleman, "I believed I could see at least a gleam of light. Whether or not it goes out . . ."

"Well, don't look at *me*," protested Isabelle de Sancerre. "I'm utterly befogged!"

"We are all befogged, Isabelle," her husband said almost with cheerfulness, "except the legal pundit there. A question for you, O Solon. Whoever may be behind this business, what has Voodoo got to do with it?"

"A great deal, I believe, though in an oblique way. And we

have need of official sanction; we must have official sanction! I
wish Sergeant O'Shea would get here!"

Four full-length curtained windows faced front towards St.
Charles Avenue. Macrae, who had been listening, nodded towards
them.

"I rather think," he suggested, "there's a carriage coming up the
drive. If that's Sergeant O'Shea now ..."

"Nonsense!" said Jules de Sancerre. "Your messenger left here
a bare twenty or thirty minutes ago. He can't possibly have driven
to City Hall and back again!"

"There's certainly one carriage, perhaps two. Hadn't I better go
and ...?"

"Yes, go and see. Let's hope we can settle *something!*"

Macrae strode out into the hall and made for the front door.

Ursula's carriage and Jared again waited outside. Up the drive
came spanking an English-style gig, two wheels and one horse.
There was enough light from the front door and from carriage-
lanterns to show massive, red-haired Sergeant Timothy O'Shea,
with his freckled face and his bushy side-whiskers, handling the
reins of the gig. Just behind him Walter drove the other *calèche*
and Harry.

Sergeant O'Shea drew up the gig with a flourish. He got down
from it, mounted the front steps, and swept off his high beaver hat
to greet Macrae.

"And is it yourself, now, sir?" he began in his hoarse voice. "A
very good evening to you, though be all the omens it's a bad 'un
and no mistake!"

"A good evening to *you,* Sergeant O'Shea. How did Mr. Ludlow
get from here to City Hall and back in so short a time?"

"Frankly," said Sergeant O'Shea, with the air of one imparting
a secret, "'twas not at City Hall we met. 'Twas a bit nearer, like.
And when I say the young gentleman and I ran into each other—
faith, now, that's no figure o' speech in anybody's book. It's a
grand town, New Orleans!

"I was at Brannigan's, St. Charles Avenue, refreshing the inner
man with a potation or two to stand by me if this thing should be
a joke or a fool's errand, and I'd be catching hell from the D.A.

tomorrow morning! Being already on the way out here, you see . . ."

"You were already on the way out here?"

" 'Deed and I was: no lie! I was driving the hired gig I always drive, like the gentleman I am not but would like to be, when I've wherewithal in me pocket to hire one."

"Well! Leaving Brannigan's, now, I own I may have been on the wrong side of the road. But how could I have crossed over before the other rig comes bowling up? Whether I sideswiped him, or he sideswiped me, is no odds to anybody now. And there was no damage done either, bar a lick o' paint gone from both of us, and bar that the open-handed young lordling, in a brand-new silk hat he bought only this morning, runs his head smack into the back of the seat behind the coachman and smashes his new tile to blazes. And then, glory be to God, it turns out *he's* looking for *me!* Yes, it's a grand town."

Harry, the ruined hat in his hand, had approached with the look of one who would have agreed with the sergeant's last remark. Sergeant O'Shea was in full cry.

"Then, sir, he begins to tell me a tale the like of which I've not heard even when I was a constable with the detective police in London. The young lady *is* gone, it seems. And old Judge Rutherford: *he* takes a header with worse results than this young gentleman's header, and five witnesses there but nobody near him. But I said I'd better speak to the witnesses meself, and here we are."

"Sergeant, how did it happen that—"

"I'm no genius at police work, Mr. Macrae; I'm no Jonathan Whicher or Charley Field. But I was born in Limerick; I'm no fool either, and there's worse hands than Tim O'Shea at the kind o' game this may turn out to be. Since I'd already got the word there was something wrong here . . ."

"Yes," Macrae almost yelled, "that's what I've been trying to ask. How did you happen to be on your way here in the first place?"

Sergeant O'Shea put his hand into his pocket.

"You'd better see this, sir. It was stuck in the pigeonhole that's mine of the rack outside the office six of us use in the west wing. I can't tell you who stuck it in the pigeonhole; there's people about there at all times, even at night. It might have been ten o'clock I found it, and for the life of me I couldn't decide whether 'twas honest or somebody was having me on.

"I don't usually dither, it's God's truth I don't; but I dithered and dithered *this* night. It must have been far past eleven when I started out in the gig; and I may have stopped for a nip at maybe two or three other pubs before I got to Brannigan's at all. Anyway, here you are."

From his pocket he took a white card, perhaps four inches by two or three, and handed it over. Macrae held it up to the light. On one side the sergeant's name had been printed in ink with small, neat block capitals done by a fine-nibbed pen. The other side read:

Voulez-vous faire votre devoir? Allez toute de suite à la
maison seigneuriale de Jules de Sancerre, Avenue St. Charles.
Mademoiselle de Sancerre a disparue, ou peut-être la disparition
n'est pas encore arrivée. Et alors?

Toujours à vous,
Papa Là-bas.

"Many's the time," said Sergeant O'Shea, "I've been tipped the wink for information received, from one source or another. But it's not often I get it from the devil's own self."

10

Fifteen minutes later, in the big downstairs hall, Macrae faced Senator Benjamin.

Sergeant O'Shea, with many apologies and a winning manner which in England or Ireland would have been described as smarmy, had taken charge. His voice could be heard now behind the closed door of the library, in session with Jules de Sancerre, Barnaby Jeffers, Harry Ludlow, and Tom Clayton.

Isabelle de Sancerre, evidently wanting to impart something in private, had taken Ursula upstairs. They were dismissed with Sergeant O'Shea's blessing.

"We'll not be troubling the ladies," he had said jocosely, "or troubling their heads either, at this unholy hour. No, sir," he had added to Jules de Sancerre, "and I'll *not* say no to a drop o' Bourbon, thank you very kindly!"

Judah P. Benjamin, hands dug into his pockets, stood in the hall and mused. Several possibilities were going through Macrae's mind; he approached one of them.

"Those two cards we saw," he said. "Both written in French, both signed Papa Là-bas, both hand-delivered by someone who wasn't seen. The card Mr. Jeffers showed us—the one he's kept calling a 'note'—ran simply, 'Take care. Your turn will come.' What do you make of the other?"

"The message to Sergeant O'Shea?" Mr. Benjamin stirred and raised his head. "That, if memory serves, went like this. 'Do you want to do your duty? Go at once to Jules de Sancerre's mansion,

St. Charles Avenue. Miss de Sancerre has disappeared, or perhaps the disappearance has not yet occurred.' Then that sneering, 'Well, what about it?' followed by 'Ever yours,' and the signature."

"Yes, Senator?"

Mr. Benjamin took a brisk little turn towards the staircase, then swung back again.

"I am assuming," he said, "that Judge Rutherford's death *was* an ingeniously contrived murder, though at present there seems no way of proving it. Very well. Whoever wrote that card—both cards—either is the murderer himself or is someone cognizant of the murderer's plans and abetting him. You agree?"

"Yes. It's inescapable."

"What follows from the evidence? For argument's sake we will postulate that the writer of the card, Papa Là-bas, is someone associated with the murderer rather than the actual assassin. He knew that Margot de Sancerre would vanish, or would be made to vanish, though not the actual time at which it would occur. He also knew, in all probability, that the disappearance couldn't be prevented."

"Couldn't be prevented? What are you saying?"

"Well, consider. At whatever time tonight the card was put in Sergeant O'Shea's pigeonhole at City Hall, O'Shea found it at ten o'clock. If the good sergeant had come here at once, or even reasonably soon, he might well have arrived before Margot herself. The writer of the card must surely have felt the vanishing-trick was all but foolproof, to risk summoning this far-from-stupid police-officer as a potential witness?"

"It sounds reasonable enough," Macrae said stubbornly, "when you put it like that. All the same! Unless we also postulate Margot herself as a party to some conspiracy, possibly even to the murder . . . ?"

"No, my friend, no! I don't believe the young lady knew (or knows) the least bit about it. But I don't believe she is in any danger either."

"Then, as Barnaby Jeffers would say, aren't we still straying from the point? If a murderer does lurk in the background, who is he and where do we look for him? You weren't there last night when Madame de Sancerre told me that the leader of the mob who wrecked Delphine Lalaurie's house was young Horace Rutherford, his lieutenants being Barnaby Jeffers and George Stoneman of the Planters' & Southern Bank. But I imagine you've heard of this?"

"Yes. I've heard of it."

"Mr. Jeffers is sure the son of Rosette Leblanc has returned, a dark-browed avenger, to execute justice on all three. It may be the elusive 'Steve White,' though Tom Clayton states sound reason for thinking it can't be. What's your view?"

Senator Benjamin rubbed a furrowed forehead.

"To answer that question," he replied, "is extraordinarily difficult without being over-cryptic or misleading or both. May I make a suggestion? It's late, it's very late; but I have no inclination for sleep. Instead I have a fancy to stroll round towards the back of the house and get some air. Will you accompany me, while we continue to thrash at these perplexities?"

"With pleasure."

Taking their hats from a table in the hall, they went out the front door and down the portico steps into a cool, fragrant night. Senator Benjamin, motioning towards his left, led the way along the gravel drive towards the west side of the house, which was the right-hand side as you faced it.

"We have been speaking of a conspiracy," he went on; "not the first time one has been mentioned. For seven weeks or thereabouts something or somebody has been 'at' Margot de Sancerre. For the same length of time something or somebody has been 'at' you. This sensation of being followed and spied on . . ."

"Don't ask me to describe the feeling; it can't be expressed in simple terms."

"I think I understand. Last night, no doubt, you felt it at its strongest when some visitor flung through the window-pane the object we at first took for a human head?"

"Yes!"

"Have you felt it today or this evening?"

"No, not once."

"And you're sure the presence is malignant?"

"Well, put yourself in my place. Suppose you felt eyes boring into *your* back, heard footsteps that never materialized into a person, kept expecting something that didn't happen? How would *you* feel?"

"Exactly as you have. Yes, of course. H'm."

They had rounded the side of the house, walking very slowly. The broad gravel drive, greyish under a luminous sky, stretched straight ahead with a scattering of rounded whitish stones at its edges. Senator Benjamin had taken out his leather cigar-case, but he did not open it.

"And now, with regard to the possible mechanics of what we believe to have been a murder," he resumed, "I will ask you to indulge briefly in a wild flight of fancy. Are you willing to do that?"

"I am always willing to do that."

"There (imagine!) stands Judge Rutherford, poised and teetering at the top of the stairs. Tom Clayton has talked of his being pushed. But suppose him not to have been pushed at all; what if it were something else? Suppose, finally, that a presumed witness to this happening was in fact the murderer himself?"

Macrae's fancy did take wing, more wildly than he could control.

"I think I see what you mean. The judge wasn't pushed: he was pulled!"

"*Pulled?*"

"And the murderer needn't have been one of our group of five. It could have been somebody standing behind us, somebody we never saw."

"Explain that, please!"

Macrae groped.

"Senator," he said, "tonight you told us one fishing story. I am going to venture on another.

"There stand the five of us in that high hall. Behind us stands the murderer: with rod, with a length of fishing-line so fine as to be invisible by gaslight, and with a hook at the end of it. He casts; he casts over our heads; he is a fisher of men. Judge Rutherford, already precariously balanced, pitches forward as the hook catches in his coat. The murderer gives a yank, dislodging the hook and—and—"

Suddenly appalled at the grotesque image he had conjured up, seeing its full ludicrousness, Macrae stopped short.

"It won't do, will it?" he asked.

"Frankly," his companion told him, "I fear it won't. To imagine our murderer giving any such performance—flourishing a fishing-rod, making his cast, drawing back the line: all totally unseen and leaving no mark on the victim's coat—is not a spectacle that can be viewed without emotion of some kind. But don't apologize, I beg! Never apologize for imaginative boldness; there is all too little of it in this world."

"I shouldn't have perpetrated any such damned idiocy!"

"On the contrary, you were right to perpetrate it. Pity the man who won't speak for fear of talking nonsense; he may be a model of temperance, but he is infernally dull."

"And yet . . ."

"You misunderstood the direction of my approach, that's all. There *is* a way in which the thing could have been done: simply, and, to my mind, quite feasibly. However, since it has no shred of supporting evidence and is open to at least one grave objection, it had better be kept in abeyance for the moment." Senator Benjamin replaced the cigar-case in his pocket. "Shall we walk on a little further? I have also a fancy to see Margot de Sancerre's room in her absence."

"If you wanted to see Margot's room," said Macrae, glad to be on firm ground again, "why didn't you go upstairs when we were in the house?"

"And meet Isabelle and be forced into explanations? I think not. The young lady's room, if memory serves, is at the other side of the house. But there is a gallery with an outside staircase leading up to it."

They had reached the angle of the house at the back, where they paused. Macrae glanced over his shoulder.

"Though there may be no pursuer on my trail tonight, somebody is following us along the path now."

It was only Jules de Sancerre. He came bustling up out of the gloom, hatless and with a sardonic look on what they could discern of his face.

"I was dismissed, gentlemen," he announced. "I was dismissed in my own house. With great deference, I allow; that blarneying Irishman, who seems to know a thing or two, also knows how to lay it on with a trowel. But I was dismissed none the less, once I had spoken my piece. The Irishman now communes with poor Barnaby, who insists on having protection and is assured he will get it. You two, it seems, are not to be troubled with questions. Are you looking for anything in particular, may I ask?"

And he swept out his hand, as though calling attention to the house's southern aspect.

Along the back, at the level of the floor above, ran an iron-railed gallery with a roof against rain. The two halves of the drive, west and east, united at a rear door and continued straight on between tall shrubs towards the carriage-house and the stable. At the eastern end of the south side, a covered way stretched from the back of the dining-room to the kitchen, a separate brick structure. Here on the west side, at the end of a short beaten path branching off the drive, stood another separate structure: this one of wood painted white. Though larger than the average smoke-house, it was smaller than the kitchen; it had a north window and double doors secured by a padlock on staples.

Senator Benjamin surveyed all this.

"Looking for anything? No, nothing at all," he said with a straight face. "Are you?"

"I must pay a visit to the carriage-house," replied Jules de Sancerre. "It wouldn't interest you to visit the carriage-house, I suppose?"

"No, not particularly. By the way, what is that small white edifice with the north window? It might almost be an artist's studio."

"So it is, in a way. That's Cicero's workshop."

"Cicero's workshop?"

"Uncle Cicero," their host assured them both, "is much more than a coachman, great though his skill with horseflesh. He was a famous carpenter; he belonged to Mr. Sturdevant before I won him in a poker game years ago. And he can work in iron and leather; he can turn his hand to anything; he makes us whatever we need.

"Cicero's wife is Thisbe, Margot's Mammy. When Margot was seven or eight years old, he made her an elaborate play-house complete in every detail. All I did was supply the cash for him to buy materials, and that play-house became the envy of every child in the district. Margot used it until she grew too tall to stand up inside the rooms. Well, well, if *you're* not interested in carriages, *I* am."

"Indeed?"

"Yes. And our Irish bluebottle says he won't go on questioning much longer tonight; please feel free to leave without ceremony whenever the spirit moves you. Ta-ta, gentlemen!"

Off he went at his brisk gait, down the drive between tall shrubs towards carriage-house and stable.

With an exaggerated air of secrecy, moving on tiptoe, Senator Benjamin led Macrae to the iron stairway ascending the back of the house to the gallery above. Feeling rather like a burglar and wondering why, Macrae followed him up.

Of the five rooms set in a line at the back, all but the centre-most, Jules de Sancerre's study, appeared to be dark. From the study's two tall windows shafts of gaslight pierced out on the gallery between heavy rep curtains not quite drawn shut.

Still moving slowly, the investigators peered into the windows of the first room they passed. There was just light enough for them to make out the form of the dressmaker's dummy, of a massive wooden sewing-machine, of several chairs shapeless in gloom.

Through the windows of the next room, a spare room, they could discern little except the dominating headboard of the bed. Then they were outside the study.

With more assurance, almost as though enjoying himself, Mr. Benjamin used his finger-tips to push up the lower half of the first window to its full height. He stepped through, parting the curtains, and beckoned his companion after him.

It was a good-sized square room with brown-papered walls, a

clutter of armchairs, and several open gas-jets burning in flattish glass dishes. Steel engravings of dead statesmen ornamented the walls, notably a dyspeptic-looking Andrew Jackson and John C. Calhoun with brow of thunder, above bookshelves casually arranged. The opened parcel of books lay on Jules de Sancerre's desk. A scent of cigar-smoke still hung heavy. And the door still stood wide open.

Senator Benjamin, pulling at his right side-whisker, wandered out into the upstairs hall. He went to the head of the steps and peered down. Turning round, he bent over to look at the carpet. Finally, unenlightened, he came back into the study, only partly closing the door, and bent over the opened parcel on the desk.

"Here," he continued, "are the books Jules and Judge Rutherford were examining not long before the tragedy. This one is called *The Courtship of Miles Standish*. Here," and he lifted two quarto volumes, "we have a pirated American edition of *Little Dorrit*, Mr. Dickens's latest, which in England is still appearing in monthly parts. The pirates have got there first, as they always do."

He stood back from the desk, weighing the books in his hand, a twinkle in his eye.

"Into *Bleak House*, some five years ago, the same author wove a full-scale murder mystery as an important part of his plot. The chapters dealing with the death of old Tulkinghorn, and the surprising identity of his assassin, form a separate entity which may be read by itself. Though it's a device invented for the short story by the late Edgar Poe of Virginia, and soon abandoned by him, let's hope it won't be lost. Let's hope Mr. Dickens, or perhaps some younger writer, will give us a novel in which the solving of a mystery, through appropriately sensational events and with all the clues in sight, shall form the whole theme of the book. It might be called the novel of sensation or even, more fancifully still, the 'detective' novel. What a prospect!"

Senator Benjamin's face glowed. Macraé studied him.

"You know," Macrae said, "you really do seem to be enjoying yourself!"

"In a ghoulish sort of way," the other confessed, "I'm afraid I am. Don't underestimate man's appetite for the sensational. I believe that in fairly recent years a countryman of yours, the novelist G. P. R. James, was British Consul at Norfolk, and married an American lady before leaving us. Is he still in the government's service?"

"Yes. He is now consul-general at Venice."

"Mr. James's works used to delight me. Little mystery, unfortunately, but roaring sensationalism in plenty. More than a decade ago, when my mother was still alive, I used to read aloud from those books to my mother and my sisters.

"I did worse than that," Senator Benjamin admitted guiltily. "For the edification of mother and sisters I would tell a series of the most fearsome ghost stories I could remember or concoct. I told the stories in near darkness, piling horror upon horror, working up slowly for effect, and then shouting, 'Boo!' at the *dénouement*. It would do me little good if my present-day clients learned that. Can you imagine any pursuit more childish?"

Macrae swung round to look at the open window behind him.

"For a moment," he replied, feeling a cold chill at his back, "*I* imagined my own ghostly pursuer had returned, and was standing there looking at me. Just a moment."

He went to the window and put his head out between the curtains. He closed the lower half of the window, which slid down almost without noise, and turned back.

"There's nobody outside," he said, "or there seems to be nobody. But look here! If you want to see Margot's room, hadn't we better get on with it before we're interrupted?"

"As a matter of fact," said his companion, "that suggestion was only a *ruse de guerre* in case someone should be listening. It was this study, and the hall outside, I really wished to see. In the young lady's room I had no interest at all."

The study door suddenly opened. They had heard no approach over soft carpet. Ursula Ede stood in the aperture, one hand pressed under her heart and a look of consternation on her face.

"Forgive me!" Ursula cried. "But if you don't want to see Margot's room—really, that's just as well. Because she's there now, and I don't think she'd let you. She's come back, do you understand? Margot's come back!"

Senator Benjamin's mood changed in a flash. "When did this happen?"

"A little while ago," Ursula appealed to Macrae, "Aunt Isabelle and I came up here. You may have seen us."

"I saw you."

"Aunt Isabelle said, 'Do you think, before Margot left here tonight, she may have left a line of explanation for me? Just a word or two on a bit of paper, so I wouldn't worry myself ill? Let's go and see.'

"We went to Margot's room, and opened the door without even knocking. The lights were full on. There was Margot, standing in front of the dressing-table mirror and straightening her gown: though she wasn't even very untidy, really."

"Where had she been?"

"That's what Aunt Isabelle asked. And, 'What do you mean by frightening us to death?' and so on. Margot wasn't in a very good mood. She said, 'Get out of here and leave me alone! Please get out of here and leave me alone! Do get out of here and leave me alone!' She took each of us by one shoulder and practically ran us out by main force.

"Aunt Isabelle ran downstairs: to fetch Uncle Jules, I supposed. Anyway, she went into the library and hasn't come up again. Margot is still in her room with the door locked, and won't answer it."

"Is she there in the dark?" asked Macrae. "There was no light to be seen when we came in from the gallery."

"She'd drawn the curtains, that's all, and you know what thick curtains they are!"

Ursula, who had advanced into the room, appealed once more.

"Anyway," she went on, "Margot's back safe and sound. That's the main thing and the only thing. And I *must* go home; really I must; I can't stay a minute longer. And may I drive *you* home, please, just as I brought you here? And can't we go *now*?"

"Well . . ."

"I've been pacing the floor up here, mainly in Aunt Isabelle's room at the front. Then I wandered back along the hall, and heard your voices. But I must get home; my conscience is all over me; and can't I persuade you to come along? If you're thinking of Harry, Tom Clayton will be glad to give him a lift. When I plead with you, as I'm doing now . . . !"

"My friend," Senator Benjamin said weightily, "accept a suggestion from me and do as Miss Ede asks. No leave-takings, if you please! I will make your excuses; and, as you heard Jules de Sancerre say, no leave-takings are necessary. However, I begin to see more light in this business. If you will both do me the favour of meeting me here tomorrow, say at four o'clock in the afternoon, I will try to unravel *a little* of the tangle. May I depend on you? Very well! 'Stand not upon the order of your going, but go at once.' "

A few moments later, after Ursula had run to Isabelle de Sancerre's room and fetched her silvery cape, they were on their way downstairs, with the senator following. Instinctively they made as little noise as possible.

Some sort of commotion seemed to be going on behind the closed door of the library. Ursula had taken Macrae's arm, and he steered her quickly past that trouble-spot. Senator Benjamin nodded farewell from the foot of the stairs. Marcus Brutus materialized from nowhere to open the front door and close it after them.

"It's number 33 Carondelet Street, isn't it?" asked Ursula, as they climbed into the waiting carriage. "You hear that, Jared?" Then she spoke in a whisper. "Quentin, what's the matter?"

At the moment he had no opportunity to answer. Jules de Sancerre, evidently returning from his visit to the rear of the premises, bustled round the west side of the house, mounted the portico steps, and opened the front door. During that brief interval, it became evident, the commotion in the library had boiled over.

As Jared flicked the reins, the two in the carriage were too far from the portico to see who had just run upstairs. But they heard a last thud of footsteps before those footsteps reached carpet at the top. And the hoarse voice of Sergeant O'Shea, as he came shouldering out of the library with Barnaby Jeffers in his wake, left little doubt.

"Ah, be hokey," yelled the sergeant, "but what would yez be doing now? Come back here, Mr. Clayton! Come back and—"

Jules de Sancerre closed the front door. The carriage bowled away.

"Oh, no!" breathed an agonized Ursula. "Not more ructions, for heaven's sake? Not Tom on the war-path *again?* Still, there's not much we can do to stop it either. And what *is* the matter with you?"

"Matter?"

"Am I too forward? Don't you like me any longer?"

"Merely to be here beside you, Ursula, were paradise enow. The trouble is this business of driving me to Carondelet Street before *you* go home. You live fairly near here, don't you?"

"Yes; it's not far away."

"Then why not go there and let Jared call it a night? I can easily walk home, as I did the first time we met. Also, if your father should happen to be awake on this occasion, I can always explain . . ."

"You don't know my father. He's well disposed towards you now; he has been since that day we saw you shooting beside the lake. He says you're a capital shot and carry yourself like a gentleman. What he'd say if a total stranger brought his daughter home at nearly two o'clock in the morning, especially if you tried to explain where you picked her up . . ."

"Do you think I'd say anything like that?"

"Don't say anything at all, please! I can get out of this on my own. I may have to stretch the truth a good bit, in spite of my insistence on being honest with Aunt Isabelle. But every girl has to do that so often, especially with her own family, she never thinks twice about it." Ursula looked at him sideways. "There's something *else* troubling you, isn't there?"

There was. What troubled him was Ursula herself: her eyes, her lips, her arms and shoulders so close as to cloud the judgment. Though hardly a ladies' man, he could not have failed to see that his attentions had not been distasteful to her so far.

And yet . . .

They sat mainly in silence, each beginning several times to speak but stopping short. Again a lurch of the carriage all but threw them into each other's arms. The church clocks had struck two before the *calèche* rolled in at number 33 Carondelet Street and stopped under the covered way beside the main staircase to his living-quarters.

Macrae climbed down from the carriage. Ursula extended her hand, and he took it.

"Thank you!" she whispered. "Thank you for everything."

"No; thank *you*. We meet tomorrow, don't we?"

"Margot's house, four in the afternoon. I'm looking forward to that." The light of the right-hand carriage lantern shone in Ursula's eyes. "And you needn't be so *very* discreet, if you don't want to be. Good night, Quentin."

"Good night, Ursula."

He pressed her hand and released it. He waited until the carriage had gone. Then he ran up the steps and unlocked the door.

A dim point of gas burned blue in the foyer. Stout Tibby, Sam's wife, had been occupying a straight chair underneath the gas-jet, and started up in terror as the door opened. Though reassured when she recognized him, she remained a frightened woman.

"Tibby! How is it you're still up at this hour of the morning?"

Round her head Tibby wore the red bandanna which the law ordained for all free women of colour, though not all of them obeyed it. Tibby, unlike Sam, had received a very fair education at a church school.

"Here it is, Mr. Richard!" Tibby blurted, taking something from the pocket of her apron. "Here it is! Someone sneaked in and left it on your desk, the desk downstairs in the office, not long after you'd gone tonight. Something else was left on the desk too. But do you think I'd touch *that*? No, sir! Catch me fooling with *that*!"

She held out an oblong card of a sort with which he had become familiar. Macrae brightened the gas-jet and examined the card. On one side his name was neatly printed with a familiar fine-nibbed pen. On the other side was:

> A la maison hantée, rue Royale. Cherchez-moi là vendredi à minuit ou un peu plus tard. Je jette ce défi, cher monsieur, et j'ai l'honneur d'être
>
> Toujours à vous,
> Papa Là-bas.

"Tibby, can you read this?"

" 'Course I can read it!"

"What does it say?"

" 'At the haunted house, Royal Street. Look for me there Friday at midnight or a little later. I send this challenge, dear sir, and have the honour to be always yours, Papa Là-bas.' "

"What else was put on the desk, Tibby?"

"Sir?"

"You said something else was put there, something that's frightened you half out of your wits. What is it?"

Tibby shrank back from him.

"It's a snake, Mr. Richard! A dead snake!"

I I

ON THE FOLLOWING MORNING, FRIDAY, MACRAE SAT DOWN
to breakfast, as usual, at half-past eight.

Memories of the small hours still tumbled in his mind. After
locking away Papa Là-bas's card in his desk, after disposing of
what else had been on the desk, he had gone to bed at once. He
was just dozing off when he heard another carriage roll up outside,
and heard Harry Ludlow, who had been provided with a latchkey,
tramp to the guest-room.

Though he had not expected easy slumber, in fact he slept quite
well, dreamed of Ursula, and awoke alert. A shave and a cold bath
further refreshed him.

Friday was another overcast day. In his dining-room, a place of
heavy furniture adjoining the drawing-room on the floor above the
courtyard, he had just attacked bacon and eggs when Harry, rosy
of face, entered the dining-room with the air of one who has been
through a great spiritual experience.

"Well, Harry?"

"Well, sir, I can't write home and say I'm not seeing life. That
Sergeant O'Shea *is* something to write home about, isn't he?"

"Sorry you got your new hat smashed, Harry."

"That's no odds, sir. Lots more hats where that came from.
And hats—or Sergeant O'Shea either—are the very least of it. Oo-
er! *I say!*"

"Tom Clayton brought you home, I suppose?"

"No, sir. Tom couldn't; he was still involved in the row. The

old gentleman with the Louis Napoleon beard and moustache very
decently ordered out another of their carriages, and here I am."

"There was a row, was there?"

Harry, in his fashionable short-coated lounge suit, did a little
dance beside the table.

"Was there a row? Oh, blow me to Babylon, was there a *row*?"

"Steady! Control yourself! What happened?"

"I'm not sure how much you saw or heard before you left,
sir."

"Margot returned unexpectedly. Madame de Sancerre ran down
to the library . . ."

"She was looking for the old gentleman, sir. But he'd gone out
somewhere . . ."

"I know that too. Go on from there."

"Madame de Sancerre told us Margot had come back, but still
refused to say where she'd been. That was all right. Or at least it
wasn't so bad until Madame de Sancerre said she didn't know
what the younger generation were coming to, because her own
daughter had taken her by the shoulders and slung her out of the
room. Tom Clayton looked at her for a second or two, and then
blew up all over the place.

"Out he went, with the rest of us after him, and up the stairs
three at a time. When I got there he was shaking the knob of the
girl's door and hammering on the door with his fist. She wouldn't
answer. Then he said, 'Now, you spoiled brat,' he said,"—Harry
had caught the inflection exactly—" 'do you open this door *tout
de suite*, or do I break it down?'

"He'd have done it, too. He was crouching to charge, when all
of a sudden the door opened. There she was, looking just as she'd
looked when she stalked out of the quadroon ball, except that she
was holding a heavy hand-mirror.

"She yelled back at him and called him an overbearing so-and-
so. Good girls aren't even supposed to know that word, though
I've heard my sister use it. She called him an overbearing so-and-
so, and she threw that heavy glass straight at his head.

"It missed him and broke against the opposite wall, but that
only made him madder. Before she could close the door again, he

was in at her. And he did," whooped Harry, clearly torn between discomfort and an unholy joy, "he did just what he said he was going to do earlier in the evening. He sat in a chair; he held her face down across his knee; and he . . . he . . ."

"Steady! I can imagine."

"It wasn't as embarrassing as it might have been, even if he did lift up her skirts at the back. Under their skirts, you see, sir, they wear a thing like a pair of white trousers with lace and frills on it. His left hand was underneath her. In the middle of the tanning she twisted her head down and bit his hand to the bone.

"That did it.

"Tom stood up, picking her up bodily, and chucked her away from him. He was trying to throw her on the bed. But he threw her too hard and too far; she landed face down on the floor beyond the bed. She wasn't hurt; she was up in a second, crying, 'Will nobody avenge my honour? Will nobody avenge my honour?' Tom said, 'Why? Have you lost that too?' And he walked out of the room while she was still looking round for something else to throw.

"Afterwards, sir, there was a right royal rumpus. I don't think I need say too much about that . . ."

"No. You have sketched in the highlights already."

". . . though I think Madame de Sancerre was more concerned about Tom's bitten left hand, which she bound up, than with the injury to her daughter's dignity. And the old gentleman seemed to be rather enjoying himself."

"What did Sergeant O'Shea have to say?"

"He just said the police couldn't concern themselves with lovers' quarrels. All the same, sir, how will those two fare when they get married? Do people in New Orleans usually go on like that?"

"No, of course not! And don't judge too hastily. Let any person anywhere work himself up into an over-excited state; he—or she—will behave just as childishly as Tom and Margot did. That's not even funny; it's simply human nature. Now one last question, and we can drop the subject. What was Senator Benjamin doing throughout all this?"

"The m.c. with the glittering eye? During the main action, as you might say, I hardly noticed him. Afterwards he asked Madame de Sancerre some questions. Was Margot accustomed to using a lot of perfume, or very little perfume, or no perfume at all? As a rule almost none, her mother told him, though last night rather a lot. Then the m.c. wandered away somewhere; before I left somebody said he was walking home."

Tibby had brought more food to the table. Settling down, Harry pitched with such despatch into bacon, eggs, toast, and coffee that he finished before his host.

"Thanks, sir, but I don't smoke," he said, as Macrae offered a paper of cigars. "Better for the wind if I keep off it. Now what do I do this morning? Any instructions?"

"Well, yes."

"I'm ready, sir. Fire away."

"Every consular representative, within twenty-four hours of taking up a new post, is supposed to send a brief report on the situation he finds there."

"*I'm* to do that?"

"Not the situation you've been describing, of course; we mustn't shock 'em out of seven years' growth. What they really want is a word about trade, business conditions, and so on."

"Sir, I don't know one ruddy thing about . . . !"

"No, but you can easily work it up. Last year, for instance, the port of New Orleans did three hundred and fifty million dollars' worth of business. If you're anxious to impress the Foreign Office . . ."

"Sir, I've *got* to impress 'em!"

"In my office downstairs, on the shelf to the right of the fireplace beside the city directory, you'll find some printed reports that will help. Go down and do some work. The consulate officially opens at nine; it's a quarter to nine at the moment. As soon as I've smoked a cigar and drunk a last cup of coffee, I'll come down and turn you out. Then you can work in the drawing-room through there." Macrae pointed. "The consular bag goes out tomorrow, Saturday. If you're conscientious about preparing the report, it's just possible somebody at home may actually read it. Now cut along."

Harry rose to his feet.

"Drawing a bow at a venture," he said, extending his left hand as though gripping the shaft of a bow, and pulling his right hand back to his chin. "I don't think H. Ludlow's first report is going to make 'em stagger with joy. But I'll have a try at it. See you later, sir."

Off he went. One of the doors in the drawing-room opened on the outside gallery with the staircase to the courtyard. As Harry descended, full of determination, Macrae carried coffee-cup and cigar into the drawing-room.

Macrae sat down at a table by one window. He was turning over certain problems in his mind, thinking himself a little nearer solution, when Tom Clayton on a fine saddle-horse rode slowly into the courtyard, dismounted, and gave the reins to a waiting Sam.

Tom's frock coat this morning was bottle-green, his left hand heavily bandaged. Macrae signalled him through the window; he strode up the steps, swept off his hat as he entered, and faced his friend with powerful Byronic gloom.

"Harry has been telling me, Tom, about your emotional spree last night. Have you recovered from it?"

Macrae's heavy walking-stick was propped against the wall near the table at which he sat. Tom snatched up the stick as though about to make a lunge at fencing. Thinking better of this, he replaced it against the wall.

"If you're asking me whether I'm ashamed of myself . . . ?"

"I didn't ask you that. I said . . ."

"Well," Tom roared, "*I am*." Then he controlled himself. "Walloping a woman's behind," he said, "is only fair, proper, and righteous; it's what she ought to expect. Hitting her or manhandling her, which is what I did, can under no circumstances be described as gentlemanly conduct. Why does the damn girl make me so *mad*?"

"Probably because you're in love with her."

"Judging Margot's own conduct by the same criterion," Tom told him, "her passion for me must be boundless. But I don't believe it; I can't believe it; it's too easy."

"Has she condescended to explain what she was doing between the time she vanished out of the carriage and the time she materialized again in her own bedroom?"

"No; she won't say a word. Have *you* anything to report?"

"A little, possibly a good deal. First you'd better hear what I found when I got home."

He described the card signed Papa Là-bas, quoting it verbatim. He also mentioned the dead snake. Tom paced back and forth, in and out amid tables and chairs, fuming to himself.

"Dick, old son," he decided, "it's more of the haunting and no mistake. The snake was left on your desk, eh? What kind of snake was it? Poisonous?"

"No. So far as I could judge, it was a perfectly harmless species about two feet long. At least, it hadn't the arrow head of the viper."

"Somebody'd killed it, you mean?"

"I don't think so. Again without benefit of post-mortem analysis, the snake seemed to have died a natural death. Tibby wouldn't touch it, so I threw it down the drain at the back of the courtyard."

Macrae put his cigar on the edge of an ashtray and stood up.

"Much more important, for what I have in mind, is the card from Papa Là-bas. I have been dared to visit Delphine Lalaurie's house, the famous haunted house, tonight at midnight or a little later. There's an almost donnish flavour about the phrasing. '*Je jette ce défi*,'—literally, 'I *throw* this challenge,'—which is grammatically correct but a little fancy for everyday wear."

"I'm familiar with elementary French, damn it! What *have* you got in mind?"

"Tom, I am going to do something that at first glance may seem foolish or even outlandish. I am going to accept that challenge; I am going to be there."

"Then so am I, by God!" Tom lifted a clenched fist. "We'll go together, shall we?"

"Good man; I hoped you'd say that. But Harry mustn't learn anything of this, or he'd want to go too. I feel responsible for him; he mustn't get in any deeper than he need. And he won't learn anything; I've cautioned Tibby and Sam against mentioning the card or the snake. He can't even stumble on the card by accident; it's locked in my desk. Whereas you and I . . ."

"You know, Dick," Tom said lyrically, "this is far and away the best proposition I've heard in years. We'll meet old Papa Làbas, if he's really there to deliver the goods. We'll land one on his jaw, we'll kick him in the . . . never mind; you see the point: Jesus Christ, this is adventure after my own heart!"

"No, Tom."

"What do you mean, no?"

"I mean we're not going from a sense of adventurousness, or any schoolboy joy at accepting a dare. We're going for the best of good reasons."

"Such as?"

"Last night, at the de Sancerres', my wits weren't working well. They weren't working at all, in fact; I was preoccupied; I couldn't think of anything but . . ."

"You don't have to tell me, old son; I know. You couldn't think of anything but Ursula. Am I right?"

"Dead right."

"Well, who blames you? Ursula's a very attractive gal. All kinds of swain have been hanging around her since she was fourteen years old . . ."

"Why be hard on 'em, Tom?"

"I said swain, not swine! Maybe the plural is 'swains,' though I doubt it. The point is: she's never so much as looked twice at anybody, until . . . go on; figure it out. Her behaviour towards you last night stopped just short of being wanton. All we need now is for you and Ursula to land in some damn compromising position that will make General Ede burst a blood-vessel, and then the muddle would be complete."

"I can do without that, Tom."

"Oh, let nature take its course. And you're not making yourself very clear, are you? What's this strong, sound reason why you and

I must go after Papa Là-bas at the haunted house?"

"Last night Senator Benjamin said he could see at least part of the truth. Reviewing the evidence with a clearer eye this morning, I think I can see part of the truth too. Whether it's the same part as the senator's, or something else altogether, I can't yet say. In any case, he's to preside over another session at four o'clock today. Had you heard about that?"

"Yes; we're all invited. That ought to be quite a party too, if I know old Benjie. But it won't be a patch on our expedition to the haunted house: is that what you're getting at? You seriously think we can learn something if we go there?"

"I'm sure of it. We—" Macrae stopped abruptly. "Look here, what the devil's wrong with my sense of hospitality? You drop in at this hour, and I don't even invite you to have breakfast! Could I interest you in a cup of coffee?"

"I've had breakfast, thanks; but I wouldn't say no to a cup of coffee."

"The coffee in the dining-room is cold, like this cup here. It doesn't matter; Tibby's still in the kitchen. I can just cross the dining-room, go downstairs and outside for a word with her. She can have a fresh pot brewed in five minutes, and . . ."

"*I'll do it!*" yelled Tom. "Stay where you are, you blithering idiot; I said I'*d* do it! Tibby's very partial to me; she must be the only woman in New Orleans who is. But you'd better have some news for me when I come back. Even my intuition hasn't hit on this 'part of the truth' you make so much of. You're going to tell me the great discovery, aren't you?"

"I can give you a very strong indication, at least. The rest you'll see for yourself."

Tom strode away into the dining-room.

Afire with ideas, too restless even to sit down, Macrae began to pace as Tom had been pacing: between chairs and tables of his own somewhat cluttered drawing-room, resisting the impulse to talk to himself aloud. Last night, in the garden of the Washington and American Ballroom, he had divined the truth about Ursula Ede and her mission there. Correctly or incorrectly, he felt in his bones he was on the right track now. A, B, and C followed in restless progress; every piece of evidence fitted the pattern.

If he could reach a full solution ahead of Judah P. Benjamin
. . . !

The extreme left-hand window was partway open. He could hear Sam, who presumably had taken Tom's horse to the stable, pottering in the courtyard below. Decisive footfalls thumped on flagstones as some newcomer entered from the street. Some words were addressed to Sam, who replied with an indistinguishable rumble. Then the newcomer raised his voice.

"Announce me to your master, fellow. I am Mr. Nathaniel Rumbold."

Macrae went back to the table at which he had been drinking coffee, and looked down from the window. Last night, seeing him only at a distance and under grotesque circumstances, he had thought of the gambler almost as a figure of comedy.

But Square Nat Rumbold could not be called a figure of comedy.

His age might have been the late thirties. He was tall, as tall as Tom Clayton, and carried himself with a swagger. In contrast to sober black frock-coat and trousers, to a soft black hat and brown moustache that were unobtrusive enough, his embroidered waistcoat bore a design of scarlet and black poppies set off by gold buttons. A big diamond glittered from his beruffled shirt; there were more diamonds on the fingers of his left hand. His mean-looking eye he could mask with the superficial charm of manner necessary to his profession. But he was not troubling to mask it as he addressed Sam.

"Did you hear what I said, fellow? Announce me to your master."

Sam, standing in front of the stairway to the gallery, mumbled something to the effect that Mist' Richard was not down yet, and couldn't be disturbed. The gambler's voice rose to a snarl of rage and contempt.

"Out of my way, nigger!"

Sam shrank back. Without more ado Square Nat Rumbold bounded up the stairs, checked himself as he reached the gallery, tapped very lightly at the door, and opened it.

A thin smile was pasted like a wafer under the spreading moustache. All courtesy sounded in his voice.

"You are the consul, sir?" he began. "Forgive so early a call. I had hoped I might be of some slight service to you in your unfortunate predicament. If in fact I can be of service . . ."

Macrae looked at him, restraining his own wrath.

"You might begin," he said, "by using better manners towards my servants."

"Manners?" exclaimed the gambler. His smile slipped a little, but not the courtesy of his bearing. "It was a question of manners, sir, that emboldened me to call. At the home of Mr. Leonidas Clayton I was informed that Mr. Clayton's son might be found here. My name—"

"I am acquainted with your name, Mr. Rumbold. You are here uninvited. If you insist on entering . . ."

"Between the younger Mr. Clayton and myself, sir, there is a matter which may no longer be deferred. Perhaps it was only a misunderstanding. In that event, I am prepared to act magnanimously. Where is Mr. Clayton?"

There was no need for an answer. Tom, scratching at his scalp over the right ear, wandered in from the dining-room.

"The coffee," he reported, "will be ready as soon as—" Seeing who was before him, he stopped short. "It's *you* again, is it?"

"Surely you must have expected me, Mr. Clayton? I warned you, did I not?"

"Well, what do you want?"

"You will find me magnanimous, sir. I am prepared, even now, to accept your apology."

"Apology, for God's sake? Apology for what?"

"For what you may have done thoughtlessly, in the heat of humiliation at being rejected by the pretty quadroon whom you were annoying with your advances. Failing an apology," said Square Nat Rumbold, "I must insist on the satisfaction one gentleman owes another. Be good enough to name a friend to whom I may send *my* friend."

"Now look here, you be-diamonded pipsqueak! If you're proposing what I think you're proposing . . ."

"You apprehend perfectly, Mr. Clayton. Will you meet me, or will you not?"

"I will meet you," roared Tom, "anywhere, any time, with any damn weapon you care to name. But let's keep it a secret, shall we? Why trouble our friends? There's no need for me to be seen with you in public, even at *that* game."

Then Tom spoke with a sense of grievance.

"Who are you, anyway? Where do you come from? You go up and down the river, up and down the river, like a bale of spoiled cotton nobody will pick up. Just who *are* you?"

"Permit me," said Square Nat Rumbold, "to introduce myself like this."

From his pocket he yanked a pair of kid gloves. His arm had gone back, to slash the gloves across his adversary's face in traditional fashion, when attack was forestalled by counter-attack.

Again Tom uncoiled his weight. His bandaged left fist jolted hard into the middle of the gambler's stomach. His right fist whipped over in a murderous short cross to the side of the jaw.

The gloves flew wide. Once more Mr. Rumbold reeled backward, this time into a padded chair whose castors carried him only a foot or two before the chair fetched up against a table. Winded but snarling, he bounced to his feet like an India-rubber cat.

And then everybody went into action.

Already Macrae's hand hovered near the head of the heavy walking-stick against the wall. The gambler's own hand had darted inside his coat. Macrae saw the double-barreled derringer pistol that was almost small enough to be concealed in a man's palm. He saw the barrels tilt up towards Tom. And with the full power of his arm he brought down the stick across Square Nat Rumbold's wrist.

It finished Square Nat, who could not quite repress a cry. He stood helplessly, shoulders bowed and both hands hanging down. The fallen pistol had skittered across the carpet to Tom Clayton's feet. Tom gathered up pistol and gloves, weighing them, before he addressed the latest visitor.

"We'd better get you out of here," he said not unsympathetically. "You've had enough, my fine-feathered friend; and enough, in my book of maxims, is too much for anybody. Here are your gloves; I'll stick 'em in your pocket. The other little toy I'll return when I'm sure you can be trusted with it. And I shouldn't have manhandled you last night; I'm sorry; there's the apology you wanted. —Dick, thanks for saving my life! But you might give me a hand with him, eh?"

Together they escorted to the gallery door a gambler who had recovered much of his poise and dignity. They escorted him downstairs. To Macrae, abstracted, it seemed that the courtyard had suddenly become crowded with faces, though in actual fact there were only two persons besides Sam, one of them a woman.

Square Nat Rumbold had a final word to speak.

"I could have helped you," he proclaimed in ringing tones. "I meant what I said; I could have helped you! But now, when all you've done is set on me and break my wrist, you'll have to find out for yourselves."

Away he went, under the covered way to the street. And at Macrae's ear a Cockney voice rose up.

"Jack Dowser, sir, the sailorman as wos 'ere to see yer Wednesday night! Mind if I present me young lady?"

12

Stocky, square-jawed in pea-jacket and flat-crowned hat, Jack Dowser stood with pride beside his young lady, whom he proudly introduced as 'Miss Nadine Belly, of this city.'

Miss Nadine Belet, a vivacious little brunette of nineteen or twenty, clearly was no nymph of dubious calling or repute. Nor had she the air of waitress or barmaid. She wore a pink poke-bonnet as well as her brave, not unsuccessful attempt at a fashionable crinoline of the same colour. She might have been, and probably was, a superior shop-girl from the Old Square.

"Thees Jack!" she said roguishly, tapping her companion's shoulder. " 'E 'as tell me so much about thees great *ambassadeur* he meet . . . !"

"I am a consul, Miss Belet; I have not the honour to be our ambassador."

"You spik for your *patrie*, don' you? You rep-re-sent *l'empire de la Grande Bretagne en Amerique?* Ees all one, *vraiment?* Well! Thees Jack weesh to marry wit' me. I say, 'No, no!' I say, 'You 'ave wife in every port, *n'est-ce pas?*' Jack swear 'e 'ave no wife at all, not even in Irish-town or Algiers over de river. And 'e is *gentil* for one stupeed *anglais*, so maybe I marry wit' 'im after all."

Jack Dowser faced Macrae with a stateliness of accusation and reproach.

"Now, sir, I asks yer! 'Come back tomorrer,' yer says to me. That's wot yer says Wednesday night: 'come back tomorrer!' And I did come back tomorrer, which was yesterday. But I didn't see yer, I couldn't see yer, 'cos yer wasn't 'ere to be seen!"

"Please accept my apologies. I had a good deal on my mind, but that's no excuse; I ought to have been in my office."

"Well, sir, wot's done is done. Could I see yer *now*, maybe, and in strick privacy? It's awful important!"

"Yes, by all means."

Harry Ludlow, his hands full of papers, emerged from the passage leading to the office and addressed Tom Clayton in near stupefaction.

"Square Nat Rumbold!" Harry exclaimed. "I saw him go up there; I heard thumps on the ceiling and Lord knows what. Crikey, Tom, what did you do to the fellow this time?"

"We taught him a lesson," said Tom. "Now a lesson for you too, young fellow! In both your country and mine there's an ancient prejudice against hitting a man when he's down. And we don't laugh at him either."

"I wasn't laughing, Tom!"

"Tom," Macrae said, "the coffee should be ready by this time. Go on back upstairs and try it. You too, Harry. I must attend to our seafaring friend here; I must pay at least some attention to business."

"Haven't you got an explanation to give me, Dick?" Tom demanded.

"Yes, but in good time. Now up you go, both of you! This way, Dowser. Miss Belet . . ."

"Nadine m'gel," the sailor had become powerfully proprietary, "you just stop outside 'ere and wait. Wot I 'as ter say to the gentleman, and get advice about, is men's concerns and not for no pretty 'ead like yours."

"I don' like thees! I don' like thees one beet! You say you take me. I say I be good girl, and I *am*. Then you shove me out; you 'ide t'ings from me; you are not *gentil* at all!"

Their voices seemed to echo each other, whether the mutual lack of aspirates could be called French or merely Cockney.

"So 'elp me, *chérie*," swore Mr. Dowser, "I'm not 'iding nothing from yer and never 'ave! Wot I 'as ter tell 'im, *and* get advice about, is wot yer knows as well as yer knows me good intentions.

Won't yer please *be* a good gel and shut up?"

Accepting her fate with philosophy and cheerfulness, Nadine Belet immediately addressed herself to Sam. Though Sam could neither read nor write, he could jabber French twenty to the dozen. The two appeared to be getting on very well as Macrae led Jack Dowser to the office.

The broken window had been repaired. But the day was growing so dark with threatened rain that Macrae struck a lucifer and lit the gas-lamp on his desk. Sitting down behind it, he motioned his visitor towards the armchair.

Jack Dowser would not or could not sit down.

"I'm a-thinking, sir," he announced, after staring hard at the window that had been smashed. "I'm standing 'ere, as yer might say, a-thinking long thoughts. Now, sir, 'bout the matter as brings me 'ere Wednesday night. I 'inted—I didn't say straight out; I sorter 'inted—it 'ad to do with a gel I'd got much on me mind. And you've just met 'er, sir; you've met Nadine! Trim, tight little craft, now ain't she?"

"She is delightful. I congratulate you."

"Thank'ee kindly, sir. Well brought up, too, by an old uncle as makes dolls and sells 'em in Royal Street. We'll come to that in arf a mo'. But there was one thing I did say, as straight and frank and fair as you'd let me, and you'll bear me out if I remind yer I did."

"Oh? What was it you said?"

"Voodoo!" returned Jack, his strong dramatic sense manifesting itself again. "You'd got Voodoo on *your* minds, you and the 'andsome elderly lady and the other gentleman too. I said me own woes might be much closer to yours than you ever dreamed on. And that's true, sir, as true as the first mate bein' at the rum when the skipper ain't looking! Voodoo!"

"You also uttered a stern warning against it, if I remember. You and your girl haven't been dabbling with Voodoo, have you?"

" 'Dabble,' sir? Now wot's '*dabble*'?"

"I asked you—"

"Nadine ain't been at it, no, 'cos I wouldn't let 'er even if she wanted to. Me? No, not me ezzactly either. She asks me to do something; I done it, but what's to be done next? 'Fore I lets go me anchor, I wants ter be sure o' the sounding. Mind if I tell it?"

"That's what you're here for, I understand. Go ahead."

"Nadine and 'er uncle, now, the one as makes dolls and brought 'er up. Wot's the French for 'doll,' sir?"

"*Poupée.* P-o-u-p-e-acute-e."

"Aye, aye, that's it! It's on the shop-winder, see, in big letters underneath 'is name. And I first see Nadine, as sweet and pretty as a doll 'er own self, a-looking at me past the dolls in that winder.

"This uncle, sir. 'E means well, I know; 'e brought 'er up a treat, like a real lady; and 'e's got a tidy bit put by, Nadine says, that ought to be Nadine's one day. Not that *that* means a rope yarn as far as I'm concerned, 'cos it don't! I've got me 'ealth and me strength; I can give 'er wot she wants; I may get me mate's ticket any time.

"But these furriners, sir, 'specially these furrin gels! They're dead set on not a-getting married 'thout a dough, which means a dowry. And this furrin talk! 'Jack,' Nadine says to me, 'you are a nice boy and I love you; but you are not *pratique*.' That means practical, don't it? And the 'ole trouble, sir, is this damn Louise from Algiers!"

"Who?"

"Cousin called Louise; lives at Algiers t'other side the river. Uncle Pierre means well, as I've said. But 'e's old, 'e's cranky, 'e'll get into a state and give Nadine wot-fer! 'Specially if 'e thinks she's too bobbish, or she up and sauces 'im like wot she sauces me, 'e'll threaten to turn Nadine out and bring in Louise. 'Be warned, wretch and ingrate,' he'll say in his furrin talk; 'be warned, I counsel yer, afore the hour 'as struck.' And 'e'll carry on like the ruddy furriner 'e is!

"'It ain't fair!' Nadine's said to me, and many's the time she's said it. 'After all I've done for me pover onkell—cook for 'im, wash for 'im, serve in the shop too—it ain't fair this 'orrible Louise should run foul o' me and capsize me in ten fathom.'

That's the sense of it, not the French talk. On Wednesday arternoon, which is 'er arternoon off, she says something else. We wos in Jackson Square, under the statue of the general with 'is 'at lifted. And Nadine says, sorter w'ispering in me starboard ear, there might be a way to capsize Louise first. And she asks me if I've ever 'eard of Marie Laveau."

Macrae, glancing out of the window beside his desk, could watch Nadine Belet in animated talk with Sam.

"I think I see what's coming," he remarked. "But no comment need be made until you've finished, and I won't interrupt again."

Jack at last consented to sit down. He took the straight chair rather than the armchair, hitching it forward with an air of intensity, and putting his hat on the desk.

" 'Course I'd 'eard o' Marie Laveau, and what they says she can do with 'er magic. I don't doubt she can do it, neither! Us coves as knocks round the world, sir, we sees and understands things they don't see and understand in Poplar or Stepney. But that's just the trouble.

"I argued with Nadine, mind! 'Steer wide o' these Voodoos,' I says to 'er; 'let 'em come athwart your 'awse and you're done. Besides,' I says, 'this 'ere Cousin Louise may be a lubber and a wrong 'un, but she's your own flesh and blood arter all. Yer don't want 'er *killed*, now do yer?'

" 'Killed?' says Nadine, with a kind o' screech. 'I don't even want the slut *'urt!* Just a fall down some stairs, maybe a twisted ankle or a broken 'ead, anything that'll keep 'er away from my onkell w'ile I smooth 'im down and make 'im promise me a dowry. Marie Laveau could do it as easy as wink.'

" 'You worn't a-thinking,' I says, 'you worn't a-thinking you'd *go* to Marie Laveau, now? That you won't do,' says I, bein' masterful, 'cos I won't let yer.' 'No, I can't go,' says Nadine; 'but *you* can. Wot!' she says. 'If some of the best people in New Orleans can buy *gris-gris* from the great Queen o' Voodoo, is my Jack too proud or too afeared to see 'er 'is own self?'

"I dunno if it's ever 'appened to you, sir, a swell like you? A-sitting on a bench somewheres, and a pretty gel snuggled up ter you and w'ispering in yer ear? Afore yer knows wot's wot, 'less yer looks very sharp, you'll 'ave promised 'er Kew Gardens on a plate.

"I kept me 'ead—well, in the main I did. The most I'd promise, then and there, wos ter take advice. This 'ere was a matter o' love, as Nadine said; maybe o' life and death and our future 'appiness too. So I'd see you; I'd see our consul, 'ooever 'e wos. And I'd ask yer straight out. Everything bein' considered, little as I liked it, mightn't it be better if I steered right in the wind's eye and got 'elp from the Voodoo Queen?

"Well, sir, yer knows wot 'appened. Between you, and the lady in the lavender dress and the other gentleman as talked like a lawyer, not one word would yer let me get out! I got a bit of an idea, right or wrong, the Voodoo people wos after you too. When the big jar come slap through that winder there, and busted it to blazes as I was telling yer 'bout them savages wot cut off Sullivan's 'ead, it give me a turn I'd not deny if me life depended on it. The next day, yesterday . . ."

"Aye, aye, sir; I come back. But not afore Nadine 'ad been at me again, with 'er coaxing ways. And this time, so 'elp me, I couldn't resist her. 'Orl right,' I says; 'orl right; I'll do it! I'll go to the 'ouse o' shadders and take me chances with the spooks. Only I'll not go at night-time, thank'ee. I'll go this afternoon, in the broad light o' God's day, and see wot magic's for sale in 'er den.'

"Not that you could call it a broad light, sir. It were a dark day, almost as dark as it is now, with rain-squalls once or twice. The nearer I gets to that poky little place in St. Ann Street, as well-known 'ere as the 'King's Arms' in the Ratcliffe 'Ighway at 'ome, the more me legs drag; the more I wants ter spit on me 'ands and can't. I'm a bold man up the ratlines or in the shrouds; I can take me own part if a fight starts in a pub. But the thought o' the dark night and wot might be a-waiting there . . . Well, sir, that's different.

"It's a poky little 'ouse, as I've already said, and kind o' dark too, though it's furnished beautiful inside.

"Well! The door's opened by a brown-faced gel maybe sixteen

or seventeen years old, 'oo asks me something in French. I ask her if she speaks English, and say I'd take it kindly if I could see Madame Marie Laveau. I said *madame*, yer see—French like, and as polite as though I'd been in Sunday school.

"The gel says she does speak English, thanks. She takes me to a little front parlour with a elegant varse on the mantel and a curtain over a door at the back. The gel says *sa majesté* (I think she said *sa majesté*) wouldn't keep me waiting long, and slings 'er 'ook. I wasn't kept waiting long neither. Back sweeps the curtain over the door, and . . ."

"You saw Marie Laveau?"

"Oh, ah! I seen 'er. But—"

"But what?"

"I done 'er a injustice, sir," said Jack, drawing a deep breath, "if I thought of Marie Laveau as a iggerant darky woman. She's not *really* dark, sir; not so dark as some fine Spanish ladies you'll see in Cadiz. And dignified, gracious like, sorter royal! The rest I did expect. Dark eyes and 'air, o' course; beautiful as a pictur on a wall, and so young-looking that . . ."

Macrae sat up straight.

"Young?" he repeated. "I promised not to interrupt, but this is a little too much. Have you been drinking, man?"

Jack hitched his chair forward, jaw thrust out.

"Avast there, sir! Avast, belay, and 'ware shoal! I'm as sober as a Methodist preacher; not a single drop 'ave I taken this day, caulk me dead-lights if that's one word of a lie!"

"Marie Laveau is at least sixty-three years old."

"I said young-*looking*, di'n't I?"

"Well?"

"Sir, Nadine told me about that afore I went! Marie Laveau's looks 'aven't changed one bit these past thirty year and more; Nadine's met those 'oo can remember 'er then. There's some people 'as the secret of eternal youth, and she's one of 'em!"

"Or else the explanation is that . . ." Macrae hesitated, but his companion paid no attention to the implied suggestion.

"She just looked at me, sir. A rain-squall 'it the winders; I couldn't 'a' told yer if it wos rain or shine. She knew I wos

English, knew I wos a sailorman, knew I'd come on an errand o' love."

"She hardly needed supernatural powers to decide that much."

"But, sir, she knew *everything*. Abaht Nadine, abaht Uncle Pierre, even abaht Cousin Louise from Algiers! 'I 'ave been expecting yer,' she says.

"And she takes out a little linen bag not two inch long, sewed with cotton at the top." Jack Dowser's hand dived for his own pocket, but he checked himself. "Nadine's to wear the bag, she says, on a string round 'er neck underneath 'er dress. It may take a day or two, it may take a week; but this *gris-gris* is bound ter work.

"Then I started wondering what she'd charge for it. I didn't like ter go near this; something told me I *oughtn't* ter go near it; but wot else could I do? 'About payment,' I says ...

"Gawdlummycharley, I might 'a' been offering a sixpenny tip to the Duke o' Westminster!

"'Payment?' says she. 'Let there be no talk of payment now. Return to me, if you are still so minded, when your beloved shall 'ave gained 'er 'eart's desire. Then you may contribute to Zombi's altar ...' I think she said Zombi; it sounded like that! ... 'Then you may contribute to Zombi's altar wotever you think 'is intervention 'as been worth.'

"I said I 'adn't time; I'd be shipping out in a day or two; it might be six months or a year afore I learned whether the spell 'ad flummoxed Louise and 'er little games. 'If you never return,' says Marie Laveau, 'if you lay no offering whatever upon the altar, it will be all one to Zombi and to me. That is me last word; good day.'

"And the rain strikes the winders again, and she looks at me sideways with 'er brown eyes, and I staggers out o' there, sir, as though I'd *been* 'owlin' drunk and no mistake!

"Then I gets ter thinking. This 'ere was magic, right enough. But it was *black* magic, that we're warned against by the Bible and everybody else. Wot 'ad I got meself into? And Nadine as well? Wot if this spell worked the wrong way—backfired, like—and 'urt the pore gel stead o' 'elping 'er?

"'Ere's the *gris-gris* now, sir," cried Jack Dowser, taking from his pocket a tiny cloth bag such as he had described. "Feels like herbs inside; dunno; can't smell nothing. Allow yer can't control a Voodoo spell, allow any old consekens there might be, wot wos I ter *do* with the damn thing?

"If I 'adn't gone to you, sir, where *could* I 'a' gone 'cept to a pack o' lubberly ship-mates as iggerant as meself? I come 'ere straightaway, like you told me to. But you'd gone out with a couple of friends, they said, and they didn't know when you'd be in again.

"Back I goes to Nadine in Royal Street. All *she* can do is beg me for the *gris-gris* to wear next 'er 'eart, and say all our troubles is over now. But for once I resisted 'er; I wouldn't listen. 'No, me gel,' I says, 'it stays with me. If any bad things 'appen then, they'll be on my 'ead and not yours. It stays in me pocket,' I says, 'until bright and early tomorrer morning I makes very sure o' finding the gentleman at 'ome.'"

"If you ask my opinion . . ."

"That's what I *been* a-asking, ain't it?"

Macrae looked him in the eye.

"There is no such thing as magic, black or otherwise. You have been the victim of an imposture or a trick. Throw that *gris-gris* into the fire and forget it."

"But if it won't 'urt 'er, sir . . . !"

"That is exactly the point. There is no possible way in which it can harm her; neither is there any possible way in which it can help. If your sole fear is of some devilish result attendant on wearing the bag, she may wear it until Doomsday without injury. On the other hand . . ."

"Begging your pardon, sir, but wot *is* all this?"

Jack Dowser had risen to his feet, dropping the *gris-gris* into his pocket and taking up his hat from the table.

"Yer looks at me funny-like. Yer looks at me," he said with sudden passion, "as if yer thinks I've been a-gammoning yer, or as if I didn't see and 'ear wot I did see and 'ear. Fair's fair, sir; wot *is* it?"

"I don't think you have been gammoning me, Dowser, but I am

very sure someone has been gammoning *you*. This woman you met in St. Ann Street, the woman who seems to have impressed you so much . . ."

"Well, sir, if *you* saw her . . ." The sailor glanced towards his left; his voice went soaring up. "Gawdlummycharley, there she is now!"

And then everything seemed to happen at once.

Jack's finger had stabbed towards the window beside the desk. Following its direction, Macrae saw that Nadine Belet had retreated to the other side of the courtyard. Sam, his servant, stood in the middle of it. Facing Sam, evidently having just asked some question, stood a tallish woman, slender but full-bosomed, in a dress of some darkish material with a modest-sized crinoline.

Her flat-crowned darkish hat, round the front of whose brim a white ostrich-feather curled flat, had a veil she had raised for speech. Macrae saw her face in profile: the face of a young woman, as handsome as the impressionable Jack had described, and with a look of command that could not be mistaken.

The woman looked towards her right, and Macrae saw her full-face. But she also saw him. Dropping her veil, she turned and made off in haste for the covered way to the street.

He acted at the same instant. He was out of his chair, across the office, down the passage, and into the courtyard, where a minor commotion had begun to boil.

"Mist' Richard," shouted Sam, "she make mistake. She ask is dis Petuhs & Walkuh, de brokuhs? I say, 'No'm, dis de British Consulate. Petuhs & Walkuh dey some ways up de road same side.' She don' say no mo'; she—"

Nadine Belet, much excited, also cried out something. Tom Clayton and Harry Ludlow had emerged on the gallery above. Macrae could not wait. Under a dark and swollen sky, with faint thunder growling in the west, he plunged on after his quarry.

On Friday morning, as usual, Carondelet Street throbbed with business. The banks were being besieged; many of the offices too. Cabs, carriages, and wagons struggled past in both directions. The veiled woman could not possibly have reached the brokerage firm of Peters & Walker, if in fact that had ever been her destination.

But he saw no sign of her either; it was as though the street had swallowed her up.

Macrae, hesitating on the *banquette* at one side of the entrance, observed a momentary break in the crush of wheeled vehicles. He detected no flash of fire on the opposite side of the road. With so great a din of hoofs and wheels on cobbles, he barely heard the explosion of the pistol-shot. But he felt the wind of the bullet's passing; he heard the bullet whack into the wall behind him a short distance above his head.

Then the skies opened and the rain tore down.

13

AT HALF-PAST THREE THAT AFTERNOON, CANTERING EASILY on the saddle-horse he had hired from Likins's livery-stable, Macrae rode west along St. Charles Avenue.

Several showers of rain had come and gone since the first one that morning. Though a dark cloud-mass still hung heavily, shafts of golden sunlight pierced through. Macrae was approaching the intersection of Jackson Avenue when Tom Clayton, who had lagged a little behind, cantered up beside him and resumed a familiar burden.

"That pistol-shot, if I may refer to it again . . . ?"

Macrae reflected.

"The house directly opposite number 33," he said, "is built in *Vieux-Carré* style like the consulate. Next door to it is Hookson's Bank, then a wine-merchant, then—but that doesn't matter.

"What does matter is that the house opposite has a covered way, a courtyard, half a dozen business offices, and at least two other ways out besides the front entrance.

"Hang it, Tom, you ought to know that! No sooner had somebody loosed off a pistol from under the covered way, than you came charging out of my house. Then both of us, in the driving rain, charged across the street and searched those premises. We didn't find a soul who conceivably could have done the shooting; but we didn't actually expect to find him, did we?"

Tom's reply seemed something of a *non sequitur*.

"I told you I had to leave as soon as we'd searched the place! I

150

told you I had to go, didn't I? I promised my old man I would drop in at his office and sign some papers for him; there you are.

"Why he keeps that Canal-Street office is anybody's guess. You see, the old man can't decide whether he's a country gentleman or an ex-diplomat still deeply involved in politics. He keeps bombarding our bigwigs with letters of advice, and hopes the southern wing of the Democrats will nominate him for president in '60. He hasn't a chance, as he ought to know; they'll nominate John Breckinridge if they nominate anybody; but it does serve to keep the old man in a good humour.

"All right! I saw the old boy; I lunched with him at the Boston Club; I didn't get back to your place until half an hour ago. Now, then! This yarn spun for you by the Cockney Jack Tar: about a Marie Laveau in her sixties who's discovered the Fountain of Youth and is recreated as a handsome piece not a day over thirty if she's that . . ."

"Well, Tom, what about it?"

"I didn't even get a look at her; she'd lowered her veil by the time I emerged. But what was *she* doing at the consulate? Could she really have mistaken the address? As for the marksman over the road, it was damn poor shooting if he really meant to hit you: like a woman's shooting. Could it have been the woman herself who dodged across the street and . . . ?"

"No, Tom."

"What do you mean, no?"

"I mean the *modus operandi* is all wrong. Whoever the Voodoo crowd may be and however they're concerned in this business, they have a very different form of approach. It may be little less subtle than cutting loose with a bullet, but it's more devious and a good deal more secret. The point is . . ."

"The point is," Tom retorted, "you promised me at least a partial explanation for the tangle that's shortening my life, and now you won't even open your mouth. Aren't you a kind of a cheap skate?"

"Possibly, though I don't think so. The explanation is not suppressed; it's merely deferred. First let's hear what Senator Benjamin has to say, shall we? There'll be no harm in telling him what we've learned today, either about Square Nat Rumbold or about Jack Dowser and the visit to St. Ann Street. In fact, if he's on the right track he'll have to know. But not a word to anybody, mind, about dead snakes or cards from Papa Là-bas; and above all no mention of our projected visit to the haunted house tonight! Is that understood?"

"You bet your boots it's understood! All the same," and Tom shifted in his saddle, "let's hope we find more enlightenment at the haunted house than we seem to have found at your house. As for the gathering at Papa de Sancerre's, aren't we half an hour too early? And where's Harry?"

"There's no harm in being too early. Will Likins at the livery-stable has reserved a horse for Harry, who will be with us as soon as he's finished a little task I set him. And yet I understand your state of mind."

Macrae meditated ruefully.

"There was a time this morning, Tom, when it seemed to me that half New Orleans must be crowding in at number 33 Carondelet Street. What I hope is that we've now met everybody connected with the blasted business! If more people keep turning up and calling for our attention, like characters in a book introduced so fast you can't keep 'em straight . . ."

"Everybody connected with it, did you say?" asked Tom, glancing over his shoulder. "Everybody?"

Not many persons were abroad in the Garden District at that hour. Up behind them, also coming from the direction of town, loomed an equipage of the most conservative variety: an open carriage spick and span behind two bay horses. The coachman's livery was so inconspicuous as hardly to seem livery at all. In the carriage, appearing more than half asleep, sat an impressive figure who would have been still more impressive if he had not been so very fat.

Glossy hat, black frock-coat with silk lapels, Ascot tie and striped trousers, were all matched by the silver-headed stick trailing from his left hand. And the fat man was far from being asleep. His heavily pouched eyes opened; he said something from the corner of a rat-trap mouth; the carriage slowed and stopped.

Tom, checking his fine stallion Brigadier, rode up at one side while Macrae approached from the other.

"Good afternoon, sir," Tom greeted him. "I won't ask about the state of the banking business. I won't even ask whether any widows and orphans have been swindled today. Despite the purity of my intentions, I have a feeling such queries might be taken amiss. Dick, I believe you've met Mr. Stoneman, of the Planters' & Southern?"

"I am acquainted with Mr. Macrae," said George Stoneman, folding his hands over the head of his stick. "I wish I weren't acquainted with *you*, you young pup! However, since I must reluctantly confess to knowing you . . ."

"Haven't you left your den of iniquity rather early, sir? Or are you bound for the de Sancerres' too?"

"I am on my way home," the banker said with dignity, "because, as usual, I have a job of work to do there. If you want a thing done right, never trust it to any slave; do it yourself! I am of ample girth, as you see; but I am neither too fat nor too proud to work with my hands as my father taught me.

"Yes, yes," he added quickly, "I have heard of Horace Rutherford's death! Don't expect me to shed salt tears; if he had not brought about his own end in one way, he would have brought it about in another. And no, no, distinctly I am *not* going to Jules de Sancerre's! The rest of you will attend, I gather, with one exception. Don't expect Barnaby Jeffers; *he* won't be there."

Tom cocked an eyebrow.

"No harm has come to Barnaby Jeffers, I trust?"

"No, no harm has come to him; he is taking very good care it won't. What an old woman Barnaby is! He turned up at my office today, with a police-officer in tow . . ."

"Sergeant O'Shea, was it?"

"No, though a certain Sergeant O'Shea was mentioned. In his misery Barnaby has insisted on having a bodyguard at all times, and has been given one. Sergeant O'Shea, it seems, has been trying all day to trace some character named Stephen White: a hopeless task, I should have thought, even if they had some information other than a most inadequate description."

"Sergeant O'Shea, we understand, is on night duty."

"Well, District Attorney Tappan has put him on round-the-clock duty. His quest for Stephen White . . ."

"You don't take that very seriously, do you?"

Mr. Stoneman's jowls swelled and shrank like those of a breathing dragon.

"No, I do not. Just what *is* poor Barnaby's tale of woe? That the son of Rosette Leblanc has left off weeping at Delphine Lalaurie's grave to turn on her enemies twenty-four years later. That with some mysterious lightning-bolt he killed Horace Rutherford in public, and will next direct his lightning at Barnaby or at me. Twenty-four years later, forsooth! Now what should I say if some client of the bank came to me and asked me to advance cash on the strength of *that* story?

"Three of us were once young fools; I concede it. The older I grow, however, the more I become convinced that we are all fools, and that the only proper course is to avoid being a damned fool. I am not a damned fool; I can look to myself. Good day, gentlemen. Jean-Baptiste, *en avant!*"

He raised his hat formally, ducked a little bow, and fell somnolent again as the carriage rattled away.

"Against the money-changers in the temple," observed Tom, "how shall we stand when *they* take a stand? It had better be *en avant* for us too; come on!"

Heels touched horses' flanks. The two riders clattered forward, and before many minutes turned into the drive at the end of which Jules de Sancerre's home reared its three white floors above oaks, magnolias, and pecan trees.

Once more the iron-grilled gates were wide open. At the portico stood General Ede's carriage, easily identifiable by its oystershell-coloured upholstery, with Jared again in attendance. A stable-boy waited at the carriage-block to take their horses as Tom and Macrae dismounted.

Marcus Brutus admitted them into the hall; daylight also entered through long windows at either side of the door. Isabelle de

Sancerre, controlling agitation pretty well, emerged from the front drawing-room and swept towards them.

"It was good of you to come, both of you. Benjie's back there," and she indicated the rear drawing-room on the right. "No, there's nothing unpleasant now; the undertaker came for Horace Rutherford long ago. Benjie's back there, I say; he had a bad time with Amelia Rutherford this morning. Tom, how's your poor left hand?"

"My poor left hand is in excellent shape, thanks," Tom assured her, flexing the fingers by way of illustration. "If a certain young lady gets uppity again, it's still ready to hold her while the right hand does yeoman service as of old. And I still say I was right to wallop her, Mama de Sancerre, though I apologize to you yourself. Where *is* your sharp-toothed daughter, by the way?"

"Still in her room, and won't come out. Ursula's with her; Ursula's the only one she'll see. Tom, do go back and speak to Mr. Benjamin! Mr. Macrae: a word aside with *you*, if you please."

Away went Tom, his footsteps clacking. Madame de Sancerre grew confidential.

"Poor Ursula!" she said. "No mother to counsel her; only those aunts. Such a sweet girl! But she reads too much; she dreams too much; it'll be *such* a relief if she's found . . . oh, never mind. But do be careful, Mr. Macrae! Ursula hasn't said much, of course. I do gather, though, that when she drove you home this morning you wanted to take *her* home and then walk the rest of the way?"

"That's what I ought to have done."

"Mercy on us, it's exactly what you *shouldn't* have done, and you can thank your lucky stars you didn't! It was past two o'clock when Ursula did get home. And she stumbled into something in the dark; she knocked over a lamp; she woke up the whole house. Down came the four aunts, curl-papers and all. Down came General Ede, with a drawn sword in his hand. What would have happened if he'd found *you* there I shudder to think of."

"I am not a home-wrecker, Madame de Sancerre."

"No; but who except ourselves is likely to know that? Now

listen: we've concocted a story for the benefit of our own friends and of General Ede too. How far it'll be believed I can't say; let's hope the general believes it.

"Last night was an opera night at the Théâtre d'Orléans; they were singing Hernani. Our story is that Margot and Ursula went to the opera. No man was concerned; the girls weren't anywhere they shouldn't have been, let alone that awful Washington and Jefferson place. But do be careful, I say. And never, never again in the future keep Ursula out as late as you did last night!"

"Before we have finished, no doubt, the whole evening will be my fault. No matter. Provided I do see Ursula again—"

"Oh, you'll see her!"

"I am content to accept the responsibility for anything."

"You wouldn't say that if you'd met General Ede. Now I must find Jules; he keeps eluding me. Why don't you go and see Mr. Benjamin?"

Macrae walked slowly to the back drawing-room. He hesitated for some time, pondering many matters, before he opened the door.

The back drawing-room, its ceiling sixteen feet high like that of the others, was as cluttered as the front drawing-room with furniture and with pictures round the walls. In one corner stood a piano, in another corner a harp, in a third corner a huge folding screen decorated with brightly coloured figures of ballet dancers. In the fourth wall-angle, also cater-cornered, loomed a gigantic grandfather clock.

Nobody was actually in the room. But on a sort of porch, outside four tall open windows at the back, Senator Benjamin in his grey frock-coat and trousers sat in an iron chair at an iron table, smoking a cigar as he listened to Tom Clayton recount that morning's events.

Shafts of sunlight struck from the west; the gallery above was like a roof; Senator Benjamin stood up as Macrae went out to join them.

"You seem, both of you, to have had an unusually full time of it before lunch," the senator said. "Beginning with Square Nat

Rumbold, and going on to the rest of it. Rumbold was deflated when he left you, was he?"

There were half a dozen chairs within reach; Tom dropped into one of them.

"I almost pitied the poor devil," Tom said. "He won't be dealing cards—or pulling triggers either—for some time to come."

"And yet he has the reputation of being ambidextrous, of being a crack shot, and of carrying two pistols. If he had been *very* bloody-minded, I fear, he could still have drawn and fired with the other hand. Is he the sort of bully who collapses at a show of spirit? Or . . . The fact remains, you see, that nobody knows anything about him. You have been thinking of him in one capacity. It would be curious, would it not, if in fact he figured in quite another capacity?"

"What capacity?"

Senator Benjamin did not seem to hear.

"Then," he mused, pulling at his left side-whisker in an anguish of concentration, "there is the entrance of a youthful, rejuvenated, recreated Marie Laveau! It's an infernal nuisance, of course, and yet it fits in. Yes, by the mysteries of Eleusis, it all fits in!"

"Will someone kindly explain," roared Tom, "just what the hell it fits into? Dick here, after giving his solemn word to explain at least a part of the truth, has broken the promise and shut up like a clam. You, Senator, said you were prepared to do the same thing. Are you prepared, sir?"

"Yes, I am prepared."

"Well, then?"

"I should have preferred," said Senator Benjamin, "to clear up one point before making the charges I am bound to make. The point, I feel sure, could have been elucidated in five minutes' talk with Barnaby Jeffers. The trouble is that I have been unable to find Barnaby Jeffers."

"Barnaby Jeffers," Tom informed him, "has been roaring around town with a police-officer as his bodyguard. Coming out here, Dick and I met George Stoneman from the bank. Our esteemed historian turned up in George's office today, dithering a good deal and taking the Steve White threat as seriously as George scorns it. According to the lord of finance, Barnaby won't be coming here at all."

"I know he won't."

"You know?"

"On my way back from the Rutherfords' this morning," a shadow crossed Senator Benjamin's face, "I called at Mr. Jeffers's house and had a word with his manservant, whom he has christened Edward Gibbon. Apparently he regards *our* company as dangerous, and prefers to visit only well-frequented places with the bodyguard forever at his elbow, though why he should feel safer at Arnaud's Restaurant or in the bar of the St. Louis Hotel I am at a loss to determine."

"But about this explanation, now . . . ?"

"I am prepared," said the lawyer, sighting along his cigar, "to forgo elucidation of the point I mentioned, and proceed at once with such answers as I now have. The difficulty there—"

He stopped. Fluid chimes rang from the grandfather clock in the back drawing-room, a whole storehouse of Mallard furniture. As the clock whirred in its throat and struck four, Isabelle de Sancerre and her husband emerged from an open window to join the group. Jules de Sancerre, in a red smoking-jacket of the so-called Turkish variety, was combing his fingers through his Napoleon III imperial.

"Yes?" he prompted. "What *is* the difficulty? Damme, man," he added cryptically, "I've given you the padlock-key you asked for. You haven't gathered us together under false pretences, have you? What *is* the difficulty?"

Tom Clayton sprang up and pushed forward chairs for the two newcomers, who sat down gingerly. Senator Benjamin looked uncomfortable.

"We are all friends here; we know each other well," he said. "And yet most of what I have to tell you concerns your daughter; it will be of a fairly intimate nature. Isn't this a little too public, a little like shouting secrets from the rooftops? If first, for instance, I were to take the young lady aside and ask her certain questions in private . . ."

"She wouldn't answer you," cried Isabelle de Sancerre. "She wouldn't even see you! When Mademoiselle High-and-Mighty *becomes* high and mighty, there's no handling her or controlling her except by Tom's method, and even that's no use in the long run. I'm sure *I* can't control the girl; Jules doesn't even try. When matters have reached their present pass, what is a mere mother to do? If she has done something disgraceful . . . !"

"Reassure yourself, Isabelle. She has done nothing disgraceful."

"Well, by this time the whole town thinks she has. If you're trying to spare Margot's feelings, or my feelings or Jules's feelings, for heaven's sake forget it. There is altogether too much consideration for young people nowadays. If I had ever carried on to one-tenth the extent Margot's carried on, I know what *my* mother would have done even if I can't. Very well; that's my failure. But at least let's hear what there is to hear!"

"Senator," Tom Clayton interposed with a kind of pounce, "do you know how Margot vanished out of that carriage?"

"Yes, I think I do."

"And that's half the battle, isn't it? Mama de Sancerre is right: let's hear what there is to hear! Is there one damn clue to how Margot disappeared like a soap-bubble?"

"There is more than one clue, believe me," replied the lawyer. "For instance! Do you recall telling me on Wednesday night, Isabelle, that about a month ago Margot rather inexplicably drew out five hundred dollars from her own account at the bank?"

"Yes! But—"

"I say 'inexplicably,' ladies and gentlemen, because a young lady of well-to-do family is not as a rule in much need of pocket-money. Should she wish to make a purchase, her own credit or her father's credit will be good anywhere. A sum like five hundred dollars suggests some concrete purpose in which credit could not be used. What did she want the money for?"

Margot's mother was galvanized.

"Are you saying, Benjie, the poor girl has been paying *blackmail*?"

"No, Isabelle. You read too many novels; we all do, I fear. Any suggestion of blackmail, though sensational enough to suit even my own tastes, is a little far-fetched when we have a much more probable explanation at hand."

"She wanted to bribe somebody, you mean?" demanded Tom.

"No, not that either. She had no need of bribery for what she had in mind."

"And with five hundred dollars," Tom groped in the air before him, "she could vanish slap-bang before our eyes?"

"In one sense she could. Do you insist, all of you, that I proceed with the solution at this minute?"

"I can't speak for my husband," said Isabelle de Sancerre, settling her crinoline and looking up defiantly, "because Jules never insists on anything. Let's have an end of this; I insist!"

Senator Benjamin threw away his cigar into the drive and turned back to face them. Easy, persuasive, no longer a prey to nerves, he might have been addressing the jury in a courtroom.

"It cannot as yet, of course, be a complete solution. A complete solution must explain too many other factors, from the strange death of Judge Rutherford to the curious conduct of a gambler named Rumbold. But at least a part of the truth lies open before us. We may say at the beginning that—"

Once more he stopped. Harry Ludlow, subdued but hearty, crossed the back drawing-room and came out among them.

"Excuse me," he began; "the butler said you were all here. I couldn't help overhearing what you were telling them, Senator, and I'm glad to hear it. But I have some news for my superior officer." Harry fixed his eyes on Macrae. "He's back, sir! That gambler's come back again!"

14

"WE ARE HAPPY TO SEE YOU, MR. LUDLOW," SAID ISA-belle de Sancerre. Then she began to lose control. "But what's all this about gamblers? I have heard nothing of any gamblers! What on earth would *Margot* have to do with gamblers?"

"So far as any of us can tell, nothing whatever," Senator Benjamin assured her. "The reference is to an unpleasant incident at the British Consulate this morning. Square Nat Rumbold was looking for trouble, and got it. Tom handled him roughly enough; Mr. Macrae broke his wrist with a walking-stick. You say he has returned, my boy?"

Harry assented heartily.

"I was in the office, polishing up my first report to their majestics of the Foreign Office, when I saw him come back through the courtyard. He must have gone to a doctor; he was carrying his right arm in a sling. Tibby met him at the foot of the stairs to the drawing-room. He wanted to see Mr. Macrae; he insisted on seeing Mr. Macrae. When Tibby told him Mr. Macrae was out, he said he'd wait and followed her upstairs without a by-your-leave.

"I didn't intercept the fellow; I had no authority to throw him out. Anyway! I don't carry firearms; I avoid those who do, and Square Nat had an ugly look about him for all he was as polite as butter. I left there; I picked up the horse that had been reserved for me, and here I am. I hope I did right?"

"The man you call your superior officer," said Senator Benjamin, as Macrae nodded, "would agree you did absolutely right.

Here in the dining-room, last night, he was telling me something about you. Are you settling in satisfactorily?"

Harry beamed.

"Can't say whether it's been satisfactory to Mr. Macrae, sir. It's been very satisfactory to *me*. As I told him when I arrived yesterday morning, about the one anticipation that was really troubling me . . ."

Harry glanced at Macrae. His eyes so clearly begged permission to speak that again the latter nodded.

"Yes?" enquired Senator Benjamin. "The one anticipation that was really troubling you?"

"This American politicial situation, North versus South! So far not a soul in New Orleans has said one word to me about politics. And yet it's all they could go on about, hour after hour, wherever else I've been. Southerners, you know, are popularly supposed to be fire-eaters. All the same, apart from people like Tom there, I'm not so sure. At Willard's Hotel in Washington, for instance, I met a man from Charleston, North Carolina . . ."

Macrae looked at him.

"Charleston, *South* Carolina."

"Yes, sorry; I knew there were two of 'em! 'Old Buck's not so bad,' the South Carolinian said." Here Harry appealed to Senator Benjamin. "He meant President Buchanan, didn't he?"

"He did indeed. Mr. Buchanan, though from Pennsylvania, is a conservative Democrat who tends to favour the South. Anything else?"

" 'Old Buck's not so bad,' " this South Carolinian said. 'But you can bet your bottom dollar, young man, there'll be trouble if the God-damn Republicans get in at the next election.' " Harry checked himself, stricken. "Oh, I *am* sorry, Madame de Sancerre!"

"Now at long last," murmured their hostess, casting up her eyes, "I have heard a man apologize for using bad language in this house. Pray *don't* apologize, Mr. Ludlow, refreshing to my ears though the novelty of an apology may be."

"That's one for me, as usual," observed Madame de Sancerre's husband. "You'll hear bad language in plenty, Isabelle, if the God-damn Republicans *do* get in at the next election: as, with the

Democrats so hopelessly split, they probably will."

"Anyway," Harry continued, "that's the worst I heard on one side. But on the other side . . . Boston, Cambridge, anywhere in New England . . . oh, crikey! They not only eat fire; they spit the coals in your face before they've finished. They seem to want more than freed slaves; they want blood. And—hang it, I dunno! Maybe I'm all wrong or not very intelligent, but I can't be as shocked by slavery as people at home think I ought to be." This time he appealed to Macrae. "What do *you* say, sir? As fellow-Britons in a strange land . . ."

"As fellow-Britons, Harry, you and I can hardly afford to sing pious hymns on that subject. Slavery has been abolished in our own empire for a bare quarter-century. And we're not here to debate slavery, are we?"

"No, sir; I was coming to that!"

"More comments, Harry?"

" 'Fraid so, sir. When somebody asks me about my impressions of New Orleans, I'm bound to admit my first impressions are rather a peculiar lot that don't do the place justice. Deuce take it! I think of Tom at the ballroom grabbing that gambler and slinging him like a chucker-out at a pub. I think of old Judge What's-his-name standing there looking down at you before something invisible grabbed *him*. I couldn't even go for the police without having Sergeant O'Shea's gig sideswipe the carriage and nearly knock *me* silly. And then—no, enough said! It can't always be like that, but what *is* it like?"

Tom Clayton arose in towering sternness.

"If you'd just shut up for one minute, young fellow-me-lad, we might have a chance to find out. When you came butting in with your unwanted reports, you prevented the master of ceremonies there from explaining how Margot could use five hundred dollars to vanish like a soap-bubble!"

"That," acknowledged Senator Benjamin, "among other things that may give Mr. Ludlow an impression of our city still more weird and wonderful. We must deal with matters more secret than a girl's adventure at a masquerade ball; we must skirt the fringes of Voodoo itself."

The space in which they had gathered formed a kind of lower gallery some four or five feet above ground. Senator Benjamin's eye strayed towards the iron stairway to the gallery above. Then he rubbed his chin, squared himself, and addressed the whole group.

"I have said that I approach explanations with reluctance. Margot's mother, as you have heard, thinks me over-considerate of the young lady if I would avoid embarrassing her even in her absence. And yet the closer we are to a person, surely, the more careful of trampled feelings we must be?

"May I plead that I have a daughter too? I see her only once a year, when I visit Ninette and her mother in Paris. But I walk warily when I am there. I will offend any stranger, and be damned to him; is there need to ride roughshod over those nearest and dearest? We insist that our children must not mock us or wound our small vanities; have we therefore the right to mock them or wound theirs? My own feelings, perhaps from self-defence, work the other way. With Ninette at least, when I have pressed too much or pried too far, it is I who feel the embarrassment and turn my head away. As for Margot . . ."

A new voice spoke.

"If my own family had ever been as reasonable as that," the voice said, with a little laugh underneath it, "there would have been no need to show my worst traits nine-tenths of the time."

Head up, shoulders back, not in defiance but in apparent sweet co-operation, she came with light, swift steps down the stairs from the gallery above.

Though it was not the first time Macrae had seen Margot de Sancerre, it was the first time he had been given any opportunity to meet her. His impressions last night had been of bad temper and a certain theatricality. But last night might never have existed. Allure Margot had in full measure; she chose to exercise it now.

Shafts of sunlight, kindling the dark hair, were reflected back from amber eyes. In afternoon dress and crinoline of virginal white with a design of silver fleur-de-lys, she seemed all reasonableness and sugar-candy. To each person present, including Tom, the amber eyes gave a coquettish little glance along with her smile. She captured the undivided attention of them all, with one exception.

Just behind her was Ursula Ede, today wearing colours of orange and tan. After one look at Ursula, who would not quite meet his eye, Mr. Richard Macrae decided that he could look at nobody else.

But he had to look elsewhere. Macrae was formally presented to Margot, as was Harry Ludlow. Whether or not Margot had so much as noticed Harry the night before, she devoted flattering attention to him now. Then she sat down facing Senator Benjamin and resumed her air of sweet co-operation.

"I don't like this," she announced, "and I can't pretend I like it. Still! Let's all be kind and sensible, shall we? If you've got anything to say to me, Uncle Benjie, please do say it. *Have* you got anything to say to me?"

"I need hardly remind you, need I," the lawyer studied her, "that you have worried your mother badly?"

"No, you needn't remind me. Mother herself has been reminding me, all day and every day, without ever once changing the subject. She'll go on reminding me of some enormity or other, I suppose, as long as there's breath in her body or mine. I said it a moment ago: if only my own family had been as reasonable as you are, I needn't keep showing *all* my worst traits."

Isabelle de Sancerre stood up in wrath, crinoline ballooning out.

"If we had been reasonable? If *we*—! Oh, this is too much; I bear nothing but crosses and vexations! Land sakes alive, Margot, what do you *want*?"

"A little dignity, Mother. A little privacy, Mother. Some measure of freedom (shall we say?) from interrogation in the daytime and spying at night."

"You call your own mother a spy?"

"What could anybody call it?"

"Getting down to cold facts, Margot," Jules de Sancerre interposed, "you can't seriously claim you're being ill-used?"

"Not by you, Father; never by you! You let her dominate you and talk you down, that's all. But it's not your fault; you can't help it; I don't blame *you!*"

"She doesn't blame her father; she holds nothing against him. Really," said Isabelle de Sancerre, "that's most generous and magnanimous of her! Benjie, aren't you even going to *correct* this wretched girl?"

"I call for charity towards her," Senator Benjamin replied. "You and I, as parents, demand indulgence for our vanities. Let's not forget young people have their vanities too."

"Vanities, Uncle Benjie? Are you trying to say," Margot screamed incredulously, "that *I* am vain?"

Again the lawyer studied her.

"If there were any indictment against you, my dear, it would be on two counts: a greater and a lesser. Let us first deal with the lesser, which is relatively unimportant, and can be cleared up by a little demonstration I have already arranged."

He turned sideways to look south across the grounds. The two arms of the driveway, meeting at the back door, stretched straight southwards, between rows of vividly coloured shrubs higher than a man's head, in the direction of carriage-house and stable. Somebody appeared to be lurking behind the nearer row of shrubs, hidden as though behind a hedge.

The lurking did not go on. Senator Benjamin raised his arm in signal. Round the side of the hedge appeared the face and top-hat of massive Uncle Cicero, whose eye the senator caught.

"Cicero," he called clearly, "do as I have instructed you. Go back and fetch out the little carriage. No horse, remember! You are big enough and powerful enough to get between the shafts and draw it yourself. Pull it just far enough so that we can all see the carriage from where we are. You understand?"

Cicero bowed and retreated.

"Now I, even I," exclaimed Jules de Sancerre, bouncing up to stand beside the senator, "will rise to a point of order. There's nothing wrong with that carriage, nothing at all! I said last night I would examine it, and I did; you and Macrae were both present when I went out there. I was thinking . . ."

"Father—!" began Margot, gripping the iron arms of the chair.

". . . I was thinking someone might have built a kind of secret panel, *Mysteries of Udolpho* style, to let the girl slip out and flummox us as she's so fond of doing. Cicero's a famous carpenter; he adores Margot. But there's no hocus-pocus of any kind; it's an ordinary carriage; she couldn't possibly have left it unseen."

"Quite right," agreed Senator Benjamin. "And yet what *might* have happened?"

Tom Clayton was also on his feet.

"I can't stand much more of this," he swore. "Answer your own question, O Sage: what *might* have happened? It's the damn disappearance that's got to me worse than anything else. It's the damn disappearance . . ."

"Of course it is, Tom," Margot said sweetly, "as we all ought to have known long ago. *That's* why you lost your temper, went completely berserk, and treated me as you'd never have treated one of the black mistresses I don't doubt you keep in secret. That's your constant preoccupation, isn't it; else what were *you* doing at the quadroon ball?"

"Want some more of it, do you?" yelled Tom. "Don't ask me more of what; you know what. The good right hand is already itching—"

"There will be no more losing of tempers," said Senator Benjamin, suddenly seeming to tower. "We have no time for it, not to mention patience. *Is that* understood?"

"Oh, all right," Tom conceded, "if only because I won't have her mother upset again. Answer me this much, anyway! Were Ursula and Dick both telling the truth?"

"Oh, yes."

"Then the damn disappearance is the hardest part of the problem after all?"

"On the contrary," said Senator Benjamin, "it is the only easy part."

Tom went over and smote his head against one of the iron pillars supporting the gallery. At the same moment Cicero appeared in the drive, between the shafts of the little black carriage, with a massive hand clamped round each. Senator Benjamin motioned; he stopped.

"One last try," declared Tom, wheeling round from the pillar, "and then my lips are forever sealed. *May* I say it?"

"Say what?"

"*I've* been toying with the notion that, when some girl got into the carriage outside the Washington and American Ballroom, it may not have been Margot at all. It may have been only a kind of duplicate Margot who looked like her. She went in one door and straight out the other; she had slipped away before the carriage left that courtyard, and before Dick and Ursula were watching."

Ursula Ede spoke for the first time.

"But we *were* watching; we were watching the whole time; you've just heard Mr. Benjamin say so. Between last night and this morning I've been called a liar about so many other things that I can't tell you what a relief it was to hear those words!"

"The Sage of the Senate, Ursula," argued Tom, "said only that you were both telling the truth. He didn't say you couldn't have made a mistake. If at *some* point last night, either before the journey began or during it, Margot or the duplicate Margot made her escape without being noticed . . . ?"

"Tom," Macrae said with some vehemence, "will you get one thing through your head? It makes no difference whether the occupant of the carriage was Miss de Sancerre or someone who looked like her. How did *anyone* get out of there? And the passenger was certainly the young lady we see before us. She was there just before the carriage turned into Royal Street and headed west; she looked out of the window; I saw her. Will you confirm that, Miss de Sancerre?"

"Really," answered Margot, lifting her shoulders and smiling at him, "I hardly like to confirm anything. It may only make Tom lose his filthy temper again; who can predict the result when that happens? He *threw* me last night, you know; he picked me up and threw me with real intent to hurt. The next time it happens, if there is a next time, he may play the cave-man he likes to think he is, and try to beat my brains out with a club. Wouldn't you *like* to take a club to me, Mr. Cave-man?"

"Thanks for the suggestion, light of my life; I'll remember it. But I prefer to learn what you did before I take the proper remedy. And that's just where we're up against a blank wall." Tom appealed to the others. "We don't know *when* she got out of the carriage, we don't know *how* she got out of the carriage . . ."

"No," interrupted Senator Benjamin, "but what do we know? The very shortest reflection supplies us with an answer, and the time has now come for that answer. —Michael!"

Standing on the lower gallery and facing south, he gestured towards his right. Round the west side of the house strolled a Negro in sober dark garb. Though almost as big as Cicero, and wearing gardener's gloves, he had the air of an indoor hand. Macrae correctly judged him to be Senator Benjamin's man-servant.

"Michael, you have the key I gave you? There is the building; go out and unfasten the padlock. When I signal, follow the rest of your instructions. Look sharp, please!"

Some twenty-odd feet south and to the right, at the end of the beaten-earth path branching off the drive, loomed the white-painted frame structure with the double doors and north window like an artist's studio. But the window was so dusty as to be opaque; it did not reflect such sunlight as touched it sideways.

Taking a key from his pocket, Michael addressed himself to the padlock that held the double doors. Up went Senator Benjamin's admonitory forefinger.

"Cicero, as we have been reminded, is a famous carpenter; there is his workshop. What else do we know of him? Before our friend de Sancerre won him in a poker game years ago, he employed his skill for Mr. Sturdevant. And to what end?"

Here the senator looked at Macrae, his eye gleaming.

"You must often have seen, almost opposite your consulate, the sign reading *Sturdevant & Sons, Coach-Builders*, which crosses the whole front of the premises. But Cicero is much more than even a first-class carpenter. He is a jack of all trades; he can work in iron or leather; he can construct anything."

Then Senator Benjamin addressed Margot, who had become expressionless.

"Last night, my dear, your father explained that Cicero had once made a play-house, complete in every detail, which was the joy of your childhood. All your father did was give him the money to buy materials.

"This, I suggest, must have occurred to you years afterwards. For your vanishing-trick, a seeming miracle, you could not use the regular carriage which we see there on our left, and in which you were so fond of riding. It would be too carefully examined afterward, as in fact it was. But what *could* be done?"

Somebody said, "Well?" Macrae could not be sure who spoke.

"Granted Cicero's skill and devotion, I say, there could be constructed a duplicate carriage outwardly indistinguishable from the first. We have heard talk of a duplicate passenger. But a duplicate carriage, surely, is more likely and more feasible? Now, Michael! The rest of you look there!"

Michael, at that good-sized white-painted structure in a clearing of trees, threw open the double doors and stood back. They saw the interior, with work-benches round every wall and another dusty window towards the west. In the middle, shafts touching the ground, stood a little black carriage with red-spoked wheels. It was not possible to compare the second vehicle with the first. No sooner had Senator Benjamin said, "Now, Michael!" than Cicero, the expression of whose face could not be read at that distance, suddenly wheeled round and, still dragging the original carriage after him, retreated out of sight.

Rather vaingloriously Senator Benjamin hooked his thumbs in the armholes of his waistcoat.

"The workshop, we may note, served a double purpose. Cicero had been given money to buy materials, we know by whom. He was accustomed to tinkering there; he excited no curiosity on the part of the household, and in any case he could not be spied on through such grimy windows. The workshop, then, served both to conceal the construction of the duplicate carriage and to hide the finished product when it was no longer needed.

"You will find, of course, one difference between the two carriages. This I discovered when very late last night, with the aid of a lantern, I examined both before I went home. There are two keys to the workshop's padlock. One is Cicero's; the other belongs to our friend de Sancerre. To make my examination I borrowed the second key from our host, as you heard him say a while ago."

"Just a minute!" blurted Tom Clayton, groping in the air. "*One* difference between the two carriages?"

"Of course. there had to be. The seat inside the real carriage is a solid affair, heavily padded and upholstered in red. The seat inside the duplicate carriage seems solid enough if you merely look at it, but . . ."

Tom did not hesitate. Shaking his fist, he ran down the steps of the lower gallery and plunged out to the workshop. Once inside, he dragged open the door of the carriage and climbed into that. Harry Ludlow had made a move to follow. But one glance from the far-from-stricken Margot, a glance incandescent with allure and appeal, held Harry rooted where he stood.

After perhaps thirty seconds Tom reappeared, slamming the vehicle's door as he climbed out. He walked slowly back to join them, fist again lifted.

"Well, well, well!" Tom said. "She wasn't seen leaving the carriage because she never did leave the carriage until it came safely home. The whole top of the seat lifts up like a lid on invisible hinges. The inside of the seat is nothing but a kind of long and deep box, also padded so she wouldn't bruise her knees, and with some near-invisible air-holes.

"Women's crinolines *look* large enough. But they can be compressed into spaces smaller than a little carriage or even the box she was hiding in. She didn't crawl into her hidey-hole until the carriage was almost home. Cicero drove the fake carriage around the side of the house; he unharnessed the horse and pushed the fake carriage into the workshop before taking the horse back to the stable beside the carriage-house with the real *voiture* in it. She got out, and hid somewhere in the grounds until she marched up the gallery stairs to her room as bold as brass!" Tom smote his forehead. "That's the whole story, damn me to hell and back again! *That's* her notion of the world's funniest joke to play on us!"

"Oh, no," said Senator Benjamin.

Once more he addressed Margot.

"Let me try to read your conduct, *chère nièce*, both according to the evidence and according to your character as I have observed it.

"The vanishing-trick, I think I can assure your parents, was no mere prank to stun the minds of unsympathetic elders and contemporaries hardly more sympathetic. It had a purpose. You did not *necessarily* mean to vanish at all. It was only a bastion of defence you had prepared in the event of trouble at the quadroon ball.

"There have been hints that you more than half expected trouble. Very well. If no *contretemps* overtook you and no fireworks burst, you could return serenely home after establishing another triumph of beauty and charm. If something went wrong, on the other hand, the 'miracle' was ready to be sprung like a mine.

"And that is what happened. You could be fairly sure Miss Ede would follow, and that there would be other witnesses too. You had given orders to have the front gates opened and left open; there could be no mechanical difficulty about your return.

"But your mother was now certain to learn where you had been, and to be as scandalized as we see her at this moment. For a short time—an hour or two at most—you would let her worry about what *might* have befallen you. You would then reappear in your room, as you did. Relying on her sure relief at finding you back safely after all, you could count on a minimum of fireworks if you confessed the whole story today. But—"

"If only I could *convince* my mother," Margot said suddenly, "that my intentions were perfectly good! Years ago a girl named Cécile de la Plage went to a quadroon ball without any harm coming of it; why fuss so much about *that*? And I—I did one thing, Uncle Benjie, that even you don't seem to have guessed. When I crawled out of that dreadful little box, which left my knees black and blue and all but smothered me, I couldn't let anybody suspect the carriage I had been travelling in wasn't the real one."

"Ah, the duplicate carriage." Senator Benjamin pointed to it. "We should have realized what happened long before we did realize it. Almost every witness who followed the carriage home testified to the smell of perfume that haunted its interior. But both windows had been lowered. Any smell of perfume will soon dissipate in open air: unless, of course the presumably missing person is still there. You were saying, Margot?"

Margot shook her head as though to clear it.

"I was saying," she answered, "that (for the time being, at least!) I couldn't let anybody suspect the carriage I had been travelling in wasn't the real one. I had left my black mask on the seat when I crouched down inside underneath the lid. But it mustn't stay there. So I went to the carriage-house. I put the mask on the seat of the real carriage, which hadn't been away from the place . . ."

"And a little while afterwards," interposed Ursula Ede, "I went out there and took the mask. Please don't ask me what I wanted it for, any of you! It's all over now, or at least I hope it is." Ursula hesitated, pondering something. "Margot . . ."

"In another minute," Margot flared out, "you'll be asking me why I was agitated and upset! On top of everything else, could I guess Judge Rutherford would choose last night when I was absent to fall downstairs and kill himself?

"I don't mind telling you how I learned. I decided to wait, as Uncle Benjie said, and I did wait. I went to the arbour beside the croquet lawn over there," she swept her arm towards south and east, "and sat down there. I had no watch. But I could tell time by the church clocks; time never seemed to pass so slowly. At half-past twelve or a little later I went back to the house, and up the gallery stairs to my room.

"The door of my room was an inch or two open; I could hear some men shouting in the downstairs hall. I peeped out and I saw them, though they couldn't see me.

"You were there, Uncle Benjie. You too, Father. And this other gentleman: Mr. Macrae, isn't it? You were shouting about Judge Rutherford being dead from falling downstairs, and it was an accident or had somebody pushed him?

"Delightful homecoming, wasn't it? Murder, murder, murder! If somebody had pushed him, that meant policemen too. Had I done anything I could be arrested for?

"And it did mean the police. You three went into the library; Mother joined you; the same shouting began in the library. Presently Mr. Macrae came out to meet that Irish sergeant, the one who drinks so much. And then the real fun started.

"I'm supposed to be a fairly calm and collected person. But do you wonder I wanted privacy and freedom from badgering? When Mother and Ursula burst in, and Mother instantly began badgering all over again, do you wonder I drove them out and locked the door? Finally, when that irresponsible maniac there," she stabbed her finger at Tom Clayton, "banged on the door and swore he'd break it down unless I admitted him . . . oh, God, do you wonder at *anything* that happened?"

"Let it be conceded," replied Senator Benjamin, "that you had more on your mind than was generally known." His gaze moved to Margot's parents. "By the way, you saw Cicero bolt as the knots were being unravelled. I had to pledge him my solemn word he would land in no trouble for what he did. You will honour my word, won't you?"

"Oh, we'll honour your word," cried Isabelle de Sancerre. "Who blames Cicero? Who *could* blame Cicero?"

"I am gratified to hear you say it."

"But Miss Hoity-Toity-High-and-Mighty is a very different proposition, don't you think? It's easy for *you* to be indulgent, Benjie. It's not your daughter who's concerned; it's not your daughter the whole town will be talking about, and saying heaven knows what! Since you seem to think she has nothing to answer for . . ."

"Did I say she has *nothing* to answer for?"

"Well, what do you say?"

Senator Benjamin, standing above Margot, looked down into her eyes.

"Forgive me," he continued, "if I now speak in sterner guise. Of two possible counts against you, we have disposed of the lesser and pass on to the greater. I hope—if I were a man of stronger religious views I could say I pray—that your adventure has been extraneous to our true problem: that you have no real concern with the black and ugly business, an affair of murder and conspiracy, through which at present we are stumbling half blind. Your part in it, if any, can be determined by frank answers to one or two extremely personal questions."

Margot met his look.

"You shall have your frank answers," she told him. "I don't go back out on one thing I've said or promised. What on earth are you trying to find out?"

"I am trying to find out," said Senator Benjamin, "whether or not you have become enmeshed in Voodoo. To begin with: When and where did you meet Marie Laveau's daughter?"

PART III:

Daybreak

15

Margot's expression changed slightly.

"I—I don't understand what you mean!"

"Do you understand the question?"

"Not very well. *Marie Laveau . . . Voodoo . . .*"

"Let me try to assist your memory. For some seven weeks, Margot, your preoccupation both with Delphine Lalaurie and with Marie Laveau has become notorious."

"Mother told you that, didn't she?"

"Who else is so concerned for your welfare? And are these the frank answers you promised?"

"If you'd just explain what you're talking about . . . !"

"I will do so. There is only one Delphine Lalaurie, now dead and buried. What of Marie Laveau? When I discussed the matter with your mother at some length on Wednesday night, I asked whether there had been any contact between you and Marie Laveau. She assured me that there had not; she scoffed at the notion that you would even consult (I quote) 'a dirty, dingy old witch-woman with a pet snake.'

"Both of us, of course, referred to the notorious Voodoo Queen, now in her sixties, who has dominated the secret life of this city for over thirty years. And I agreed that you would be unlikely to heed such a counsellor.

"I had not then learned what I learned on Thursday, and imparted to the group in the library last night: that Marie Laveau's eldest child is a daughter, born in 1827. This daughter, now only thirty-one years old, would be at the peak of good looks inherited from a beautiful mother and a handsome near-white father.

"For there *is* such a person, you know. Marie Laveau the younger—impressive, well mannered, probably well educated too —now exists and moves among us as the *only* Voodoo Queen.

"You see what they have done?

"The elder Marie, as I also informed your mother on Wednesday, has long controlled a secret organization of her own. In perhaps half the households of this city, households both exalted and humble, she has spies and adherents to keep her informed and do her bidding at need. And now, as a last stroke to spellbind the credulous, they have gone even further. By substituting the daughter for the mother in public appearances, they have created the legend of a Voodoo Queen defying time. She is eternal, she is immortal, she cannot even grow old!

"Very well. The possibility of some such person's existence had occurred to me even before I learned of the daughter ..."

"Oh, had it really?" asked Margot, now watching him as though from behind a barrier. "Why should you think of that?"

"Because *somebody* has been visiting you in secret, by night, and exerting influence over you. Some person, probably on more than one occasion, has crept up those gallery stairs to your room. For some considerable time, I am told, a chosen slave has watched your windows every night from sunset until dawn."

Margot whipped round in her chair.

"And you say, Mother, you have *not* been spying on me?"

"Really," exclaimed Isabelle de Sancerre, regarding a point above her daughter's head, "one would think I am here to account for my behaviour, not you to account for yours! If a mother mayn't choose the best course for a child with no sense, what's the good of anything we've *ever* been taught? The one who's been watching is Willie, Marcus Brutus's son, the most trustworthy boy we have. He says you've never left the house at night; that's *all* he says!"

"Will it shock you, dear Mother, if I ask whether I'm supposed to have a lover? Some good-looking young man like . . . no, not like Tom; he's hideous! But someone," her eye strayed very slightly towards Harry, "I don't dislike and do find rather attractive?"

"I thought of that, if you must know! But Willie swears not, and your Uncle Benjie says—"

"May I entreat you," Senator Benjamin interrupted, "to remember the mentality of those who serve us? No slave, least of all a house-servant with an easy job like Willie's, would ever dare tell lies about a clandestine love-affair on the part of his owner's daughter, the most serious offence Margot could commit or a servant conceal. Such is our society in the nineteenth century.

"I see no clandestine love-affair here. I see merely a mentor, another woman: no dirty, dingy old witch-woman, but the very reverse of that in appearance, speech, and appeal to the young imagination."

"Do you mean Marie Laveau the younger?" asked Isabelle de Sancerre.

"I do. Remember that spider-web of Voodoo worshippers, stretching its filaments invisibly into so many houses! If a watching slave had seen any man go up the stairs, he would have told his master or his mistress. But if he had seen the Great Voodoo Queen, with all her awesome powers to curse or to destroy, he would have had his tongue torn out before he betrayed her."

Jules de Sancerre sat up straight.

"Voodoo influence *here*? In *this* house? It's preposterous, man! It's absolutely preposterous!"

"It is not in the least preposterous, believe me. Nor is Voodoo influence always malignant; it may be used to bless and defend as well as to curse, if you can credit a blessing administered upside down. And it would explain much that still remains dark. Come, Margot, have you nothing to tell me? What *has* the woman been saying?"

"I—"

"If she suggested only that you attend the quadroon ball and score a triumph, never mind; we may forget that. Was there anything of a darker, more sinister sort? I ask in sober earnest, though I don't think there was. Even at the unkindest view of your character, I am inclined to acquit you."

"What *is* the unkindest view of my character, Uncle Benjie? Do tell me!"

"We are not here to discuss your character . . ."

"But that's exactly what you've been doing, isn't it? Come on; I challenge you! If I have any outstanding faults, as may very well be the case, I am most anxious to correct them myself. Do have the kindness to speak!"

"We all love you, my dear. As a general thing you can do no wrong. Though it is true that you are sometimes vain, inconsiderate, and self-indulgent, with a tendency to make mysteries for the sake of making mysteries, nevertheless . . ."

Margot had sprung to her feet.

"I can endure much, as you know. But the accusation of being vain—*vain?*—is a charge I will not hear from any person who walks the earth. Vain, indeed! You are not the police, Mr. Benjamin; you have no authority here. I can't be forced to answer your questions, however much I may be badgered and berated!"

"Nobody is trying to force you, Margot."

"Then there's an end of it." She drew a shuddered breath. "And now I am stifling; I need fresh air; I must go for a stroll in the grounds. Will you accompany me, Mr. Ludlow?"

Harry, flustered, made deprecating gestures.

"Wouldn't it be better," he suggested, "if we both sat down and . . . ?"

"I said I was going for a stroll in the grounds. If you care to accompany me," Margot gave him an intimate glance, "you will be very welcome. If you don't care to accompany me . . ."

"Accompany you with pleasure, of course! Which way?"

Margot hooked her arm in Harry's. They descended the steps and turned left in the drive towards the east side of the house. Passing under the open covered way which led from house to kitchen, they were lost to sight in a screen of trees beyond.

"*Well!*" breathed Isabelle de Sancerre.

Senator Benjamin drove his right fist into the palm of his left hand.

"I handled that badly," he said in a low voice. "It is inadvisable to tell any woman the truth about herself. If you wish to learn something from her, it's worse than inadvisable; it's hopeless. Yes, I handled that badly; it would have done me no good in court."

Throughout all this Macrae's gaze had seldom strayed from Ursula; Ursula, the intense but gentle, as contrasted with Margot, the intense and flamboyant. Macrae was content to have it so. Ursula looked at him.

"I shouldn't mind a stroll either," she said, "though maybe not for the same reason. Will *you* accompany *me*?"

"I was about to suggest it."

"Yes, go!" urged Senator Benjamin. "Perhaps everybody had better go for a walk. You have had a momentary overdose of truth; you are surfeited. But don't close up your minds, any of you; there is still a long way to travel."

"*I* think—" began Isabelle de Sancerre.

Ursula and Macrae did not hear what she thought. She made so long, impressive a pause, as though on the brink of awful revelation, that they had drifted down the stairs and east, in the same direction Margot and Harry had taken, before Madame de Sancerre resumed speaking.

All threat of rain seemed to have passed over. A golden glow bathed lawn and trees. Beyond the covered way to the kitchen, with its brick floor and its white-painted wooden supports, they found a grass avenue stretching south between lines of oaks.

Ursula hesitated before emerging into sunlight. Seductive in her orange-and-tan silk dress, head up but eyes far away, she seemed to have much on her mind.

"Have you guessed," she asked, "what really upsets Margot so much?"

"Since she lost her temper about half a dozen times . . ."

"It's *Tom Clayton* who upsets her. Couldn't you feel that behind every word she spoke? But not, of course, for the reasons she says he does. Tom doesn't really have all those black women she accused him of keeping, now does he?"

"No, of course he doesn't!"

"I don't think Margot believes it either. But he did go to the quadroon ball; she does think he was looking for a pretty quadroon of the sort she pretended to be!"

"*I* was at that ball too."

"It's no business of mine to ask why *you* were there."

"As a matter of fact, I was there as a sort of chaperon for Tom
and Harry. On the other hand, if you had actually been the pretty
quadroon *you* were pretending to be . . ."

"What would you have done?"

"The answer is not even problematical; it's certain. Ursula, have
you any notion how infernally attractive you are? And with none
of what's been called Margot's damned crinkum-crankum; you're
too human."

"Oh, I'm human enough; that's the trouble! I'm no good at all
I'm a broken reed!"

"Hardly a very well-chosen description."

"But it's true. You heard what Mr. Benjamin said: 'Don't close
up your minds; there is still a long way to travel.' Here we are in
the middle of the most ghastly mess; just to know Margot hid in
duplicate carriage doesn't solve anything at all! How did Judge
Rutherford die? What's *going on?* And yet all I can think about are
my own ridiculous troubles and misadventures!"

"Why call them ridiculous?"

"Because that's what they are. Did Aunt Isabelle tell you about
the rumpus when I did get home last night?"

"Yes."

"I was afraid she would; I do so wish she hadn't!"

"Is there any good reason for keeping it dark? Anyway, all she
said was that you knocked over a lamp and roused the house
Today, apparently, you and Madame de Sancerre concocted
story that you and Margot went to an opera at the Théâtre d'Orlé
ans."

Ursula retreated a step, her hand at her throat.

"*I* concocted that story! I made it up on my own, at past two
this morning, to pacify my father and my aunts. Towards daylight
they stopped calling me a liar; they believed me. I even said I'
met you there."

"You had met me where?"

"At the opera. And it was all right; my father didn't seem
displeased. I want him to meet you, you see; I'm anxious for him

to meet you, though not when he's waving a sword and remembering the Mexican War. So with everybody in a good humour again, or almost, it occurred to me that I could ask him to invite you to dinner tonight."

Ursula spread out her hands.

"Only, unfortunately, he'd already accepted an invitation for the six of us—my father, the four aunts, and myself—to have dinner at ex-Governor Corliss's plantation down the river. We ourselves don't know Governor Corliss very well. Also, since it's twenty-four miles away, they dine very late, and we're unlikely to get back until past midnight, I couldn't very well ask to have you included too, or I'd have done it. Is *that* very forward of me?"

"On the contrary, Ursula, it's the sort of thought I most appreciate. But I'm afraid I couldn't have accepted in any case."

"You have another engagement, have you?"

"Not a social engagement, no. Anything of that sort would be broken instantly if it meant being with you. Tonight Tom and I have an errand whose outcome may prove vital to the outcome of this business and the solution you were calling for a moment ago. It won't begin until midnight, but we must be prepared before then. And the nature of the errand must remain a secret for the time being."

"Mayn't I even *ask* about it?"

"I'd rather you didn't. It should be possible to tell you afterwards. Yes, it should be possible to tell you afterwards!"

"Is it your habit," demanded Tom Clayton, appearing suddenly from among the trees behind them, "is it your habit always to say you'll explain something afterwards, and then never do it?

"You had a part of the solution, remember?" Tom went on. "Whether or not it was the same as old Benjie's part, you promised to tell me as soon as he'd had his say. Have you done that?"

"The promise still holds good. I've been waiting for an opportunity when we could catch the oracle alone."

"Well, you won't catch him alone just yet; he's still in conference with Papa and Mama de Sancerre. *Is* your part of the solution the same as his?"

"No, though he did touch on one point I want to develop. The wonder is that he himself didn't develop it. He can't have missed it, surely?"

"Old Benjie doesn't miss much. But how the hell," Tom burst out, "are you going to do any explaining without mentioning the things we've agreed not to mention?"

Clearly Tom referred to the written challenge from Papa Là-bas and the dead snake on the desk; he was corking himself down with difficulty.

"It has occurred to me," Macrae said, "that I can develop my small thesis, and ask the oracle's opinion, without bringing up anything except points he already knows. When we do find him alone . . ."

Tom brooded for a moment. Then, fishing in his right-hand pocket, he suddenly produced the wicked little derringer with its two barrels, one above the other.

"Here's the damn thing," he announced, "still loaded as I took it from Square Nat. But I'm not carrying this with me tonight, thanks; I might be tempted to use it. For me, Dick, it'll be a stout walking-stick of the kind you wielded. —Ursula, you ought to see this fellow go into action; he's greased lightning. Yes, it'll be a stout walking-stick for your obedient servant. Then, if a certain character shows his ugly face in the halls of infamy, I'll swat the bastard as I'd swat a fly."

"Good heavens," cried Ursula, "what *are* you two about? Pistols! Walking-sticks! 'Took it from Square Nat'? 'Halls of infamy'? 'Swat the—' Never mind. If I'm not to ask questions I won't ask questions. But you tell me, Tom! This errand tonight: is it going to be *dangerous?*"

"It may be; probably it will be; who cares?"

"But—!"

Tom dropped the pistol back into his pocket.

"Ursula, honey," he said with indulgence, " 'no questions' is distinctly the right attitude. Just take us both on trust—Dick will tell you the same thing—and don't go fretting your pretty little head.

"You two are going in that direction, aren't you?" he added, pointing south along the little avenue. "That way leads to the croquet lawn; it's not my way. I'll return to the house and keep my eye on old Sir Oracle. Good luck, my children!"

Then he was gone.

Side by side, not looking at each other, Ursula and Macrae drifted along. Moving noiselessly in grass, they stopped as they heard voices beyond the end of the avenue.

It was a regulation-size croquet lawn, with six hoops and two pegs, its cropped turf green and gleaming in late-afternoon light. The voices belonged to Margot de Sancerre and Harry Ludlow, but they were not playing croquet.

They stood facing each other at the entrance to a rustic arbour in the middle of the lawn's east boundary. Harry had his back turned; Margot, though seen diagonally, could be seen full face. Presumably they meant to play croquet; on the ground behind Margot a big wooden box, open, displayed four heavy wooden balls coloured red, blue, green, and yellow. But other matters preoccupied these two. Margot had again grown intense and Harry defensive.

"I asked you a question, Mr. Ludlow. By the way, may I call you Harry?"

"Wish you would; everybody else does. Shall I call you Margot?"

"Please do." Margot drew herself up. "Now, Harry, my mother has told me about this man known as Steve White, the character who has frightened poor Barnaby Jeffers so badly. You're the only one who's seen Steve White, or at least will admit having seen him. And I ask you a question, I say!"

"With the best will in the world, Margot, what can I tell you by way of description that I haven't already told you and Sergeant O'Shea too? Average height, clean-shaven, brown hair: average in every way, as far as I could see."

"Age?"

"Older than I am; I can't say how much older. Dash it all, I didn't ask the fellow for his birth-certificate!"

"He lived in New Orleans, he said?"

"Either lived here or had once lived here; I can't remember which. Last night in the library, when they were going on about Steve White being Rosette Leblanc's son, how was I supposed to know that just by meeting him aboard the boat? Anyway, Margot, why are you so interested in him? And if you're going on about Voodoo, as Mr. Benjamin did a while ago . . ."

"I am not going on about Voodoo. I have confessed to you," Margot said clearly, "that I *am* acquainted with Marie Laveau's daughter. They don't understand that woman, Harry. They don't realize the frightful handicaps she's had to overcome, and *has* overcome to her eternal credit. They look down on her, I imagine. What philistines they are!"

"If that's what you say, Margot, it's my view too. All the same . . ."

"Not one word," Margot went on in the same clear voice, "has she ever spoken to me of Voodoo or of any would-be magic. She *has* told me of Delphine Lalaurie: the famous, some would say infamous, Madame Lalaurie. Madame Lalaurie tortured no slaves and committed no crime; she was a much-wronged woman. The younger Marie's mother, our Voodoo Queen, grew absolutely devoted to her when she was the great lady's hairdresser in far-off years. Marie the elder would have done, and would still do, anything for the clearing of a cherished name. And if the son of Rosette Leblanc *has* returned to avenge his mother's benefactor after nearly a quarter of a century, then I say strength to his arm!"

About to cross the lawn and intervene, Macrae glanced behind him as Ursula plucked at his coat. In the avenue a little way back stood Tom Clayton, finger at lip, making fierce beckoning gestures.

They hastened to join Tom, who had assumed an air of profundity.

"If you want a word with Sir Oracle," Tom said, "you'd better catch him now. The de Sancerres have withdrawn, and Sir Oracle is still on the terrace: which is not a terrace, but I trust I make myself clear?"

"Right. Back to the house, then!"

"May I go with you?" asked Ursula, taking Macrae's arm. "Please, may I go with you?"

"Yes, by all means. Come along."

When they returned by the way they had gone, no trace remained of the recent demonstration with duplicate carriages. The double doors of the workshop were padlocked; Cicero and Michael had gone.

The man called Sir Oracle, a pencil in his right hand and an unlighted cigar in his left, sat in the iron chair at the iron table, making notes on the back of an envelope.

"Tom intimates, my dear Macrae," he said, "that you have a good deal on *your* mind. Have you anything to add to our present theorizing?"

"Yes. It's not much, but it does seem worth consideration."

"Well, sir?"

"You yourself remarked last night, Senator Benjamin, that two forces appear to be working in this business. One force is the actual murderer, whoever he may be. The other force is a kind of close-knit conspiracy which, if not actively aiding the murderer at his work, is at least conscious of his every move and stands in his support."

"That is what *I* believe, certainly."

"Barnaby Jeffers receives a card intimating that he had better look sharp. Sergeant O'Shea receives a card suggesting that he come out here and investigate Margot's disappearance. Both are signed Papa Là-bas; both are in French; both, it should be obvious, are a part of that same conspiracy. It's a *Voodoo* conspiracy, isn't it?"

"Yes, I think it is. But—"

Macrae looked from Senator Benjamin to Ursula and Tom, and back to the senator again.

"That's a very large *but*," he agreed, "and seems ultimately to provide only more puzzles. How do I fit in as another if minor victim of that conspiracy? All three of you know that for some time I have been followed and spied on and subjected to petty annoyances. An earthen jar is thrown through the window of my office. I could cite a further instance, though more evidence should be unnecessary. My knowledge of Voodoo is nil; I have had no contact of any kind either with Marie Laveau the elder or Marie Laveau the younger. What can they possibly want of *me?*"

Senator Benjamin put down his pencil and took the cigar in both hands as though to study it.

"You have reasoned well," he replied, "but you may not have carried the reasoning far enough. That apparent contradiction may itself provide the answer. If only I could have questioned Barnaby Jeffers today, as I may still be able to question him tonight . . . !"

"Finally, with regard to Steve White . . ."

"Ah, yes; the elusive Steve White. Any suggestions there?"

Macrae, who had considered telling him of Margot's recent outburst on the croquet lawn, rejected the whole idea. It was information gained through eavesdropping; to use it would be a sneaking and underhand stab. Besides, once Margot had recovered from the hurt to her vanity, she herself would be quick to pour out in public what she had already poured out in private. Macrae said:

"Steve White, under that name or another, is somewhere in New Orleans. He may be an avenger; he may be a red herring. Let Sergeant O'Shea find and question him, let the sergeant hammer some questions at Marie Laveau too, and we may get the facts that at present we so conspicuously lack."

"*I* can tell you a *little* more," declared Isabelle de Sancerre, appearing at an open window, and marching out in an almost regal way. "I said last night there was something about Rosette Leblanc's son I couldn't quite remember, but I remember now. And it's two things, really.

"You know, Benjie, in a way I can still see that fourteen-year-old boy, thin-faced and brown-haired, worshipping Delphine Lalaurie as though she'd been a goddess. For one thing about him, he was an uncanny mimic. He could imitate an old coloured woman, and hit her off to the life. He could do a Creole speaking broken English with such perfection you could swear you were actually listening to Jean de Courcelles or Raoul Longueval.

"The other thing I remember is his accuracy with a boy's slingshot. Do you know what I mean, Mr. Macrae? In England I think they call it a catapult. It's a heavy piece of wood shaped like the letter Y, with rubber or elastic to pull back and discharge stones of different sizes. Delphine tried to discourage him from using it, but she never succeeded. He could knock a bird out of a tree; he could hit anything you pointed at; he—" Isabelle de Sancerre broke off.

"Benjie, what's the matter with you?"

An almost frightening change had come over Senator Benjamin's face. His eyes opened wide, then narrowed. He broke the cigar in two pieces and dropped them on the table. While Isabelle de Sancerre retreated to the back drawing-room, muttering something they could not catch, Judah P. Benjamin rose to his feet and went to the western end of the gallery, where he seemed to be staring at the setting sun beyond the trees.

"There's something here, I think," Tom Clayton proclaimed, "we all ought to see. But our good Mama de Sancerre is right. What's the matter with you, Sir Oracle? What are you up to now?"

Senator Benjamin turned back, his face again smoothed out and unreadable inside its half-circle of whisker.

"In one sense," he replied, "it might be said that I am again at my favourite sport. Devil-fishing."

16

FOR THEIR EXPEDITION THAT NIGHT, THEY HAD DECIDED, THERE was no need of a carriage or of saddle-horses either. They would go afoot.

"If we have dinner at Arnaud's," Tom had said, "it's only about ten blocks from Bienville Street to where we're going. We're both in good health; walking will be best anyway."

Macrae had a question. "Delphine Lalaurie's house: do we need anybody's permission to enter the place?"

"No; we just go there and walk in. The trouble, so far, has been to *get* people inside. The house has gained so bad a reputation, as you've probably heard, that nobody will live there."

"Still a ruin, is it?"

"Not a bit of a ruin, as far as I know. It's been redecorated several times for tenants who said they wouldn't mind alleged spooks, and the decorations were still new when the tenants cleared out in a hurry. What the hell *is* there, do you think?"

"Probably only the house's reputation. Anyway, we'll see."

So it had been arranged.

It was very late, almost nine o'clock, when they met to dine at Arnaud's Restaurant in Bienville Street. Tom carried a heavy oak walking-stick, which he left at the *vestiaire*. Macrae, though not armed even with a stick, deposited at the *vestiaire* a small parcel in wrapping-paper. Nor was it an occasion for evening dress; both wore day clothes of an old and comfortable sort. Both were a little on edge, though neither would admit this or show it.

Arnaud's used no gaslight. Only a sheen of many candles fell across napery, silver, china, and walls papered in dark red patterned with gold. They sat long at their meal, lingering afterwards over coffee, brandy, and cigars. It was only then that Tom even remotely approached the subject on their minds.

"You know, old son," he said, "I had a sort of idea you were seeing Ursula this evening."

"That's what I should have liked, but it couldn't be managed. The whole family are having dinner at some place twenty-odd miles away; they won't be back before midnight."

"Then this time, at any rate, you'll have no chance to keep the poor girl out until all hours and compromise her again."

"If that's an attempt to be helpful . . ."

"To tell you God's truth, Dick," observed Job's comforter, smiting the table, "I shouldn't have minded seeing Margot. No matter; that can't be helped either! As for Margot . . . I don't really think Harry is trying to beat my time, though once or twice today I wondered. Where *is* Harry, by the way?"

"At work, still struggling with his report to the Foreign Office. Tibby gave him something to eat, and he locked himself in his room. He has no difficulty in writing letters; I still have half a dozen he sent from various cities. But some people get a kind of stage-fright at composing anything for the official eye. His report is to be finished tonight and on my desk for dispatch tomorrow morning." Macrae straightened up. "Now what's on your mind about Margot?"

"You shouldn't have left the de Sancerres' quite so early this afternoon, Dick. You missed the rest of the fireworks."

"Fireworks?"

"Not fireworks of the earlier kind, thank God! Margot had turned as nice as pie. She apologized to old Benjie for flying out at him, and told him what he wanted to hear. She does know Marie Laveau's daughter; met her one day at D. H. Holmes's. This Marie the younger seems to be quite a woman. So as not to embarrass Margot in public, she's taken to calling at night, just as old Benjie thought. But it hasn't been to whisper about Voodoo; it's been to explain the handicaps she's suffered from and to defend Madame Lalaurie as a much-wronged innocent."

Tom then recounted a tale with which Macrae was already familiar, and the latter nodded.

"I know, Tom."

"You know?"

"I overheard the same thing on the croquet lawn. Now hadn't you and I better be getting on to our destination?"

"But the appointment at the haunted house, if we have an appointment, is for midnight. And at the moment, old son, it's not quite half-past *ten!*"

"It might be best to go on ahead and reconnoitre, don't you think?"

"All right; fair enough. You see, Dick," Tom continued, as Macrae paid the bill and they made their way towards the *vestiaire*, "the fact is that Margot's idealistic. You mightn't think so, but the idiotic wench *is* idealistic. Her 'preoccupation,' which worried Mama de Sancerre so much, has been nothing but starry-eyed concern both for a handicapped Marie and a wronged Delphine. It's very noble of Margot, but it does make for a certain disappointment."

"Why disappointment?"

"From this expedition tonight," Tom said with a kind of pleased ferocity, "I've been hoping for something fairly lively. And we're not going to get it, Dick. There may or may not be such things as ghosts. But you can't have the ghosts of tortured slaves in a house where no slave was ever tortured and no crime was ever committed. You can't even make a pretence at it by rattling chains or groaning in a cupboard. It's a hoax and a sell; Delphine Lalaurie was innocent."

"Just a moment, Tom!"

"Well?"

"Delphine Lalaurie may have been innocent. But Marie Laveau the elder or Marie Laveau the younger, whoever is behind these Voodoo attempts pretending to be Papa Là-bas, can't be as innocent as Margot likes to think. They've done their best to shake my nerves with following footsteps, prying eyes, a water-jar through the window, a dead snake on my desk. Allied with them in some way is the murderous joker who killed Judge Rutherford and may kill others before he's finished. And now they've challenged me to meet 'em on their own field. There may be results of a livelier nature than you anticipate."

"Then I'm ready for it," declared Tom, taking up hat and stick. "Let Papa Là-bas show his ugly face just once . . . !"

"Tom, for God's sake be careful! Just because Margot blew up today, don't you blow up and do something before you understand what you're doing. Control yourself, can't you?"

"My conduct shall be a model of decorum, I promise, unless somebody tries to get gay. What's that you've got in the wrapping-paper?"

"A dark lantern. Want to see it?"

" 'Dark lantern' *sounds* very fetching and mysterious," Tom commented, as his companion undid the paper. "But that's not much to look at, is it? Just a flattish little black-metal lamp, with the stump of a candle, a reflector, and a slide to close when you don't want it seen. Are you going to light the thing now?"

"No, not yet. Part of the handle is wood, as you see, but it can get infernally hot if it's carried for very long." Throwing away the paper, Macrae slipped the dark lantern into his pocket. "Outside, now! Then over to Royal Street, a left-hand turn, and we're on our way."

The night air had turned damp and heavy under a black sky. The restaurant-attendant who saw them out into Bienville Street said he could smell a thunderstorm coming.

Thirty seconds later they strode east along Royal Street at a pace that ate up distance. Though many windows showed yellow stars of light, they encountered few wayfarers once they had passed the glittering façade and great dome of the St. Louis Hotel. A little later Tom spoke.

"I forgot to tell you," he said, "what happened just before we met at Arnaud's. A friend of the old man's gave me a ride to town in his carriage, and dropped me off at Canal Street. I was crossing over when I came face to face with Sergeant O'Shea, in a state of some excitement. I kept my mouth shut; he got nothing out of me. But then I got nothing out of him either, except that he'd been tracing Steve White. How he'd been tracing the fellow he didn't say.

"Whereupon I commenced speculating. I don't mean I used what we humorously call a brain," Tom tapped his forehead, "for rational thought about this mystery or the murderer's identity. What I did was give way to the wildest speculations that could occur to me. How would the mystery be solved in a sensational romance? Do you understand what I mean?"

"I understand very well; I've been playing the same game. Any results?"

"We've drawn our sights so exclusively on Steve White that we haven't even aimed anywhere else. And that's bad even as common sense. The name isn't unusual. There must be a dozen Steve Whites within hailing distance, all of 'em innocent; the man O'Shea pursues is probably innocent too.

"Any sensational romance," argued Tom, "would provide an unexpected development to turn the whole affair upside down. We've been thinking of three potential victims: Judge Rutherford, George Stoneman, Barnaby Jeffers. One of those *is* a victim; he's dead. But what of the other two? What if . . . ?"

"What if one of the prospective victims, standing by in apparent innocence, should actually be the murderer himself? Last night, it seemed to me," Macrae told him, "Senator Benjamin suggested something very like the same possibility."

"Is that the line old Benjie's working on?"

"He hasn't given any real hint of what line he's working on. But is it what *you* suggest?"

"It can go even further," declared the simmering Tom. "Let's look at *everybody* who was young when the case of Delphine Lalaurie blew up. There's Jules de Sancerre, a man of such outwardly blameless life that he's almost bound to have a guilty secret on his soul. It would be a crashing surprise ending, wouldn't it, if Papa de Sancerre should turn out to be Papa Là-bas?"

"You don't really believe that, of course?"

"I said I was romancing, didn't I? But we've got to think of *something*, dammit, or forget the whole business and go home to bed! And there's still another field for conjecture, giving us one development that's occurred to nobody so far."

"What is it?"

"Steve White," answered Tom, "really is the murderer after all. The lover of Rosette Leblanc, remember, has never been identified. Could it have been Horace Rutherford? Barnaby Jeffers? Even Jules de Sancerre? Rosette's son, roaring for blood, returns like a destroying angel. Though he doesn't know it and has never suspected it, one of the men he wants to kill is his own father. I have gone as far as I can in the realm of lunacy; I will now shut up."

Tom had slowed his walk to a saunter. He did shut up, except for muttering to himself, while intersection after intersection fell away behind them.

Apart from themselves and their own footsteps, Royal Street had become as deserted and silent as a thoroughfare in Pompeii. Distant thunder made a vibration rather than any noise. They had been walking on the left-hand or north pavement; as they neared the intersection of Hospital Street, Tom touched Macrae's arm and they crossed to the other side.

Delphine Lalaurie's house, a darker mass against darkness, lifted its three floors at the street-corner only fifty or sixty feet ahead. Macrae did not care to confess, even to himself, that dread touched his heart as through with a finger. He countered this by chuckling softly; they must not yield either to enemies or to bogles. And it was now time to light the dark lantern.

Taking it from his pocket, he ignited a sulphur match with the edge of his thumb-nail and, when the flare of sulphur had burnt away, easily kindled the lantern's wick. A beam of light perhaps a foot wide ran out and touched a shop-window. In white letters across the glass he saw the name *P. Belet*; underneath it, in French, *Dolls and Toys*. Ranks of witless doll faces stared back with an illusion of mimic life. Then the beam moved to the left, and found human figures.

At a recessed door between two windows of the same shop, a girl with a pink dress—facing outward, eyes closed—stood in the arms of a young man the back of whose pea-jacket and flat-crowned hat seemed more than familiar. As the light brushed

them the girl, without even opening her eyes, disengaged herself
enough to grope sideways with her left hand for the brass bell-pull
to the right of the door.

Macrae closed the slide of the dark lantern and hurried his
companion on.

Next door to the doll-maker's shop was another shop, unidenti-
fiable in darkness, and then the house they sought. Past a line of
shuttered ground-floor windows the entrance to its covered way
gaped like a cavern. Macrae spoke in a low voice.

"You recognized those two back there, didn't you?"

"It looked like the sailor and his girl who visited you this morning. What about 'em?"

"I can suggest a theory too. If I adopted your own style, Tom, I
should say that the real villain of this piece, disguised as a common sailor with a Cockney accent, has contrived all the dirty work
not managed by Marie Laveau & Co. How does he get so much
shore leave, if he's what he pretends to be? But then I don't know
the ways of the sea."

"And I don't want any more theories, thanks. We're here."

"We are. Steady, now!"

Conscious of the dark lantern's increasing heat, Macrae opened
its slide enough to send a narrow beam ahead. There was no main
staircase under the covered way, which had a heavy smell of
damp, of greenery, and of rotting vegetation. But in the courtyard
beyond, its garden a jungle and weeds thrusting up between the
paving-stones, a broad staircase with rusted iron handrails led up
to a three-sided gallery off which the house's principal rooms
obviously opened.

Thunder rumbled closer as they went through to the courtyard.
Macrae directed his light at the stairs. Both still spoke in
muttering voices, even when they spoke with emotion.

"If the place is locked up . . ." Macrae began.

"If the place is locked up," said Tom, "we must just break a
window. It won't be the first time that's happened here. By God,"
he muttered, lifting the heavy walking-stick as he started up the
steps, "if Marie Laveau & Co. are up to their games . . . !"

"Steady, I said!"

"I *am* steady. In case somebody's following us, that's fair warning. . . . No trouble about getting in," he added a moment later. "Double doors here; they're unlocked, and the hinges don't creak. Everything seems damn dusty, though. Come on *up!*"

Mounting the steps to the gallery, Macrae found that the double doors in question gave on a spacious central hall with a graceful staircase to the floor above and rooms still more spacious opening out of the hall on either side.

He bent over to examine the lock of the double doors. Then, light probing, he led the way as they began to explore.

No windows on this floor were shuttered, but many had been broken: whether from malice at the house's reputation or from the carelessness of urchins throwing stones. The big rooms, with hardwood floors and once-satiny wallpaper, seemed to have suffered from little more than neglect or decay. Great patches of damp stained the paper; gilt cornices and the gilt outlines of wall-panels had alike turned black; dust festooned the pendants of crystal chandeliers; trailing cobwebs brushed your face where spiders had spun unmolested across doorways. No furniture remained except a little table, its marble top chipped and cracked, left behind in what might once have been a Creole salon.

They made a slow, careful circuit of the whole floor. One side looked down on Hospital Street, another on Royal Street; the windows of the third side showed a tangle of low roofs westwards; the fourth side, at the rear, had no windows except those giving on the inner courtyard. Though two or three times a rat scuttled across the floor, there seemed no other sign of life. And yet oppressiveness, an oppressiveness of the spirit, weighed down on these two intruders as they returned to the central hall.

"At risk of being called fanciful or superstitious," muttered Tom, "I don't like the *feel* of the damn place. But the atmosphere oughtn't to be so wrong, ought it? Since no violence was ever done here . . ."

"On one occasion at least, when the mob sacked and wrecked it in '34, there was an overdose of violence that may have left repercussions. I was wondering—"

"Yes; what's on *your* mind?"

"I was wondering," Macrae muttered back, "if somebody has been using the house as a kind of lair. But that can't be! We're leaving tracks in the dust, as you can see; and nothing else has left tracks except the rats."

"Wait!" Tom said suddenly. "There's a whole mess of scuffed tracks we didn't make! It leads . . . turn your light towards those stairs to the floor above! Yes, it heads there. That'll be the bedroom floor, and we'd better go up. Stir your stumps, can't you?"

Up the staircase, on the Royal Street side towards the front, they followed a double line of tracks, going and returning, which someone had made and then half-obliterated so that the footprints could never have been studied or measured.

The staircase, so solid that it did not creak, led to a cross-passage with doors to bedrooms at the front of the house. They were now on the topmost floor; the wrong atmosphere had become an oppressiveness you could almost have touched.

Macrae's legs felt light and shaky. Opposite the head of the stairs, beyond a wide-open door to the principal bedroom, momentarily he did not need the beam of the lantern to see smashed windows or silver-white wallpaper that had rotted and peeled down in strips from damp.

The windows went white with lightning; a shock of thunder smote across chimney-tops and rolled in tumbling echoes down the sky. With Tom following close at hand, Macrae marched pretty steadily into the bedroom and swept his light round.

"Found it, haven't we?" Tom whispered. "Look there!"

On a wall once silver and white, the south wall with the door to the passage, some crude drawing had been done with a stick of charcoal.

Under the initials H.R., behind what may have been intended to be the outline of a judge's bench, the judge in his black robe dangled by a rope round the neck from the sketch of a cross-beam above. To the right of this, under the initials G.S., was a kind of counter with stacks of coins piled high, and an immensely fat figure also neck-dangling from a second cross-beam. Both drawings might have been the work of a child. But both watchers knew no child had drawn them.

Tom's hacking whisper was barely audible.

"It's easy to draw a judge and a banker," he said. "All the same! If H. R. stands for Horace Rutherford and G. S. for George Stoneman, what's being conveyed beyond the suggested fate of both? Is G. S. already dead, or only threatened?"

"There's no way of telling."

"Dick, what time is it?"

Holding the lantern in his left hand, Macrae fished out his watch, opened it, then shut the case and replaced it.

"Ten minutes past eleven. But it really doesn't matter."

"Doesn't matter?"

"There'll be nobody here tonight, Tom. We were meant to find the drawings, that's all. Whoever did them made sure of doing the job early, avoided the risk of being caught, then left a trail that can't be followed and made off."

There was a pause. Then Tom spoke almost against his companion's ear.

"Dick, put out that light! Close the slide, you hear, and then stand perfectly still!"

The bedroom went pitch-dark. Macrae's return whisper was a mere breath of sound.

"All right; there you are. What's the game?"

"You're wrong, Dick. Somebody's here and following us. I heard him on the stairs just now, and I think he's outside the door."

"The 'he' may be a 'she,' you know."

"It's no woman, not with a tread like that. It's the damn joker come to gloat, but he won't gloat much longer. Stand perfectly still, I say, while I make for the door on tiptoe. I'll count to twenty and then charge."

"Tom, if you do something foolish . . ."

"This isn't foolish, it's the only proper course. Easy, now!"

"Tom—"

There was no reply. Darkness pressed down like an extinguisher-cap. The lantern, feeling as hot as though it contained fifty candles instead of one, Macrae juggled from one hand to the other. He himself commenced counting. Would Tom count slowly or quickly? Very quickly, in all likelihood. One, two, three, four, five, six . . .

He had not even reached seven when it happened.

Lightning opened a white eye at the windows. In that brief dazzle Macrae recognized, or half thought he recognized, the one standing outside the door. But it blinded the man with his back to the stairs. There was no time to warn Tom, who clearly had seen nothing and would have heeded no warning. Even the ear-splitting assault of the thunder, the cloudburst of rain that followed, could not blot out other sounds as the oak walking-stick smashed down on hat and head. A heavy body went over backwards and rolled downstairs, awaking tumultuous echoes from every corner.

Macrae, hurrying out into the passage, fumbled at the slide of the dark lantern and sent its beam up instead of down.

"I walloped him, didn't I?" roared Tom's triumphant voice. "We've got the murdering devil now! Put the glim on him, Dick; let's see who he is. And what do we do next?"

By this time Macrae hardly needed to look at the man who lay spread-eagled on his back at the foot of the stairs, breathing stertorously, the remnants of a shattered hat round bushy red sidewhiskers. But Macrae directed the light. When he addressed Tom, he himself could not tell whether his tone was indulgent or sardonic.

"Yes," he said. "Now that you have successfully walloped and knocked out the police-officer who has been following to give us protection, what *do* we do next?"

17

Sᴇʀɢᴇᴀɴᴛ ᴛɪᴍᴏᴛʜʏ ᴏ'sʜᴇᴀ, ᴘʀᴏᴘᴘᴇᴅ ᴜᴘ ɪɴ ᴀ sᴇᴀᴛᴇᴅ ᴘᴏsɪᴛɪᴏɴ against the wall of the central hall downstairs, raised somewhat rheumy eyes, lifted his fist, and addressed the invisible ceiling.

"Ah, now, bejasus," he begged, "and will ye give over, gentlemen? Will ye cease and desist, for the sweet saints' sake? I'm not mad; I'm not mad one bit! 'Twas an honest mistake, Mr. Clayton. So many mistakes have I made in me own life that it's glad I am o' the chanst to overlook yours. Besides! This twenty-dollar bill I find stuck mysteriouslike in me waistcoat pocket . . ."

"You won't call it attempted bribery, will you?" asked Tom.

"I will not, thank'ee kindly, sir, and I'm not too proud to accept it. It will much more than buy me the new hat I need, getting the hat smashed being a particular hazard o' this investigation. Mr. Macrae, sir! If ye *could* take the light out o' me eyes for just wan second . . . !"

Macrae turned the beam of the lantern away.

"It was the hat that saved you from concussion or worse," he said. "The hat got the main force of the blow before it struck your skull. But the time is close on midnight; it's taken us half an hour or more to bring you round. Mr. Clayton went out and bought the bottle of brandy you'll find in your side pocket . . ."

"Thank'ee kindly for that too, gentlemen! It's a great comfort!"

"And is what I've been suggesting the true explanation? That you followed us with some idea of offering protection?"

"Protection, is it? Now what protection would *you two* be need-

ing, saints preserve us? No, not that ezzactly. I met Mr. Clayton
this evening, as ye may have heard. He's a well-meaning gentleman, is Mr. Clayton; but of all God's crayturs he's not the crafti-
est or the most discrate. Says I to meself: 'Tim,' says I, 'there's
something up.' So, after I'd had supper and taken advice from Mr.
Benjamin, I stood in the street opposite Arnaud's until yez both
came out."

"Taken advice from Mr. Benjamin?" repeated Tom. "Is old
Benjie in this? Is *he* in it too?"

"He is that, sir; he's in up to his neck. And at the moment he's
no great distance from here; he'd be glad of a word wid yez both
before the night's over."

"We ought to have told him!" groaned the remorseful Tom,
knuckling his forehead. "We ought to have told him the whole
story this afternoon!"

Tom then gave a full account of their errand, beginning at its
inception the night before and ending with their discovery of the
drawings on the bedroom wall. Rain still drove at the roof-slates,
and at one place had found its way through; they could hear it
splashing somewhere upstairs. But the rain had slackened; it was
dying.

Sergeant O'Shea struggled to his feet and braced himself against
the wall.

"Now, sir!" he said. "Mr. Macrae was right: there'll be nobody
here tonight; 'twas the drawings they wanted ye to see. And reassure yourselves, both of yez! The president of the Planters' &
Southern Bank is a rare headstrong sort, with more pepper than
milk o' human kindness. But he's all right and he'll *be* all right,
glory be to God—spite of insisting, with all that weight he carries,
on doing repairs to his own house and not letting a naygur touch
it. So I'll just . . ."

"Sergeant," said Tom, "you took one hell of a knock; I can't
apologize often enough. If you'd like to take the same stick for a
return wallop at me and *my* hat, that's only fair and I stand
ready."

"I'm satisfied, sir, if you are. I'll just take a pull at the brandy
to recoop me energies . . . aah, that's better! . . . I'll go upstairs for

a look-see at the art masterpiece; and then . . ."

"But hadn't we better get you to a doctor?"

"Doctor, be hokey? Devil a doctor would Tim O'Shea be need-ing, that once went twenty rounds with the Bristol Smasher and lives to tell of it! And, no, Mr. Macrae, sir, I *don't* need the dark lantern; got some matches here that'll do me. Stay there, gentle-men; back in a moment!"

Shaky but indomitable, he struck a match as he mounted the stairs. It was barely half a minute before he returned, bottle again in hand and a benevolent look on his face.

"Arragh, now! The rain has stopped; the gig is outside. To play the game properly, be your leave, we'll wait until the town clocks strike midnight and give Papa Là-bas his chance to turn up. He won't turn up, bad cess to him! Then, having hoisted our colours and sailed without challenge, it's off to the senator we'll be."

"Where *is* Sir Oracle, by the way?" asked Tom.

"In an upstairs room at the Gem Saloon, t'other end o' Royal Street."

"Judah P. Benjamin? In a common saloon?"

" 'Tis no common saloon, begging your pardon. At the Gem, in January of '57, the honourable gentlemen of the Pickwick Club met to organize the Mistick Krewe of Comus and get up our first torchlight procession in carnival-time. So 'tis no bad place even for *him*. All day, ye may mind, he's been saying he wanted to find Mr. Barnaby Jeffers for the answer to a devilish important ques-tion?"

"Well?"

"He's seen Mr. Jeffers; he's found the answer; the answer may surprise ye. The night's not over yet; you'll see!"

A few minutes later, after the last stroke of twelve had died away from many steeples, they left the house without regret. Ser-geant O'Shea's gig had been left under the covered way to shield its horse from rain. There was just room for all three of them. Macrae, the dark lantern blown out and stowed away, sat on the outside with Tom in the middle as Sergeant O'Shea sent the vehi-cle spanking west along a flooded Royal Street.

Puddles steamed outside the gaslight of the Gem Saloon. The

three wayfarers descended. They were at the door of the main bar, Sergeant O'Shea leading, when they came face to face with Barnaby Jeffers and a tall, lean, saturnine man of Southern European aspect.

"Ah, sir!" Sergeant O'Shea greeted the former. "Saw you here some time ago, I seem to recall. Didn't know you'd stayed on."

"As a matter of fact, Sergeant," replied Mr. Jeffers, who was tipsy but carrying it fairly well, "I did not stay on. I visited several other places and dropped by again in passing on my way home." Adjusting his oblong spectacles, he indicated his companion. "Officer Fiala and I, having already made a day of it, are now doing the same with the night. I have taught him cribbage; he has taught me pinochle. At the first pastime I won from him a sum of money which he has more than won back at the second. Officer Fiala will remain with me, I trust, until the police have snared their quarry and set me free. And now, I think, a last bumper at the St. Charles Hotel. Then home to Second Street for more cribbage or more pinochle, as the mood may direct."

"Senator Benjamin still there, sir?" Sergeant O'Shea jerked his thumb upwards.

"He is still there; he seems rooted to the spot. Now good night, Sergeant; good night, Tom. And good night, Mr. Macrae; I wish you joy of the hand *you* have been dealt!"

Away went the historian towards Canal Street, with Officer Fiala at his side.

"Now what did he mean by that?" asked Macrae, as the sergeant led them through the downstairs bar. "Have I been dealt any particular sort of hand?"

"You have, sir, and in one way it's a beauty! Don't ask me, though; Senator Benjamin will tell you!"

Had there been a touch of glee in his manner? Ominous though the words sounded, Macrae did not comment or question further. At the rear of the bar-room a flight of steps ascended to a central passage through the house from back to front, with doors on either side.

The door of the front room on the right was open. At the doorway, hand on the knob and bending forward to address someone inside, stood a portly man in a dignified frock-coat, though with a bartender's curl on his forehead. He straightened up and stepped back as the three newcomers approached.

Gaslight sang thinly. In a room with rough-plastered walls, a low ceiling, a long table, and quite a number of chairs, Senator Benjamin sat in a cane-bottomed chair at the nearer narrow end of the table, on which he had built an elaborate card-house. The left-overs from two packs of cards lay scattered at his elbow. Also at his elbow stood a glass containing what remained of some brownish-coloured beverage.

Senator Benjamin, his eye twinkling, arose and bowed when first Tom Clayton, then Macrae, then a suddenly self-effacing Sergeant O'Shea went in to join him.

"The Sazerac cocktail," he announced, looking at Macrae and indicating the glass on the table. "I might say *the* original cocktail: brandy, sugar, and aromatic bitters well iced. Christened Sazerac from a favourite cognac manufactured by Messrs. Sazerac-de-Forge et Fils of Limoges in France, but invented decades ago by a Creole apothecary named Peychaud. —Mr. Daniels!"

The portly man with the bartender's curl marched in; he was introduced as Mr. John Daniels, one of the Gem's two proprietors. Again Senator Benjamin pointed to the glass.

"Might we have three more of those?" he asked. "No, better make it four; that one is almost gone. Might we have four more of those?"

"It'll be a pleasure, Senator! I'll send up one of the boys."

"Now, Mr. Daniels, concerning the gambler you were telling me about . . ."

"Nat Rumbold? The way these professionals carry on ashore," said Jack Daniels, shaking his head wisely, "ought to learn the rest of us a thing or two. They'll get off at New Orleans and lose to the faro-dealers every penny they've taken from mugs on the river-boats. It's not gamblin' losses on Nat Rumbold's mind, though."

"You think it's not?"

"I know it's not. Somebody broke his wrist for him. He's dead drunk and sleeping it off in one of the rooms up here; been swill-ing it down by the bucket since before noon today. It's not what we like or encourage; I've knowed him nasty drunk too. But he spends pretty freely and don't give much trouble, as a general thing. We'll *let* him sleep it off, I reckon."

"Might I speak to Mr. Rumbold, do you think?"

"Not if you want to get any sense outa him. Even when he *could* talk, all he'd say was that he's got to get back up-river by the *Governor Roman* tomorrow morning. That, or mumble some words about hair-dye. If you ask me . . ."

"Very well; we will let him sleep."

"Drinks coming up, Senator!"

And Jack Daniels withdrew, closing the door. Senator Benjamin addressed the others.

"Be seated; be comfortable. Though we are almost ready to close in on our quarry, as Barnaby Jeffers would put it, there is still much to be settled. Do I detect an aura of adventure about you, Sergeant O'Shea? Or about you, Tom? Or about you, Bonhomme Richard?"

"It might be called adventure," Macrae answered, "or it might be called by a name less polite. Tom said we should have told you the whole story this afternoon, and he's right. You had better hear it now."

Whereupon he gave his own version of what Tom had already poured out to the sergeant. He started with the challenge from Papa Là-bas and the dead snake on the desk, clear evidence of Voodoo work; he ended with the hat-breaking and near skull-breaking in the house of Delphine Lalaurie.

Senator Benjamin listened intently, smoothing his side-whisker.

"Every turn of this affair, I fear, has lacked the dignity that should be associated with high crime." He looked anxious. "But it ended well, at least? You're all right, Sergeant O'Shea?"

"I'm as right as rain, glory be!" said the sergeant, who had perched himself on the edge of the table without disturbing the card-house. "I'll accept the same any time, sir, at twenty dollars a whack and the bottle o' brandy I'll just take the liberty of sampling before the other drinks are served. Your permission, sir? Thank'ee!"

"I also, in my own way, have had a minor adventure."

"*You* have had an adventure, Senator?" asked Macrae. "We met Mr. Jeffers on our way in; he seemed to think you hadn't stirred from here all evening."

"He did not know. Let me see, now!" mused the lawyer, settling back in the chair and putting one finger at his temple. "I think, Sergeant, it was just on ten o'clock when you left here to take up your vigil opposite Arnaud's Restaurant? And Mr. Jeffers was still with me?"

"He was that, sir!"

"He left soon afterwards," said Senator Benjamin, "to sample the fruit of the vine elsewhere. When I had pondered deeply, one course or another, I did what it seemed to me I must do. I summoned a cab and was driven to the home of Marie Laveau, St. Ann Street."

Tom was simmering again.

"Marie Laveau, eh?" he echoed. "Yes, we're all in it now. Good for you, Sir Oracle; good for you every time! You wanted to put the fear of God into her?"

"On the contrary, Tom, I had no intention of putting the fear of God into anyone just yet. Against my will I visited those premises (what *would* clients say?) to question and to listen and to observe."

"Well, sir?"

"I did not see Marie the younger. After some difficulty with a mulatto girl who answered the door, I did succeed in meeting the famous mother, in my opinion much the more wily character of the two, who had hidden some documents in her chair just before I entered a little back room. She is no longer very pretty, but she showed both physical well-being and a mental agility quite astonishing.

"As a matter of fact, I hardly expected to see the daughter. When I was driving up there, I could have sworn I saw . . . never mind. I was there barely half an hour before I returned. The point is that we shall get little change out of Marie the elder, still a dominant personality for all her withered looks. Even when the trap is sprung and the deadfall snaps, she will tell the police only what it suits her to tell. She . . ."

A knock at the door made him pause; it was a waiter with four Sazerac cocktails. The waiter departed, and they were just lifting their glasses for a toast when Jules de Sancerre, wearing evening dress as the others were not, burst in with an air of some excitement.

"Then you received the message I sent by Michael?" asked Senator Benjamin. "I thought it only fair you should hear what I have to say."

Jules de Sancerre put down his hat at the far end of the table where the others had left theirs, with the exception of a police sergeant who had no hat.

"I got your message, yes," the little Creole replied, "but that's not the main reason I'm here." Then he burst out. "Tom, do you know where Margot went tonight?"

"Margot?" blurted Tom, spilling some of his cocktail. "For God's sake, sir, you're not saying she's disappeared again?"

"Not disappeared in the sense you mean. She did go out in spite of us, and nobody knows where or why."

"But she said she was staying in! After all the hullabaloo on Thursday night, Margot said, nothing would tempt her out of the house tonight. She had quite a conference with Ursula about it. Don't you remember, sir? Once she broke down and admitted to Sir Oracle there that she *was* acquainted with Marie Laveau's daughter . . ."

"Broke down and 'admitted' it?" raved Margot's father. "Broke down and *admitted* she knew the accursed woman? Egad, Tom, she boasted of it; she waved it like a banner! That's the trouble.

"I'm a patient man. I've got no objection to young people as long as they're only misbehaving themselves or doing what they oughtn't to do, which is perfectly right and natural. When they scare and infuriate me is when they think they have a principle to defend or a disinterested cause to argue. It ceases to be argument or debate; it becomes a holy crusade for which they will do battle in fury until the sun falls and the skies rain blood. They're like abolitionists; they're worse than abolitionists, if anybody can be worse. What do you say, Benjie?"

"I have little affinity with abolitionists, Jules. And yet, even though they take no active steps in the matter, the time may come when of our own accord we shall agree with them."

"Do I hear *you* saying slavery is wrong? *You?* Is Saul also among the prophets?"

"I do not say slavery is wrong, as I do not say owning any property is wrong. I say merely that it may cease to be economically sound."

"What are you talking about?"

"I myself was once part-owner of a sugar plantation down the river. You are a plantation-owner. So is General Ede; so are several of our friends. What I say may be true only of Louisiana. But consider:

"The work of your field-hands, particularly on the levee or in irrigation-ditches, is hard and dangerous. Many die or are incapacitated there; others die from yellowjack, cholera, snake-bite, and kindred ills we are all prey to. A good field-hand represents an investment of twelve to fifteen hundred dollars; lose him, and you lose your whole investment. If instead of using slaves you had hired the many Italian or Irish immigrants who for small pay are accustomed to labours far more dangerous, surely you would have found it cheaper in the long run?"

"Nonsense! Cotton is king; our position can't be challenged as long as there's cotton to be sold. I don't believe this 'economic' talk; I don't think you believe it either. A hard-headed fellow like you . . . !"

"My hard-headedness," said Senator Benjamin, "is notorious throughout the state. In my plantation-owning days I was hardheaded enough to sink half a fortune in an ice-making machine that never worked. I was also hard-headed enough to back a friend's note for sixty thousand dollars, and all but lost the plantation when he couldn't pay up. Let me stick to the practice of law, which I understand.

"And I wrestle so much with politics in the Senate, old friend, that I have sworn an oath not to tackle it outside those halls. We were not discussing politics, I may remind you. We were discussing your daughter and her idealization of the younger Marie Laveau, which subject . . ."

". . . which subject," supplied Jules de Sancerre, "has got me badly worried and sent her mother almost into hysterics again. Is *that* the reason she went out tonight? I don't like to think so, and yet I don't know what to think. She left before anybody knew she was gone, after assuring us all she meant to remain at home. Cicero's been forbidden to drive her anywhere. But she managed to persuade Hezekiah, who serves as deputy coachman. And away she went in that same accursed little carriage—the real carriage, not the dummy one—she's always been so fond of using."

"When did she go, sir?" asked Tom.

"About an hour after dinner, as far as we can determine. The Edes are in town, you know. My first notion was of sending some-one to Louisiana Avenue and asking whether Margot might be there, but her mother seemed to think . . ."

"The Edes aren't in town tonight, sir. They're dining some-where miles away, as Dick will tell you. Anyway, what's to be done now?"

Throughout Jules de Sancerre's recital Senator Benjamin had grown more and more grave.

"You bring disturbing news," he said, "especially since . . . well, no matter! In reply to Tom's query, there seems little enough we *can* do at the moment. Before you arrived, Jules, I was about to harangue them again. With the end of the case in sight, I was about to clear up one misunderstanding which should carry us a long way towards solving the central mystery. Can you bear to sit down and hear it?"

"Frankly, I can't even bear to sit down."

Jules de Sancerre caught up his hat and jammed it on. He bustled to the door, where for a moment he stood massaging his Louis Napoleon moustache and imperial.

"I am going somewhere," he added, "though for the life of me I can't decide where. That's a sad confession, eh, for one of mature years and would-be dignity? It has even been suggested that Margot herself, with her Voodoo ally, may have had some hand in all this deviltry."

"Now who suggested *that?*"

"Let's say," returned the other, "it emerged in one of those family conclaves at which everybody shouts and nobody thinks. It's more than disturbing; it's horrifying; but who can keep out a random thought? Shall I complain of my wife's vapours when I am no better? So I shall go: whether home or to Irish-town or to the devil hardly seems to matter. Good night."

The door closed after him.

Tom Clayton, swallowing what remained of the Sazerac cocktail at a gulp, pointed the empty glass at each man in turn.

"Several of us, this evening, have tried our wits at picturing a grotesque solution to this problem. I tried it; Dick tried it. Now Papa de Sancerre joins the club. *Margot* concerned in Voodoo persecution and in murder? Tell me, Dick: can you imagine anything more insane?"

"I should prefer, for a change," Macrae told him, "to imagine something sane. You, Senator, said you were about to clear up a misunderstanding which seems to have impeded our progress. Who has done the misunderstanding?"

"You have," answered Judah P. Benjamin.

"I have?"

"It was reasonable that you should misunderstand, but none the less undeniable that you did. My own knowledge of Voodoo tactics is patchy and incomplete. I needed Barnaby Jeffers's encyclopaedic information to draw on, and I drew on it. Now consider. This Voodoo persecution, or seeming persecution, to which you have been subjected for some time . . ."

" 'Seeming' persecution?"

"Yes. You may say, if you like, that one of the two Maries sent an agent or agents from afar to follow you, spy on you, and perform the various acts of which we have heard. But it is more probable that the agent or agents may be found in your own home. As servants you employ a married couple, usually referred to as Sam and Tibby. I believe their surname is Glapion. Is that correct?"

"It is."

"No very common patronymic. From my notes last night," up went Senator Benjamin's forefinger, "I read out the name of the man who for nearly thirty years was Marie Laveau the elder's husband *derrière l'église* until his death in the odour of sanctity on June 26th of 1855. His name was Christophe Glapion."

Macrae stared at the lawyer.

"Are you trying to tell me," he demanded, "that *Sam* and *Tibby* . . . ?"

"Sam most probably, with Tibby's knowledge but without her active complicity. Because Sam is totally uneducated, because he seems so hearty and carefree, don't underestimate him. You show the same shocked incredulity our friend de Sancerre showed when I suggested Voodoo influences in *his* house. And you are still misunderstanding."

"How am I misunderstanding?"

"You have not looked far enough for motive. When I asked you whether you were sure this force or presence was malignant, you indicated that you were very sure. And you countered with what seemed cogent questions. 'Suppose,' you said, 'you felt eyes boring into *your* back, heard footsteps that never materialized into a person, kept expecting something that never happened? How would *you* feel?' "

"Well?"

"I replied that I should feel exactly as you did, because under those circumstances I should have misunderstood too. May I state a hypothetical case?"

"Of course."

"Let us suppose," said Senator Benjamin, his eye far away, "let us suppose I have a client who possibly, just possibly, may be in some personal danger? To protect him, unknown to himself, I hire a bodyguard. This bodyguard is some innocent-appearing member of his own household. The bodyguard has instructions to keep an eye on my client, to follow him at times, to make sure no harm comes to him, and then, returning home, to become again the innocent servant the bodyguard appears to be.

"But what is my client apt to think? He won't know my motive or the bodyguard's. He will be conscious only of the probing eye, the following footstep, the presence that is sometimes there and sometimes absent. What *can* he feel but that he is the victim of malignant persecution? And yet, when he feels that, he will be wrong.

"This was the thought which occurred to me last night. I could not state it: I lacked knowledge; I must first draw on the great store of information which would be provided by Barnaby Jeffers. And he has told me what I wished to know."

Senator Benjamin put down his own glass and rose to his feet.

"All Voodoo influence, remember, is not used to curse or to destroy. It may be used to defend and to bless, though with a blessing given upside down. That is the way of those who worship the snake-god; it has been their way in your case.

"You may reassure yourself, sir. Your faithful servant, Sam, really is a faithful servant. But he took his directions from a certain house on St. Ann Street; he acted according to Voodoo pattern. In everything Sam did, with the possible assistance of Tibby, these people had no thought of being inimical to you. On the contrary, they were giving their own public sign that they wished you well and hoped for your protection. It was no warning to take care or look sharp lest harm befall. They were saying, in the only way they knew how, 'Let this man walk in the peace of Papa Là-bas, and may his house be blessed.' "

18

"THEY'VE WORKED FOR MY BEST INTERESTS IN EVERY-
thing, you say?"

"I believe I could so demonstrate. Don't forget the blessing
given upside down."

"It's not only the blessing," Macrae pointed out, "that seems to
be upside down. So does everything else."

"For instance?"

"It was a sign of *protection*, was it, when they threw a damn
great water-jar through the window of my office?"

Senator Benjamin took out his cigar-case.

"A jar of that type is sometimes used to catch rain-water in
courtyards, yes. According to Barnaby Jeffers, it is also a sacred
vessel at Voodoo rites. From it the high priestess drinks strange
concoctions; it may contain an alcoholic beverage or it may contain blood. The manner of its delivery to you may have been
crude, but then all Voodoo is crude; Sam could hardly have
walked in and solemnly handed it over. Since the point still seems
to perplex you . . ."

"I'm perplexed, right enough!"

Senator Benjamin bit off the end of a cigar, lighted it from a gas-
jet on the room's east wall, returned to his chair, settled back
luxuriously, and eyed the card-house on the table before turning
again to Macrae.

"Considering that I myself was present on Wednesday night,"
he resumed, "permit me to explain. Actually, what startled us so

much when that sacred vessel came crashing through the window? It was the coincidence that the young sailor had been telling his tale of the severed head: a tale which, with both windows closed, could not possibly have been overheard by someone standing in the middle of the courtyard to throw. If you still think the gesture was malign rather than benevolent, remember the two windows."

"The two windows?"

"If the jar had been thrown through the right-hand window, it might well have smashed the lamp on your desk and set the place afire. Since Sam chose the left-hand one, with no obstruction beyond it, what harm was done except the trumpery damage of a broken window?"

Macrae pondered.

"There's a kind of upside-down consistency about the business, let's admit. But surely there was malice and intimidation in the culminating act of leaving a dead snake on my desk Thursday night?"

"On the contrary! To these people the serpent is a religious symbol; it is *the* religious symbol. Voodoo being a perfectly genuine religion in their eyes, they would no more have used a snake for intimidation than any good Christian would have used a cross. They were still blessing you."

"I hope nobody will mind," interjected Tom Clayton, "if I add my own two cents' worth to the discussion. They weren't exactly blessing him, were they, when they left a card, written in French and signed Papa Là-bas, challenging him to go where we did go? Sam can speak French well enough, but he's quite illiterate. He didn't write *that*, did he?"

Again Senator Benjamin eyed the card-house.

"Of course not, Tom. Sam no more wrote that message than he wrote the one to Mr. Jeffers or the one to Sergeant O'Shea; he merely carried it to the consulate. All three were the work of the directing brain from St. Ann Street, who has adherents enough to leave cards all over the place.

"And was it a challenge? Again ask yourself what actually happened. You did not meet Papa Là-bas; you did not meet anyone. You found only a couple of crudely done charcoal drawings: one of Judge Rutherford, who is dead; and one of Mr. George Stoneman, who so far as we know is very much alive. Sergeant O'Shea! You did say, I think, that no harm has befallen Mr. Stoneman?"

"Ah, now!" grunted Sergeant O'Shea.

Getting up from the edge of the table, he sank into a cane-bottomed chair and, having long finished the cocktail, refreshed himself with another pull at the bottle.

"I said it, sir, and he is so! Leastways: he was in rare good health and rare bad temper, bedad, when I saw him just before dark, and he'd given over doing some repair-work that might 'a' hurt him without any evil craytur comin' near. You'd not think, wouldja, that a man as cantankerous as Mr. Stoneman would have four married sons: all livin' with him, all devoted to him, all hoverin' round him as if he was a statue of the Virgin? No evil craytur will get at him because no evil craytur could get near him!

"I've not said much, sir, though I've talked a hell of a lot, as me countrymen do. I've not said much about *your* plans, I mean, even when I joined these two gentlemen and came back wid 'em to the saloon. All I told Mr. Macrae was that what you learned from that history man—about the Voodoo people being on Mr. Macrae's side, helping and not hurting—was going to surprise him." He looked at Macrae. "And it surprised the daylights out of ye, sir, now didn't it?"

"Yes, it surprised me," a shaken man admitted. "But, even accepting these people's twisted logic, what do they think they're doing and why should they be doing it?

"Listen, Senator! There has been talk of 'protection,' as though for some reason I needed it. I've asked you before this why anyone should be harrying or persecuting me. Well, why should a Voodoo conspiracy be protecting me either? And protecting me from what?"

"Remember," said Senator Benjamin, smoking reflectively, "remember the unspoken message I suggested. 'May this man walk in the peace of Papa Là-bas, and may his house be blessed.'"

"Is that supposed to mean something? Does it have any bearing on the solution of the mystery?"

"It has the very greatest bearing, believe me. You don't see the answer to the single question of why they are protecting you?"

"I do not."

"And yet the answer stares us in the face. When we have reached a complete solution, you will quickly understand."

Once more Tom shouldered into the debate.

"'When we have reached a complete solution,'" he quoted. "I have reached a state of morbidity where I can see symbolism on all sides. Every few seconds, Sir Oracle, you will look over at that card-house on the table; you seem much too interested in it. Now there's a murderer among us, Sir Oracle . . ."

The oracle did not comment.

"And you—assisted by Sergeant O'Shea, who talks a lot without saying much—are out to trap him. But you don't seem happy about it. Does the card-house represent a plan of capture you've constructed, which the least touch or shake may send toppling?"

Senator Benjamin studied the card-house.

"It does not represent my own plan," he replied. "It does represent my adversary's."

"Your adversary's?"

"There's a murderer among us, as you say. With great cunning, with infinite patience, he has reared an edifice as elaborate and handsome as the card-house, but fully as fragile too. That is the trouble with most such schemes. They are too shaky for the amount of patience they require; the fragility remains even when it passes unnoticed and the culprit escapes.

"On such an edifice the murderer has gambled heavily, has gambled everything, has gambled his life. A Voodoo conspiracy is backing him to win. No, Tom, I am not happy about what I must do. This murderer, vicious to the core, deserves no mercy or pity. And yet I am not happy. As a man of humanitarian principles, or perhaps only of weak nerves . . ."

"Weak nerves, eh?" exploded Tom. "Weak nerves, for God's sake?"

"I fear so. You can't sympathize with that?"

"Can't sympathize? Hell's fire, Maestro, it's the thing I sympathize with most! My own nerves are jumping like a hooked fish;

they're in a state nobody could be proud of. Margot's gone out into the night; something tells me Marie Laveau the younger has also gone out; it's a very fair bet the two of 'em are together. I give you a last, God-awful vision of nightmare. The vision is of Marie Laveau *and* Margot, in Delphine Lalaurie's house, drawing designs in charcoal on a ruined wall. How do *you* like it, Dick? If Margot—"

He was not permitted to finish. After a discreet knock at the door, the door opened to admit portly Jack Daniels. In a subdued rush the proprietor made straight for Her Britannic Majesty's consul.

"Excuse me," he said, "but could you come downstairs and step outside for just one minute? It's a lady: a very handsome young lady in a little black closed carriage. She can't come in, naturally; but, being as she's so particular to see you . . ."

Macrae's wits were still spinning. Handsome young lady? Little black closed carriage?

"To see *me*?" he repeated. "Are you sure you've got the right man? Or the right name?"

"Your name's Macrae, ain't it, and we was introduced?"

"Yes, but . . ."

"My mother was Scotch; I wouldn't forget a Scotch name. Well?"

"You'd better go, Dick," Tom advised him. "It's Margot, all right! What she should want with you is anybody's guess. But take it easy; no false moves. This business is about as bad as it can get. With one murder on our hands already . . ."

"I myself," said Senator Benjamin, "am more concerned with the murder we have not yet heard of."

"Would it be Mr. Stoneman ye'd mean, sir?" cried Sergeant O'Shea. "You're not thinking *he's* kilt too?"

"Oh, no. The one I mean should be apparent; I have already given certain instructions." Senator Benjamin looked at Macrae. "But Tom is right; you had better go."

Macrae took up his hat and left at just short of a run.

The main bar downstairs had grown fairly crowded. A light mist hung in the street, blurring without veiling the outlines of several equipages, including Sergeant O'Shea's gig. The carriage he sought stood last in line, facing towards Canal Street, with a youngish coachman on the box. He had almost reached it, hand extended for the door, when he stopped short. This carriage's wheel-spokes were not painted red; they were painted brown and yellow.

Then inspiration came to him, and an exhilaration he could not suppress.

There was just enough light from the saloon. He saw the tawny hair, the soft gold-and-white complexion, the grey-blue eyes that were first lowered and then lifted as he opened the carriage door . . .

"Yes, it's me," said Ursula. "You're not very pleased to see me, are you? You look so dumbfounded that . . ."

"Of course I'm pleased to see you. But I *am* surprised. When they said a little black closed carriage, I thought . . . we all thought . . ."

"You thought it was Margot? Really and truly, though, almost everybody has a carriage like that; we own one too. Anyway, Margot's safe at home. I'm the shameless one this time."

"You're the what?"

"What I said. I've been following you for half the night. You and Tom were so horribly mysterious about this 'errand' that . . . and there's another reason too."

"Ursula, you're supposed to have been miles away at ex-Governor Somebody's. Since you do happen to be here, what about your family and how did you manage things?"

"I planned it with Margot before I left the de Sancerres' this afternoon. She's staying at home, having had enough gallivanting. We were due to leave for Governor Corliss's at half-past seven. Margot wrote a note, sending it over with one of the boys, that she *must* see me tonight on a matter vital to her future happiness. My father didn't like it at all, but he said we did owe a duty to our friends.

"The rest of them left in the *calèche découverte*; I borrowed this carriage and Eustace to drive me. You see: you said you wanted to be with me. Well, though I oughtn't to say this, I wanted to be with you. But I didn't get much of a chance. And I was a dreadful liar to my family, wasn't I? Are *you* going to be cross with me?"

"No, just the opposite. But . . ."

"I waited in Carondelet Street until you walked over to Arnaud's, where Tom joined you. After a while that Irish policeman drove up in his gig; he was waiting too, but I took good care he didn't see me. You and Tom left the restaurant; the Irishman followed you, and I followed him.

"Then I waited outside that dreadful house that's supposed to be haunted. The carriage protected me from the rain between a quarter past eleven and almost midnight. I begged poor Eustace to take shelter under the covered way where the Irishman had left his gig. Eustace wouldn't go a step nearer that house; he's wearing a waterproof, and said he didn't mind at all.

"There had been bumps and crashes from inside. Tom came out, and went back with a bottle of something he'd got down the road. I was frightened, not knowing what had happened. But I simply hadn't the courage to go inside . . ."

"And face the ghosts?"

"No; to face you and Tom. But it seemed to be all right. At a little past midnight the three of you left in the gig and came on here. So I waited again . . . it's been all waiting . . . until I felt I couldn't wait one minute longer, and sent a message by Eustace. It's been *all* waiting, as I say!"

Though in Ursula's presence Macrae felt as exuberant as a boy in his teens, he could not avoid certain responsibilities.

"There must be no more waiting," he told her. "Ursula, Margot is *not* at home tonight; there may be the very devil to pay. She went out about an hour after dinner, at whatever time that means. The general view seems to be that she's with Marie Laveau."

He told what he knew of Margot's second disappearance. Ursula did not seem either alarmed or disconcerted.

"Marie Laveau again? Well, Margot changed her mind about staying in tonight; she's forever changing her mind. She was so full of Marie Laveau I ought to have expected it! What do we do now?"

Macrae consulted his watch.

"We try to mend our fences," he said, "though it's a quarter to one in the morning; the damage has been done. I will leave a message for Tom that I have been called away. After which, despite hell, high water, and a military father on the war-path, I am escorting you safely home. This is the second night in a row it's happened; they'll be waiting up for you."

"But they won't be waiting up for me!"

"What makes you so sure of that?"

"Drive back in all that rain? They'd never have done it! They won't have left until after midnight; it'll be another hour at least before they're here. I can slip in before they arrive, and then send you home in this carriage. Yes, leave your message for Tom; I have some instructions for Eustace."

Macrae went back briefly to the Gem. He requested Mr. Daniels to convey his excuses to Tom Clayton, adding only that the girl who summoned him was not the girl both he and Tom had expected. Returning to Ursula after hardly more than a minute's absence, once more he ran full-tilt into the unexpected. The carriage, which had been facing west in Royal Street, was now turned round to face east.

He dragged open the door and swung himself up. Ursula, in a shimmering silvery gown, compressed its crinoline around her. There was just room for them to sit close together in those narrow confines, Ursula at his left side. The whip cracked and the carriage moved away as he began his protest.

"Ursula, what's going on here? This isn't the way to the Garden District; we're headed straight in the opposite direction! What are you up to now?"

"It's all right! There's loads of time!"

"If you insist. But why are we going in the wrong direction? What did you tell the coachman?"

"Before he starts for home, he's to drive along St. Ann Street past Marie Laveau's house. Everybody's heard of that place, and what's said to go on when they hold their rituals in the back yard. If Margot's there tonight . . ."

"It's never been suggested Margot's there: only that she went somewhere with the younger Marie."

"Yes, this daughter! Margot may think she's a wholly admirable character, but how can she be? If she's taken over her mother's part as high priestess, this stately, beautiful creature also does suggestive dances and drinks blood. Anyway, if Margot is there we'll know; the carriage will be there too."

"You don't want to visit the place, do you?"

"Good heavens, no! I wouldn't even dream of *stopping* there; I've shown what a coward I am! Can you tell me what happened to you and Tom at the haunted house tonight, or is that still a secret?"

"No, it's no secret."

So he told her in full as the carriage rattled on. A strange look had come into Ursula's eyes.

"Tom's awfully impetuous, isn't he? I sometimes wish . . . !"

"You wish what?"

"It doesn't matter. All three of you, you and Tom and the sergeant with the bump on his head, went to the Gem and met Mr. Benjamin. And *he* thinks—?"

Macrae gave her a fairly complete if discreetly edited account of what had been said in the upstairs room. The carriage turned left into St. Ann Street as he began; it was nearing the intersection of Burgundy Street before he had finished.

"They're closing in, Ursula; the sergeant and Sir Oracle are closing in. But who's their quarry? If they've given any indication of that, I've been too dense to see it."

"Dense?" Ursula breathed. "*You* dense? Oh, Quentin, you're the cleverest one of them all! Think of the Washington and American Ballroom, and how you reasoned it out about me and everything else!"

"That was only because it concerned you. The rest of the business—"

He stopped. Ursula had seized his left arm with her own left hand, and was pointing out of the window.

"There it is!" she whispered. "Across the street on the left. There's Marie Laveau's house now!"

Already driving at a careful rate through slight mist on streets mired from rain, Eustace had slowed the horse to a walk. Macrae followed the direction of Ursula's pointing finger.

Slatternly and weatherboarded, painted a dingy white, the cottage had above its ground floor a peaked roof which might have hidden upstairs rooms just high enough to stand up in. The whole place was dark except for one place on the cottage's right-hand side towards the back. Yellowish light struggled out into mist through a window only partly curtained.

"There seems to be a fair-sized plot of ground at the back," Ursula was whispering. "But no carriage is there. And you couldn't take a carriage *into* the yard; there's only that gate in the picket fence. Margot's not here. We can go on and . . ."

Macrae had lowered the window of the carriage on his side, and put his head out to speak to the driver.

"Stop!" he called. "Pull over there and stop!"

Obediently they swung to the left through mud. Ursula looked at him as he sat down again.

"*You* want to stop?"

"Just for a moment. Evidence!"

"What evidence?"

"Senator Benjamin saw Marie the elder in a little back room. When a sailor named Jack Dowser met Marie the younger, she emerged from a back room, on the right-hand side of the house, with a curtain over the door. You see the light in that window?"

"I—I see the light. But I don't follow you at all!"

"Your instincts have been right, though. Marie the younger or Marie the elder, perhaps both, will have a good deal to answer for. They may not have committed murder, but they've been backing the murderer to win. If they choose to deny everything, as they will, it's hard to see how their complicity could be proved in court. And yet it's possible—not probable, but just possible—that *some* bit of evidence can be found.

"I am getting out, my dear, for a look through that window. Stay here; don't move, but don't be alarmed either. I shall be gone only a minute or two."

"You'll be careful, won't you?" Ursula pleaded. "You *will* be careful? If the Voodoo Queen has as many secret disciples as Mr.

Benjamin told us she has . . . !"

"Yes, I will be careful."

To avoid stepping on Ursula's skirt, he descended from the carriage on his side and went round the back of it.

A little broken gate sagged open in the white picket fence. Beyond the gate a brick path stretched through a wilderness of mud to the front door, after which it branched to the right and continued round the side of the cottage. Though very wet, it was at least not slippery to walk on.

There seemed no sign of life anywhere. He followed the path to the side from which the one light gleamed out. Was it Ursula's warning or some atavistic instinct of his own that made him walk warily, loosening his shoulders as though in preparation to meet attack?

Or, the thought occurred to him, could Voodoo magical ceremonies practised here, even sham magic of barbaric crudity, have left strong emotional residue that breathed from the earth even when no torches were lit, no drums throbbed, no stamp of bamboula dance inflamed the night?

Where *were* such rites performed? In the back yard, more than one person had said. The thin white mist, clammy of touch, varied its density from one point to another. At the rear of the cottage, where a semicircle of stunted trees lifted their foliage as though guarding this side of the ring, the mist, thick and opaque, shifted like greyish smoke.

Here it did not even impede sight. The sill of the lighted window, now less than a dozen feet away, was at about the level of Macrae's chest. Loose, ill-fitting, with a number of oblong panes rather than one clear-glass sheet, it seemed a large window for so small a cottage. Coarse curtains had been less than halfway closed. For the moment disregarding caution, Macrae strode to the window and peered inside.

19

"Somebody has been careless," he said aloud.

The little room was empty.

It had the air of a back parlour, full of cheap, gaudy furniture and not over-clean. There was a table just underneath the window. An oil lamp with a yellow-glass shade burned on a round table in the middle of the room, beside which had been drawn up an old armchair whose cushion partly disguised its sagging seat. From underneath the cushion projected paper-edges, as though documents had been hastily thrust out of sight by someone who no longer sat there. One such edge resembled roughish paper of the sort used for commercial telegrams; the rest might have been notepaper of any kind.

In the wall opposite the window there was a flimsy door with an iron latch. By craning his neck to the left Macrae could see, beside the fireplace of a brick chimney-stack upreared through the east wall, a brown curtain covering the doorway to a front room.

They had made one effort at painful respectability. On the grubby wall beside the door opposite the window, a religious picture in garish colours showed Abraham about to sacrifice Isaac. But a little clay model of a snake lay on the centre table under the lamp. And always Macrae's gaze returned to the table beneath the window, to the objects he had seen at his first glance.

A little pile of white cards, perhaps three inches long by two inches wide. An inkstand brimming with its black contents. And a pen with a very fine nib. Yes, somebody *had* been careless. But . . .

Macrae stiffened and drew back.

The iron latch of the door opposite the window had lifted; the door was moving. When it did open, which of them would he see? A withered but still mentally agile elder Marie, who customarily occupied the sagging armchair? Or the younger Marie in her beauty and impassiveness, as he had seen her in the courtyard of the consulate that morning?

He never learned.

"If the Voodoo Queen has as many secret disciples as Mr. Benjamin says she has . . ."

The memory of those words may have tapped a warning to his brain. It may have been some noise in the mist at the rear of the cottage. As he whirled round to the right, retreating a step or two the way he had come, rage and hatred flew at him like an arrow released.

The wiry mulatto youth, nineteen or twenty years old, charged out of mist and along the brick path. He wore tattered clothes and some kind of sandals. His mouth was pulled square with fury. Then Macrae caught the glint of the knife; his own wrath kindled too.

Through his head flashed the Sicilian's advice to those who would use steel: "Your thumb on the blade, and strike upwards!" If the mulatto youth had done that, his adversary might have been a dead man.

But the boy did not do it. His right arm had whirled up and back; he was too intent to stab blindly for the neck.

Macrae's left hand seized the wrist and wrenched. His right forearm went up under the other's chin; the heel of his right foot hooked behind his opponent's left. The knife tinkled down on bricks. The youth, already off balance, was toppling when Macrae caught him in a Cornish wrestling-grip he had not used since his days at Oxford.

The youth, who had been trying to speak past bubbling rage, gasped out six or seven words in French.

"Who are you?" he blurted. And, "What do you want?"

Still they swayed for a moment before Macrae, now as enraged as the boy, with a powerful heave of both shoulders lifted into the air the body of an opponent suddenly gone rigid with terror.

Macrae shouted back in French.

"Here," he said, "is a return gift for the sacred vessel they threw at me!"

And he flung the mulatto youth head-first through the parlour window.

The crash of glass exploded in a quiet night; its remaining fragments clattered down. Though Macrae's attacker pitched beyond the table under the window, the instep of one foot caught briefly between table and wall. The table went over too, bringing down cards, pen, and inkstand in a gush of black liquid across the floor.

There was still nobody in the parlour except the entrant who had landed there face down. Dazed and shaken but apparently unhurt, not even cut by the glass, he picked himself up and made in haste for the door. His late antagonist did not wait to see him open it.

For a full minute, drawn well back from the light, Macrae stood facing the back yard in challenge should other attackers appear out of the mist. Nobody did appear; nothing had been disturbed except a barking dog in some nearby yard. Macrae gave it a little longer. Then, his pulses having slowed but still hammering, he returned and joined Ursula in the carriage.

No sooner had he sat down, slamming the door, than the whip cracked and the carriage rattled away towards Rampart Street.

"It's all right!" Ursula said. "I told Eustace; we're on the way home." She hesitated. "All that noise back there . . ."

The window on Ursula's side had been lowered; she raised and closed it. Far from being fearful or shaken, she seemed in a very different mood. The firefly gleam of a carriage-lantern touched heightened colour in her face; it was as though she had been through an emotional experience too.

"He came at you with a knife, didn't he?" she asked. "I couldn't see it, but I heard everything. He came at you with a knife; you made him drop it; I heard the knife fall. Then I heard what you did, and what you said when you did it!"

"Since you also heard my earlier report," he told her, "you

know that for some reason these Voodoo Queens are supposed to be protecting me. I can now claim I am protecting them in the same way by chucking one of the company through Marie La-veau's window. The plain truth, Ursula, is that I lost my temper and my head."

"But I'm glad you did! Oh, I'm so glad! You seem so very quiet, and yet you're not quiet at all. You should lose your head more often! And you're not really sorry you did that, are you?"

Macrae's pulses were still hammering.

"No, I'm not. Beyond doubt I ought to be, but actually I'm not sorry at all."

"Did you find the evidence you were looking for?"

"That room is Papa Là-bas's workshop. There are cards for the messages; there's ink; there's the right sort of pen. Those things could hardly have been on display when Senator Benjamin visited the place earlier tonight or he'd have mentioned them. They'll soon be hidden away again, if only in process of cleaning up the mess. I don't know whether it's any good just to testify I've *seen* the stuff."

"Did you see Marie Laveau, either of the two?"

"I didn't see a living soul except the young fellow with the knife. Someone else started to come in, but thought better of it. Speaking of evidence, Sir Oracle did mention some 'documents' Marie the elder had been hiding in her chair. I noticed the edges of those papers under a pillow in an armchair. They must have a meaning, since our amateur detective laid stress on them. What meaning they have seems as obscure as everything else."

"But you're not harmed; you're safe and sound; *that's* the point!"

"No, Ursula, it is not the point. The whole point and the whole trouble . . ."

He fell silent, brooding, for a long time. The carriage clattered along Rampart Street to Canal Street, crossed, and followed the latter thoroughfare south until the St. Charles district loomed up. Then, turning off to the right, they were on exactly the same course they had pursued in an open carriage some hours earlier the previous night.

Consulting his watch by the light of a match, he found it was past one in the morning. The whole downtown St. Charles neighbourhood was dead and dark except for lights burning in some business premises on the ground floor underneath the St. Charles Hotel: to be exact, the office of the Grand Bayou Steamboat Line.

"And only this morning," he said bitterly, "I thought I might beat Judah Benjamin to a solution!"

"You may do it yet, you know!"

"I will not do it; it's a vain hope; I am not even sure I want to do it. To achieve a complete solution, every irrational puzzle-bit must fit into a coherent pattern. Which is what it won't do so far.

"I am almost tempted to adopt the theory that the guilty person *is* our mysterious and elusive Steve White, Rosette Leblanc's son. This is more than indicated by two charcoal drawings on a wall. The actual death of Judge Rutherford, the overweening implied threat to George Stoneman. And yet . . . oh, never mind! There are better things to think about!"

"What things?"

He did not answer. But he let his mind dwell on those better things.

Yes, it was the same route they had followed on Thursday night: out towards the Garden District, with the carriage swaying and the dark streets slipping past. He was even closer to her now.

"Ursula, do you remember the first night we met? In February, when you ran away from somebody's masquerade?"

"Of c-course I remember! Why do you ask that?"

"This time, serenely and sedately, we are headed for your house to take you home. Where exactly is your house? You said it's fairly close to the de Sancerres', I think?"

"It's fairly close as distances go, yes. But it's some way further on. It's St. Charles Avenue and Louisiana Avenue, the very fringe of the district out in the country."

"You left somebody's masquerade. You hailed a cab and told the cabby to drive anywhere. When he drove you towards town, and must even have taken you there, he was carrying you in the opposite direction *away* from your home, so that at the end of it you had to turn round and go back again?"

"I was upset; I was not myself; I couldn't think. Yes! The Hendersons' house, where they held the masquerade, is closer to town than ours is. Wh-what *is* all this?"

"You will see presently. Eustace has quickened the pace; he knows he is going home. In some minutes, Ursula, we shall be passing the spot where we first met. We can't put up a plaque or dedicate a drinking-fountain; no local historian would consider the place or the occasion as important as I consider it. And yet it seems fitting that it should be commemorated in some way."

"Commemorated?"

"Yes. The high gods spun a comedy that night; the real became topsy-turvy and the topsy-turvy became real. As for the place we met . . .

"Well, there it is!" he added presently, after both of them had fidgeted in silence for some time. "Look out of the window. It's on the other side of the road, but there it is. The old Cavendish house, I think you called it. It was lighted that night. And by the living jingo, as somebody says in *The Vicar of Wakefield*, for some reason it's lighted tonight! Possibly the people who live there now know the importance of the occasion, and they're commemorating it for us."

"What *are* you talking about?"

"You know, don't you? Outside that house, on the night of February sixteenth, I jumped into a cab going towards town. And you, fearing I would take advantage of you, ordered me out."

"I've already explained—!"

"That night you were upset; you were not yourself. Are you yourself tonight?"

"Oh, never more so!"

"You have called me quiet-seeming but not quiet at all. 'Quiet,' Ursula, is the word most often used to describe you. Is it a true word, an accurate word? Or would some other word be better after all?"

Though the lights might be across the road, their glow reached the interior of the carriage. Never had he been so conscious of her nearness: of the supple body in the silvery gown, of the eyes lifted and searching his face.

"And surely," she whispered, "surely *you* know the answer to *that?*"

Then he had her in his arms, holding her tightly against him, kissing an open mouth whose response was as instant and as intense as the pressure of her arms round his neck. Nobody spoke during the chaotic interval before, so to express it, they disengaged themselves without letting go.

"If I know the answer to that, Ursula, I am the owner of everything on earth. I love you, you saintly little devil and sugar-candy witch! I love you completely, blindly, and to very near a point of idiocy."

"I do so hope you mean that," Ursula whispered back, as they gripped each other again. "It's the way I feel about you, only more so, as I make painfully clear every time we meet. Yes, you may be almost as far gone as I am. You called me 'my dear' and didn't even realize you'd said it."

"Then I must go on so calling you. Do you believe in long engagements, my dear? What are you thinking?"

"If I told people in general what I'm thinking now," said Ursula, releasing herself for an instant, "they'd call me a shameless hussy and they'd probably be right. Go on; kiss me; never stop! As I told you last night, don't be afraid of carrying *anything* too far! Oh, Quentin . . . !"

With talk no more intelligent (but no less human) than the foregoing, with the conviction—and who shall say they were wrong?—that they had found a kind of immortality, these two grew lost to the world for some ten minutes, until the coachman rapped on the roof with the handle of his whip.

"Much though I hate it," Ursula whispered, "I've got to get home *some* time, and I think we're almost there. It *is* in the wilds, isn't it?"

Still in his arms, she leaned across him to lower the right-hand window. Together they put out their heads.

The sky had cleared; the edge of a setting moon shed diffused silvery light. Mist no longer breathed from the ground. On the right, just before the intersection of Louisiana Avenue, a gravel drive past open iron gates sloped for some distance and rather steeply to the pillared red-brick house atop a slight hill. The carriage turned in and climbed.

"I hope I haven't rumpled you too much, Ursula. Those dresses tear very easily, it's said."

"Oh, what could it *matter* how much you rumple me? Evening gowns do tear easily, as a general thing. But this one's of sterner stuff; I don't think it's torn at all."

"Ursula, look there! That carriage beside the portico! If your family has got here ahead of us . . ."

"But they haven't! Darling, look at the *carriage!* You'll see it better when we get closer. It's like this one; it's *just* like this one! And I think it's got red wheels."

"Margot?"

"Probably."

"Seeking sanctuary?"

"Maybe, though that's not like her. When we get there, Eustace," Ursula called upwards, "you're not to put anything away. Turn around in the drive; in a minute or two you'll be taking Mr. Macrae back to Carondelet Street." She swung back to the gentleman in question. "There's somebody getting *out* of the carriage. And it's not Margot; it's not tall enough for Margot. It's Aunt Isabelle!"

"That's Cicero on the box, surely? Yes; what are we thinking of? There are two such carriages: the real one, and the duplicate just like it except for the hiding-place under the seat. Margot took the real one. It's her mother in the duplicate, though what she's doing here at this hour of the morning . . ."

It was in fact Isabelle de Sancerre, the Empress Eugénie shawl over her shoulders. She had descended before a dark house, and stood awaiting them in the glow of one carriage-lantern.

Eustace pulled up. Retrieving his hat from the floor, Macrae, himself somewhat rumpled from Ursula's attentions, got down and assisted her to alight. Ursula, though with curls all awry, seemed as much a model of poise and propriety as though the evening were just beginning instead of ending.

Isabelle de Sancerre began on a note of grievance.

"I *told* Jules it was no use looking for Margot here," she said. "I told him that hours ago, before he went rushing away to meet Judah Benjamin at some drinking-den in the *Vieux Carré*. But, when Vivienne Stoneman, George Stoneman Junior's wife, dropped by on her way to fetch Dr. Andrews, and told us what happened to poor George Senior . . ."

Trouble wheeled back again like a vulture.

"Mr. Stoneman, the banker?" Macrae demanded. "Is he dead?"

"Dead? Mercy on us, of course he's not dead! Physically, he's not even hurt. It's an incredible story, absolutely incredible. Vivienne said she could almost have laughed, if it hadn't been so horribly serious. And he might have been killed; he should have been killed! The shock to the poor man's nervous system . . ."

"Forgive me, Madame de Sancerre, but what happened and when did it happen? He was all right when Sergeant O'Shea saw him just before dark."

"And he'd still be all right, Mr. Macrae, if he hadn't been so stubborn and pig-headed about the roof. George weighs two hundred and fifty pounds; you'd never *dream* he had so much strength in his arms and shoulders!"

"Aunt Isabelle," stuck in Ursula, "will you please just tell us what *happened*?"

"I've been trying to, only you keep interrupting. It was the roof, didn't I say so?"

"What about the roof?"

"He *would* insist on fixing the tiles himself, when the house is higher than ours or yours either. He went out through a dormer window; God knows how he balanced himself on the slope, but he did. And there were the four sons and their four wives, all watching him from one point or another, and crying out, 'Father, do be careful!' until George swore he'd disinherit the next person who said a word."

Isabelle de Sancerre made a dramatic gesture.

"Well! He did that from the time he got home from the bank until it was beginning to get dark. Then, for the moment, he stopped. As they were all sitting down to dinner, he said, 'That roof's not finished; I will finish it later this evening.' They all told him he couldn't work in the dark. They begged him, if he insisted on such antics, to wait until tomorrow, Saturday, because the bank would close at noon.

"George only snarled at them. 'I can't work in the dark, can't I? Light half a dozen kerosene lamps; have a boy stick 'em out on various parts of the roof where I'm going to work. I said the job would be finished today; and, by the Lord God Jehovah, it will be.'

"They warned him it was going to rain, but would he pay any attention to that? It was almost a quarter to eleven when he climbed out again with the lamps burning. Three of the sons and their wives were watching from the ground. Only George Junior and Vivienne had their heads out of a dormer window up there. And nobody *dared* to speak."

"Then we gather he didn't finish the job after all?" asked Macrae.

"But he did finish it, all but one tile! That's one miracle among other miracles. It happened about a quarter after eleven, with thunder and lightning going, though nobody's sure what did happen.

"He was working down near the edge of the roof, about twenty feet from the back of the house. His tool-box, which had been slung on a strap around his neck, was balanced on the iron gutter. George Junior and Vivienne were watching from the dormer window. But nobody else saw him at that height. Though at the back of the house near the gutter-edge there's a big maple tree that some stable-boys wanted to climb so *they* could watch, Arthur Stoneman wouldn't let them do it.

"Vivienne and young George could see Father clearly, although the light might have been better. All of a sudden, alone there, bending over with nobody near him, he slipped or stumbled. His foot kicked the tool-box, which went over the edge and down fifty feet on to gravel. George fell forward against the tiles. His feet slid over the edge; most of *him* slipped over the edge, until he grabbed the gutter with both hands and hung there. And, just before he did that, the storm burst and the rain came down.

"Well . . .

"On the ground," continued Isabelle de Sancerre, who seemed almost rapt, "there was a good deal of scurrying to fetch a ladder. At first the boys couldn't find a ladder; you know what boys are. It must have been a good fifteen minutes, Vivienne says, before they propped one up against the house.

"The rain was torrential. It put out the lamps and drenched George; he might have been struck by lightning at any time. But still he hung there, an elderly banker with all that weight, and *wouldn't* let go."

"What happened finally, Madame de Sancerre?"

"They got the ladder against the house. George climbed down under his own strength, saying he was all right and complaining only of a slight pain in his left side. But it was no pain in the side. It was the horrible nervous effect of thinking back to what *might* have occurred. He collapsed of it as he was changing into dry clothes, and before they could even ask him how he came to fall. After they put him to bed, Vivienne Stoneman went for Dr. Andrews at around midnight. On her way past our house she stopped to tell me about it, before some grotesquely distorted version should become current. George is all right; I have had a note from her since then. But I think you are aware, Mr. Macrae, how worried we have been about Margot?"

"Yes. Your husband was at the Gem for a short time, also at shortly past midnight."

"From there Jules came straight home; he said he had seen you. I had been pacing the floor and wondering, pacing the floor and wondering. After which," and Isabelle de Sancerre turned out her wrist, "Jules and I thrashed over the same old matters in the same old circle."

"Did you arrive at any conclusion?"

"Was it likely we should?"

"No; but—"

"I had already told Jules it would be useless to seek Margot at Ursula's. However, as more and more time passed into eternity, I myself began to wonder. At long last I decided it might be worth a try. Jules offered to go; I packed him off to bed with a hot toddy. I called Cicero, who had driven Jules, and bade him make ready the duplicate carriage of Margot's most unamusing hoax.

"And really, Ursula dear, what do I find when I get here? A house as lightless and deserted as a hut in the forest! I arrived prepared to offer my excuses for calling at so unearthly an hour. And to whom can I offer those excuses? Only to you and your escort, who, with an air which means much to the eye of experience, arrive even later than I do.

"I won't ask where you have been tonight, Ursula. I have no right, and by this time I am afraid to ask that question of anyone. Revising an earlier opinion of you, I am now inclined to suspect that at defying your own nearest and dearest you are as bad as or worse than Margot herself. But there is one saving grace. When you outrage convention or spurn your elders' advice, at least you do so in the company of a man as reliable and responsible as Mr. Macrae." She looked at him. "Have you any comment, sir?"

"I can't say whether I am a reliable or responsible man, Madame de Sancerre. I do know I am a very happy one."

"Happy?"

"It has been a night of alarms and excursions. But that's finished now, or I hope it's finished. The clouds divided, the sun shone out—in short, all became gas and gaiters—as soon as Ursula and I reached an understanding. Since I asked her to marry me . . ."

Ursula reared up. "You never asked me!"

"Well, will you?"

"Yes!"

"Then that's settled. What I like about the present generation," murmured Isabelle de Sancerre, with a kind of luxuriance between benignancy and cynicism, "is their disposition to shout tender utterances at each other as though they were hurling insults over a back fence. Whatever else my husband may say of me, I have not lost my sense of humour." Her tone changed. "Are *you* happy, Ursula?"

"I'm sorry, Aunt Isabelle, but I can't help it: I'm wonderfully happy!"

"Never apologize for that, Ursula; I beg of you, never apologize for *that!* Cherish happiness, thank your stars for happiness. One day soon, I hope and believe, Margot will be happy too."

Then Margot's mother appraised them both.

"Take good care of Ursula, Mr. Macrae. She is a sweet girl, though she must be indulged in some foibles. I warned you, I think, that she reads too much; she dreams too much . . ."

"About the wrong things, Aunt Isabelle?"

"Oh, not necessarily the wrong things," said the other woman, answering Ursula but addressing Macrae. "And that reminds me. My husband, as you may be aware, is fond of meeting and taking up with extraordinary characters, whom he brings home for my delectation or the reverse. The latest acquisition, some days ago, was a young river-pilot named Clemens or Clements: Sam Clements. Young Clements, though a little too brash, was most amusing. He spent a whole evening arguing that the novels of Sir Walter Scott have been the curse of the South, infecting us with grandiose notions of a chivalric code no society could possibly carry out in practice.

"Ursula, I must warn you, is passionately addicted to Scott's novels, in particular those of exaggerated romanticism. *Ivanhoe, The Talisman, Quentin Durward* . . . Now why, Mr. Macrae, do you wear so strange an expression when I mention *Quentin Durward?*"

"It was not a strange expression, Madame de Sancerre. It was merely . . ."

"And you, Ursula! What are *you* looking at down there?"

Ursula, at the moment, did not seem to be looking at anything 'down there.' Eustace had turned the carriage round so that its horse's head now pointed towards the front gates; he was bending down while Ursula stood on tiptoe and whispered to him. Then she plucked at Macrae's arm and drew him apart out of earshot.

"Please," she whispered with desperate urgency, "will you do me a very great favour?"

"Ursula my sweet, will you do *me* a favour? Whatever you do, don't mention this 'Quentin' business to Tom Clayton. He'd think it was the funniest joke in the world; he'd never let me hear the end of it. 'Good morning, Rob Roy, and how are all the Clan Macgregor today?' "

"Please, please, this is *serious!* I must say good night in a moment. Meanwhile, there's something very, *very* private I must tell Aunt Isabelle. Will you get into the carriage and wait there until I tap on the window? *Will you?*"

"For you, Ursula, I would wait in the Black Hole of Calcutta or in hell. Here goes."

And then it happened.

No sooner had he climbed inside, without even the opportunity to close the door or sit down, than he realized that Ursula, in all loving kindness and with the best intentions, had committed an act of treachery.

Eustace made the whip whistle with real intent to sting. The horse bolted, flinging Macrae against the forward panel and crushing his hat. It plunged downhill like a thoroughbred released, dragging the carriage at an ever-increasing speed. The right-hand door was jarred shut. The passenger, thrown first back against the seat and then against the left-hand door, managed to lower the window and put his head out.

"What the hell do you think you're doing?" he yelled to the driver. "Stop!"

"—orduhs take you home. Yo' bein' *tuck* home! Jump now, jump enatime, yo' break yo' naick!"

That was when Macrae saw what Ursula must have seen in St. Charles Avenue.

Up the drive, at a speed not matching that of the little carriage but at a very fair pace, came a *calèche découverte* with two mired horses and five passengers. The passengers, four women and a man, had the bedraggled appearance of those who some time ago have passed through at least part of a thunderstorm.

Two ladies sat with their backs to the driver. Two other ladies faced them. Between the latter two, standing up as though to encourage Walter on the box, towered a gentleman of Homeric proportions, his right fist lifted high. Even the thunderstorm had not much reduced the bristle of his formidable grey moustache.

If this was what Ursula wanted, she must have her way. Macrae sat down, putting aside his crushed hat. Before the little carriage bucketed out into St. Charles Avenue, the *calèche découverte* had stopped at the house's portico.

He was too far away to see anything. But in the night's quiet he could not help hearing, and remembering, a powerful voice.

"*Ursula*," the voice thundered, "*who was that man?*"

20

How long he had been dreaming he could never afterwards have said. It was only the very end of the dream he remembered, and even that for no more than a second or two.

It seemed to him that he had been trying to reach Ursula across some shadowy, undefined waste of ground, and that all would be well if he could touch her outstretched hand. But always faceless beings, evil of intent, interfered to impede him and hold him back. One of these beings held a knife, another a derringer pistol; still a third wore pirate's costume with skull and bones on the hat. He was fighting his way past these when the enemies became Voodoo shapes of nightmare, stamping in a bamboula dance or drinking blood from a dark-brown jar. Macrae reached Ursula, touched her hand, and experienced the shock of waking.

He was in his own bed in his own bedroom at the consulate. Through the windows streamed the morning sun of Saturday, April seventeenth. Stout Tibby, her red bandanna round her head, had just drawn back the bed-curtains and put down a tray with teapot, milk-jug, cup, and saucer on the table at the bed's head.

"Morning, Mr. Richard. It's eight o'clock."

"Tibby!"

"Sir?"

Macrae cleared his throat. Propping himself on one elbow, he poured the first steaming cup of tea and added milk; he took no sugar.

"This may not be the proper time to tell you what I propose to tell you. But I had better mention it while a dream keeps it fresh in mind. I understand, Tibby, it was you and Sam—or, rather, Sam with your connivance—who favoured me with those delicate reminders of Voodoo power: sacred drinking-vessels, dead snakes, and so on. Do I make myself clear?"

"Oh, my God!" blurted Tibby.

She retreated, flapping her arms, and did not even attempt denial.

"I swear to the Good Man, Mr. Richard, it wasn't anything against you! I told Sam it was wrong; I told him that! *He* meant no harm either, and only did what they told him he had to. He's ignorant, Mr. Richard; never had a day's schoolin' in his life. But he's *just* ignorant; he's not ornery or a bad actor. You've been too good to us for Sam to act up, or me either. And yet we did do it! And now you'll fire both of us, I expect?"

"No, Tibby, I am not going to give you the sack. You have both served a stranger too well for me to stand on outraged dignity or waste time with preaching. Let there be no more of this; I will say no more either. Is *that* clear?"

"God bless you, sir, and we'll see you don't regret it! And Mr. Clayton's here already, and wants to see you. What shall I tell him?"

"Tell him? Why, tell him to come in!"

Tibby scurried out. Tom Clayton, resplendent of frock-coat and fancy trousers, appeared in the doorway.

"Thanks, old son," Tom said. "I heard that little exchange; you do have a way with servants. Now hear me: hear the voice of doom and destiny."

"Well?"

"All hell has broken loose this morning. For the next hour or so, until the whole business blows up, there'll be no peace for you or for me either. Glance down from the window, will you?"

Climbing out of bed in his nightshirt, Macrae donned dressing-gown and slippers and padded to a window overlooking the inner courtyard. Still another *calèche découverte* waited there. On the box was a Negro of vaguely familiar aspect, though without coachman's uniform. In it sat Senator Benjamin. Beside it stood

Sergeant O'Shea, addressing the senator with what seemed to be measured oratory.

"It's old Benjie," Tom reported, "who's hired a carriage this morning. That's Michael driving it, as you see. Sir Oracle wants us to be in at the death, and what a death it's likely to be! But never mind that, for the moment. Personal news first; I'm bursting with it."

"Can you make yourself comfortable while I shave and go through a bath?"

"Dick, for God's sake! Shave, by all means; but there'll be no time for a bath, or for breakfast either, until later in the day. Don't you even want to *hear?*"

"All right; come and watch me shave."

Macrae gulped down tea. Then he made for the adjoining bath-room, where Tibby had left his hot shaving-water in a brass container. While he washed and removed the stubble from his face, Tom lounged against the wall.

"I was up betimes this morning, Dick. I have visited the family of de Sancerre, and held communion with them."

"Were they up at this hour, Tom? It's early enough for you, but the night-owls of St. Charles Avenue and Holywell Street . . ."

"They were up, old son, for the inescapable reason that nobody went to bed. Papa de Sancerre, I understand, had been dispatched in that direction at the virtuous hour of one-thirty A.M. But he didn't get to bed. When Mama de Sancerre returned from General Ede's, and Margot also turned up . . ."

"Margot's back, is she?"

"Margot is back, yes. But presently, presently! Before we treat of my humble affairs, let's deal with yours. It has come to these ears that you, escorting Ursula home at some similarly virtuous hour, were sent flying from the scene when your inamorata caught a distant sensory impression of her old man, on his way back from Governor Corliss's and roaring for blood. Then . . ."

"More trouble, I suppose?"

"Not so much as a prophet might foretell. Dick, you'll never have a better friend than good old Mama de Sancerre! She was the one who smoothed the general down. She told lies by the bucket;

did you ever know a woman who *couldn't* tell lies by the bucket? She said you and Ursula (and Margot too) had been in her company for most of the evening. When she added that you and Ursula were engaged to be married: always subject to the old man's approval, of course . . ."

"How far was the situation smoothed down?"

Tom made a broad gesture.

"Listen, Dick. General Henry Clay Ede, when not under the impression that single-handed he won the Mexican War, is a pretty good sort after all. And there are practical considerations as well. He knows you've got an independent income; if Ursula's misguided enough to marry you, he knows she won't exactly starve. He still thinks you'll be up to your games with his daughter if you're given half a chance. But, always provided you don't land the poor girl in another compromising position worse than that one, he's at least willing to accept the thesis that you may be a pretty good sort yourself."

Macrae dried the razor and put it away. Giving his face a last rinse, he returned to the bedroom and began to dress. Midway through it he reverted to the subject.

"In that case, Tom, no real damage was done last night?"

"No real damage was done? What do you mean?"

"I mean the attack on George Stoneman, if it was an attack and not accident. You heard about that, I imagine?"

"You bet I heard about it!"

"Mr. Stoneman might have killed himself or been killed. But he wasn't. Apart from the fact that he got a drenching in the rain as General Ede got a drenching, the only actual damage was to the dignity of them both. Since every man among us has been in at least one damnably undignified fix so far, we haven't fared too badly. At least there's been no other tragedy, no second murder . . ."

"No other tragedy?" Tom stared at him. "Dick, for God's sake! Now that we're off personal matters and love-affairs, there's the ugly part of what I came here to tell you. There *has* been a second murder. Late last night the body was fished out of the river by two men shooting at alligators on a sandbar just below town."

"Whose body? Who was killed?"

"That's what Sir Oracle and the O'Shea won't tell me, though I've asked till I'm blue in the face. This murder was done with a knife; it's butcher's work of the worst sort, they say.

"Look at 'em down there!" raved Tom, striding to the window and pointing. "They were on duty, or on guard, when I got here. The four of us are going somewhere, and it shouldn't take too long. Anything else I could get out of 'em consisted of cryptic hints and innuendoes. 'Well, who was killed?' I said. 'Was it Barnaby Jeffers?' 'Come!' says Sir Oracle. 'Under the circumstances, how *could* it be?' Mama de Sancerre is right about something else she keeps saying. When old Benjie becomes all Oriental and mysterious, wrapping his smile around him, it makes any sane person want to land him one with a blunt instrument. *And how much longer will it take you to finish dressing?*"

"Only this cravat to tie; than I'm ready."

Macrae, who had rung the bell for Tibby after drawing on trousers and shirt, turned from the mirror to find Tibby in the doorway.

"I shall have to go out for a little while," he told her. "You might hold up breakfast until nine o'clock, if you will, and tell Mr. Ludlow."

"I'll tell him, sir. You sure you'll be back by nine?"

"Better make it half-past nine, just in case. Or even ten. It's Saturday morning; there's not a great deal to do.

"This way, Tom," he added. "Straight through the passage; and then round the corner into the hall, down the stairs under the covered way, after which the carriage with the cryptic ones will be in sight.

"My own personal affairs," he continued, when Tibby was beyond earshot, "you have dealt with in a terse and lucid way. What of your own? Margot has returned, you said. Where did she go and what was she doing?"

"She *was* with Marie Laveau the younger, just as everyone thought. Drove to St. Ann Street for the witch-queen's daughter, just as the witch-queen's daughter has been calling on her, only Margot paid her call without secrecy. As for where the two of 'em

went, old son: you'd never guess that in a million years, so I won't
waste time asking you to guess. They were at a school."

"At a what?"

"At a school! It's the School of Poor Children and of Orphans,
L'Ecole des Pauvres Enfants et des Orphelins, on a little street off
Esplanade Avenue in the Creole section. Marie Laveau is one of
the founders and chief patronesses. Are you following me?"

"Closely."

"There's no doubt Margot actually went there; she brought
back photographs taken some time ago, and could describe the
place at night when no pupils were on the premises. You see, Dick,
L'Ecole des Pauvres Enfants is a charity day-school with stand-
ards to match those of any private school in the country. As
teachers it will employ only women of the highest educational
and moral qualifications; each pupil is provided with two hot
meals a day free of charge. And that's where we run slap into the
unexpected."

"Again?"

"Yes, again! Up to the time she'd visited Marie Laveau and
visited this school," Tom explained, "Margot couldn't sing her
heroine's praises loudly enough. In theory, at least, she's strong
for modern ideas and progress: enlightenment, women's rights,
good works, up with the downtrodden! When she comes into actual contact with all this . . ."

"Disillusionment sets in?"

"It was partly that, yes. Doing good to people often just means
bullying 'em. If you ask me, though, Margot's disillusionment
stemmed mainly from going to the St. Ann Street house and seeing
this woman in what Margot called unbelievable squalor. 'She's
personally clean; she's neat without being drab,' Margot said;
'need she *live* in such dirt and disorder?' "

"The cottage is squalid enough, I can testify," Macrae agreed.
"She would have been still more shocked if she had visited it late
at night, and seen the dirt and disorder following a fight outside
the back-parlour window. Then Margot's herself again; the world
has come right; and with you, too, all is gas and gaiters?"

"At least it's a good deal better. 'I promised to visit their school in the daytime,' she said, 'and yet I don't think I shall bother. You lead a sterile and unproductive life, Tom, but I *am* rather fond of you.' Yes, she's seeing my sterling qualities at last. On the other hand, old son, the business we're embarked on this morning isn't likely to be gas or gaiters either. Look there!"

They had passed through the hall, where Macrae paused to tap a barometer at set fair. They descended the stairs under the covered way, and emerged into the courtyard. Senator Benjamin and Sergeant O'Shea now sat facing each other in the open carriage. Before he even hailed them, Macrae went in for a brief look at his office. He glanced at the austere furnishings, at the neat, swept desk-top, at every chair now in place. Then he and Tom joined the other two in time to catch the end of what seemed to be an argument.

"Sir," Sergeant O'Shea was proclaiming, "I'll give yez every bit o' credit there is to be given! Ye've raysoned it out from A to Zed; ye've got the spalpeen in a corner! But—"

"But what?" asked the other.

"This killer's more than a killer, sir. Behind that mask he's a vicious degenerate. Never mind the weapon he used on Judge Rutherford and Mr. Stoneman. He's got a knife; he's used that too; and I'd give yez odds there's a barker up his sleeve. 'Tis all very well for the likes o' me. I've got a barker meself," Sergeant O'Shea slapped his pocket, "and anyway it's me job. But you, now! A United States senator, a man o' substance and standing, and not a young man at that. It's rough work there may be at any minute. Do you think *you* should go?"

"Accept my assurance, Sergeant," replied Senator Benjamin, "that the whole of the district attorney's detective force could not keep me away. Will it be the first time I have hunted the devil-fish?"

Tom Clayton raised his voice.

"This is to inform you, o descendant of Hibernian kings, that Dick and I are now at your service. You don't mind taking *us* along?"

"No, sir, that I do not. Take any man ye like, give him knife or barker or pitchfork or shillelagh: as God's me witness, sir, I would back you—or Mr. Macrae either—to tackle the murtherin' swine and bring him down! Climb in, gentlemen, and we'll be off."

Tom sat down beside Sergeant O'Shea with his back to the driver. Macrae was at Senator Benjamin's elbow. Michael on the box flicked his reins across the horses' backs. Out they rattled, turning left for Canal Street and, when they reached Canal Street, making a broad right-hand sweep towards the south.

"It would help considerably," observed Tom, "if we had some idea of where we were off to."

"Patience, Mr. Clayton, only a little patience! All will be clear in wan moment!"

A warm sun glowed on the pastel colours of the buildings along Canal Street. Two-horse omnibuses plied in both directions.

"Look here, Sergeant," Tom persisted, "just how long is one moment? If we're not to learn anything until we actually get there . . ."

"Patience, I said, and all will be plain sailing!"

Tom sat up straight.

"When you mention plain sailing, Brian Boru, something tells me in a loud, clear voice that our destination must be a steamboat landing on the levee. Is that so?"

"It's as right as religion, sir! If ye guessed that from a clue like 'plain sailing,' what might ye not have guessed from the other clues?"

"Other clues?"

"They've been all over the place, Mr. Clayton; they've been as plentiful as rain in Ireland. Senator Benjamin . . ."

The senator addressed Macrae.

"Sergeant O'Shea," he said, "seems to think I ought not to be here at all. In one way, of course, he is quite right. I should be in Washington, where I hope to return in a day or two. Washington is not a beautiful city; it has little glamour. However, with the Supreme Court housed in the Capitol at no great distance from the Senate, I have no difficulty in carrying out my double duties as legislator and as advocate. There are other compensations as well.

To browse through the old Library of Congress, to play cards with David Yulee and Clement Clay, to sample the free lunch in the bar at Willard's Hotel . . .

"But we are not assembled to discuss my life in Washington, or indeed my life anywhere. Most of the big steamboats, as you must be aware, leave for St. Louis at five in the afternoon. Those of the Grand Bayou Line, notably the *Governor Roman*, depart at eight-thirty in the morning.

"It is now well beyond half-past eight. But we have tried to make sure—or, rather, Sergeant O'Shea has tried to make sure—that the boat in question will not leave before our arrival."

"He spoke to the captain, did he?" Macrae asked.

"He spoke to the captain, yes, though the captain is not quite the all-powerful autocrat so many think. The man of real authority is the pilot. Each craft carries two pilots; when the boat is *en route* they take alternate watches of four hours at a time. Sergeant O'Shea has taken counsel with both captain *and* pilots; so far as I know, it has been arranged. And now, I think, we had better say no more until we are closer."

They did say no more. In scant minutes the carriage, with a sweeping right-hand turn at the foot of Canal Street, clattered at a spanking pace along the road paralleling the levee. Except for those knots of loungers who may be seen anywhere, there were comparatively few people to watch a morning departure. Tall steamboat chimneys, white decks, paddle-boxes with names painted in scarlet and gilt, towered past in showy parade.

But Senator Benjamin had grown restive.

"I don't like this," he declared.

"Nor me either!" said Sergeant O'Shea.

"But it's all right, isn't it?" asked Macrae. "I can see the *Governor Roman* ahead. There's very little smoke from the chimneys: There would be a good deal of smoke, surely, if they were preparing to back out into the river and go?"

"On the contrary," said Senator Benjamin. "Steamboats usually *arrive* with a flourish of black smoke and a great screaming of steam through the gauge-cocks; it's part of their performance. Departure is a quieter business. We are coming abreast now. Observe the captain on the texas with his hand lifted. And the two deckhands standing by to heave in the landing-stage. Yes, somebody has been bribed. Michael, pull up! Gentlemen, we had better hurry!"

The carriage stopped; the four of them leaped down.

"Hold hard, there!" Sergeant O'Shea shouted at the steamboat. "Name o' the law!" he added.

There were calls, humorous or ribald, from passengers lining the rails of the decks above. Across this babble smote the clang of a brass bell. Macrae heard the engines begin their clang and thud. Past deckhands and roustabouts he saw fire from furnace doors in the cavern of the lowest deck.

A broad landing-stage, on the point of being hauled in, projected from the *Governor Roman's* port side near the bow. Across that bridge Sergeant O'Shea flung his bulk to the deck. The stout little lawyer bounded after him with surprising agility. Tom Clayton's long stride covered the same distance just before the landing-stage itself bumped aboard.

Great paddle-wheels churned the muddy water to froth. A gap widened between deck and levee, and widened still further, as the boat backed its way towards mid-channel. And on the dock . . .

"Jump for it, old socks!" somebody shouted encouragingly to Macrae. "Don't let 'em leave you behind!"

Good advice, he decided. Drawing well back for purchase, Macrae ran. His flying leap carried him from the edge of the wharf to the edge of the lowest deck, where he lurched, staggered, and righted himself when Tom caught his arm.

Round the four newcomers boiled deckhands, roustabouts, and main-deck passengers who might not share the amenities of their betters above.

"Where *is* the spalpeen, now?" bellowed Sergeant O'Shea. "Didn't seeum at the rail, didja?"

"The person in question," said Senator Benjamin, "will try to remain as inconspicuous as possible for some time. It's a stateroom we want, I think. Those stairs to the upper deck, now . . ."

Once they had mounted the stairs in question, they entered a different world. On this level would be the bar and the barbershop,

as well as staterooms which included a bridal suite lavishly decorated. But before them now stretched the white-and-gilt tunnel of
the *Governor Roman*'s main cabin or salon, two hundred-odd feet
long by twenty-odd feet broad: pillared, deep-carpeted, with luxu-
rious chairs at the line of round tables on which food would be
served, gleaming with mirrors, resplendent from the polish of its
grand piano to the polish of its spittoons.

"You want a stateroom; all right!" panted Tom Clayton. "Do
you know which stateroom?"

"We know the name of the stateroom," Senator Benjamin replied. "It's *Kentucky*, I think the sergeant said. However, since I
am unfamiliar with this boat . . ."

"I'm familiar with it, though!" roared Sergeant O'Shea. "Starboard side; look sharp; follow me!"

Leaving behind them a cabin which would not assume radiance
until the clusters of oil-burning globes were kindled at night, and a
much-advertised orchestra played at the far end, they hurried out
through one of the archways into a side passage from which a line
of doors gave access to staterooms opening on the outer deck.
Though lighted only by a porthole fore and aft, the passage held
enough sunshine to show the name of a state, together with its
appropriate marking, painted on each door.

Kentucky was well forward on the starboard side, its door
closed. Sergeant O'Shea wrenched at the knob, which resisted him.
Then, hammering his left fist on the panel, with his right hand he
drew from his pocket a heavy revolving pistol of Smith & Wesson's
new model, rim-fire with metallic cartridges.

"Open up here!" he yelled. "Will yez open up, bejasus, in the
name o' the law?"

There was no reply. Sergeant O'Shea hurled his massive shoulder at the door, which looked flimsy enough. At the first impact it
shivered. At the second impact the lock was torn out bodily and
the door flapped back.

Having completed its manoeuvre and swung to port, the *Governor Roman* was forging upsteam. A slight vibration shook
through every bulkhead. The spires of New Orleans slid past the
porthole of the stateroom revealed when the door flew open. But

nobody glanced at what was outside.

Macrae and Tom Clayton were staring in a kind of paralysis at the man who stood looking at them from beside the bunk under the porthole, and who also had a revolving pistol in his hand. Mouth distorted, with something inarticulate between a yell and a howl, their quarry whipped up the Colt's 'Navy' and fired almost in their faces. The bullet went wild, smashing a lamp against the bulkhead before it drilled through into the stateroom adjoining.

Sergeant O'Shea fired and did not miss. Flung backward by the impact of a bullet in the chest, the one they sought sprawled face upwards across the bunk while his weapon thudded down.

Macrae's ears were still ringing from the two shots. Tom, half dazed, stepped gingerly into the stateroom and pointed at the recumbent figure before turning towards Senator Benjamin in the doorway.

"Do you mean," Tom said incredulously, "that *he* . . . ?"

"Yes," replied Senator Benjamin. "That's the murderer. That's the real Steve White. But don't let it trouble you; don't be cast down if you failed to penetrate an excellent disguise. Since Thursday morning he has been calling himself Harry Ludlow."

21

ON THE EVENING OF SUNDAY, APRIL EIGHTEENTH, FOUR
guests—Ursula Ede, Tom Clayton, Richard Macrae, and Judah
P. Benjamin—had dinner at the home of Jules de Sancerre, Isabelle de Sancerre, and their daughter.

Darkness had deepened before coffee and liqueurs were served.
Margot and Tom, a chastened Margot and an almost equally subdued Tom, excused themselves to go for a stroll in the grounds.
The others repaired to the library, where Marcus Brutus had kindled the lamp on the centre table.

The de Sancerres, Ursula, and Macrae drew up chairs round
Senator Benjamin, who had sat down behind the centre table and
lighted a cigar.

"These murders . . ." began Jules de Sancerre.

Senator Benjamin sat back comfortably.

"Though some parts of the pattern must remain conjectural,"
he remarked, "all the principal threads are in our hands. And the
main design is soon visible. Steve White, Rosette Leblanc's son,
returned from Paris to wreak havoc on those he had sworn to kill.
At first his plans were vague; he would pose as a travelling Englishman seeing the sights; and he seems to have loitered in St.
Louis for some time. Then fortune handed him a gift. In St. Louis
he met and made friends with the real Harry Ludlow, a forthright,
talkative soul who kept a diary. It occurred to Steve White that his
plans could brilliantly be furthered if he killed Harry Ludlow and
took the latter's place, an imposture for which he was uniquely
fitted. Am I clear so far?"

Ursula, in an elaborately frilled gown of light-blue tulle, put her elbow on the arm of the chair and took her chin in her hand.

"Forgive me," she said, "but there's one thing I can't quite grasp even yet. That fair-haired, ingenuous-seeming boy was actually a man in his late thirties?"

"Correct," agreed Macrae. "It did occur to me, when I first met a grown-up 'Harry Ludlow' at the steamboat on Thursday morning, that he was one of those people who remain extraordinarily youthful-looking at an age well past maturity. But we have all known such characters; I thought nothing of it."

"You never suspected him of *anything*? You even accepted him as another Britisher?"

"I never suspected him, and I did accept him as such. His speech was entirely authentic, even to the new slang term 'absquatulate.' Since he seemed to make no mistake of any kind . . ."

"It should not be forgotten," said Senator Benjamin, "that during his life's most plastic phase he really was at school in England. The details of this (with other details as well) we now know from his confession before he died of a bullet-wound on Saturday afternoon. His years between fourteen and eighteen he spent at Rugby under the headmastership of the great Dr. Arnold. Add to this his genius for mimicry, add to it the fact that he lived in Paris and had all the money he needed; the late Delphine Lalaurie freed him from want long ago. He could visit England whenever he liked, both to preserve the authenticity of his accent and to keep himself up to date.

"In actuality he was neither fair-haired nor ingenuous, as we shall see. And he made many mistakes, but seldom the kind of mistake an impostor might have been expected to make. That also we shall see. As the tale progresses . . ."

"Yes," put in Isabelle de Sancerre, "as the tale progresses! Why not begin at the beginning and tell us the whole story? No, don't start at the beginning! Commence with your first suspicion of him, and go on from there. How did you come to suspect anybody so innocent-looking?"

Senator Benjamin smoked reflectively, his left hand at his left whisker.

"It began," he answered, "with that sense of wonder which is the inception of suspicion. Cast your minds back to Thursday night, after Horace Rutherford had fallen to death down the stairs. With the exception of Miss Ede, I interviewed each witness separately in the dining-room."

He looked at Macrae.

"Your testimony, my dear fellow, was extremely suggestive. You had seen Judge Rutherford fall and die. At that moment you looked at all those who were there with you in the hall. You described Jules de Sancerre; you described Tom Clayton; you described Barnaby Jeffers,* even to the look on their faces. You did not describe Harry Ludlow or even mention him."

"I didn't see him, it's true. But I assumed he was there, as the others did too. Afterwards he said he was there, and the others seemed to agree."

"Very well; they assumed it too." The senator rubbed his forehead. "Was it possible, I asked myself, that you failed to describe him because in fact he wasn't there? If so, where could he have been?

"Up to this point, bear witness, it was not even suspicion. It was only the wonder that induces suspicion. But you had done more than give your own version of Judge Rutherford's death. You had also told me a good deal about Harry Ludlow: his background, his travels, his arrival that morning, certain of the things he said and did; I rather incautiously reminded him of this at a later date. For your own account led to still more wonder."

"How so?"

"You acknowledged to me, as I believe you had previously acknowledged to Tom, that you had not set eyes on Harry since he was a boy of ten. But you believed you could not mistake him. At the steamboat you saw a strongly built, young-looking man with fair hair and an expression of not over-intelligent good nature. You never doubted he was your friend's son because it never occurred to you that he could be anyone else. And yet, within two

* See page 84.

minutes of meeting you, he professed never to have heard of Bourbon whiskey."

"But surely . . . !"

"A small point, I agree: merely cause for wonder. Nevertheless, consider. Already he had visited several cities, including Washington and St. Louis, and written you letters from there. It was conceivable that a young Englishman, a convivial one like himself, might have spent some time in Boston, Philadelphia, even New York, without being offered Bourbon or so much as hearing of it. That he should have remained in the same ignorance after visiting both St. Louis *and* Washington, to say nothing of travelling down-river by steamboat, was (at the very least) less likely.

"It caused me to look more closely at what we knew of Harry Ludlow. Here in the library, that same Thursday night, I myself first heard of a certain Steve White and his passionate hatred of three men. Somebody named Steve White, it seemed, had shared a stateroom with Harry Ludlow on the journey from St. Louis; after which, apparently, he slipped ashore and ran away.

"Bear witness that Harry Ludlow was not with us when the discussion of Steve White arose; he had been sent to fetch the police. But he had been with us for some time previously. Well, remembering that I had some slight cause to be suspicious of this ostensible youngster who said he feared blood and violence, what else *did* we know of him?

"He would do much and dare much. The trials he complained of—having no work to do, meeting inexplicable violence wherever he turned—were borne with smiling fortitude. Far from seeming unintelligent, a hearty athlete who scorned books, his remarks showed very good sense, and he made a pointed reference to the satire on the Circumlocution Office in Mr. Dickens's latest work, the only-just-appearing *Little Dorrit*. He would follow his consular superior anywhere; he would do, in general, what he was asked to do. But under no circumstances could he be persuaded to *write* anything."

Jules de Sancerre bent forward.

"I remember!" their host said. "Macrae asked him to write a

brief note to Sergeant O'Shea. It was a simple enough request, entailing no difficulty. But he wouldn't do it; he made excuses; he had his way. Yes, of course! Since the real Harry had written a number of letters, which Macrae may have kept . . ."

"Which Macrae did keep, Jules."

". . . the false Harry could never risk a comparison of handwriting! Is that it?"

"Yes; and we have much more evidence. Already that day Tom Clayton had offered to introduce him to the manager of Hookson's Bank. He refused, on the grounds that he had sufficient cash: which was true enough in a double sense. His real reason, of course, was that in identifying himself at the bank, even with so respectable a sponsor as Leonidas Clayton's son, he would have had to sign his name.

"Still, that is only unimportant corroboration, which might have meant nothing. For important or even clinching corroboration, let us momentarily leap ahead to Friday."

Again Senator Benjamin looked at Macrae.

"You asked your assistant, I think, to prepare a brief report for the Foreign Office. Did he do it?"

"No, he did not." Macrae reviewed events. "He was working on it, or professed to be working on it, all day Friday. But he would let me see nothing. I told him it must definitely be on my desk Saturday morning. When I glanced into the office on Saturday morning, the desk-top was still bare."

"Deplorably, I fear," said Senator Benjamin, tapping ash from his cigar, "we have anticipated the course of events. Let us return to the Thursday night which found me in such a quandary.

"Harry Ludlow had also claimed to be ignorant of the amenity called a free lunch, and asked that it be explained to him. The free lunch, though invented here, has in fact spread to other cities. I myself have partaken of it in the bar at Willard's Hotel in Washington, where confessedly he himself had stayed. The little points were piling up. 'Harry Ludlow' might not be Harry Ludlow at all; he could even be the elusive Steve White. And he *could* have killed Judge Rutherford, if . . ."

"That's a suggestion I see," cried Isabelle de Sancerre, "if you'll forgive a poor downtrodden housewife for speaking up. The fourteen-year-old Steve White, as I told you, visited this house before it was quite completed. He ran up and down stairways inside and out. The only outside staircase is at the back, and leads to the gallery behind five rooms, with Jules's study in the middle.

"Allowing 'Harry Ludlow' to be Steve White, anybody as obsessed as he was would never have forgotten so vivid a childhood memory. When poor Horace appeared at the head of those stairs, Steve White could have counted on the attention of the other witnesses being so fixed on Horace they'd never have noticed *him*, then or afterwards.

"He could have slipped around to the back of the house and up the gallery stairs. In the study, with the door open as it was, he'd have been in a direct line behind Horace some twenty feet away. He couldn't possibly have been seen by anyone standing in the hall below. But where could he have learned of Horace's bad heart, or Horace's habit of standing so precariously balanced that a shove would topple him?"

Senator Benjamin crushed out the cigar in an ashtray.

"With your permission, Isabelle," he said, "we shall come to an explanation in good time. On the Thursday night in question, however, the problem of how it was done seemed insuperable. Venturing out to get some air with Macrae, I observed at the side of the driveway a number of stones rather smaller than an egg and quite round. I remembered the bruise in the middle of Judge Rutherford's back. Yet it seemed more than doubtful that any murderer would have risked throwing a stone, and what happened to such a stone afterwards?

"Friday brought the answers to several riddles at once. A fairly strenuous afternoon was climaxed when you provided us with two pieces of information: (1) the erstwhile Steve White's genius at mimicry and (2) his uncanny skill with the slingshot or catapult.

"Eureka!

"Before you provided the information, that same Friday afternoon, 'Harry Ludlow' had faced us on what has been called the terrace behind this house and given proof of his powers as a mimic. He imitated a gentleman from South Carolina with such accuracy that I could have imagined myself back at Port Royal.

"His deliberate mistake in assigning Charleston to North Carolina, like his deliberate mistake about Bourbon whiskey, at first glance seemed no more than the sort of natural blunder we might have expected. It was (or so he thought) another deft character-touch for the part he had set himself to play. This man was more than a mimic; he was a remarkably fine actor who could spellbind his audience when he chose."

"He failed to spellbind *you*, Senator," Macrae pointed out, "and it's just as well for all of us he failed. As for his mimicry, you should have heard him at the breakfast table on Friday morning. He imitated Tom Clayton bellowing at Margot's door before the episode of the spanking, and he 'did' Tom to the life.

"Something else occurred at the breakfast table," Macrae added, "though it failed to impress me at the time. A *propos* a different matter, with a remark like, 'Drawing a bow at a venture,' he held out his left hand as though literally gripping a bow-shaft, and drew back his right hand to the chin. But an archer draws the bowstring high to the ear. The motion he made, so instinctive that probably he never realized it, was the motion of one pulling back the elastic of a slingshot to fire a stone. It brings us to the second piece of information you stress: his skill with what could become a formidable weapon."

"Ah, the slingshot!" repeated Senator Benjamin. "Does any of us ever forget a boyhood sport at which we excelled? Have I forgotten devil-fishing? Did Steve White forget his own particular kind of marksmanship?

"Ladies and gentlemen, I had hoped to show you the heavy Y-shaped slingshot, with strong rubber propelling-mechanism, which hospital attendants removed from his pocket when they put him to bed. The wood is American hickory, they tell me; he manufactured it in this country. He had a knife, he had a pistol, and he also prepared the slingshot against the eventuality which did arrive. But I can't show you the weapon. It has been impounded by District Attorney Tappan as evidence against a murderer who may no longer be prosecuted in this world."

Ursula Ede raised her hand like one in a classroom.

"Forgive me," she said, "if I'm less interested in the slingshot than in the false Harry Ludlow's character. He *was* a mixture, wasn't he? Did he betray himself in any other way besides those you've mentioned?"

"Well, yes. To Jules and Macrae he said Judge Rutherford was looking down at *them*; he did not say '*us*.' He further betrayed himself in a conversation with Margot, beside the croquet lawn and also on Friday afternoon."

"I know!" Ursula sounded apologetic. "Mr. Macrae and I overheard the conversation. You know about it; afterwards, when Margot admitted to you she was well acquainted with the Voodoo Queen's daughter, she repeated what she and this man said virtually word for word. But what was so betraying about it?"

"Margot questioned him about Steve White; as a last twist of irony, she questioned him about *himself*. Let me see if *I* can recall some of his words. 'Last night,' he said, 'when they were going on in the library about Steve White being Rosette Leblanc's son, how was I supposed to know that just by meeting him aboard the boat?'

"Apparently an unanswerable reply. But a betraying one. When the subject of Steve White came up for discussion in the library, remember, 'Harry Ludlow' was not there. He could not have heard what he professed to have heard. But he *had* heard rumbles and rumors of what we were about; he was trying in desperation to discover how much we might have learned or guessed. Margot, also ironically, praised Steve White and wished strength to his arm!

"It is now time to sum up the whole sad affair.

"Having determined by Thursday night that the alleged Harry was probably an impostor and might himself be the actual Steve, I could tell Sergeant O'Shea how to go about 'tracing' Steve White on Friday.

"The alleged Harry, in his private interview with me, had told me what he had told Macrae and Tom: he had travelled by the *Governor Roman* with Steve White, a rather peculiar character who kept him aloof from other passengers and hurried ashore as soon as the boat docked. The description he had given me (and given Sergeant O'Shea) was the same as he afterwards gave on the croquet lawn: a clean-shaven man with brown hair, older than twenty-four years. It was a truthful description of himself, though meant to mislead: he *looked* no more than the twenty-four years Macrae attributed to him, and his hair had been brown until he dyed it blond the night before the steamboat touched New Orleans.

"One day before long, no doubt, they will succeed in laying the transatlantic cable that so far they have failed to establish. With a transatlantic cable in operation, we could have asked Paris immediately about a Stéphan Leblanc who became Stephen White on this side of the water. Lacking such an opportunity, Sergeant O'Shea must proceed with what information we did have.

"The *Governor Roman* was still here. It would remain here, of course, for the customary forty-eight hours before plying back to St. Louis. Crew, waiters, and other attendants could be questioned about two passengers who shared a stateroom on the journey down.

"According to the records of the Grand Bayou Line, a Stephen White and a Harry Ludlow had booked from St. Louis to New Orleans, and had shared a stateroom. Witnesses among the crew testified that these were, or appeared to be, two young men of about the same age: both of them travelling Britons. They did keep aloof from other passengers, but at which one's insistence?

"*Our* Harry testified to the other man's slipping ashore in the morning; he said a waiter had told him this. No waiter had told him anything of the sort. One of that pair vanished overnight, and was not seen again. If he vanished overnight, it could only have been because the other had disposed of him. Q.E.D., surely?

"You see the inevitable course of events. Having determined to take the real Harry's place, the false Harry waited until the last moment, and let him send a perfectly authentic telegram from Baton Rouge. The talkative Englishman with the diary would have supplied Steve White with authentic details of his background and of the Foreign Office, which the murderer need only remember for a daring imposture next day. On the river, that night, he slew his victim with a knife and dropped the body overboard. He dyed his hair fair to ape the other man's hair; who would particularly notice him in the bustle of arrival?"

Macrae intervened.

"Then what we have been thinking of as the second murder, Senator, was actually the first? At the Gem Saloon, late Friday night, Tom made some comment about the tragedy we had on our hands. You said you were more concerned about the murder we had not yet heard of. By that, I take it, you meant the murder of the real Harry Ludlow?"

"I did. Having been washed down the river, the body was not recovered until early Saturday morning; it may be accounted as singular that the body was recovered at all. And now let me proceed with the final summing-up.

Senator Benjamin paused for a moment.

"Miss Ede has expressed curiosity about the murderer's true character. What was he really like, behind the face he kept so constantly on display? We can reconstruct that character partly from our knowledge of his movements and partly from his own dying confession.

"When he met the real Harry Ludlow in St. Louis, it was as Stephen White, another young Englishman, who himself had formerly lived in New Orleans. At the beginning—or so the dying man claimed; I am inclined to believe it—he had no thought of killing the consular assistant or impersonating him. His original scheme had been very different.

"He had been at St. Louis for some time, as I think I mentioned. In furtherance of his original scheme he had been in communication by letter with Marie Laveau the elder, who knew all about him. That is how both Marie Laveaus (or should it be Maries Laveau?) enter the story."

"Yes!" exclaimed Jules de Sancerre. "*Enfin*, Benjie, how *do* they enter it?"

"Ask yourself why he should be exchanging letters with the elder Marie. To carry out his original scheme, of averting suspicion by posing as a sight-seeing young Briton while he attended to three men marked for death, there were certain things he felt he must do.

"It would be natural that he should call on the British Consul. But he would do more than this. What better way to avert all suspicion than to strike up a friendship with the consul, as he could strike up a friendship with almost anyone he chose? He would haunt the consulate; he would become something of a fixture at the consulate; it would become his home from home.

"Hence a word to Marie the elder seven or eight weeks ago, before he had any notion that a consular assistant would arrive out of the blue. 'Come, *chère Marie!* Draw on your Voodoo resources. Some delicate little attentions, please, to show that your eye is on the consul, the consulate, and all who gather there. Invoke your inverted blessing; one day soon you will be blessing *me!*'

"Though I explained all this on Saturday night, Jules, I explained it after you had left the Gem. Repetition now would serve no good purpose. Suffice it to say that Macrae here was watched and spied on, though with the reverse of evil intent, before a would-be murderer in St. Louis had worked out the ultimate design.

"For what happened? When the real Harry Ludlow appeared, a confiding young man who talked much of himself, Steve White's original scheme seemed only strengthened and improved. What better entry to the consulate at New Orleans than the friendship of its new assistant?

"Then, a little later, the dazzling inspiration already outlined: kill Harry Ludlow and take his place. It became still more vital for Voodoo attentions to be directed towards Richard Macrae. It became still more vital to whisper, 'Let this man walk in the peace of Papa Là-bas, and may *his house* be blessed.' The final plan, I suggest, tells us much of Steve White's true character.

"If his intent had been *only* to avenge the wrong done Delphine Lalaurie long ago, at least we should have understood. Though it would have been idolatry gone mad, and we could not have sympathized, we could have understood. But was it only a twisted vengeance? Cold-bloodedly to kill this young Englishman, with no purpose other than that of feeding the murderer's vanity by averting suspicion still more? And to kill him with six stab-wounds, as you will discover if you examine a decomposing body fished from the river: what shall we call *that*? Steve White really enjoyed doing murder; it warmed his shrivelled heart. In most respects, I fear, he was the vicious degenerate Sergeant O'Shea named him.

"From St. Louis he sent Marie Laveau a last letter, explaining what his new identity would be in a few days. He warned her she must never attempt to communicate personally with him after he had landed, as he would never attempt to communicate personally with her. Then he and his victim boarded the *Governor Roman* for New Orleans.

"I think, though I cannot prove, that somewhere *en route* he sent the elder Marie a cryptically worded telegram, as the real Harry telegraphed to Macrae from Baton Rouge. With his butcher's work finished on Wednesday night, with the victim's diary, papers, and money transferred to his own person at the same time the victim's luggage went overboard, he was ready to meet all contingencies the next morning.

"A story had to be told to account for the disappearance of Steve White. He had kept his victim away from the other passengers, and the fact of two young men travelling together would have excited little curiosity on so cosmopolitan a highway as the Mississippi River. But, if *no* explanation were given, it was just possible somebody might remark and remember.

"He improvised well, as he always did. Steve White, having served his turn as a sight-seeing Briton, became a mysterious American who chose to fade from the scene. A refreshed avenger could look towards his principal target, Judge Horace Rutherford.

"It was as though chance and good fortune were showering every benefit upon him. That very same night he got his opportunity.

"A few moments ago I was asked how 'Harry Ludlow' could have learned of Judge Rutherford's infirmities and his disposition to stand precariously balanced on stairways. Don't forget that correspondence with Marie Laveau.

"The elder Marie would not help him to do murder; for all these years she has kept too carefully on the leeward side of the law. But she cherished Delphine Lalaurie's memory as much as he did. She would aid or abet in every passive way. And she had kept him well posted about Horace Rutherford.

"A few minutes before the murder on Thursday night, as though still further to encourage the murderer, Isabelle de Sancerre commented on every circumstance which made the judge an ideal victim."

"I did?" cried Madame de Sancerre.

"You did. Though I myself was in the back drawing-room at the time, your words have been repeated to me. A small black carriage, with your daughter apparently missing, arrived before the portico of this house. Two other carriages, one with Miss Ede and Macrae, the other with Tom Clayton and a predatory companion, drew up immediately afterwards. You emerged from the house and announced that Judge Rutherford was upstairs in the study.

"'And I do wish,' you presently added, 'I do wish Horace Rutherford, with his lame leg and his bad heart-condition, wouldn't prance around and strike poses everywhere. If he had a fall it would kill him.' You said that, did you not?"

"I—I daresay I did. I don't remember what I said!"

"Then Barnaby Jeffers arrived: were all the doomed men being served up on a platter? As Miss Partridge continued to exercise her lungs, Judge Rutherford himself came shouldering out to the head of the stairs.

"And a murderer opportunist instantly seized his chance. Did anyone take note of the presumed Harry Ludlow at that time? Nobody did. He slipped round to the back of the house, Isabelle, just as you suggested. He had not forgotten what he saw when the house was under construction long ago. Though he had three weapons at his disposal, only one could be useful here.

"He chose one of the round stones available beside the driveway. In the study, unseen, and with a direct sight-line to his target past the open door, he launched his missile as our tame soprano reached a high note of *Oft In the Stilly Night*. He had returned to the hall, as innocent-faced as he was unsuspected, in a matter of seconds later.

"If the stone that bruised the victim's back had fallen down uncarpeted stairs to an uncarpeted lower hall, the murder-method would have been betrayed. It did not do so; it fell in the upper hall. With the upper hall so thickly carpeted, with Miss Partridge's din filling all ears, nobody saw and nobody heard."

"But you yourself asked the question!" interposed Jules de Sancerre. "What happened to the stone?"

"It was found by your major-domo, Marcus Brutus: who, you remember, kept going up and down that staircase. Marcus Brutus *says* he paid no heed to the fact: that he thought someone had carelessly dropped the stone, and he threw it away without mentioning so trifling a circumstance. Marcus Brutus may be no intellectual giant, but he can hardly have been as obtuse as that.

"We must now revert very briefly to Marie Laveau and her hidden web of adherents. You, Jules, have denied with passion that there could be any such in this house. I suspect that Marcus Brutus himself—who bolted in fear from the front door when he heard too much mention of Voodoo practice, but would not mention this when he reported Margot's disappearance to you—may have been one of those adherents. And his son, Willie, watched your daughter's room by night without reporting the visits of Marie the younger.

"Don't take it out on Marcus Brutus or Willie, I beg! Don't sell them in the slave-mart at the St. Louis Hotel; don't punish them or even curse them too much. Over and over I have assured you these people hold no malice towards you or your family. Lecture them, if you like; then forget the whole thing as Macrae has forgotten similar activities at the consulate.

"But the subject of this discussion is the progress of a brutal killer; to that happy soul we must return.

"With Judge Rutherford out of the way, he could turn his attention elsewhere. But he could not turn it towards Barnaby Jeffers. Our local historian was far too well guarded, with a police-officer quite literally at his elbow every moment. The next step, obviously, must be towards George Stoneman."

Isabelle de Sancerre made the gestures of one groping through cobwebs.

"That's all very well!" she said. "And we *won't* be too hard on

Marcus Brutus or Willie, whatever they may deserve. But the masquerading Harry Ludlow hadn't been in New Orleans for twenty-four years. He remembered the arrangement of rooms in this house; he had good reason to remember, having seen the place last in the company of his goddess. And yet he had no such good reason to recall anything about George Stoneman! How did he even know where to *find* George?"

"Did Marie Laveau tell him that, too," asked Macrae, "in one of the letters she seems to have been so free with?"

Senator Benjamin looked at Macrae, his expression one of sardonic relish.

"She might well have told him," he replied, "though by the confession of a dying man she didn't. *You* told him. Or, to be exact, you made it easy for him to track down George at home. Ah! I see by your expression that light begins to dawn, doesn't it?"

"Light dawns," Macrae agreed, "in bitterness and self-castigation. When I instructed Harry to consult some commercial figures in preparing his report to the Foreign Office, I said he would find this printed information in my office on a shelf beside the *city directory*."

"Once more," said Senator Benjamin, "we must revert to Marie the elder and the secret band who serve her, after which the subject will be closed.

"At disseminating information from one end of town to the other, the Voodoo grapevine is faster than any electric telegraph; it really does approach the supernatural. As soon as Judge Rutherford was dead, the news reached St. Ann Street.

"The Voodoo Queen, who has her tentacles in so many homes that she even knew what was passing in a doll-maker's shop on Royal Street, and could have her daughter astonish a sailor named Jack Dowser with seemingly supernatural insight, knew also that the next victim of a murderer would be either Barnaby Jeffers or George Stoneman.

"She could not have known which one, having been forbidden— see murderer's confession—to communicate with him. But it hardly mattered. Having already written a card to Barnaby Jeffers and a card to Sergeant O'Shea, that same Thursday night she sent a card to the British Consul and suggested he meet Papa Là-bas in the haunted house at midnight on Friday.

"Of course he was never meant to meet Papa Là-bas or anyone else. On Friday she would—and did—send another of her many adherents to draw on the wall the sketch of a dead Judge Rutherford and a threatened George Stoneman. Perhaps the adherent had been told to draw Barnaby Jeffers as well, and broke off or was interrupted. We are never likely to learn; nobody will persuade the woman to speak out, and nothing can be proved against her. *Verba scripta manent*, by which I mean the letters from Steve White; but by this time, beyond doubt, his letters and his telegram have been destroyed.

"Now what of Steve White's last stroke?

"Here, apparently, he had been offered the most golden opportunity of all. Reconnoitring at the banker's home when he was believed to be working at the consulate, he found a target wide open to assault by slingshot.

"The President of the Planters' & Southern, with a thunderstorm approaching, was at work on the edge of a lighted roof-top fifty feet above ground. At the rear of the house, quite close to it, the false Harry discovered a tree from whose branches he had a direct sight-line to his quarry at convenient firing-distance. If certain stable-boys had also climbed that tree as they wished to do, the encounter would have been interesting.

"The murderer discharged a stone, which struck the victim in the side. It ought to have toppled him from the roof, and almost did. The storm burst in a clap of thunder which drowned out the noise of the missile's fall. The rain came deluging down. But this particular victim gripped an iron gutter as he slid over it; he *would not* give way or let go.

"Certain of George Stoneman's business associates, I understand, have made very merry over the spectacle of this weighty banker clinging to the gutter in a thunderstorm. They should not make merry, nor should we. If war ever does come, that is exactly the sort of man we shall need.

"The banker, complaining only of a pain in the side where he had been hit, went indoors and thence to bed. No longer could the murderer get at him with any weapon; he was surrounded by worshipful sons and daughters-in-law. The murderer's prospects, so splendid-seeming only twenty-four hours before, were dimmed at that instant. He had struck at an easy victim, and most dismally he had failed. Luck might well have deserted him. Since he had known by mid-morning that his whole scheme was threatened, this could foretell the beginning of collapse."

"What do you mean, his whole scheme was threatened?" Macrae demanded. "He couldn't have suspected *you* were on his track. And nobody else was after him."

"Oh, but somebody was," said Senator Benjamin. "May I remind you of Mr. Nathaniel Rumbold?"

"Square Nat, the gambler? Senator, how does *he* fit into all this? When we made our dash for the steamboat yesterday morning, I wondered if you were going to produce Square Nat as the murderer. The night before he had been dead drunk at the Gem Saloon, repeating that he must leave by the *Governor Roman* next day."

"And muttering something about hair-dye, remember."

"Well?"

"I could not question him on Saturday night; he was dead drunk, as you say. But we had evidence enough already; and I had no wish to involve so unsavoury a character in a case already unsavoury enough. I once remarked, by the way, that a person who seemed to figure in one role might well figure in another role . . ."

"Not as a murderer?"

"No, as a witness." Senator Benjamin inhaled deeply. "Even after you had broken his wrist on Friday morning—he was handled very roughly, after all—he stood in the courtyard shouting that he could help you, as he had already said in the drawing-room.

"How much he guessed or suspected by that time is not easy to determine. Any professional gambler must keep his eyes open. Though on the voyage down the river he had small reason to observe two young men who did *not* play cards with him, 'Harry

Ludlow' was very much in evidence at the Washington and American Ballroom on Thursday night. Square Nat may perhaps have noticed that a *Governor Roman* passenger with brown hair had overnight acquired fair hair.

"I am inclined to think that it was Square Nat who fired the mysterious shot at you from across the street after he had taken his departure on Friday morning. He was not trying to hit you. He is ambidextrous; he carries two pistols; he is a crack shot. He could have warned you about 'Harry Ludlow,' as his every word indicated. But he had suffered injury; worst of all, his dignity had suffered on two successive occasions; he would not speak out. So with his left hand he fired a shot meant to go wide. It was his own way, a peculiar way but characteristic of gambling gentry reluctant to commit themselves about anything, of saying, 'Look out; take care; there's someone near you who means bad luck!'

"Your consular assistant, after one chance encounter with Square Nat at the quadroon ball, took good care to avoid him afterwards. But there can be little doubt he overheard Square Nat bellowing in the courtyard, and knew he might be under suspicion.

"After the fiasco with George Stoneman, he was finished. This Steve White, this superman of cold blood and burning idolatry, was a mass of nerves; he was all nerves. He could take no pressure; he broke. On nights before a sailing of one of their big boats, lights burn very late in the office of the Grand Bayou Line. Sergeant O'Shea, calling there late on Saturday night, discovered that passage for St. Louis had been reserved in the name of Stephen White. He was bolting; he was getting away; the time had come to close in.

"You all know what happened. Cornered in the *Kentucky* stateroom of the boat, he felt his strength deserting him even as he fired that futile shot.

"On his deathbed, witnessed only by Sergeant O'Shea, he reverted to type: he became a boasting, snarling, screaming youth whom the world had injured as it had injured Delphine Lalaurie. He revealed freely the part played by Marie Laveau the elder in giving him encouragement. But, since he signed no confession and the words were heard only by Sergeant O'Shea, they would be very doubtful evidence in a court of law. Let me repeat that the Voodoo Queen, who unquestionably has destroyed the documents I myself saw without reading them, is in no danger of being prosecuted for her passive role.

"In conclusion, then: a wily double murderer made no very good end. Having cursed his bad luck, he cursed all of us, individually and collectively. Then, having cursed everyone except Delphine Lalaurie, he cursed God and died. That is all."

"All?" echoed Ursula, sitting up straight in her chair. "It *does* seem to have ended happily, if not quite in the best romantic vein. Margot, completely disillusioned with Marie the younger because the daughter is so fond of *good* works, has discovered how fond she was of Tom the whole time." Ursula extended her hand to Macrae, who took it. "As for Qu—as for Richard and myself, we're happy, aren't we?"

"Very happy."

"But we're only two in a great number, and there are others to consider. What does the future hold for us all?"

Meditatively Senator Benjamin took out his cigar-case.

"A large question, Miss Ede, for one of my modest attainments to answer. Troubles may well lie ahead; change, dark days, and the disruption of our ordered world. Still, whatever these changes may be, we can see the dangers we must face; they are not such as are brought about by the breed of Steve White. His like, I hope and pray, we shall never meet again."

NOTES FOR THE CURIOUS

1

OF THE AMATEUR DETECTIVE

With the exception of Judah Philip Benjamin, every character with lines to speak in this story is fictitious. The Senator Benjamin of 1858 has been chosen somewhat arbitrarily to act as detective. His character as depicted here has been drawn for the most part from the best biography of him, *Judah P. Benjamin, Confederate Statesman*, by Robert Douthat Meade (New York: Oxford University Press, 1943). See also the earliest full-length biography, *Judah P. Benjamin*, by Pierce Butler (1907).

His favourite sport really was devil-fishing. He did back a friend's note for sixty thousand dollars, and met the obligation when the other failed. Of Latin authors his favourite was Horace; in earlier years he greatly enjoyed reading aloud from the romances of G. P. R. James and frightening his sisters with ghost stories. For other sentiments he is made to express I cannot quote chapter and verse, but the sentiments seem characteristic. During the War Between the States he was successively Attorney General, Secretary of War, and Secretary of State in Jefferson Davis's Cabinet. At the end of the war he escaped to England, was admitted to practise at the British bar, and became an immensely successful barrister before his death in 1884.

2

OF DELPHINE LALAURIE

The real-life history of Delphine Lalaurie, still the city's most famous sensation, was the inspiration for this detective story. An account of it has been given by almost every writer on New Orleans from the time of Harriet Martineau to the present, usually with an admixture of hearsay and legend.

At the height of her social career she was in fact accused of torturing slaves, as the present story relates. A mob wrecked her house on April 15th, 1834. She fled abroad with her third husband, and died there in 1842. The 'haunted' house may still be seen at the southeast corner of Royal Street and Governor Nicholls (formerly Hospital) Street. Beyond such certainties lies only a question mark.

One admirable modern historian, the late Stanley Clisby Arthur, takes the view—see his *Old New Orleans* (sixteenth printing, 1966)—that Delphine Lalaurie was a much-wronged woman, in the main a victim of early yellow journalism. The view seems probable, and has been adopted here. But at this point I must plead guilty of blending fact with fantasy. The ringleaders of the mob who wrecked her house were not the imaginary young men of the narrative; so far as is known, no dire fate overtook anybody. Rosette Leblanc and Rosette's murderous son never existed either; they were invented to provide a surprise villain for the last chapter. Again so far as is known, Madame Lalaurie had no connection with Marie Laveau, even to the extent of being acquainted with her.

3

OF MARIE LAVEAU

Though both Marie Laveau and her daughter were very much real-life persons, they cannot be called characters in the story. The younger Marie makes a brief appearance in the twelfth chapter, but she says no word we hear and departs forthwith into limbo (or charity). Marie the elder, whose grave is in St. Louis Cemetery No. 1, does not appear at all. She has been the subject of a biography, *Mysterious Marie Laveau, Voodoo Queen,* by Raymond J. Martinez (New Orleans: Hope Publications, 1956), which, despite its sensational title, is a careful study dealing in fact rather than romance. Those interested in the cult of which she was high priestess should further consult *Voodoo in New Orleans,* by Robert Tallant, newest edition (New York: Collier Books, 1962).

Marie's history is chronicled with accuracy in the novel, apart from her presence on the outer fringe of a fictitious murder case. But she walked many dubious ways; she might have been concerned in anything. To preserve the tradition of Victorian story-telling, no character in the novel makes mention of the fact that, in addition to being Voodoo Queen, she was also a noted procuress. The house you see today is not her original cottage, which was demolished in 1903.

4

OF THE BRITISH CONSULATE

The actual British Consul in 1858 was a Mr. William Mure. Taking up the post in 1849, he was still there at least as late as the outbreak of hostilities between North and South. William Howard Russell, the celebrated correspondent of the London *Times*, visited him in the early summer of 1861. We find mention of this in Russell's *My Diary North and South* (London: Bradbury & Evans, 1863), reissued in modern dress as *My Civil War Diary* (London: Hamish Hamilton, 1954).

The consulate of those days, as listed in a contemporary city directory, really was at number 33 Carondelet Street. But don't waste time trying to place it today. Buildings lining the present thoroughfare are of a massive modern sort; and, anyway, all New Orleans street numbers were changed in 1894.

5

OF THE QUADROON BALL AND OTHER AMUSEMENTS

The newspaper advertisement for the quadroon ball in the story is authentic. The first person to describe these affairs in print seems to have been Frederick Law Olmsted, the landscape architect who in 1857 was appointed superintendent of New York's Central Park, then under construction. Also in 1857 he travelled south and gathered materials for a book published two years later: *Journey in the Seaboard Slave States* (New York: Mason Bros., 1859). Olmsted's New Orleans local colour is excellent, though he describes the famous St. Charles Hotel—perhaps truthfully; nobody now knows—as 'stupendous, tasteless, ill-contrived, and inconvenient.' He discusses the institution of the quadroon ball, quoting the advertisement for such a 'society' gathering to be held on October 16th at the Globe Ballroom.

Through the efficiency and courtesy of my friend Mr. Charles Stow and his staff at the Greenville County Library, Greenville, South Carolina, I was able to study microfilms of the New Orleans *Picayune* for the entire year 1858. The month of April is particularly interesting. Another such society ball will be given at the Washington and American Ballroom ('formerly Globe') at the actual address used in the story, on Thursday, April 15th, and every succeeding Thursday. The opera *Hernani* is to be sung that week at the *Théâtre d'Orléans*, while a minstrel show occupies the St. Charles Theatre.

Finally, we can establish from Stanley Clisby Arthur's *Old New Orleans* (page 26) that on January 10th of 1857 a group of gentlemen did in fact assemble in an upper room at the Gem Saloon to found the Mistick Krewe of Comus (*sic*). Who's dreaming now?

6

OF ADDRESSES REAL OR IMAGINARY

The murder of Judge Rutherford is committed in the home of Jules and Isabelle de Sancerre, described as being at St. Charles Avenue and Holywell Street. There seemed small harm in assigning Barnaby Jeffers's house to Second Street or General Ede's to the corner of St. Charles Avenue and Louisiana Avenue. No dirty work occurred at the former address; and, at the latter, only embarrassment for Ursula Ede and Richard Macrae.

But carefully to define the location even of a fictitious murder might cause confusion with some real house or annoy those who live in it now. There is no Holywell Street in the Garden District. And the address of George Stoneman, who escaped death by so narrow a margin, is never mentioned at all.

7

OF THE BACKGROUND IN GENERAL

There are almost too many books about the Crescent City. Apart from those already cited, a few which can be recommended without reservation are *Fabulous New Orleans*, by Lyle Saxon (New York: Century Co., 1928), *The French Quarter*, by Herbert Asbury (New York: Alfred A. Knopf, 1936), *Lake Pontchartrain*, by W. Adolphe Roberts (New York: Bobbs-Merrill, 1946), *It's An Old New Orleans Custom*, by Lura Robinson (New York: Vanguard Press, 1948), *Queen New Orleans*, by Harnett T. Kane (New York: William Morrow, 1949), *The Romantic New Orleanians*, by Robert Tallant

(New York: E. P. Dutton, 1950). Both *New Orleans*, by Stuart M. Lynn (New York: Bonanza Books, 1949), and *Louisiana, A Treasure of Plantation Homes*, by J. Wesley Cooper (Natchez: Southern Historical Publications, 1961), are volumes of striking photographs.

For readers curious concerning steamboats, the library at Tulane University houses a vast collection of material about the great age of river travel, including some nine thousand photographs. The *Governor Roman* of the story is fictitious, unlike other steamboats named. Perhaps I should apologize for including a reference to the youthful Mark Twain when he was plain Sam Clemens. But his dissertation on Sir Walter Scott's novels as the curse of the South, together with much fascinating lore, will be found in *Life on the Mississippi*.

Though there is not much about firearms in the story, the new model Smith & Wesson (1857) carried by Sergeant O'Shea and the Colt's 'Navy' carried by the murderer were both authentic pistols. *The Revolver, 1865–1888*, by A. W. F. Taylerson (New York: Bonanza Books, 1966) also deals with revolvers well antedating 1865.

8

OF LEGENDS AND THEIR MAKERS

That tireless talker, Isabelle de Sancerre, is made to discuss the fashion in New Orleans of adding to the effect of a picturesque story by making it still more picturesque with legend. Andrew Jackson and Jean Laffite provide good examples. That the buccaneer did so spell his name, not Lafitte as usually given, has been established by Stanley Clisby Arthur with *Jean Laffite, Gentleman Rover* (New Orleans: Harmanson, 1952).

Nor is this all. When next you are on the ground, visit the Wax Museum in Conti Street. As a connoisseur of such displays, I can testify that this one is as good as and more imaginative than either Madame Tussaud's in London or the Musée Grévin in Paris. You will see Andrew Jackson and Jean Laffite. You will also see Delphine Lalaurie, and Marie Laveau's cottage with a little black carriage waiting outside.

Yes, already the legends are multitudinous. Having here said frankly how much is true and how much is all a damn lie, shall I be too much blamed for adding to their number?

CARROLL & GRAF

MYSTERY/SUSPENSE
AVAILABLE FROM CARROLL & GRAF

☐ Allingham, Margery/THE ALLINGHAM CASE-BOOK	3.95
☐ Allingham, Margery/BLACK PLUMES	3.95
☐ Allingham, Margery/DEADLY DUO	4.50
☐ Allingham, Margery/DEATH OF A GHOST	4.95
☐ Allingham, Margery/DANCERS IN MOURNING	4.95
☐ Allingham, Margery/THE FASHION IN SHROUDS	4.95
☐ Allingham, Margery/FLOWERS FOR THE JUDGE	4.50
☐ Allingham, Margery/MR. CAMPION'S FARTHING	3.95
☐ Allingham, Margery/MR. CAMPION'S QUARRY	3.95
☐ Allingham, Margery/MYSTERY MILE	4.50
☐ Allingham, Margery/PEARLS BEFORE SWINE	4.95
☐ Allingham, Margery/POLICE AT THE FUNERAL	3.95
☐ Allingham, Margery/TETHERS END	4.95
☐ Allingham, Margery/THE TIGER IN THE SMOKE	4.95
☐ Allingham, Margery/TRAITOR'S PURSE	4.95
☐ Allingham, Margery/THE WHITE COTTAGE MYSTERY	3.50
☐ Ambler, Eric/BACKGROUND TO DANGER	3.95
☐ Ambler, Eric/EPITAPH FOR A SPY	3.95
☐ Ambler, Eric/PASSAGE OF ARMS	3.95
☐ Ambler, Eric/THE SCHIRMER INHERITANCE	3.95
☐ Ball, John/IN THE HEAT OF THE NIGHT	3.95
☐ Bentley, E.C./TRENT'S LAST CASE	4.95
☐ Block, Lawrence/ARIEL	4.95
☐ Block, Lawrence/COWARD'S KISS	3.95
☐ Block, Lawrence/DEADLY HONEYMOON	4.50
☐ Block, Lawrence/THE GIRL WITH THE LONG GREEN HEART	3.95
☐ Block, Lawrence/NOT COMIN' HOME TO YOU	4.95
☐ Block, Lawrence/SUCH MEN ARE DANGEROUS	4.50
☐ Block, Lawrence/YOU COULD CALL IT MURDER	4.95
☐ Block, Lawrence/THE TRIUMPH OF EVIL	3.95
☐ Brand, Christiana/DEATH IN HIGH HEELS	4.95
☐ Brand, Christianna/FOG OF DOUBT	4.95
☐ Brand, Christiana/TOUR DE FORCE	4.95
☐ Boucher, Anthony/THE CASE OF THE BAKER STREET IRREGULARS	4.95
☐ Carr, John Dickson/BRIDE OF NEWGATE	4.95
☐ Carr, John Dickson/DARK OF THE MOON	4.95
☐ Carr, John Dickson/THE DEVIL IN VELVET	4.95

❏ Carr, John Dickson/THE EMPEROR'S SNUFF-BOX	4.95
❏ Carr, John Dickson/FIRE, BURN!	4.50
❏ Carr, John Dickson/NINE WRONG ANSWERS	3.95
❏ Carr, John Dickson (writing as Carter Dickson)/ CURSE OF THE BRONZE LAMP	4.95
❏ Gilbert, Michael/ROLLER COASTER	4.95
❏ Kitchin, C. H. B./DEATH OF HIS UNCLE	3.95
❏ Lansdale, Joe R./ACT OF LOVE	4.95
❏ Lansdale, Joe R,/THE DRIVE IN: A DOUBLE FEATURE OMNIBUS	5.95
❏ Lansdale, Joe R./THE NIGHTRUNNERS	4.95
❏ Lansdale, Joe R./WRITER OF THE PURPLE RAGE	5.95
❏ McGivern, Wiliam P./ODDS AGAINST TOMORROW	4.95
❏ Muller, Marcia and Bill Pronzini/BEYOND THE GRAVE	3.95
❏ Muller, Marcia and Bill Pronzini/THE LIGHTHOUSE	4.50
❏ Pronzini, Bill/SNOWBOUND	4.95
❏ Rogers, Joel Townsley/THE RED RIGHT HAND	4.95
❏ Sandra Scoppettone/A CREATIVE KIND OF KILLER	4.50
❏ Sandra Scoppettone/DONATO & DAUGHTER	6.95
❏ Sandra Scoppettone/RAZZAMATAZZ	4.95
❏ Sandra Scoppettone/SOME UNKNOWN PERSON	5.95
❏ Stevens, Shane/THE ANVIL CHORUS	4.95
❏ Stevens, Shane/DEAD CITY	4.95
❏ Stout, Rex/A PRIZE FOR PRINCES	4.95
❏ Stout Rex/THE GREAT LEGEND	4.95
❏ Stout, Rex/HER FORBIDDEN KNIGHT	4.95
❏ Stout, Rex/UNDER THE ANDES	4.95
❏ Symons, Julian/BOGUE'S FORTUNE	3.95
❏ Westlake, Donald/PITY HIM AFTERWARDS	4.95
❏ Waugh, Hillary/A DEATH IN A TOWN	3.95

Available from fine bookstores everywhere or use this coupon for ordering.

Carroll & Graf Publishers, Inc., 19 West 21st Street, Suite 601, New York, NY 10010-6805

Please send me the books I have checked above. I am enclosing $ _____ (please add $2.50 per title to cover postage and handling). Send check or money order—no cash or C.O.D.'s please. New York residents please add 8 1/4% sales tax.

Mr. / Mrs. / Ms. _____

Address: _____

City: _____ State / Zip: _____

Please allow four to six weeks for delivery.